Never Say Goodbye

LINDA KAVANAGH

POOLBEG

Published 2011
by Poolbeg Press Ltd
123 Grange Hill, Baldoyle
Dublin 13, Ireland
E-mail: poolbeg@poolbeg.com
www.poolbeg.com

1

A catalogue record for this book is available from the British Library.

ISBN 978-1-84223-496-9

Typeset by Patricia Hope in Sabon

Printed and bound by CPI Group (UK) Ltd, Croydon, CR0 4YY

www.poolbeg.com

About the Author

Linda Kavanagh is a former journalist who has worked for various Irish newspapers and magazines, and was a staff writer on the *RTÉ Guide* for fifteen years. She lives with her partner and dog in Dun Laoghaire, Co Dublin. Her previous four novels, *Love Hurts*, *Love Child*, *Hush Hush* and *Time After Time*, are also published by Poolbeg.

Author email: **linda@lindakavanagh.com**

Also published by Poolbeg

Acknowledgements

Sincere thanks to Paula Campbell and all the Poolbeg team, and to editor Gaye Shortland for her amazing attention to detail. Special thanks to my wonderful agent Lorella Belli for her encouragement, support and belief in me. Thanks also to the Irish Kidney Association and the British Renal Society for information on kidney transplants – hopefully, I haven't misinterpreted any of the information so generously given, but if I have, the fault lies entirely with me. Thanks also to Pascal Rosenstock and Raphael Rosenstock for discussions about first love and its impact on vulnerable young male minds. These discussions required several enjoyable sessions in the pub . . . cheers, and here's to many more! Special thanks to my partner Mike Gold for suggestions and support, and to Scruff for licks and tail-wagging. I couldn't have done it without you all!

Finally, a big thank you to all the readers who helped to turn my previous novels into bestsellers – I hope you enjoy this one!

In memory of Mick Slattery,
poet and much-missed friend.

CHAPTER 1

I feel sick with fear when the school bell rings at the end of the day. Why am I the one this is happening to? It's been going on for ages now, and I don't know how much more I can take.

"Oh my God – how could I not have known?"

Claire Ross bit her lip so hard that it bled, but she was oblivious to everything but the words she was reading. She'd just discovered her late sister's diary, and its revelations left her reeling. Suddenly, everything she'd believed about Zoe had been overturned in an instant.

As she began turning the pages, her eyes filled with tears. So Zoe's death hadn't been an accident. Her thirteen-year-old sister hadn't been snatched from the beach by a freak wave, as had been claimed at the time, because the proof was here, in Zoe's own handwriting.

Claire felt all the pain of loss well up inside her again. How could all this have happened to her sister without her knowing about it? Had their mother been aware of what was going on? And what about the school? Surely someone had been aware of the situation? Oh my God, Claire thought, it's like walking into a nightmare. Now I really know why Zoe died. And the world as I've known it has just been turned on its head.

As Claire read through the entries, anger rose in her throat and formed a lump that almost threatened to choke her. A month after her sister had written the final entry in her diary, her body had been found floating out at sea. Memories of that day came flooding back into Claire's mind. On that day she had, in effect, lost her mother too. Although her mother's drinking had been bad before her sister's death, the aftermath had been even more horrendous. From the day Zoe died, her mother was rarely sober again, and Claire had suddenly been thrown into a bewildering and frightening world of loss.

As a small child, alone and terrified, she'd crawled into Zoe's bed that first night without her sister, hoping to find comfort from contact with Zoe's possessions. She'd put on Zoe's pyjamas and pressed them tightly to her body, as though they might somehow connect her to her beloved sister again.

As the weeks went by and before social services waded in, her mother had consumed even greater amounts of whiskey to dull her own pain, and Claire watched broken-hearted as her mother retreated from her, sinking deeper into her own world of despondency and despair. Despite their shared sorrow, they hadn't been able to comfort each other, and Claire longed to scream at her mother: You had two daughters – one of them is still living – why can't you find some joy in me? Why do you miss the dead one more than you love the one who's alive?

Claire had been nine when her older sister died. Now, at thirty-eight, there hadn't been a day that passed when she hadn't thought of her sister.

Claire wiped her eyes. Was it only an hour ago she'd stepped into the gloomy interior of her mother's house? It felt like a century. Having recently inherited the house on her mother's death, she'd reluctantly made the journey back to the seaside village of Trentham-on-Sea where she'd grown up.

Opening the blinds, she'd glanced around the dusty, stuffy drawing room, feeling a pang of guilt that this house was now hers. It was years since she'd had any kind of relationship with her mother, but now that she was gone Claire felt her loss acutely. All those lost opportunities to say the things that mattered.

As she wandered around, picking up and touching things as she went, Claire had been filled with sadness and regret. Perhaps she should have made more of an effort to understand and support her mother. On the other hand, it had been difficult, if not impossible, to deal with a belligerent drunk who hadn't been sober in years.

Claire surveyed the old cooker, fridge and pantry with distaste. Nothing had changed since she'd left all those years ago. In fact, nothing had changed since her father left, a lifetime earlier. Her mother had made no attempt to modernise or replace anything. The same old pots filled the cupboards, and the ironing board wore the same piece of scorched gingham material that she remembered from her childhood.

Claire shuddered. They'd all have to go. In fact, the entire house would have to go. After today, she'd no intention of ever setting foot in it again. She intended getting a local estate agent to put it on the market immediately. Then, when the house was sold, she'd set a date to marry David. For the first time since she'd arrived, a fleeting smile crossed Claire's face. Her fiancé was the best thing that ever happened to her, and she knew that Zoe, wherever she was, would be happy for her.

Claire had then made her way into the room that housed the old-fashioned roll-top desk that had originally belonged to her father. It seemed like aeons since he'd been part of the family, and Claire wondered where he was now. He was probably dead himself. His departure had been the turning point in all their lives. Before that, their mother had been a happy woman. But after he left, she began drinking heavily, and her two daughters' young lives had been turned upside down. Not only had they to deal with the grief of losing their beloved father, they'd also had to contend with a mother who was becoming increasingly out of control. If he hadn't deserted them all, their mother wouldn't have started drinking, and maybe poor Zoe wouldn't have died.

Opening the roll-top desk, Claire gazed inside. There were bundles of bills accompanied by matching receipts, carefully rolled-up pieces of string, and out-of-date coupons cut from newspapers. Claire was suddenly overwhelmed with grief as she surveyed the trivia that represented her mother's life. In truth, the poor woman hadn't had much of a life. With the benefit of hindsight, Claire was seeing her mother as someone who once had hopes and dreams of her own.

The first two drawers were empty, but in the third drawer Claire discovered a pile of ancient newspapers, their pages yellowed and fragile. Gingerly opening the first of them, Claire found herself staring at the local newspaper's account of her sister's drowning. She shuddered. It was ghoulish of her mother to keep such mementoes, but as she smoothed out the papers' tattered edges, Claire realised these newspaper accounts had represented her mother's last link with her eldest daughter.

The first account detailed the discovery of the missing child's body. Claire remembered the hushed tones of Doctor Barker and the local policeman as they arrived at the cottage to give her mother the devastating news. Then, as nine-year-old Claire was taken away by a kindly neighbour, she heard her mother's screams and sobs behind the closed drawing-room door.

Another newspaper, dated a few days later, detailed Zoe's funeral, displaying a photograph of all the pupils from The Gables School for Girls lining the route from the church to the graveyard.

Claire's lip trembled. What hypocrites they'd all been! Once their moment in the limelight was over, they'd left Claire and her mother to their lonely and tragic existence, without a helping hand from that day onwards.

As the light began to fade, Claire had abandoned the newspapers and wandered into Zoe's bedroom. Everything was exactly as it had been the fateful evening she'd left, never to return. Idly, she touched Zoe's duvet, as though it could act as a conduit that would somehow link her to her sister.

Blinking back a tear, she wondered how different her life

might have been if Zoe had lived. With each other to lean on, they'd have struggled through, and eventually they might even have got their mother the help she needed. But it had been too great a task for one little girl to tackle, and now, many years later, Claire was left among the tragic remnants of three women's lives.

Claire lifted her sister's hairbrush and held it to her face. As she felt her sister's hairs against her skin, she remembered the times they'd sat together on Zoe's bed, whispering and laughing, making plans for the future – a future Zoe had cruelly been denied.

Looking around the room, Claire decided she'd just take a single memento of Zoe with her. She dismissed the bedclothes, the books and the hairbrush – she'd look for something more in keeping with the Zoe she'd known. Her sister had enjoyed art at school – if she could find one of Zoe's paintings, she could frame it and hang on her apartment wall. Then Zoe would always be with her.

Getting down on her knees, Claire looked inside Zoe's bedside locker, but it yielded nothing of interest. Bitterly disappointed, she leaned on it to steady herself as she got up. But it toppled over, and Claire ended up on the floor beside it.

Swearing, she hauled herself up onto the bed, angry and determined to leave the house as soon as possible. If ever she needed proof that this house was cursed, she'd confirmed it now!

As she reached out to put the locker back in its upright position, Claire noticed a book attached to the back, held in place with sticky tape. She tingled with excitement as she peeled it away from the locker. It was a diary, the kind companies gave away free to customers, and it advertised a well-known breakfast cereal on the front. Claire now remembered Zoe being thrilled when a local shop-owner, Mr Leonard, gave it to her. She hadn't even waited until January to begin writing in it – she'd filled the entire frontispiece and title page with her writings!

As she opened the diary and began reading Zoe's childish writing, Claire expected to discover details about Zoe's homework assignments, her favourite film stars and her dreams for the future. Instead, she found something very different and shocking. And as she read, a swell of anger rose up inside her, threatening to overwhelm her with its ferocity. Oh, Zoe, she whispered as the tears ran freely down her face, I'll avenge you, no matter what. I swear I'll make them pay for what they did to you.

CHAPTER 2

Anne Ellwood looked through the morning post. There were the usual begging letters, entreating her to intercede with her husband on the writer's behalf. As the wife of an MP, she was well used to people targeting her to find a route to her husband, The Right Honourable Clive Ellwood.

But this envelope was addressed in her elderly mother's handwriting. Then she remembered. Her mother had mentioned she was forwarding a letter that had arrived at the family home, addressed to Anne under her single name, Anne Morgan.

Tearing open the envelope, Anne was surprised to discover an invitation to attend a reunion of her school year. Her initial smile quickly changed to a frown, and her heart began to beat uncomfortably. She wouldn't go – she *couldn't* go.

Her bitterness was also tinged with anger – she'd actually like to go to the lunch and lord it over all those other girls who hadn't married as well as she had! But she wouldn't go. It would only bring back the past – that awful time from which she still tried so hard to distance herself.

Over the years, Anne and her three friends had tried desperately to forget about that tragic event that shaped their lives. It coloured everything they did, and it was always there between them. No matter how happy the moment, the spectre of Zoe Gray would suddenly creep out from the shadows and cast a pall of sadness over everything.

Anne looked at the invitation again. Presumably her friends Fiona, Jennifer and Emma wouldn't want to go either. Besides, she didn't need to lord it over anybody – her three friends gave her all the feedback she needed. None of them had married as well as she had – and Emma hadn't married at all – and over the years, she'd revelled in their envy. Clive had often expressed surprise that she still kept in touch with these friends from her school days. He thought her kind and loyal to maintain contact with people she'd left behind socially, but the truth wasn't quite so clear-cut.

Anne had made a career of being an MP's wife, and it was a career she took very seriously. She saw her job as ensuring that Clive's life ran smoothly, and his home was organised with the precision of a military campaign, so that his every comfort was taken care of when he was present. During the week, while he was away at the Commons and staying at his luxury Westminster flat, she'd plan menus, stock up on supplies, supervise the housekeeper and gardeners, all aimed at enabling them to spend quality time together at weekends. There were no children, so Anne devoted her entire life to Clive. He was her world, and before his arrival each Friday evening, she'd have her short dark hair trimmed, washed and blow-dried at her local salon, so that she always looked attractive and elegant for her adored husband.

Anne stared angrily at the invitation in her hand. Would she and her friends ever escape from that terrible tragedy that haunted their lives? It angered her that her emotions could so easily rise to the surface and threaten the composure she'd cultivated over a lifetime.

Angrily, Anne tore the handwritten invitation in two. Tonight, she'd phone each of her three friends, and confirm their collective decision not to attend. In the meantime, she needed to get on with planning the forthcoming garden party. Some South American diplomats would be attending, and she needed to theme the event in their honour. She'd get bunting in their national colours, and prime the musicians to learn some of their national songs.

Of course, she always invited, Fiona, Jennifer and Emma to these events, even though neither Fiona's nor Jennifer's husband would ever fit in with the calibre of people who'd be present. Fiona's weedy little solicitor husband Edwin became even more boring as any event wore on. As for Jennifer's uncouth and loutish husband, Benjamin Corcroft . . . Anne wrinkled her nose. She was well aware that Jennifer stayed with him only because he made obscene amounts of money. He built ghastly little boxes that masqueraded as houses, and they seemed to proliferate all over the country. Then there was Emma, who could always be depended upon to disgrace herself when she'd had too much to drink. Her career as a writer of children's books might add cachet to some events, but her ability to become a nuisance after her third glass of wine was guaranteed.

Still, they couldn't all be as fortunate as she was. She'd set out to marry a man of distinction and substance and, as soon as she'd met Clive Ellwood, she'd known he could be moulded into something worthwhile.

They'd met during their last year at university, and Anne, who'd been studying fine arts, immediately saw his potential. He'd already been approached by the various political parties and was leaning towards the Liberals, but Anne steered him towards the Conservatives, seeing little point in going into politics if you weren't ultimately aiming for the highest office. With equal determination and speed, she'd taken him up the aisle of her parish church in Trentham-on-Sea, before anyone else got the chance to snap him up.

And her hunch had paid off – Clive had become a very successful politician. In fact, the prime minister had recently assured Clive that in the next cabinet reshuffle, he'd definitely be in line for a ministerial post.

In the kitchen, Anne threw the fragments of the invitation into the bin, and made herself a cup of coffee in the state-of-the-art surroundings. She was relieved that today was Mrs Hill's afternoon off. In her present unsettled mood, she couldn't have endured her housekeeper's endless chatter. The woman was a great worker, but right now Anne just wanted to be alone. Tonight she'd talk to each of her friends, and they'd all take their lead from her, as they'd always done.

Looking out the window, Anne could see that the two gardeners were trimming the edges of the lawn. She nodded approvingly. All was looking good on the Ellwood estate. The lawn and the flowerbeds were looking marvellous, and everything would be perfect for the garden party at the end of the month. As always, everything would go like clockwork, since she demanded the highest standards of everyone who worked for her.

Turning away from the window, she bit her lip angrily. What a pity her private life wasn't as orderly and controlled as events at The Grange. No matter how often she tried to bury the past, it always returned to haunt her.

CHAPTER 3

Benjamin Corcroft removed a piece of gristly breakfast bacon from his mouth and put it on the side of his plate. He glanced surreptitiously at his wife Jennifer, who despised his table manners. But he could never match up to his wife's expectations, no matter how hard he tried. Which, of course, he didn't. Truth be told, he often deliberately misbehaved at the table to annoy her. He liked living up to his wide-boy image, especially since he knew how much it irritated her.

"Benjamin, please – you're setting a bad example for the children." Jennifer wrinkled her nose in disgust.

"Sorry, Jen," he replied, glancing across at his wife, who was sitting opposite him. But he was smiling as he said it, so she knew he didn't mean it at all. And the children knew it too.

As usual, his wife was pushing her food around on her plate. Benjamin wondered if she was anorexic, since she rarely seemed to eat anything. He'd also noticed that she ate even less just before her regular Wednesday bridge nights in London.

He belched loudly as he placed his cutlery neatly on his plate, purposely avoiding Jennifer's glare. Of course, he knew she'd put up with him no matter how bad his behaviour was. He provided everything she could possibly need and a lot more besides. She could buy anything she wanted, go anywhere she wanted, drive what she wanted. Right now, she had a Range Rover sitting out on the gravel driveway, and a Maserati in one of the garages.

Both children had heard their father belching, but knew their mother would be livid if either of them acknowledged it or derived amusement from it. Nevertheless, thirteen-year-old Vanessa gave her father a wink that lifted his spirits.

Benjamin glanced at fifteen-year-old Alan, who looked as though he couldn't wait to get away from the table and back to that incessant music he played on his guitar upstairs, which could be heard through the ceiling and often gave Benjamin a headache. Alan had recently announced that he wasn't going to university when he finished school in three years' time – he was joining a crowd of wasters who were forming a rock band. Well, he hadn't exactly used the word 'wasters' – that was Benjamin's own interpretation.

Benjamin looked closely at his son, and felt a stab of pity for him. The teenage years were a horrible time – you thought you knew everything when in fact you knew nothing, and your dick gave you endless trouble. And while Benjamin felt annoyed with Alan for throwing away the kind of chance he'd have given his right arm for, it gave him a sneaking sense of joy to see his wife so disconcerted by it. He suspected that Alan's rebellion would be short-lived, and that he'd dutifully go up to Cambridge when the time came. But, in the meantime, he was deriving pleasure from seeing Jen's feathers so ruffled. Although he was fond of his wife, her delusions of grandeur often drove him to retaliate.

Looking at Vanessa again, Benjamin couldn't help but smile. Jennifer had been trying to turn their daughter into a carbon copy of herself, but Vanessa was ferociously resisting. The child had no interest in designer clothes, expensive cars or meeting the right people. She was happiest when she was out on her pony, Grey Star, or watching the deer, rabbits and foxes who wandered through the gardens of The Old Vicarage, and Benjamin got a kick out of seeing Jennifer's efforts thwarted. Nevertheless, how many kids did he know who had their own pony at thirteen?

Where he came from, kids were lucky to have a bike at that age.

Reluctantly, he admitted to himself that he found it hard to deny his kids anything they wanted. Perhaps a few weeks working on his brother's fruit stall at Walthamstow market would teach them some lessons about life, but of course Jennifer didn't allow him to 'embarrass' her or the children by associating with his lowly family.

Benjamin grimaced to himself. Years before, he'd been more than willing to fall in line with Jennifer's wishes. Back then, he'd been making his way up the corporate ladder and, at Jennifer's behest, he'd severed contact with his family and invented a poor-but-genteel background.

Of course, he'd never managed to fool those toffee-nosed friends of Jennifer's. That trio were the snootiest bitches he'd ever met, although Anne Ellwood's husband Clive was a decent bloke, and Fiona's husband Edwin was a nice enough chap too. How on earth had such nice guys hitched themselves to such harridans?

Benjamin pushed back his chair, and stood up. "Jen, I'm off to the Clara Court site. I'll stay at the hotel overnight."

His wife gave an indifferent shrug of her shoulders. He probably had some bimbo lined up, but she didn't really care. It was Wednesday, and she had plans of her own for the evening. Their housekeeper, Mrs Quick, was staying over to mind the children.

Vanessa turned towards him. "When will you be back, Dad?"

Benjamin smiled at his daughter. She was the only one who ever seemed to care whether or not he was there.

"Probably tomorrow evening, poppet."

"Then can we go and buy a new saddle for Grey Star when you get back? I've saved the money, Dad – you won't have to pay for it."

Benjamin smiled at her, his heart filled with love for this earnest and adorable girl. She was a most remarkable child, genuinely helpful and generous without being asked. Benjamin suspected that she'd decided to be the exact opposite of her mother.

Looking across at his wife, Benjamin nevertheless felt a surge of gratitude. Jen might be demanding, and a pain in the arse most of the time, but he'd be eternally grateful to her for giving him two great kids.

He turned to Vanessa. "Alright, love – we'll do it then."

Benjamin glanced across at his wife again, as she daintily chewed a sliver of toast. He'd known Jen was a snob when he met her, and it had been a challenge to get her interested. Also, at the back of his mind, he'd known that a classy wife could get him to places he'd never get to himself.

When they'd met, he was already climbing up the corporate ladder at one of the country's then leading construction companies. He'd made it from brickie to site foreman, then on to senior management, and finally to board level. But eventually he'd wanted to go it alone. He had the ability, but not the contacts. However, Jennifer's friends got him to a senior bank official who'd liked his business plan and was prepared to lend him the capital to fund his first building project. This enabled him to go head to head with the company he'd just left – and win.

Now he was running one of the country's largest building companies, specialising in cheap housing nationwide, and he'd cleaned up over the years. He was a millionaire many times over, and he was well aware that, but for Jennifer's contacts, he'd still be working for someone else. Nevertheless, he couldn't find it in his heart to be grateful to them.

Benjamin smiled inwardly. He still got a kick out of disconcerting Jen's posh friends. He got savage enjoyment from sometimes showing his barrow-boy background, and watching how embarrassed everyone became.

Giving Alan a mock punch, Benjamin kissed the top of his daughter's head, then father and daughter exchanged a conspiratorial smile.

The permanent state of war that existed between their parents at mealtimes was a source of amusement to Vanessa and Alan, and they often took bets on who would win the next round. This time, in Vanessa's opinion, her father had won hands down.

CHAPTER 4

Her mind in turmoil, Claire slept badly. Although exhausted from the long drive home from Trentham-on-Sea and the tragic revelations about her sister, sleep evaded her for most of the night, and she awoke feeling as though she was suffering from a monumental hangover. If only the contents of Zoe's diary had been a bad dream! A breakfast of tea and toast managed to quell the nausea she was feeling, but her mind was still on high alert. Claire hoped a shower would help her to feel a little better, since she had a morning full of clients ahead. After leaving her mother's cottage the previous evening, she'd driven out of the village in a state of shock and disbelief. She'd been stunned by what had happened to her sister, and she'd had to make a deliberate effort to calm down. Otherwise, she'd have put herself at risk of having an accident. After a three-hour drive she'd reached her apartment and, safe within the confines of her own four walls, she could finally allow herself to weep.

Luckily she hadn't arranged to see David that evening, because she'd been in no mood to see anyone. Besides, she'd already made the decision not to tell him about the diary – at least for the present – and last night she'd been too emotional to be able to hide her feelings from him.

Now in the shower, she turned the water to 'Hot' and allowed it to soothe her aching muscles. As a psychotherapist with her own busy practice, she ought to be well used to controlling her feelings. Clients came to her for help in dealing with the most tragic and desperate situations, and she was expected to offer support in a calm, professional manner. But this was different – this was an issue at the heart of her own family.

In a way, Claire wished she'd never found the diary. If she hadn't fallen and grabbed the bedside locker, she'd never have noticed it. She'd simply have left the house and never returned, getting an estate agent to sell the house and leaving the new owner to bin the diary, along with all the other useless and dated items in the house. It would have made her life so much easier.

But now that she knew what had really happened to her sister, how could she not want to avenge her death? It would be an insult to Zoe otherwise. And she wanted revenge for herself. After all, she'd been cheated out of a lifetime of her sister's love. Claire knew that if Zoe had lived, they'd always have been close, and Zoe would now be helping her to plan her wedding.

Claire eyed the diary on her bedside table as she stepped out of the shower and began dressing. She now had the proof, in her sister's own handwriting, that Zoe's death hadn't been a straightforward drowning. She'd been driven to take her own life by the bullying she'd endured at the hands of four classmates whom she'd named. Why had her kind and gentle sister been victimised?

Although she'd read through the diary at her mother's house, Claire knew she'd need to read it over and over again, to ensure she didn't miss even the tiniest snippet of information that might uncover why Zoe had been victimised.

Picking the diary up, Claire opened the inside cover, where Zoe had enthusiastically begun writing as soon as she'd been given it. The early entries told of Zoe's efforts to keep their little family together in spite of their mother's drunkenness. By now, the tears were cascading down Claire's face as Zoe's handwriting brought the past so vividly to life. Claire now remembered the last Christmas Day they'd spent together – their mother had been semisober and she'd managed to join her daughters at the kitchen table for the meal Zoe had prepared. It had been a very happy day for Claire and Zoe, because they'd felt like a real family.

Claire also read Zoe's description of New Year's Eve – the last one Zoe ever experienced – when the two sisters had stood in the garden and gazed up at the stars, and dreamed that one day their lives would get better.

Claire felt a lump in her throat. If only she could turn back the clock and have that New Year's Eve night with Zoe again!

Overwhelmed by sadness, Claire skipped through the pages. The vicious campaign of bullying had begun when Zoe returned to school after the Christmas holidays, and Claire felt a deep hatred for these people who'd destroyed a whole family by taking her sister away from her.

In early January, Zoe had written:

Now that I'm back at school after the Christmas holidays, four girls in my class have started calling me names. They wait at the crossroads and shout nasty words as I go by. I don't know what I've done to deserve this treatment.

As the year progressed, Zoe's regular entries documented her distress at having to face her tormentors after school.

Claire found it odd that the diary entries stopped at the end of May, and the centre pages, which would have contained the months of June and July, were missing. Perplexed, Claire looked at the jagged scraps of paper still attached to the centre of the diary. Had Zoe ripped them out in anger, regretting what she'd written, or had she accidentally spilled something on them?

The missing July pages were of no importance since Zoe died on the last day of June. But if she'd written anything in June, Claire longed to know about it. It would be odd if Zoe, who'd written daily in her diary, hadn't kept writing right up until her death. If so, what had happened to those pages?

Claire sighed. It probably didn't matter, since the rest of the diary contained enough information to name and shame the bullies who'd driven her sister to her death. She bitterly regretted being unable to help her sister at the time, but she'd been only nine, and while she'd suspected something was bothering her sister, Zoe had always insisted she was fine.

But now it was clear that something had been terribly wrong, and the last remaining entry proved it. On the last day of May, Zoe had written:

I don't want to be hurt anymore, but I don't know how to stop it. Sometimes I wonder how much longer I can keep going. I'm going to have to do something about it soon.

A month later, her body was found floating in the sea.

For a long time, Claire sat gazing into space, imagining what it must have been like for poor Zoe. How tragic to feel so alone, and unable to ask anyone to help her. Had she walked straight into the sea, or jumped from the cliff? Why hadn't she told a teacher about the bullying, or even her mother? Despite their mother's alcoholism, Claire felt sure she'd have done her best to help. On the other hand, their mother did have a knack for making things worse, so maybe she could understand Zoe's reluctance to involve her. But why had Zoe chosen to kill herself, rather than tackle the problem in some other way? Claire felt a sudden flash of anger towards her sister – Zoe had promised to always be there for her. But just as quickly, she was overcome with guilt for even entertaining such a thought. How could she possibly judge her sister, when she herself hadn't been able to help her?

Claire felt exhausted from the sheer mental effort of reliving Zoe's tragic last days. She closed the diary and looked at the clock on the wall. If she didn't get moving, she'd be late for her first client of the day. Perhaps today's hectic schedule would distract her from thinking about Zoe for a while. And later, she was spending the evening with David.

For the first time since she'd left Trentham-on-Sea, Claire's spirits lifted.

"I thought you were going to get rid of the cottage?" said David, gently massaging Claire's shoulders.

"Yes, well, I suppose I will eventually – but not just yet."

They were in David's apartment, and Claire had been filling

him in on her visit to the cottage. But she hadn't told him about finding Zoe's diary.

David leaned forward and kissed the top of her head. "I can understand why you're not in a rush to sell – all your childhood memories are tied up in that house."

Claire nodded. The mere mention of the cottage upset her. It brought back all the memories of her miserable childhood, and the tragic circumstances of Zoe's death. She was filled with anger every time she recalled Zoe's diary, and thinking of it also made her long for revenge.

"You're very tense – do you want me to rub your back?"

Claire nodded. "Okay – thanks, love."

Leaning forward, Claire tried to relax as David's strong fingers teased the knots from her shoulders, and she made a conscious effort to close her mind to everything but his ministrations. She was lucky to have someone who cared for her so much, and she was determined not to let her anger spill over into her relationship.

They'd met a year ago at university, where Claire was taking an evening course in trauma therapy. David had been one of the lecturers, and they'd got talking in the canteen over a paper she'd written. They'd been instantly attracted to each other and before the course ended David had asked her out.

Their relationship was easy-going and uneventful, which suited her perfectly. She and David rarely had a difference of opinion and, when they did, it was resolved easily and amicably. Unlike her first marriage, which had taken place while she was studying for her degree. That had been a short-lived union, provoked by a flush of youthful hormones at the age of nineteen. With hindsight, she realised that her lonely childhood had made her desperate to belong to someone. She'd hoped Tom would ground her, but it hadn't lasted. Their ardour had cooled quickly, and after a series of stupid rows each found themselves looking at a stranger. The break-up, after three years, left Claire feeling even more lost than ever.

The only thing she'd kept from the marriage was Tom's surname. At the time, taking his name had seemed like a step on the road to a new life, and the severing of the bonds that kept her tied to her miserable childhood. Of course, it hadn't worked out that way. But her psychology degree was in the name of Ross, and while it wasn't regarded as politically correct anymore to take a husband's surname, her professional reputation had been built using it.

As David kissed the back of her neck, Claire made a conscious effort to let go of the tension she felt. If she didn't think about Zoe, she could unwind and let David get the knots out of her muscles. She could turn her thoughts to their wedding next year, and her hopes for children too. A boy and a girl would be perfect . . .

"Love you," David whispered, leaning forward and planting a kiss on the back of Claire's neck.

"Love you, too," she whispered back, feeling guilty about keeping Zoe's diary a secret.

Claire also wished she could tell David about her desire for revenge. But what if he didn't agree, and tried to dissuade her? It would undoubtedly damage their relationship if she continued with her plans in the face of his disapproval. Besides, she hadn't actually made any plans for revenge yet, and she'd no idea of what form that revenge would take. She didn't even know where to find the bullies who'd hounded Zoe to her death.

Initially, she'd thought of going to the police, but she'd reluctantly conceded that she'd little information that could usefully build a case. All she had was a young girl's diary that told of being bullied, and Zoe's desire to escape from her suffering by ending her life. But the law required concrete evidence, and how could Claire prove the connection between Zoe's suicide and the bullying she'd endured for months beforehand? And even if she could, what charge could be levelled against these people? They hadn't forced Zoe into the water – she'd made that decision herself. Besides, the police were unlikely to be concerned about something that happened thirty years earlier, and which wasn't even on their files as a cold case.

Claire felt a momentary stab of fear as she thought of the journey of hatred she was planning to embark on. But I'll find those hateful women somehow, she thought. And no matter how long it takes, I'll make them pay for what they did to my sister.

CHAPTER 5

Anne crossed to the landline in the hall. It was time to make a final decision about the reunion. Catching a glimpse of herself in the hall mirror, she surveyed herself critically. She was tall and reasonably slim, but she was a broader build than Jennifer, who was positively skinny and never seemed to eat at all. Anne admired Jennifer's ability to bypass the kind of goodies to which the rest of them were instantly drawn.

In every other area of her life, Anne maintained tight control. During her childhood, her family had always given the impression of being rich, a belief Anne had always cultivated among her friends. But the reality was that several times their home had nearly been lost due to her father's gambling on the stock market – he'd never been able to resist an insider tip – although at the last minute he'd always managed to save the day. But his wife had succumbed to several nervous breakdowns and his daughter grew up with a pathological need for financial and emotional security.

Clive had given Anne that security. Apart from his undeniable charm and political potential, he'd also given her the love she'd needed. From the outset, she felt they made a perfect team, the two of them working together for Clive's success, which also gave her the status and security she craved.

But nothing was ever perfect. Now the reunion had brought back all the shame and fear of thirty years ago. Everyone had secrets, but theirs was particularly heinous and had haunted them all ever since. Now, the reunion could once again focus attention on what had happened, and on the four women who'd been the cause of it.

Lifting the phone, Anne dialled Jennifer's number.

"So we're definitely not going?"

"Of course we're not," said Jennifer, noting the slightly hysterical tone of Anne's voice at the other end of the phone. "We'd all be bored silly – who wants to chat to a bunch of morons we've nothing in common with?"

"Have you talked to any of the others?"

"Yes, Emma rang me, said she agreed with us one hundred per cent."

There was a moment's silence, followed by a sigh. "Fiona rang me earlier – she thought it might be 'fun' to go. Can you believe it?"

"Well, if the rest of us aren't going, she's hardly going to go on her own, is she?"

"No, I suppose not."

"Well, now you have your answer. We're not going, and that's that."

In the silence that followed, both women were thinking back to their schooldays, when they'd been the ones whom all the other girls feared. It had been great fun until they'd gone too far, and what had started out as a series of silly pranks had gone horribly wrong.

Anne realised she was still unsure about what to do. Would it be better to go, or stay away? Suddenly, she had a horrific and frightening thought. If anyone at the reunion happened to know she was married to an MP, they might get the idea of blackmailing her, or telling him about her sordid past. Therefore, if they did decide to go to the reunion, she couldn't tell anyone who her husband was. Anne bit her lip. She could see her marriage disintegrating if Clive found out. He was a deeply moral man, and he'd loathe her for what she and the others had done. Dear God, would there ever be an end to this guilt and fear of disclosure? The four of them had paid for what they'd done a thousand times over! Every move Anne made still required careful consideration, in case somehow she might be linked to what had happened all those years ago. She knew her friends felt exactly the same, and each of them had as much to lose as the other . . .

"Are you still there, Anne?"

"Yes . . . I've been thinking."

"About what?"

Anne took a deep breath. "Maybe Fiona is right."

"What do you mean?"

"If we don't go, it might look bad. People might talk."

"About what?" Jennifer felt slightly unnerved. They hadn't discussed this issue in years, although it was always there between them, like an unseen spectre, an extra place at the table.

"You know."

"Look, I can't speak for you, Anne, but I'm rather busy at the moment," said Jennifer. "Since I became captain of the golf club, I've a lot on my plate. And I've my bridge in London every Wednesday night. I don't really have time to chat to a bunch of school kids I knew twenty-five years ago."

"They're not school kids anymore – that's the problem."

"Well then, I'm sure they have busy lives of their own, and don't have time for idle gossip."

Anne sighed. "I should imagine that at reunions, people talk about the past – that's why these damned events are held. And what we did was a big topic of conversation back then."

Jennifer was puzzled. "Anne, what exactly are you saying? I thought you rang me to confirm we weren't going, but now you seem to be changing your mind. I thought you said you didn't want to go?"

"I don't."

"Then what's the problem?"

"If we're not there, we've no control over what's being said about the past. About us."

"I'm sure people will be catching up on what everyone's doing now – not delving into what happened years ago."

Anne hesitated. "I hope you're right. Maybe that's why I want to make sure it stays that way."

"So you think we should go?" Jennifer grimaced. Even after all these years, Anne was still the one who dictated what happened and what the group did.

"Well, I'm just trying to take Fiona's point of view into consideration."

Jennifer smiled to herself, knowing that wasn't true. Anne would always do what Anne wanted to do. And she'd make the rest of them do what she wanted, too.

"So you're talking about damage limitation."

"Well, at least if we're there, we can steer conversations away from anything –" Anne hesitated, "– unpleasant. I think we should split up at the reception, so that we can keep an eye on things. Hear what people are saying."

"So we're going."

"What do *you* think?"

Jennifer smiled to herself. What she thought was no longer a consideration.

"I think you're probably right," she said, for the umpteenth time.

"Well, that's agreed then – but I'd better warn Fiona that we don't regard this reunion as an occasion of 'fun'."

Neither of them even considered Emma's viewpoint. As always, she'd be expected to fall in line with what the rest of the group had decided.

CHAPTER 6

Zoe's Diary

December 2

> *I miss Daddy so much, and I know Claire does too. One day we were all so happy, the next day he'd gone without even saying goodbye. Claire sometimes asks me when he'll be coming back, but I don't know what to say to her. Since he left, Mum's started drinking heavily, and we hate seeing her so sad.*
>
> *I wish there was someone who could help us, but we've never known Daddy's relatives and Mum has no family left. She inherited some money – I think that's what pays the bills and helps us to survive. I know Daddy doesn't send anything, because I always check the post for his handwriting, but no letter or money ever comes.*

Zoe looked surreptitiously at her mother, whose face was pale and gaunt. She looked old, although by Zoe's reckoning she wasn't yet forty. She was sitting in the same stained clothes she'd worn for several days, uninterested in anything that was happening around her.

"Look, Mum – why don't I run you a seaweed bath?" Zoe said,

coaxing her. "You'll feel lovely and fresh afterwards, and I'll change the sheets on your bed while you're in the bath."

"Alright – thanks, Zoe," her mother said with a sigh. "You're a good girl. I couldn't ask for two better daughters than you and Claire."

Zoe glowed with pride at this rare compliment. It made all the neglect and hard work worthwhile.

"Thanks, Mum, we love you too. Let me get you a towel –"

Encouraged by this interchange, Zoe hoped that her mother's depressive mood might be about to lift, meaning she and Claire could look forward to a few hours during which she'd be her old self again.

Since their father left, the two girls had learned to deal with their mother's moods, which followed a fairly predictable pattern. When she hadn't had a drink, she was agitated, and when she'd had too many, she was belligerent. But there were often a few hours in the morning when she was affable and communicative, and these were the moments the girls cherished. Then they saw a glimpse of the warm caring woman they used to know. On Saturday and Sunday mornings, before she began her daily descent into oblivion, she'd sometimes join the girls for a late breakfast in the kitchen. On these rare occasions, Zoe and Claire would feel like a real family again.

This evening, having run her mother's bath, Zoe urged her into the bathroom. Living by the sea meant that Zoe was able to collect wrack from the beach. It made a wonderfully soothing and relaxing bath, and the properties in the seaweed helped to moisturise her mother's skin.

"Do you need me to help you in? Please, Mum, be careful not to slip –"

"Thanks, love – I'm in now. Hmm, this is lovely . . ."

Zoe always made sure the bathroom door was left unlocked. She worried in case her mother fell asleep, slipped under the water and was too drunk to save herself.

Later, Zoe went back to check on her mother. There was no sound from the bathroom and, worried, she popped her head around the door. Her mother was dozing, her head thrown back and her mouth slightly open. In that moment, Zoe was overwhelmed with love for this sad and lonely woman, and she wished, more than anything in the world, she could make her life better.

She knocked loudly. "Mum, are you okay?"

Zoe received a monosyllabic reply. Then she heard her mother stumble from the bath, and was relieved she didn't need to worry any longer.

In the meantime, Zoe had changed the bedclothes and left a clean nightdress on the bed. Later, when she knew her mother was back in her room, she knocked on the door.

"Can Claire come in to say goodnight, Mum?"

Her mother nodded and, at a signal from Zoe, Claire appeared and Zoe slipped out of the room, feeling that her little sister needed some parental bonding time.

Sitting on the bed, Claire looked steadily at her mother. She seemed relaxed and communicative after her bath, and Claire talked about how she was doing at school. Then, sensing an opportunity, Claire decided to risk asking the question that was on her mind. She knew Zoe would kill her for asking, but she really needed to know.

"Mum, when is Daddy coming home?"

There was a deathly silence, and the atmosphere instantly changed. Zoe, who'd been about to enter the room with a cup of tea, stood frozen outside the door, her heart in her mouth. The cup rattled in its saucer as her hand shook, but she didn't dare move. If there was going to be an answer, she wanted to hear it too. As she peered through the open door, she strained to hear their mother's voice, because it had suddenly gone very low.

"Don't ever ask that question again!" she said, her face contorted in fury.

Claire was shocked by her angry response, and burst into tears.

"I want my daddy!" she bawled, and Zoe rushed in to try to keep the peace.

"Come on, Claire – Mum needs to rest!" she whispered urgently, pulling her sister out of the bedroom while still balancing the cup of tea in her other hand.

As Claire sobbed in the kitchen, Zoe hurried back to the bedroom with the cup of tea. There were a million questions she wanted to ask. Did her mother's refusal to answer Claire's question mean their father would never come back? Why had their father left in the first place? Why did their mother need to drink so much? Would their lives always be so miserable?

"I'm sorry, Mum," she said, handing over the cup of tea, "but Claire doesn't understand –"

Her mother gave a short laugh that sounded more like a bark. "All that talk about marriage being forever – well, you never really know someone until it's too late."

Zoe longed to ask her mother what she meant but the words stuck in her throat, and she felt unable to say anything.

Instead, she said, "I wish we could help you, Mum. You don't eat enough, and all that whiskey can't be good for you –"

Her mother nodded. "I wish I didn't need it, Zoe, but it helps me to cope. Someday soon, when things get better, I'll give it up –" Her bleary eyes looked sadly at her eldest daughter. "I'm sorry, Zoe – being without a father isn't fair to either you or Claire. But sometimes, we just don't have any choice in the matter –"

Her mother's eyelids began to droop and Zoe removed the teacup before she drifted off to sleep. Zoe stood by the bed watching tenderly as her chest rose and fell. The seaweed bath had done it job, and Zoe hoped she'd have a restful night's sleep. Silently, she crept out of the room.

Across the kitchen table, Claire and Zoe looked at each other as they ate their supper of bread and cheese. Claire looked chastened, and Zoe hadn't the heart to criticise her. Their mother's comments seemed to suggest their father had left her for somebody else – that would also explain the depression and constant drinking.

Zoe gave Claire a smile of encouragement. It wasn't her fault – her little sister was desperately missing her father too. "Want to play draughts?" she offered, and Claire nodded.

"Okay, I'll put out the board – do you want to be black or red?"

As the sisters settled down to their game, Zoe was still shaken by what had happened. Clearly, there was some mystery surrounding their father's disappearance and, whatever it was, their mother had no intention of telling them about it. Zoe sighed. Maybe they'd have to wait until they were grown up to find out the truth . . .

28

CHAPTER 7

Jennifer hadn't gone downstairs for breakfast. She couldn't face anyone right now, so she'd asked Vanessa to bring up a cup of coffee to the bedroom. She'd refused her daughter's offer of toast – she needed to look her best for this damned reunion, and a slice of buttered toast would add almost two hundred calories to her waistline.

Jennifer felt exhausted. She hadn't been able to sleep properly since she'd heard about the invitation. She felt weepy and confused, and suddenly out of control.

"Mum – your coffee."

Vanessa stood smiling at the side of her mother's bed and Jennifer sat up gingerly.

"Thanks, darling."

Vanessa looked concerned. "Are you okay, Mum? You look – well, you look a bit tired."

Having said it, Vanessa wished she hadn't, in case her mother thought it meant she looked old, which was something that seemed to terrify her.

Jennifer gave a half smile. "No, I'm okay – just worried about what to wear to this reunion."

Vanessa smiled enthusiastically at her mother. "It'll be great fun, Mum – I don't know why you're worrying. You always look great."

In fact, Vanessa was telling a white lie, since she didn't think her mother looked well at all. She'd been looking whey-faced and exhausted for days, and Vanessa couldn't understand why meeting up with old classmates was such a worrying prospect. She'd been so concerned about her mother that she'd even put off her trip to get Grey Star's new saddle. She wanted to be there in case her mother needed her.

"Darling, will you hand me that bottle of painkillers on the dressing table?"

Obediently, Vanessa gave her mother the bottle, worried that her mother seemed to rely on tablets and vitamin pills instead of eating properly. She was always worried about her weight, yet in Vanessa's opinion she was unhealthily thin.

"Thanks, darling – I think I'll stay in bed a bit longer," Jennifer said as she downed several painkillers and a mouthful of coffee. "I've a dreadful headache."

Vanessa longed to point out that if her mother ate, she mightn't have such a bad headache, but she was the child here, not the adult. In fact, she often found the world of adults very confusing.

After Vanessa had gone, Jennifer put her coffee cup on the bedside table and lay back on her pillows. She could hear Mrs Quick vacuuming somewhere, and in his bedroom next door Alan was twanging his guitar. Benjamin had probably left for one of his sites by now, and Vanessa was going to cycle down to the stables and take her pony for a canter. Jennifer was proud of her independent kids, although she was perturbed by Alan's insistence on becoming a musician instead of going to university. And lately he'd been so morose, but she was at a loss to know what could be wrong, and her son was unlikely to tell her.

Jennifer sighed. At least she had a few years in which to work on getting Alan to Cambridge. But there was a much more pressing matter closer to hand. This damned reunion had put them all on edge. For years, they'd all coasted along, making new lives for themselves and burying their past beneath layers of new experiences. They'd all pretended to themselves that Zoe Gray's death had been expunged from their minds, until someone had to organise a reunion and bring it all to the fore again.

What on earth were they going to do? The past that Jennifer had tried so hard to bury had suddenly returned with a vengeance. She'd been having nightmares ever since she found out about the invitation. Benjamin thought the reunion was a great opportunity to catch up with old classmates, but this was the very last thing she, Anne, Fiona and Emma wanted. After the fateful day when Zoe died, they'd never bullied anyone again, but their history would surely be remembered by their classmates. What on earth would they do if someone decided to discuss the tragedy over lunch – worse still, to point the finger at the four of them again?

Jennifer remembered every second of that awful day with astonishing clarity. And no matter how often she tried to dismiss it, it insisted on sneaking back into her consciousness, as though it had taken on a life of its own. She wasn't a woman who ever cried – unless she was using tears to manipulate a man – but now Jennifer found herself teary-eyed and unable to cope as the days advanced and the reunion got nearer. Jennifer couldn't remember anything ever filling her with quite so much fear. Except that terrifying day thirty years ago, when Zoe's body had been found by a fisherman who'd been out in the bay early that morning.

The news began to spread as the children made their way to the school. By the time the assembly hall at The Gables School for Girls was full, every girl was already aware of what had happened. There was a buzz in the air, a frisson of fear combined with a sense of disbelief. And when the headmistress, accompanied by most of the other teachers, stepped up onto the dais, she didn't have to make her usual plea for silence. The chatter had died down instantly as everyone waited for the official announcement.

"Girls, I'm sorry to have to tell you this – but yesterday there was a tragic accident. One of our students, Zoe Gray, has drowned."

No sooner had the headmistress made her announcement than the chatter began again, rising to a crescendo as children cried and hugged each other. Now that Zoe Gray's death was officially confirmed, everyone seemed to have something to say about what had happened.

"The school will, of course, provide a guard of honour for Zoe at her funeral," the headmistress added. "You'll all have the opportunity of paying your respects to your classmate and representing your school on that day."

Announcing that classes would resume after the next break, the headmistress left the dais, accompanied by her teaching staff, and the children were left to talk among themselves. Everyone looked sad, and many girls were weeping while others were consoling them. For all of them, this was their first experience of death, and Zoe's drowning made them frighteningly aware of their own mortality.

But Jennifer, Anne, Fiona and Emma said absolutely nothing. They were dazed and unable to speak. All they could do was look from one to the other, their faces drained from the shock of what they'd just heard.

"This is all our fault," Jennifer said at last. "If we hadn't made her feel so bad all the time –"

"Shut up!" Anne had said fiercely. "Don't you dare say that!"

At first, Fiona said nothing, but the tears ran silently down her face. Then she told the others that she'd known something was amiss earlier that morning. There had been a phone call for her father, and Dr Barker had rushed out of the house without even having his breakfast. But she'd never imagined it could be anything as bad as this. Now she realised he'd been called to the beach to examine Zoe's body, and pronounce her dead from drowning.

But the four knew that her death hadn't been accidental. They'd all killed Zoe, just as surely as if they'd stabbed her with a knife.

Silently, Emma had offered Fiona her handkerchief. She, too, had been consumed with guilt, and was blinking rapidly to stop the tears from running down her face.

Looking around them, the four longed to join the throng of students in the middle of the hall, but they'd felt barred from taking part or offering sympathy because the other students knew exactly how they'd treated Zoe when she was alive. It would be hypocritical and unacceptable to profess concern now.

Gradually, the four became aware of a change in the atmosphere of the assembly hall. More and more girls were looking in their direction, giving them disapproving looks and pointing at them. Eventually, their classmate Hazel Bonnington approached them and stood pointedly in front of them.

"You four did this to her," Hazel said, looking from one of them to the other. "Zoe would still be alive if it wasn't for your stupid bullying."

For the first time ever, the four actually felt afraid, especially as more and more girls gathered around them, agreeing with Hazel's remarks and adding comments of their own. It was only the ringing of the bell for class that prevented the situation from escalating out of control, and all four had known that this would be a defining day in their young lives, a day they would never forget.

As her thoughts returned to the present, Jennifer jumped out of bed. There was no point in staying there since her mind kept filling up with horrific images of that day in school. She wouldn't be able to rest until the damned reunion was finally over. Would they ever be free, or would Zoe Gray's death haunt them forever?

CHAPTER 8

Back from the stables, Vanessa appeared to be poring over the latest edition of *Pony Monthly* magazine. But she wasn't actually reading it at all – she was surreptitiously watching her mother who was chatting on the phone.

Vanessa knew that her mother was talking to a man. Even at thirteen, she'd worked out that her mother reacted differently when talking to males and females. In fact, many of her own classmates behaved in exactly the same way – if a boy was in sight, they changed from bright, intelligent girls into simpering idiots.

Vanessa was keen to know who was on the other end of the line, because this man called far too often, and Vanessa suspected her mother was having an affair. Some of her friends kept track of their parents' antics by checking the last call made or received on the phone. Unfortunately, the Corcroft landline phone was an old-fashioned one, so Vanessa had no way of checking. She suspected her mother kept the old phone purposely, to prevent her children from prying.

Once, she'd managed to sneak a look at her mother's mobile phone while she was having a shower, but most of the people listed there were already known to her. However, she'd spotted three male names that might be worth dialling, but before she could do anything further, she heard her mother coming down the stairs, so she'd quickly returned the phone to her mother's handbag and guiltily hurried out of the room.

However, Vanessa committed the three names to memory, and the following day, she launched her plan by mentioning casually to her mother that 'Robert' had called. However, this information didn't produce the guilty blushes Vanessa had expected. Her mother had simply said: "Oh, good – the plants I ordered from the nursery must have arrived. I'll collect them tomorrow."

On another occasion, Vanessa told her mother that 'Peter' had called, to which she replied: "Terrific – he's the best golfer in the club, and it's almost impossible to get a game with him. Did he say when he's free to play?"

Her final attempt, claiming a call for her mother from 'Joseph', elicited no more than a stinging retort.

"For heaven's sake – what is that idiot thinking of?" Jennifer said angrily. "I told him the hedges wouldn't need trimming for another two weeks at least!"

This time, it was Vanessa's cheeks that were burning, since she suspected that by now her mother must have seen through her pathetic little ruse.

Nevertheless, Vanessa was determined to continue with her plan to discover the other man in her mother's life. Maybe next time her mother was showering, she'd scroll through her phone and write down any numbers she didn't recognise, and ring them later to see if they really were who they were supposed to be. Perhaps her mother had disguised her lover's name, and he was listed as somebody else?

Vanessa felt deeply hurt on her father's behalf, but she'd no idea what to do, if anything. Most of her friends treated their parents' affairs as normal, but Vanessa couldn't manage to feel so nonchalant about it.

Did her father know about her mother's carry-on? Maybe he did, and he preferred to do nothing about it. Or maybe he didn't know, and the knowledge would devastate him.

Vanessa despaired of ever understanding the world of grown-ups, and she couldn't fathom why people wanted to have affairs anyway. Of course, she accepted that at thirteen she wasn't fully a woman yet, and maybe she'd feel differently when she was. But as far as she was concerned, if you married someone, forsaking all others, affairs were not part of the deal.

Glancing at Alan, who was absorbed in a music magazine, Vanessa wondered if her brother had any idea what was going on. Or if he cared. The only thing her dopey brother ever did was play his guitar out of tune, slag off the guys in his band, or play computer games on his Nintendo. Briefly, she thought of sharing her suspicions with him, but decided against it. Alan didn't give a damn about anything except his own pathetic little life.

Vanessa had gradually become aware of a strange dynamic at the heart of her family. Her father made lots of money and their family was clearly well-off, yet her mother appeared to despise the way the money was made, while still happy to spend it. Watching her parents interact, Vanessa often felt sorry for her father, who always seemed to come off the worst. Her mother seemed to use her superior education to make him look stupid. It was all done jovially, but there was always an undercurrent of aggression. Her father then reacted by making a point of demonstrating his 'lack of breeding' as her mother called it, to infuriate and embarrass her.

At other times, her mother would make nasty remarks about her father's family, none of whom she or Alan had ever met. Vanessa had often wondered why they were kept a secret – were they really so terrible? Vanessa felt angry, and cheated out of half of her family.

Vanessa longed to throw her arms around her dad and tell him his lack of a university education didn't bother her, but her mother and Alan would laugh at her if she did. Her dad wouldn't laugh, of course – she suspected he'd really enjoy it, but she was never going to have the courage to do it.

Unfortunately, the downside of all this wealth meant that her parents were seldom around. Her father was always working, and her mother was attending lunches, shopping or playing golf. And also she stayed overnight in London every Wednesday to play bridge. Or did she? Maybe, Vanessa thought, I'll make it my mission to find out what she's really doing.

Vanessa turned the page of *Pony Monthly*, and tried to look as though she was deeply engrossed in it. Her mother had just come off the phone and was looking very pleased with herself. Her last words, in a seductive whisper, had been: "See you Wednesday."

Vanessa grimaced. That was hardly the way you'd speak to a bridge partner, especially as her mother's was supposed to be a woman.

Later that night as she lay in bed, Vanessa wondered if anyone would actually notice if she wasn't there. It would probably be days before anyone missed her. Sometimes, she felt terribly alone in this family. There seemed to be very little glue holding them all together.

CHAPTER 9

The following weekend, Claire reluctantly decided to pay another – and hopefully final – visit to the home where she'd grown up. After discovering Zoe's diary, she'd become so emotional that she'd left in a hurry, without properly finishing her search of the house. But now that she'd calmed down somewhat, she felt the need to take another look around. Maybe the missing diary pages were there somewhere, stuffed in a drawer or pressed between the pages of a long-forgotten book. She dreaded going back to face her past once again, but she felt it was necessary if she was ever going to understand Zoe's final days.

She'd declined David's offer to accompany her on the drive down to Trentham-on-Sea, feeling that this was something she needed to do alone. She still hadn't told him about Zoe's diary – it was too personal and private to share with anyone else yet.

As she drove towards the village where she'd grown up, Claire's thoughts centred on how she might avenge her sister. It didn't seem fair that those responsible for her death were living normal happy lives somewhere, without ever having paid for what they'd done. Nor, to her knowledge, had they ever acknowledged their role in Zoe's death. If they'd done so, that might have been enough to appease her anger, which had been building since she'd first read Zoe's diary. It would be difficult to trace these women since, like her, they might have changed their surnames on marriage. But she intended finding them, no matter how long it took.

In the first few days after her discovery, Claire slept badly. She'd tossed and turned, unable to get Zoe's death out of her mind. In her dreams, she confronted the four women, and several times she woke up screaming. Fortunately, she'd been sleeping alone those nights – if David had been staying at her apartment, she'd never have managed to keep Zoe's diary a secret.

In her waking hours, she'd daydreamed about confronting these women, and watching the horror on their faces when she told them who she was. She liked to think of kidnapping them and bringing them all together, then killing them one by one as the others watched . . .

Claire was sometimes shocked that she could even contemplate these unknown women's deaths, although as yet they had no faces, and she'd no idea where they were – she wasn't a vindictive person by nature. But surely these were exceptional circumstances? They'd effectively killed her sister, so wasn't it only fair she should want to hurt them back? Besides, she'd no real intention of killing them – she wouldn't even know how to begin – but her thoughts were cathartic, and exorcising her hatred helped to reduce her anger and keep her sane.

She'd even looked up 'Revenge' on the Internet, and read up on the philosophies of the Bible, the Mafia, Islamic law, and numerous cultures that condoned or actively promoted taking revenge. None of it proved helpful, except that it assured her she wasn't alone in feeling that way, and that the desire for revenge was a universal human feeling.

A sudden thought made Claire smile. If one of her own clients spoke about wanting revenge, she'd feel morally bound to counsel them to reconsider!

As she neared Trentham-on-Sea, Claire felt a lump rise in her throat. She longed to turn the car around and head back to where she felt safe. She now regretted turning down David's offer of help, and she wondered, not for the first time, why she always insisted on doing things alone. She had friends, of course, but she was, at heart, a solitary person. She'd felt isolated for most of her childhood, and after Zoe's death she'd felt even more alone. She'd subsequently developed the habit of self-containment, which had stayed with her all her life.

At university, she'd got a first class honours degree, followed by a Masters, in Psychotherapy. After several years working as a psychotherapist with the NHS, then later in a group practice, Claire decided to go it alone, perhaps because she'd always lived her life that way.

Parking her car outside the cottage, Claire felt an overwhelming sense of sadness. And as she stepped into the hall of her old home, she was once again assailed by the old familiar smells of furniture polish and lavender. The house seemed to have absorbed and retained all the smells of her childhood, evoking so many memories of the past. Ghosts seemed to walk through these rooms now, and she desperately wanted to run out the door and never come back. But she needed to check everywhere again, just in case there was anything else that might help her to understand what happened to Zoe.

After spending time in her sister's room, Claire concluded there was nothing of any further help there. She'd opened and emptied drawers, searched the wardrobe, looked through all Zoe's books, pulled out the bed, stripped it and looked under the mattress. Then she searched all the other rooms in the house, but finally conceded that there was nothing of use anywhere.

Deciding to leave, Claire made her way into the hall, treading distastefully on the piles of advertising leaflets that had come through the letterbox. Surely the distributors of this stuff realised there was no one living there? Kicking them to one side, Claire noticed an electricity bill addressed to her mother, and she picked it up. She'd need to get it paid before the house was sold.

There was also another envelope on the floor, and Claire's heart almost stopped when she saw that it was addressed to Zoe.

Tears filled her eyes and she wondered if the pain of loss would ever end. Who could be writing to Zoe after all these years? Surely everyone must know she was dead?

After staring for ages at the unfamiliar writing on the envelope, Claire eventually decided to open it. She'd have to write back to the person who'd sent it, and let them know about poor Zoe. Although how could anyone *not* know after all these years?

Gingerly opening the envelope, Claire was surprised to find an invitation inside. The silver-embossed card proclaimed a 25th anniversary school reunion lunch of Zoe's year at The Gables School for Girls.

Claire blanched. Dear God, hadn't anyone on the organising committee realised they were sending an invitation to a dead person? Surely Zoe's tragic death had been a major event in her classmates' lives, so how could it have been forgotten so easily? Claire was incensed. She threw the invitation, and all the leaflets and free newssheets, into a big shopping bag and carried them out to her car. She'd dispose of them all when she got back to her own apartment.

Locking the front door, Claire cast a backward glance at the picturesque cottage that had once been her home. Hopefully, some other family would find happiness there. The Gray family certainly hadn't.

Back in her apartment, Claire threw the advertising leaflets and the invitation into her recycling bin. She was once again filled with anger at the insensitivity of the committee who'd addressed the invitation to Zoe. Maybe she'd write to them and complain. At least it might stop any further invitations arriving. On the other hand, what was the point? The house would soon be sold, and it wouldn't matter if any more invitations arrived – she wouldn't be there to receive them.

Claire grimaced angrily. No doubt the women who'd caused Zoe's death would be there, smiling and laughing while her poor sister lay in her grave! She felt certain they'd be smug, overbearing women, with no sense of decency or remorse.

Suddenly, she had a flash of inspiration. She'd attend the reunion herself! That way, she might find out what these women looked like, what their present surnames were, and where they lived.

Quickly, she retrieved the invitation from the bin, now looking at it in a new light. This invitation could be her passport to revenge! At this point, Claire had no idea how she might avenge poor Zoe. But discovering all she could about the enemy seemed like a good place to start.

CHAPTER 10

Benjamin Corcroft was a very relieved man. He'd finally got planning permission for the 50-acre Stonegate Farm and all its outbuildings. Now he'd be able to fit lots of semi-detached houses across its spectacular rolling landscape.

Of course, a bunch of old biddies from the area had opposed his planning application, and had been protesting outside the council's planning office for months. But luckily for him, deals were done behind closed doors, and all the shouting and placard-waving hadn't changed the fact that the permission had finally come through. He'd agreed with the local council to provide a percentage of social housing units, and build a community hall so the old biddies would have somewhere to hold their coffee mornings and foment further revolution against the next unfortunate sod to cross their path. Nevertheless, they'd delayed his planning approval by several months, and now the recession was seriously starting to bite.

There was also an old deconsecrated church included in the package. Although it was on the outskirts of Stonehill village, its grounds abutted the rest of the land Benjamin had bought, so it would provide the perfect entrance into the new housing estate. When the church was demolished, of course.

Benjamin's beady eyes had been quick to notice the beautiful stained-glass windows, and momentarily he'd thought of removing them and keeping them for posterity before he smashed through the end wall of the church with his JCB. But then he'd decided that, since time was of the essence, he needed to get in and out as quickly as possible before any of the old biddies could stop him. After all, it was his church – he'd paid good money for it – so he should be able to do what he wanted with it. He felt a small stab of guilt at the thought of destroying the beautiful windows. He was not unappreciative of art and craftsmanship, but when time was money, there was no contest as far as he was concerned.

He'd already arranged for a team of workers to be on site the following morning, to demolish the church and prepare an entrance onto his land before the actual building began. But since he was aware of local ill feeling towards the project, he'd decided to start demolishing the church himself under cover of darkness. In daylight, a protest could quickly escalate into a nasty confrontation, and his men would be reluctant to manhandle a bunch of old ladies. In a way, he had to admire the old dears. He'd seen them in action at some of his other developments – nothing seemed to rile old ladies more than an attempt to change the status quo.

It was late evening and almost completely dark when Benjamin drove one of his JCBs down the quiet country lane towards the church. He didn't need to do this job himself – he had hundreds of employees who could do it for him. But he was actually enjoying the thrill of it – he felt like a naughty schoolboy, about to show the locals that he wasn't to be trifled with. And by carrying out the initial demolition at night, the old biddies would all be tucked up in their beds. He chuckled to himself. By the time they realised what was happening, and got back into their corsets and stone-age underwear, there wouldn't be a church there anymore!

Quietly and carefully, with his lights now turned off, Benjamin drove in the church gate and backed the JCB up onto the lawn, so that he could get a decent run at the back wall of the church. All was looking good, there was no one around, and he'd have the wall down in no time. That would render the church unsafe, so the rest of it would have to be demolished anyway. Game, set and match! He smiled as he put the JCB into first gear and headed down the incline.

"Don't you dare!" shrieked a voice, and Benjamin stared in astonishment as a small shape jumped out in front of the JCB. Quickly he turned on the headlights, and in the beam he saw a tiny woman with thick flame-red hair waving a placard that read: HANDS OFF OUR CHURCH.

His heart sank. So much for a quick job and an easy exit. Angrily, he slammed on the brake, deliberately stopping the JCB within inches of the woman in order to scare her. Jesus! This was all he needed. And if he hadn't spotted the stupid cow, he might have accidentally run over her. That would certainly have delayed the start of his building project!

Benjamin jumped out of the JCB, angrily confronting the little woman, who looked as though she'd every intention of bringing the placard down on his head. Wrenching it from her, he threw it on the ground and danced on it until the wood began to splinter.

"You could have been killed, you daft woman!" he roared, any hope of keeping things quiet now definitely gone.

"How dare you try to destroy our church!" the woman countered. "You're not going to get away with this, you bastard! I'm going to ring the local vicar and the press, you vandal! Those stained-glass windows are priceless! Don't you know they were made by Harry Clarke, the world-renowned Irish stained-glass artist?"

He hadn't known, but Benjamin wasn't going to admit it. "Everything in life has a price, sweetheart," he said cuttingly. Looking around him, he could see lights coming on in local houses, and he suspected that before long the entire village would be on top of him.

"That's it – run away, you cowardly piece of scum!" the little woman shouted as he jumped back into the JCB and backed out of the church grounds.

"I'll be back – this is my land now, and you can't stay awake every night of the week!" he roared.

"Oh yes, we can!" she roared back. "We have people on watch every night! I'll protect this church if it's the last thing I do! Go study your history, philistine – you might learn something other than how to make money!"

Furious, Benjamin backed the JCB out of the church gate and drove it back up the road to Stonegate Farm, where his heavy equipment was stored. He punched the steering wheel angrily. He wasn't going to hang about to be berated by a load of countryside crackpots! Quickly, he parked the JCB and leapt into his BMW. He couldn't wait to get out of this godforsaken backwater, with its population of half-wits and in-breds.

Gunning the BMW, he drove to the Stonegate Farm entrance, and not a minute too soon. Coming towards him was a group of local people, led by the vicar and the redheaded woman, many of them carrying torches.

Quickly, he pulled out the gate just ahead of their arrival and drove in the opposite direction. The sweat was now running down his forehead. If he'd been a minute later, they'd have blocked the entrance to the farm, and he'd have been trapped. As he drove, the tension gradually began to leave his body and, although he was now driving in the wrong direction, it was preferable to facing the lynch mob he'd just left behind him. Christ! All he'd wanted was to quietly get started on the project, yet he seemed to have stumbled onto the set of a Dracula movie, complete with peasant procession out to get him.

As he put miles between himself and the inhabitants of Stonehill, Benjamin felt his blood pressure gradually returning to normal. The peasants seemed to have won the first round, he conceded. But, as far as he was concerned, the battle was far from over.

"Sorry, lads – I won't be needing you here today," Benjamin told his workers the following morning as they checked in at Stonehill's old church. He turned to Joe, his foreman. "But since

I'm paying their wages, they might as well start clearing the field to the left of Stonegate Farm."

Joe looked at his boss quizzically, then shrugged his shoulders. Only the day before, Benjamin had been raring to get the little church demolished.

"Okay, boss," he said, then gave instructions to the men, who left to start work at the farm. Joe then waited beside Benjamin for more detailed instructions for the day's work.

Out of the corner of his eye, Benjamin watched the gathering of villagers. They were clearly watching him and his foreman. He hated the smug look on their faces as they'd seen him dismissing his workers, but he was in this for the long haul. Let them have their few moments of victory – he'd be the victorious one in the end.

He felt particularly angry towards the little redheaded woman, who was also standing across the road with the other busybodies. If she'd been home in her bed last night, like all the other busybodies, he'd now have the site cleared!

On the other hand, he had to admit that maybe she'd done him a favour. He hadn't realised the windows were so valuable until she'd told him so. His next plan was to look up Harry Clarke on the Internet, and assuming the man's work was genuinely valuable, he'd work out a strategy for removing the windows and selling them. That way, he could make a pretty penny before getting rid of the church.

"Joe, any idea who that redheaded woman is?" Benjamin asked.

Joe grinned. "Feisty little thing, isn't she? She's an artist called Georgina Monks, but most people around here call her Georgie. I don't understand this modern-art stuff myself, but apparently she's building quite a reputation for herself." He turned to Benjamin. "It might be worth getting friendly with her, boss. If you got a good deal on some of her paintings, it could prove a better investment than building houses right now!"

Benjamin gave him a sour look, then cast a surreptitious glance in Georgie Monks' direction. In the daylight, he could see that she wasn't old at all. In fact, she was probably younger than he was, and she had a pretty, elfin face and a slim, petite figure. He hadn't noticed these details the night before because she'd been wearing a shapeless anorak and wellies. Now, she was wearing jeans and a fitted jacket that showed off all her curves.

Jumping into his Land Rover, Benjamin drove past the huddle of villagers, ignoring them completely. Why did these people have to be so damned obstructive? Hadn't they ever heard of the word '*progress*'? In fact, they were being downright selfish in not wanting other people to have houses to live in. Here he was, bringing new lifeblood to their community, and all they could do was oppose him. Benjamin felt truly put upon as he drove swiftly out of the village.

CHAPTER 11

Fiona checked her golf clubs and placed them in the boot of her car. For the past few weeks she'd been playing badly because of all the stress over the upcoming reunion. But today she was determined to make a serious effort at leaving her worries behind, at least for the duration of the game.

She, Anne, Jennifer and Emma were terrified that something awful might happen at the reunion. None of them had ever forgotten the accusatory looks on their classmates' faces when the news of Zoe Gray's death had been announced. What if someone at the reunion decided to raise the subject of Zoe's death – worse still, to point accusing fingers at them again?

Back in the kitchen, Fiona glanced out the window and saw the grocer's delivery van making its way up the driveway. She looked at her watch and smiled. She couldn't fault them, they were always on time. The staff knew about her golf date every Friday morning at noon, so their delivery was always at eleven on the dot.

The driver turned the van around so that it was facing towards the road again, while the back doors were facing Fiona's kitchen. Usually, the delivery boy jumped out, opened the back doors of the van and made several journeys to the kitchen while the van driver kept the engine running.

But this morning, things were not the same as usual. In place of the usual surly youth was a new and very good-looking young man. Hmmm, a new delivery boy – and a very attractive one too, Fiona thought. He was only about sixteen, but he had strong tanned arms that made light of carrying in the heavy boxes of groceries. Fiona smiled at him. She liked the way he reddened, it was so endearing. And she especially liked the way he got an erection when she stood close to him. She watched him closely as he carried in each box, amused and delighted at how easily she could disconcert him.

"What's your name?"

"Jim, ma'am."

"Mine is Fiona. You're a very good-looking young man, Jim – fancy staying for a cup of coffee?"

Jim went a dark shade of red. "Er, thanks, er, Fiona, but we've two more deliveries to make."

"Well, why not drop back afterwards? I'll be waiting."

Jim looked surprised and confused. "But I thought – we were told you had to be at your golf club by twelve –"

"My golf's been cancelled today," said Fiona hastily. She laid her hand casually on his arm, and watched as his erection got harder. "Wow, Jim, what a big boy you are!" she whispered, deliberately brushing the front of his bulging trousers with her hand.

Jim made a choking sound, and Fiona knew that without doubt he'd be back when his deliveries were completed.

"See you later," she whispered as Jim left the kitchen and began walking back to the delivery van. He gave a backward glance, as though he couldn't believe what had just happened, but Fiona knew he'd return. They always came back.

After the delivery van had driven off, Fiona went to the phone and dialled the golf club.

"So sorry, but I have to cancel my golf today," she said, holding her nose as she spoke. "I think I'm developing a summer cold, and I'm sure no one at the club would want me passing it on . . ."

Ringing off, Fiona began putting away the groceries with a

smile. She had better fish to fry. Who wanted to play golf with boring old farts, when she could be enjoying tender young flesh instead?

A little while later, Fiona looked out the window and saw the boy making his way hurriedly up the driveway. Before long he broke into a run, and Fiona smiled happily to herself as she crossed the kitchen floor to open the door. He'd take her mind off the reunion, at least for a little while.

"Hello again, Jim," she said as the boy reached the kitchen door and stepped inside.

CHAPTER 12

Zoe's Diary

December 5

Claire's got a part in her school's nativity play! I'm so pleased for her, and it's wonderful to see her so happy. There's only one problem – Claire wants Mum to watch her perform, but there's no way that can happen.

In the weeks before Christmas, there was great excitement at Claire's junior school. Auditions were being held for the nativity play, and Claire was thrilled to get the part of the innkeeper. When Zoe got home from school, Claire was dancing around the kitchen. Telling her sister about it was the most exciting thing in the world! She had already tried to tell their mother, but she was comatose in her bedroom and hadn't heard a word.

"When are rehearsals starting?"

"Tomorrow, after school," Claire told her sister excitedly. "Then we're performing it in the school hall in two weeks' time."

Suddenly, Claire's excitement drained away, and she looked expectantly at Zoe. "Do you think Mum might come to the school play?"

Zoe looked at her sister's earnest little face and wanted to cry. "I don't think so, Claire – Mum isn't really well enough."

"But all the other mums and dads are going."

"I know, but Mum's not well. Look, I'll go – I'm dying to see you perform! I can't believe that my little sister is playing such an important part!"

Claire smiled shyly. She was thrilled to have a speaking part, although she'd really wanted to play the Virgin Mary, because then she'd have been able to hold the baby doll throughout the performance. Since she didn't have a proper doll of her own, this would have been the next best thing.

"But I want Mum to see me," Claire said stubbornly.

"Look, it just isn't possible," said Zoe, looking sadly at her sister. "I wish it could be different, but she'd never be able to sit throughout the play without a drink."

"Other children's mums and dads don't drink until they pass out – why does our mother do it?" asked Claire plaintively, tears spilling down her little face.

Zoe enveloped her in a hug. "Look, life isn't fair, love – things will get better as we get older – I promise."

Zoe's worst fear was that their mother might actually try to go to the play if Claire continued to pester her. But the woman was incapable of going anywhere without being tanked up with whiskey, and by evening, when the play was taking place, she'd be completely drunk and might misbehave, ruining the event for Claire, and humiliating herself.

It was also ages since she'd dressed herself properly or bought any make-up, and her clothes were now old and ridiculously out of fashion. Not that Zoe cared about fashion – she just didn't want to see their poor mother becoming the butt of cruel jibes. Her attire was of little importance when she went into the village for whiskey and food. But in the minefield that was social life in Trentham-on-Sea, their mother's out-of-date clothing would be ridiculed and whispered about, and Zoe loved her too much to see her subjected to that kind of treatment.

"Look, I'll be there to watch you in the play," said Zoe, outwardly cheerful although her heart was breaking, "and when it's over, we'll go home and tell Mum all about it!"

But Claire wouldn't be appeased. "I want Mum there!" she sobbed.

"I know," Zoe soothed, "but you'll just have to make do with me." She held Claire at arm's length, smiling. "I know – I'll clap loud enough for two people, so then you'll feel as though Mum is there too!"

Claire smiled in spite of herself and Zoe's heart went out to her. Although neither ever said it aloud, they both longed for the return of the happy mother they'd once had. But they also knew it would take a miracle to put a smile on her face again.

Posters advertising the school play were displayed in all the local shop windows, and the air of excitement was tangible in the village. After hours of rehearsals, costume fittings, tears and nerves, the children at Claire's school were ready to perform for the public.

On the afternoon of the play, while Claire was at the dress rehearsal, their mother lay sleeping, as usual, in her bed. Tiptoeing into her room, Zoe decided to see if there was anything in her mother's wardrobe that would make her look older. Since she was attending Claire's play that evening, she wanted to blend in with rest of the audience, most of whom would be parents and relatives.

Zoe flicked through the clothes. There were many lovely, but old-fashioned, dresses, suits and coats, and Zoe tried on several of them for her own amusement. She was definitely getting taller, because many of her mother's dresses and coats almost fitted her.

Finally, Zoe took out and tried on one of her mother's evening dresses – a black one with sequins all over – and was pleased to find that it fitted her perfectly. She looked so grown up! She twirled around in front of the long mirror, and watched as the skirt fanned out around her, the sequins twinkling as she moved. It was a beautiful dress, and Zoe remembered seeing her mother wear it. She and their father had been going to a ball up in

London, and she had looked radiant as she left the house. Zoe also remembered the look of sheer joy on her mother's face as she'd gazed adoringly at her husband.

What a pity the dress looked so out of date now. It was also far too flamboyant to wear to a school play, and Zoe knew she'd be laughed at if she turned up in something like that! Abandoning the sequinned dress on the bed, Zoe selected one of her mother's more subdued outfits – a dark grey skirt and a black blouse that hadn't dated, and which made her look very sophisticated. Zoe decided it was perfect for the play and, looking at herself in the mirror, she felt very grown up.

Claire had already left for the school hall, filled with excitement as she anticipated her first appearance on stage. Zoe was thrilled to see her so happy, and she was looking forward to seeing the play herself. Nothing much ever happened in Trentham-on-Sea, so it was doubly exciting to have a play to attend, and one in which her very own sister was taking part.

As her mother continued to lie sleeping on her bed, Zoe leaned down and kissed her cheek, then headed out of the house and down the road to Claire's school hall. The night was dry and crisp as Zoe joined the throngs of people heading in the same direction. Obviously, there was going to be a good attendance.

Inside the hall, there was an atmosphere of gaiety and excitement. The Christmas spirit had already taken hold, and people were greeting each other and wishing their friends and neighbours Happy Christmas. Nobody spoke to Zoe, but she didn't really mind. She enjoyed sitting on the sidelines while still being part of what was happening. Anyway, the sister she loved was close by, and she didn't need anyone else to wish her well.

There was a sudden hush, and the curtains began to part. Zoe felt a surge of excitement as a group of shepherds came on stage, carrying fluffy toys posing as sheep, and before long they were visited by several angels, who told them about the Christ Child who'd soon be born . . .

In the next scene, Mary and Joseph made their weary way across the stage, and Zoe was on the edge of her seat as they approached the inn on the other side. She could see Claire in her cotton-wool beard and long cloak waiting in the wings to step out and inform them that there was no room at the inn. Claire stepped onto the stage.

Suddenly, there was a commotion at the back of the hall, and all eyes turned from the stage to what was happening at the rear. As Zoe turned to look, her blood ran cold. It was their mother, and she was wearing the sequinned ball gown Zoe had abandoned on the bed! It wasn't even zipped up properly, and was hanging off one shoulder. Her lipstick was smeared too widely around her mouth, and she was clearly very drunk. By now, everyone was staring open-mouthed at Mrs Gray, the performance on stage completely forgotten.

"I've come to see my daughter in the play!" she informed the other astonished patrons, speaking much louder than usual, as she always did when she was drunk.

Brushing aside any attempts to corral her, she began walking unsteadily up the aisle, then stumbled and fell on top of a man who was sitting in an aisle seat. Muttering angrily, he tried to push her away, just as two of the organisers rushed over and attempted to escort her out of the hall.

But she was having none of it. "That's my daughter Claire on stage!" she kept shouting. "Isn't she brilliant?"

Her cheeks red with shame, Zoe leapt up from her seat and ran down the aisle to the rear door of the hall. This was what she'd dreaded, this was her worst nightmare. Her mother was ruining Claire's performance! Several people had surrounded her mother and tried to silence her while the rest of the hall looked on, but her strident voice could be heard over everyone else's.

"How dare you try to stop me seeing my daughter's performance! I have every right to watch the play!"

Grabbing her mother's arm, Zoe began dragging her out of the hall. Relieved to relinquish her to someone else, the other people stepped back and allowed Zoe to take her mother outside. Then she heard the door of the hall slam shut with a resounding thud, and her ears were burning at the thought of what was being said inside.

"But, darling, I want to see the play!" her mother complained, swaying like a boat at the mercy of the high seas. Reaching into her handbag, she produced a half- empty whiskey bottle, opened it and drank the remainder of the contents.

"Mum – you're drunk!" Zoe hissed. "They won't let you into the hall again."

"But I must see my daughter!" she screamed, breaking loose from Zoe's grip and pounding on the door of the hall.

"Mum – it's time to go home," Zoe whispered, catching her mother's hands and tugging her away from the door. She began to lead her down the road towards the cottage.

"I'm not going anywhere until I see Claire," her mother muttered, but Zoe could see that she was gradually becoming less vociferous. It wouldn't be long before she was asleep again, and Zoe hoped she could get her home before then.

"Come on, Mum – you'll see Claire later, when she gets home," Zoe urged her. "Then she can tell you all about it."

As they stumbled along, Zoe felt as though everything was unreal, and she could only hope that Claire had managed to survive the humiliation and carry on regardless.

Back in the cottage, Zoe steered her mother to her bedroom, where the sickly smell of alcohol and vomit always pervaded. The smell seemed to have seeped into everything in the room, and even the clean sheets that Zoe washed every week did nothing to alleviate it.

Zoe helped her mother out of the sequinned dress and urged her into bed, although she was still protesting as her daughter pulled the covers over her. Before long, she'd dozed off, her face soft and open like an innocent child's. Gazing down at her mother, Zoe was filled with a mixture of love and revulsion. She desperately wanted to protect her from the nudges and the comments, but her mother didn't make it easy for her.

With a heavy heart, Zoe picked up several empty whiskey bottles, and carried them out to the bin. Before putting them in, she wrapped each bottle in paper, so that the neighbours *wouldn't hear the clink of glass when the Grays' bin was emptied. Zoe didn't know why she bothered – everyone knew that her mother drank to excess – but a sense of pride made her want to protect her in any way she could.*

Later, when Claire returned from the play, her cheeks were red with mortification. But she assured her sister that she'd played her part well, and Zoe was relieved.

"*Did anyone say anything bad to you afterwards?*" *Zoe demanded.*

Claire shook her head. "*No, everyone was nice to me – but that only made it worse. I didn't want them to pity me.*"

She looked in the direction of her mother's bedroom. "*How's Mum?*"

"*Sleeping like a baby.*"

"*Thanks, Zoe.*"

Zoe looked surprised as Claire reached out and hugged her. "*For what?*"

"*For trying to protect me. You knew what would happen if she went to the play.*"

Zoe nodded sadly. "*She didn't mean any harm – she was proud of you in her own way. Did you hear her saying she wanted to watch her daughter perform?*"

Claire nodded. She could smile at the incident now that she was safely home, and away from the condescending stares and whispers.

"*Look, Claire, no matter what happens, we have each other,*" *said Zoe solemnly.* "*Since Mum isn't well, we'll just have to get though things together. I'll always be there for you – I promise.*"

Claire nodded. "*And I'll be there for you,*" *she replied. She knew that no matter what happened, she'd always have her sister on her side. What more could any girl want?*

The following morning, their mother was alert and smiling when Zoe brought in her tea and toast.

"*I went to Claire's play last night, didn't I?*" *she asked.*

"*Yes, Mum – you did,*" *said Zoe evenly.*

"Claire had an important part, you know," said their mother as she tucked into a slice of toast. "Maybe she'll have a future in the theatre or television?"

Zoe quickly left the room. She was unable to understand heavy drinking. Clearly, her mother had no memory of the havoc she'd wreaked the night before. Zoe felt like weeping. Once she and Claire had two parents, now they didn't even have one.

CHAPTER 13

Anne tried not to show how tense she was as she led her three friends into the new plush hotel on the outskirts of Trentham-on-Sea. The reunion was due to start at noon, with a drinks reception followed by lunch. The four women had decided to arrive together in order to give each other moral support. All were dressed stylishly and expensively, except for Emma who inevitably appeared in an out-of-date flowing dress. However, Anne felt that eccentricity was acceptable in a writer of children's books. In fact, it was even desirable in this instance. Hopefully, if things got difficult, Emma could be used to distract people by talking about her writing career.

"I've forgotten my phone!" said Jennifer angrily, as she searched around in her handbag. "I left it on the kitchen table – dammit!"

"You don't need it," Anne muttered. "It's not as though we're going to be exchanging phone numbers with any of the morons here today!"

Nevertheless, Jennifer was annoyed. She was staying overnight in London, and hated being without it.

In the luxurious hotel lobby, the four women surveyed the board displaying the list of events of the day. The Gables School Reunion was being held in the Edwardian Suite.

"Remember, don't be led into any conversation about Zoe Gray," Anne warned them all, as they walked down the corridor. Like a mother in charge of a bunch of unruly children, she scrutinised their outfits, admonishing Emma for slouching and wearing ill-fitting shoes.

"You're walking as though you're constipated," Anne hissed. "Why didn't you wear shoes that fit?"

"They're the only good high heels I own," Emma muttered.

"Then why didn't you buy a new pair?" Anne hissed back. "Today is too important to us all – we've got to look calm, elegant and totally in control. You certainly won't help things if your feet are killing you, Emma."

Emma looked chastened, but inside she was furious. Why was it always *her* who seemed to draw Anne's ire?

"Smile!" Anne warned, as the four swept into the Edwardian Suite, to be faced by a throng of women, all chatting animatedly in groups.

An elegant woman rushed over to greet them, introducing herself as old classmate Jane Cartwright and ticking their names off a list she was carrying.

"It's wonderful to see you all again!" she gushed. "What fun we're all having, trying to identify old classmates!"

She handed them all name badges, but Anne pointedly refused to attach hers to her new jacket.

"Who does she think she is?" Anne muttered as they moved off. "I'm not wearing a cheap cardboard nametag – it's just like being back in school again."

"Come on, Anne – get into the spirit of things," Fiona murmured in her ear. "This whole ghastly event will be over in a few hours. Anyway, you yourself said we had to keep smiling!"

"Oh, all right," Anne retorted, attaching the badge to her lapel, and flashing a totally false smile at her three friends. The trio laughed at her, and the air of tension dissipated.

"I'm heading to the bar," Jennifer stated. "Everything will seem a lot better when I've a few glasses of wine under my belt."

"Don't drink too much, or you might slip up and say the

wrong thing," Anne warned. "Remember the wartime slogan – 'Loose lips sink ships'."

"Oh, for God's sake, Anne – lighten up," Jennifer said irritably. "The war ended sixty years ago. Besides, I'm having a glass of wine, not a bottle of neat brandy." She looked pointedly at her friend. "I think a glass of wine would do you no harm either – it might relax you a bit. You're like a coiled spring."

Nodding, Anne sighed deeply. "Okay, let's head to the bar." Then she turned to Emma. "Don't forget, lady – you can't hold your drink, so one glass will be enough for you."

Emma nodded meekly, and the others confirmed, through a shared glance, that they'd all keep an eye on her. She was the one they feared might say the wrong thing.

"Darlings! How wonderful to see you all!" A woman accosted the four as they approached the special bar that had been set up. "I'm Violet Summers – do you remember me?"

"Of course, Violet, how good to see you again," said Anne smoothly. "You remember Emma, Jennifer and Fiona?"

"Indeed!" beamed Violet, scrutinising each of their nametags in turn. "It's such fun being all together again, isn't it? I haven't been able to identify a single person – everyone has changed so dramatically!"

"I suppose twenty-five years tends to do that to people," said Anne, and only her trio of friends would have realised she was being sarcastic.

"Come and meet Sarah Bingham and Helen Seagrove," the woman called Violet entreated them, pointing into the crowd of chatting women. "We're having such a wonderful catch-up – and you can tell us what you've all been doing with your lives!"

Looking to Anne for their lead, the others were surprised when she smiled their acceptance. "Of course, Violet – we'll follow you."

As they set off in Violet's wake, Anne turned to the others. "Let's see what people are talking about," she whispered. "Fiona and Jennifer, why don't you two slip away and join some other group?" She placed a firm hand on Emma's shoulder. "Emma –

you're to stay with one of us at all times, and right now you're coming with me. And you're not to say anything, unless you're asked about your books."

Meekly, Emma nodded. She was well aware of her propensity to say too much under the influence of alcohol. And she was already grateful that she was being allowed one glass of wine today. Her nerves were fraught, and the alcohol would steady her shaking hands. She intended staying silent for the entire day, so that the others would be proud of her.

Having introduced Anne and Emma to Sarah and Helen, Violet excused herself and went to get herself another glass of wine.

"So, what are you doing these days, Anne?" Sarah Bingham asked, twirling her wineglass.

Anne longed to rub their noses in it, by telling them about her elevated position as an MP's wife, but there was too much at stake. She'd already agreed with the others that there'd be no mention of Clive, since she didn't want any connection between her past and present life. After all, she didn't care what these people thought, and hopefully she'd never have to see any of them again.

"Oh, I'm just a housewife," she said, smiling condescendingly. But she couldn't resist letting them know that she wasn't short of a penny or two. "I spend most of my time running our estate."

Sarah's eyes boggled. "Your estate? I mean, are you terribly rich?"

Anne noticed Helen Seagrove giving Sarah a surreptitious kick. "Oh, I suppose we're comfortably off," she said offhandedly, hoping that both women were noticing her expensive clothes and jewellery. On the other hand, these hideous people probably wouldn't recognise an Armani jacket if it jumped up and bit them.

But by now Helen's eyes were flickering over Anne's ensemble, taking in the cut of her clothes and eyeing the giant diamond ring that glittered beneath the wedding ring on Anne's left hand.

"And you, Helen? Has life been good to you?" Anne said, smiling benignly at her former classmate.

"Oh, fine," said Helen huffily, "but I don't have an estate like you."

"What did you do after leaving school?" Anne persisted, hoping to dispel the tension her obvious wealth had engendered.

"I became a radiographer."

"Wow – how wonderful!" said Anne, and on the principle that most people liked talking about themselves, she encouraged Helen to talk about her work, so that the women would be distracted from any other, more dangerous, topic.

"But I don't work full-time at the moment," said Helen eventually, now more relaxed. "The children take up so much of my time. Do you have any children, Anne?"

For a second, a fleeting spasm of pain crossed Anne's face before she regained her composure. "No, I'm afraid not – but my hands are full running the estate anyway."

But Helen and Sarah had both seen that split second of grief, and together they went in for the kill. They'd found a way of bringing their classmate down to size while elevating their own positions.

"What a pity you weren't blessed with children, Anne," said Sarah sweetly. "My son Rupert is starting at Oxford next year. And my daughter Jemima is in her senior year at school."

Helen decided it was now her turn to put in the boot. "My four are a lot younger, and all rather close in age, so Noel and I have our hands full!"

As Helen began to wax eloquent about her four offspring and their achievements, Anne felt that her head would burst. Unwittingly, she'd exposed her Achilles' heel, and they'd pilloried her for it. What other awful things might they say if they honed in on her guilt over Zoe Gray? As politely as she could, she extricated herself from the malevolent duo, grabbed Emma and quickly moved off.

Directing a quick glance at Fiona, who was in another group close by, Anne discreetly raised her eyebrows. That signal meant it was time to regroup before moving on. The less time they spent with any one group the better.

"You're doing great, Emma," Anne whispered to her companion, who hadn't dared to open her mouth since they'd arrived. "But I think you might actually tell people that you're an author – I mean, it's not as though, like me, you'd be worth blackmailing."

Emma nodded gratefully, oblivious to the implied insult. It would be nice to tell people that she wrote children's books. Invariably, when she met people, they assumed she did some menial job. But when she told them she was a professional writer, their eyes opened wide with surprise, and Emma basked in their adulation.

Just as they were about to move on, Emma was greeted by another classmate, and stopped to chat briefly. At the same time, a tall angular woman marched up to Anne and extended her hand.

"Hello, Anne, I wonder if you remember me?"

Anne deliberately looked vague. Of course she remembered this other woman, but didn't intend giving her the satisfaction of being recognised.

"Hazel Bonnington," the woman said, a wry smile on her face. "I can see you haven't changed at all. Still a snooty po-faced cow."

Anne seethed with rage. She longed to pass some derisive remark and put this upstart in her place, but had enough sense to know that today wasn't the day. There was no point in stirring things up, in case Hazel or someone else decided to bring up Anne's own unsavoury past.

"Hazel, I beg your pardon – of course I remember you now! How lovely to see you again."

"I'm a journalist now, working for one of the tabloids," Hazel stated, with a smile of smug self-satisfaction, which Anne longed to wipe off her face.

"Good heavens!" said Anne, reverting to type without thinking. "Weren't you able to get a job on a decent paper?"

"Once a bitch, always a bitch," said Hazel Bonnington, walking off.

As Jennifer and Fiona left another group and glided over to join her, the four women found themselves together once again.

"Everyone okay?" Anne asked, and each of them nodded.

"It's all very jolly. I haven't heard any mention of – anything," said Jennifer. "Everyone's talking about their kids, their houses and their cars. If you can believe what they say, most of the people here drive BMWs and Mercedes."

"Well, we *did* attend a good school," Fiona added. "We were all expected to do well," she directed a glance at Anne, "– although some did better than others, of course."

"Yes, it all seems pleasant enough," Anne conceded, ignoring Fiona's remark and deciding not to mention her little *contretemps* with Hazel Bonnington. "Fortunately for us, no one seems to want to revisit the past. Or else they've genuinely forgotten what happened."

"How could anyone forget Zoe's death?" asked Emma, and was quickly silenced by the other three.

"Don't mention that name!" Anne hissed, gripping Emma's arm tightly. All three women glanced around to make sure that no one was in earshot. Fortunately, everyone was chattering loudly, and no one seemed to have overheard.

"Oops, sorry!" said Emma, her face turning beetroot. Even at forty-two years of age, she was still intimidated by her three friends. They still had the ability to make her feel like a naughty child when she said something they didn't like.

"I'll take Emma with me this time," Jennifer volunteered, and Anne nodded gratefully. She was tired of watching Emma in case she said the wrong thing. Thankfully, Emma had stayed quiet so far.

"First, we're going to the bar," Jennifer announced, and Fiona and a meek Emma followed.

"Uh oh," said Jennifer as they approached the counter, but her face quickly transformed into a smile as they approached.

"There you are again!" said a beaming Violet Summers, as she took another glass of wine from the bar counter. "Are you all enjoying yourselves?"

"Yes, we're having a wonderful time," said Jennifer, deciding to have another glass of wine herself.

"It's so nice to see all our old classmates," added Fiona unctuously.

"They're serving lunch shortly," said Violet, smiling cheerfully, as she began moving off. "Wouldn't it be nice if we were all seated near each other, and could continue our chat? Byeeee!"

"I hope we're nowhere near that irritating woman!" Anne muttered, coming up behind them. "I'll go mental if I have to listen to any more of her inane chattering!"

"The Violet Summers I remember was always a mouse," said Fiona sourly. "She never said a word in class."

"Well, she's certainly come out of her shell!" Anne retorted. She also remembered that when the ghastly Hazel Bonnington had accused them of hounding Zoe Gray to her death, Violet had stood silently and supportively beside her. Anne sniffed. No wonder she disliked the woman intensely.

Anne pursed her lips. She was getting tired of trying to be on her best behaviour, and she couldn't wait for this day to be over. It was like trying to negotiate one's way through a field full of landmines. How many more calamities could occur before the reunion was over?

CHAPTER 14

On the morning of her mother's school reunion, Vanessa was thrilled to discover that Jennifer had accidentally left her mobile phone behind. She hoped her mother wouldn't miss it until she was too far away from the house to bother coming back for it. Since dawn, Jennifer had been fussing about what she'd wear, and in the end she'd left it so late that she'd dashed off in a rush, wearing a dress she claimed to loathe. Secretly, Vanessa thought the tight-fitting black dress looked too sophisticated for a class reunion. But she didn't dare tell her mother what she thought.

The four women had been phoning each other daily since they'd decided to attend, worrying about what they'd wear, how much weight they'd put on, and how awful it was going to be. Vanessa wondered why they were bothering to go at all, since the event seemed to be causing them so much stress.

Her mother's phone was lying on the kitchen table, and Vanessa eyed it as though it was some kind of dangerous creature that might attack her if she touched it. While she was thrilled at the opportunity the phone represented, she was equally scared that she might discover something she didn't really want to know.

Ultimately, the phone proved too tempting to resist, and she snatched it up, scrolling down the list of names. They were all names she knew, which was disappointing in one way, but reassuring in another. But when she came to the name 'Doreen', she had a moment of unease. Doreen was supposedly her mother's bridge partner but, as far as she knew, no one in the family had ever met the woman. Nor had she ever visited The Old Vicarage or attended any of her parents' parties. Surely you'd invite someone with whom you socialised every week?

For a second, Vanessa wondered if Jennifer could be having an affair with a woman? She'd heard about same-sex liaisons from her friends in school, but she dismissed that idea immediately. Her mother was very definitely a man's woman, and the person on the phone whom she'd been arranging to meet on Wednesday night was definitely a man.

With one eye on the driveway, in case her mother should suddenly return, Vanessa dialled Doreen's number. Her heart was thumping wildly, and she wondered if she should just cancel the number and forget all about her little plan. But suddenly, before she had a chance to cancel, the ringing stopped and she heard a man's voice on the other end of the line. In a low seductive voice, she heard him say: "Hey, Jen! Is the reunion over already? You sexy thing – I can't wait to screw you tonight . . ."

Vanessa dropped the phone as though she'd been scalded. She recognised the voice – it was Clive Ellwood! Her mother's affair was with the husband of one of her best friends!

With trembling hands, Vanessa picked the phone up off the floor and disconnected the call. She felt horribly betrayed and vulnerable. She felt as though her mother was as good as lost to her. She'd put an outsider before her own family, and this was something Vanessa found impossible to forgive. Not only was she cheating on her own husband, she was doing it with a friend's husband! Had her mother no loyalty to anyone?

Suddenly, Vanessa remembered there was something she needed to do before replacing the phone on the kitchen table. She selected the Menu, then Call Register, Dialled Calls and deleted the record of the call she'd made. Now, hopefully her mother would never know she'd used her phone. And hopefully Clive Ellwood wouldn't think to mention it either.

What on earth was she going to do? Now that she'd confirmed her mother's affair, Vanessa wondered how she could behave naturally when her mother returned home. Images of her mother astride Clive Ellwood kept creeping unbidden into her mind, and making her feel sick. Having only recently learnt about sex, such an image was more than she felt able to cope with. It had been easy enough to deal with sex in the abstract, but its illicit intrusion into the heart of her own family was more than she could bear.

Even worse, she wouldn't be able to look at her father, in case she might inadvertently blurt out what she knew. Which would only hurt him, assuming he didn't already know. And if he did know, he'd hardly want his daughter knowing about it. All of which meant that she, her mother and father were now linked in a chain of deception and subterfuge, and all because of her mother's appalling behaviour. Vanessa was filled with indignation. Maybe adults were able to cope with these situations, but she knew she couldn't possibly handle it.

Briefly, she thought of confiding in her brother, but decided against it. Aside from the fact that he didn't care about anything or anyone except himself, there was also the risk that he might inadvertently say the wrong thing, bringing their lives tumbling down around them like a pack of cards. A family unit can be such a fragile thing, Vanessa thought sadly. One wrong word could mean that her parents' marriage would fall apart, with all the attendant fallout for her and Alan.

The only one with whom she could talk things over was her best friend Jocelyn, who understood all about infidelity. Jocelyn was sanguine about her own parents' affairs, but she'd still understand how devastated Vanessa was, and she'd be able to offer advice on how to live with the knowledge of her mother's deception.

She'd also ask Jocelyn to look after Grey Star for a while, because she had just made a monumental decision. She had to get away, at least for a few days. And she had to leave soon. She didn't want to stay here a minute longer, now that she despised her mother so much. She was well aware that she couldn't stay away forever, but a break would give her breathing space, allowing her time to come to terms with her family's new and secret dynamic.

Briefly, she considered tackling her mother about her affair, but what could she hope to gain from that? Threatening to tell her father wouldn't work, since her mother would know only too well that his precious daughter would want to protect him from the hurt. Vanessa felt all alone, lost in an adult world she didn't know how to cope with.

But where would she go? She'd no relatives worth speaking of. Her mother's family were haughty and dismissive, and when her grandparents, aunts, uncle and cousins visited, she and Alan were either banished as though they didn't matter, or expected to entertain their younger cousins. Anyway, Vanessa had no wish to visit any of her mother's relatives, who might even be complicit in her carry-on with Clive Ellwood.

Suddenly, Vanessa brightened. She'd go in search of her father's family – the people her mother had dismissed as 'crude' and 'vulgar'. After all, her mother was hardly in a position to criticise others, was she?

Vanessa had never met any of her father's family. What had happened to his older brother? Suddenly, she felt ashamed that she'd never bothered to show any interest in her father's family before.

She tried to recall the little she knew about her father's past. As a small child, she'd loved hearing stories of his childhood in London, and as she'd sat on his knee he'd told her about the council flat in Walthamstow where he'd spent his childhood, and about his older brother Hugh. She especially liked the story of how they'd climbed a tall tree in the park, and Hugh got stuck up it and they'd needed the fire brigade to get him down. She also knew that her grandfather died when the boys were thirteen and fifteen, and her father freely admitted that he and Hugh had been a handful for their poor mother to cope with. Vanessa wondered if his mother was still alive, and if Uncle Hugh had married. If so, she might have cousins in London!

Resolutely, Vanessa headed for the landline. At least she knew the name of the area where her father's family had lived. But would any of his family still be there? Her starting point would be Directory Enquiries. Excited, she dialled and waited for the operator to answer.

The telephone operator quickly came on the line, and within seconds had supplied her with a H Corcroft who lived at 10 Colchester House in Walthamstow. Colchester House sounded rather posh, but the Number 10 indicated that it was some sort of apartment complex. Besides, she knew from her mother's comments that they couldn't possibly be rich. If they were, her mother would be fawning over them instead of insulting them.

Vanessa felt a surge of excitement. Would her uncle accept her when she arrived on his doorstep? She considered phoning first, but decided against it. She didn't want to give him the chance of rejecting her, at least until he'd met her.

Ringing her friend Jocelyn, Vanessa reluctantly told her about her mother's affair, but not in too much detail, since she was afraid of bursting into tears if Jocelyn was in any way sympathetic. She also told her of her plan to find her relatives in London.

"Why don't you just come and stay here?" Jocelyn said. "I mean, you don't know these relatives of yours – they could be awful. Then you'll only feel worse. If you stay here, we can muck out our ponies together and have a laugh."

"Thanks, Joss, but I need to put distance between me and Mum right now," Vanessa told her. "I can't really explain it, but I need time on my own."

Jocelyn chuckled. "They all do it, Vanessa – honestly, you'll get used to it after a while. It's a bit shocking at first – I mean, you wonder about all those 'happily ever after' stories they told us as kids. But you just need to get on with your own life and leave them to it."

Vanessa bit her tongue. She'd just been about to say that she'd thought her parents were different, but that would sound insulting to Jocelyn's parents.

The two girls arranged that Jocelyn would take care of Grey

Star while Vanessa was away. Jocelyn was also primed to cover for her friend, should anyone decide to check up on her whereabouts. But Vanessa knew that was unlikely, since her mother would be fussing about what to wear to the Ellwoods' garden party the following Saturday, so that would keep her off her case for a bit longer.

Thanking her friend, Vanessa hung up the phone. Then she hurried upstairs and filled a backpack, taking only essentials such as a nightdress, toothbrush, hairbrush, several T-shirts, a jacket and a sweater, several pairs of panties, two pairs of jeans and her laptop. Luckily she hadn't bought that new saddle for Grey Star yet! Quickly, she slid the wad of notes from her bedside table into the back pocket of her jeans. She also raided her mother's make-up drawer, hoping that some carefully applied foundation and eye-liner would fool her relatives into thinking she was eighteen.

Leaving a note on the kitchen table, informing the finder that she'd be staying at Jocelyn's, Vanessa slipped out of the house. She didn't bother telling Alan she was leaving. He wouldn't even notice, or care, if she was there or not. Her father wouldn't be back till late, and her mother was supposedly going straight to her bridge club after the school reunion, but Vanessa knew she'd be spending the night with Clive Ellwood. She smiled grimly to herself. Sometimes there were advantages in having a dysfunctional family!

Armed with a ticket to London, Vanessa boarded the afternoon train and chose a seat. Now that she'd actually made the break, she felt scared and immature. For a moment, she thought of jumping off the train and going back home, but on the other hand, what was waiting for her there? No, she'd stay put. She'd go to London and seek out her father's family. *Her* family.

Vanessa experienced a moment of sheer terror when the guard finally blew his whistle and the train began to move slowly out of the station. But it was too late now to change her mind, so she sat back in her seat and watched the countryside as it began to speed by. The hypnotic motion gradually soothed her nerves, and she began to think again with excitement of the journey ahead.

CHAPTER 15

As the attendees of the school reunion began moving to the lunch tables at the far end of the room, Anne herded Fiona, Jennifer and Emma ahead of her.

"Hopefully we're all sitting together," she muttered. "I don't think I could bear to be stuck beside some of the people I've met here today."

"Don't worry," Fiona soothed. "Since we replied to the invitation as a group, we're bound to be sitting together."

"Well," Anne sniffed, "I don't know – that Cartwright woman doesn't look as though she could organise her way out of a paper bag."

At the tables, several women were checking names off lists, and showing people to their places.

"Hello again!" said Jane Cartwright, smiling cheerfully. "Let me find your seats – Anne Morgan, Fiona Barker, Emma Durrant and Jennifer Lambe – yes, you're all at Table 3."

Anne sighed with relief. At least they were all together, and so far Emma had acquitted herself very well. And in an hour or two, it would all be over.

Yet when they reached their designated table, there were only three places vacant. And there was no place name for Emma.

"What on earth has happened?" asked Anne, barely able to contain her fury. "There must be some mistake." She turned to Fiona and Jennifer. "Can't one of you sort this out, for Christ's sake?"

Both women shrugged their shoulders.

"Someone's messed with the seating arrangements, so they could put one of their own friends beside them," Anne muttered, at the same time casting a withering stare over the other women at their table. It had to be one of those appalling creatures already in situ! If they knew my husband was an MP, she thought angrily, they wouldn't dare mess with me.

"Emma – over here!"

Turning, Emma looked across at Table 4, where Violet Summers was waving frantically.

"Emma, you're here beside me!" she called.

Giving an apologetic glance at her friends, Emma crossed to Table 4.

Anne was furious, since she couldn't keep an eye on Emma any longer. But at least that silly Summers woman was relatively harmless. And as long as Emma didn't drink any more wine, everything would hopefully be okay.

"Oh dear, you've been separated from your friends," said Violet to Emma, "and they don't look very happy about it." She cast a worried glance at Emma. "I hope you don't mind sitting beside me?"

"No, of course not. In actual fact, I'm relieved to get away from them," said Emma gratefully, sitting down and kicking off her ill-fitting shoes. "They always make me feel like an idiot. They're always afraid that I'll say something wrong – and sometimes I do."

"Like what?"

"Oh – nothing. It's just that I'm not like them. They're all sophisticated and wear designer labels all the time. I never feel well-dressed when I'm with them."

"Well, I think what you're wearing is gorgeous," said Violet supportively. "I wish I could wear something floaty like that. But I'd never look as elegant in it as you do."

"Oh, thanks," said Emma, turning pink with pleasure. No one had ever called her elegant before.

"So what do you do, Emma?"

This was music to Emma's ears. "I'm a writer – I write children's books."

"Wow! How interesting – clever old you! You always were very bright, Emma. I remember you always did very well in exams."

Emma was thrilled to be the centre of such attention. She hadn't really got great results in exams, but if that was what Violet remembered, then Emma wasn't going to disillusion her.

"What age group do you write for?"

"Mainly eight to ten-year-olds, but I've also written several teen novels. Right now, I'm working on my eighth novel, and it's due to be published next spring."

"You're amazing!" said Violet, gazing at her with admiration on her face. "You must be the most successful of all the people in our school year. I haven't heard of anyone else doing anything so interesting."

Just then, the first course arrived, and Emma smiled to herself as she tucked into her starter.

The woman sitting on Emma's left side largely ignored her, so Emma directed most of her conversation towards Violet on her right.

"What do you do, Violet?"

The other woman gave a dismissive wave of her hand. "It's so boring – I'm an accountant."

"Oh. That must mean you're very clever," said Emma, trying to return a compliment.

"Well, I'm good at figures, but it's not very exciting – not like your profession."

Emma felt a burst of joy. No one had ever considered that she had a 'profession' before.

"Do you work for a big accountancy company?"

"Er, yes."

"Who?"

"Oh – one of the big city practices."

"Which one?"

"Oh, er – Hayes, Haddon & Partners."

"That must be exciting, all the same."

Violet wrinkled her nose. "Not really. The work itself is very routine. I'd rather talk about your job – it's a lot more interesting than mine."

By the time Emma had informed Violet about the details of her next book, the main course had arrived and all along the tables women were chatting ninety to the dozen. The air was filled with conversation, laughter and the clinking of glasses.

"More wine, Emma?"

"Er, no thanks."

"Why not? You're not driving home, are you?"

"No, but –"

"Oh, come on – another glass isn't going to do you any harm."

Emma glanced furtively across at Table 3, where Anne, Jennifer and Fiona were sitting. "Oh, okay."

"That's the spirit. Isn't this chicken dish gorgeous?"

"Hmmm, it's delicious."

"So explain how you go about writing a book, Emma. Where do you get your ideas?"

For the next hour, Violet and Emma chatted about a wide range of topics. At regular intervals, Violet would turn to Emma with a look of undisguised admiration.

"I can't believe it," she'd say. "I'm sitting beside a famous author!"

Emma was thoroughly enjoying herself. No one had ever been so impressed by her before. Even her agent and publisher treated her like an errant schoolchild when she missed their deadlines. And when Violet kept refilling her empty wineglass, she didn't demur.

"What do your friends do for a living?" Violet asked, pointing across the table to where the others were sitting. "They've all turned into very attractive women. But then, they always were good-looking, even back in our schooldays. Are they fashion models? They're all so tall and elegant."

"No, Fiona is married to a solicitor and lives in Chillingham."

Now that she was away from the trio, she felt safe chatting about their achievements.

Violet chuckled. "I was always scared of your group and of Anne in particular. The four of you were always together – in fact, I was always a little jealous of your close-knit friendship. You four were the group everyone else wanted to be in, but everyone was too in awe of you all even to try."

Emma was relieved that Violet's memory of the group was positive rather than negative. And it was gratifying to think that other pupils had longed to join their little coterie. Suddenly, she found herself remembering things about her schooldays.

"Do you remember our final-year English teacher?" Emma asked.

Violet giggled. "Yes, who could forget old Frosty – she was a dreadful battleaxe, wasn't she? I wonder if the teachers knew the nicknames we had for them? And Eggers – remember her temper tantrums in French class?"

"Yes, Mrs Eglington was always in a bad mood," said Emma, remembering. "But she was a good teacher, nonetheless. Maybe she had family problems we knew nothing about."

Violet squeezed Emma's hand. "There you go – always caring about other people. You're a real sweetie, Emma."

By now, Emma was pleasantly intoxicated, and prepared to consider Violet her new best friend. She felt giddy, and pleased to be away from Anne's cold stare, which always made her feel guilty, even when she hadn't done anything.

"And Anne – what does she do?"

Emma finished her glass of wine with a gulp and watched as Violet topped it up again.

She lowered her voice. "Don't dare tell anyone I told you this – but Anne is married to an MP."

"My God! Of course I won't tell anyone – who is it?"

"Clive Ellwood."

"Wow! He's gorgeous, never mind wealthy."

"Please – you won't tell a soul?"

"Of course not! My goodness, Emma, you move in illustrious circles! Is he as nice as he looks?"

Emma nodded, unable to resist boasting. "He's very charming. And a marvellous host. We're all going to their garden party at The Grange next Saturday, and he'll be there, along with loads of VIPs."

"How exciting! But why doesn't Anne want it known that she's an MP's wife?"

"Shhhh!" said Emma, louder than she'd intended. "She's a very modest person. She'd hate others to fuss."

Violet lowered her voice. "But her old classmates would be thrilled to be in such exalted company! Isn't that why many people came here today? To boast about how well they've done since they left school!"

"Please, I probably shouldn't have told you. Don't mention it to anyone."

"Of course not. Is Jennifer married to anyone famous?"

Emma shook her head. "No, but her husband's very wealthy. He runs one of the country's biggest building companies, and they're loaded. Jennifer's also become president of the local golf club," she added, proud on her friend's behalf.

"What's her husband's company called?"

"Corcroft Construction."

"Wow! You mix in high society, don't you, Emma?" whispered Violet, her eyes alight with excitement. "But then, I suppose, being a well-known author you get invited to all sorts of exciting places."

Emma nodded, draining her fourth glass of wine. Or was it her fifth? As the empty wine bottles were replaced with full ones, and waiters topped up people's glasses, Emma held out her glass for a refill.

At the other table, Anne's gimlet eyes had observed Emma's increasing intoxication, but felt unable to do anything about it. However, by the time dessert was served, she felt that something had to be done. So with a nod to Fiona and Jennifer, she left her seat and walked in Emma's direction, stopping briefly several times as people greeted her.

"Emma, dear – are you having a lovely time?" she asked sweetly as she reached her friend's table.

Even though intoxicated, Emma was aware that Anne was displeased with her but, fortified by all the wine, she was filled with bravado. Who the hell did Anne think she was, to be checking up on her? Looking over at Table 3, she could see Jennifer and Fiona watching the interaction.

"Marvellous, thanks, Anne," Emma replied. "I hope you're having as much fun as Violet and I are having."

"And you, Violet?" added Anne. "Are you enjoying yourself?"

"Yes, thanks, Anne. Emma's been telling me all about her writing," said Violet, beaming.

"You've had a lot to drink, Emma," Anne murmured, leaning forward. "I thought we agreed you'd only have one glass of wine?" she whispered angrily. "You're pissed!"

"So what?" said Emma indifferently. "I'm enjoying myself, and please stop treating me like a child. Now bugger off and leave me alone!"

Shocked, Anne straightened up, looking around and hoping that neither Fiona nor Jennifer had witnessed Emma's insubordination. Never had she been spoken to like that! Emma was clearly out of control, and would have to be removed from the reunion as soon as possible. Clearly the wine had gone to her head.

With a thunderous expression on her face, Anne returned to Table 3, where Fiona and Jennifer were laughing boisterously at some shared joke.

"That little madam is out of control! We'll have to do something about her," Anne snapped as she sat down between them.

"Oh, lighten up, Anne," said Jennifer, still grinning. "We've all had a few drinks – why shouldn't Emma?"

Back at Table 4, Violet was pouring another glass of wine for Emma.

"I overheard what Anne said to you," she said, looking concerned. "She has no right to stop you enjoying yourself. You're a professional woman, Emma. Why did she speak to you like that?"

Emma shrugged her shoulders. "Oh, she's just afraid I might mention the 'Z' word."

"What on earth is that?"

"Oh, I'm not allowed to say it," said Emma, laughing as she downed another mouthful of wine. Her head was swimming and she felt very happy. She'd put Anne in her place for the first time in her life, and she was enjoying the sensation immensely. The chatter all around was like music to her ears. Here she was, right in the middle of all these women who were enjoying themselves. And not one person had mentioned what happened all those years ago. Anne, as usual, was being paranoid, and worrying unnecessarily.

"What do you mean you're 'not allowed'?" asked Violet.

"Oh, Anne always tries to control things," Emma replied nonchalantly. "In fact, they all do. They treat me like a five-year-old."

Violet looked shocked. "That's terrible! You don't deserve to be treated like that, Emma. None of *them* has written eight books!"

Emma nodded. Violet was right. She shouldn't accept such treatment. Violet made her feel good about herself, and she hoped they'd be able to meet again.

Violet leaned forward confidentially. "What on earth is the 'Z' word?"

Emma took another gulp of wine. She felt powerful. She could undermine Anne in an instant. Besides, it wouldn't do any harm to tell Violet. After all, she was her new friend. Well, old friend actually – they'd known each other since their schooldays.

Emma lowered her voice. "Do you remember Zoe Gray?"

Violet's face registered surprise, then shock. "Oh, God – I'd forgotten all about her! She was the girl in our class who drowned, wasn't she?"

Emma nodded. "She drowned herself because of the awful things we did to her."

"Well, that was a long time ago," said Violet calmly. "It hardly matters now. But what exactly did you do that made her drown herself?"

Emma explained about their vindictive campaign, and how they'd kept on taunting Zoe daily until she could take no more.

"Do you still feel guilty?" asked Violet sympathetically.

Emma nodded. "Dreadfully so," she whispered, a tear now running down her cheek. "If I hadn't been so weak, I might have stood up to them."

"Who?"

"Anne, Fiona and Jennifer. Things just got out of control, and I, to my shame, went along with it."

"Don't worry – it all happened a long time ago," said Violet kindly. "There's no point in beating yourself up about it now."

"Please – you won't tell anyone, will you?"

"Of course not," said Violet warmly, leaning over and giving Emma a hug. "Bygones are bygones."

Just then, the waiting staff started bringing around the desserts.

"Yummy – this pudding looks divine," said Violet. "Hmmm – it's delicious too!"

Emma nodded and began to eat. She was beginning to wish she'd never mentioned Zoe, but the wine had made her giddy and prone to talk too freely. Thank goodness it had been to someone as nice and non-judgemental as Violet.

Another glass of wine helped Emma to completely banish the painful memories of Zoe Gray, and she turned the discussion back to Violet's job.

"So you do the accounts for various companies?"

Violet nodded. "We go out to the companies themselves and audit their accounts annually."

"That must be interesting. I mean, you get to visit other companies, rather than being stuck at a desk all the time."

Violet nodded, taking a sip of her wine.

Emma hesitated. "Do you ever do accounts for private individuals?"

Violet looked surprised. "What do you mean?"

"Well –" Emma hesitated, "what I mean is – I need someone to do my annual accounts. I'm hopeless at anything like that, and as a result I'm always in trouble with the taxman by submitting them too late. Would you be able to do them for me? At your usual fee, of course, I'm not expecting any favours –"

Violet looked surprised for a moment, then nodded. "Yes, of course I can. Just phone me at the office."

"Do you have a business card?"

Violet hesitated. "Actually no, I didn't think of bringing any today. Silly me."

"Okay, I'll phone you at Hayes, Haddon & Partners next week."

When dessert was over and coffees and teas had been served, Violet stood up.

"I think I'd better be going, Emma," she said, smiling apologetically. "Perhaps you should join your friends again – some of the people at their table are also leaving."

"Oh – yes, good idea." Emma hesitated, "So – I'll ring you next week, about the accounts?"

"Great, I look forward to that. Byeee!"

Violet left the room, waving goodbye to several other women at different tables as she made her way out. Looking around her, Emma decided that since the woman on her left was still ignoring her, she might as well join the others at Table 3. No doubt she was in for a roasting from Anne, since it was obvious she'd drunk quite a lot of wine. Yet, strangely, the last glass had almost sobered her up.

"Ah, there you are," said Anne regally as Emma arrived at their table, surprising her with such a pleasant welcome.

Then she realised with relief that Anne wasn't going to refer to her earlier insubordination, since she didn't want Jennifer and Fiona to know about it. She also surmised that the wine had mellowed Anne's attitude. Jennifer and Fiona were also in a good mood, and they smiled at her as she pulled up an empty chair.

"It's over at last!" Anne murmured, surveying the gradually dwindling numbers of past pupils still at the tables. Many were leaving or had already left, and others were saying their final farewells in the hotel foyer. "Nearly everyone's gone, and we got through it without a hitch. Let's have a toast!"

"To us!"

The four clinked glasses.

"Let's hope we never have to endure another of these reunions," said Jennifer fervently.

"Definitely not!" said Fiona with a mock shudder.

"Oh, come on, it wasn't too bad," said Emma, smiling.

CHAPTER 16

Jennifer let herself into the luxurious Westminster apartment. What a relief that the ghastly reunion was over! The only problem was that she'd forgotten her mobile phone.

Quickly, she threw off her coat, revealing the tight-fitting black sheath dress that clung to her body in all the right places. Quite a few eyebrows had been raised at the reunion, when those frumpy middle-aged matrons observed that she was still svelte, stylish and elegant, even at forty-two! Smiling, she unwrapped the bottle of Bollinger she'd bought and put it in the fridge. Glancing at her watch, she sat down on the sofa and kicked off her shoes. He'd be here in fifteen minutes. Then they'd order a take-away and relax for the rest of the evening.

Their meetings were so routine now that they were almost like a married couple! Jennifer smiled to herself. What undoubtedly kept their affair so vibrant was the fact that they both enjoyed the thrill of getting one over on so many other people. His wife hadn't a clue what was going on, and he himself was like a naughty schoolboy, who got a tremendous kick out of maintaining the role of good guy on the outside, while shagging one of his wife's closest friends behind everyone's back.

The door opened, and Clive Ellwood walked in.

"Hi, gorgeous," he said, leaning down to kiss her warmly on the lips. He appraised her dress and grinned lasciviously. "Mmm, looks like I'm on a promise tonight!"

Coolly, Jennifer stood up, took his coat off and loosened his tie. "Darling, you know you're always on a promise with me."

Jennifer enjoyed every moment of her stolen hours with Clive. He was the only man she'd ever really loved, and all her sexual energies were directed towards satisfying his needs. Whatever Clive wanted, Jennifer was happy to supply, and she spent hours preparing for each Wednesday night, dressing to thrill him and combing websites and magazines for new and exotic ways to titillate him.

From an early age, Jennifer had watched how her mother wound her father round her little finger. Her mother was a beautiful but essentially selfish woman, and it was from her that Jennifer took lessons in how to deal with men. She learned that a woman was in control of the relationship as long as the man found her attractive, and that a woman's worth was based on her ability to keep her man keen.

Jennifer also learned how important it was to set your own valuation, and she'd decided that hers would be set high. From puberty, she'd kept a tight rein on her food intake, and was proud of her size-zero figure. Jennifer liked being fragile, because it seemed to bring out men's ardour and desire to protect her, so this became Jennifer's method of rating herself.

After university, Jennifer had worked as an assistant to the editor of a fashion magazine. But she hadn't enjoyed being at someone else's beck and call, and her aim was to quit as soon as she could find a wealthy husband. As far as she was concerned, there were better things to do with her time other than earning a pittance and being someone else's dogsbody. When Benjamin appeared and she'd seen the size of his bank balance, she hadn't needed to think any further. Since the man she loved was already married, Benjamin would do as a reasonable stopgap.

As Clive now took her in his arms and kissed her longingly, Jennifer could feel her own desire increasing. Sometimes however, unbidden images of Anne having sex with Clive forced its way into her mind, spoiling her happiness at the most inopportune moments. Jennifer didn't like to think of what Clive did in bed with Anne. She could only hope that her plain and unadventurous friend was unlikely to satisfy a man with Clive's appetites. Hopefully their sex was merely perfunctory, and Clive found it a duty rather than a pleasure. Or maybe he didn't bother doing it with her at all. Surely that short chunky hairstyle would put any man off bedding her.

Jennifer usually felt good in Anne's company, since she was undoubtedly the better-looking of the two. Although Anne looked after her figure, she had a thicker waist and was heavier in build, and her utilitarian hairstyle did nothing to enhance her looks. By contrast, Jennifer kept her dark-blonde hair long, which Clive adored, and which enabled her to wear it in a variety of styles, designed to tease, tantalise, and keep variety in their relationship.

When Jennifer was compelled to have sex with Benjamin, she cloaked her dislike of him in a polished and professional performance. She went through all the motions, licking, sucking and teasing, until he came, then she could mercifully give up any further pretence. In other words, she gave him what he wanted, without ever giving anything of herself. She hoped he shagged his secretaries regularly. If he was sated elsewhere, she reasoned, then his need for sex with her would be a lot less frequent.

Poor Benjamin, she thought, without any pity. He'd given her the wealth she craved, but he did nothing for her otherwise. He was a good-looking man, she supposed, in a rough, angular sort of way, but he wasn't remotely sophisticated, suave or debonair. How she wished she'd met Clive before Anne did! But she and Anne's husband didn't meet until the day of the wedding, when their attraction to each other was instant and mutual. And after the reception, while Anne was upstairs in a hotel room getting changed into her going-away outfit, she and Clive were humping furiously in a broom closet off the hotel kitchen.

"I adore you, my precious," Clive whispered in her ear, bringing Jennifer back to reality.

"You mean everything to me," Jennifer whispered back, meaning every word. If only their one night a week could be every night! Jennifer also had a delicious secret she intended sharing with Clive some day. But she'd pick her moment, because the time certainly wasn't right yet . . .

Clive walked out to the kitchen and opened the fridge. "Great – you got some champagne."

Smiling, Jennifer followed him into the kitchen and took the bottle from him, opening it with a pop and pouring two glasses.

"Your good health, darling!" she said.

"Thanks, my sweet, I certainly need it – the debate in the Commons this afternoon was hell." He grimaced. "And, as you know, we have a crowd of bloody diplomats coming to The Grange next weekend. I wish Anne would stop arranging these goddamned garden parties. All I want to do, after a tough week in the Commons, is take it easy when I go home."

"The poor dear thinks that she's advancing your career, darling."

"Well, my precious," he said, brightening, "you make the dreary days in the Commons worthwhile. Seeing you every Wednesday evening is the icing on the cake." He grinned. "Otherwise, I don't think I could listen to all those 'Learned Gentlemen' talking a load of crap every day."

Holding her champagne glass languidly and stretching out along one of the sofas, Jennifer crossed her legs so that her dress artfully fell open, revealing her long shapely legs. She knew Clive like to look at her, and she derived pleasure from wallowing in his adoration.

She also wasn't wearing any knickers, since she knew that really turned Clive on. She'd taken them off as soon as she'd arrived at the flat, and she wondered what the matrons at the reunion would think if they could see her now!

"You look lovely – as always," he whispered, and Jennifer wondered if they should have sex before or after the take-away.

Languidly, she got up off the sofa and went into the kitchen.

"Well, darling," she said, returning with the menus, "will it be Chinese or Thai or Indian tonight?"

"Right now, I'm only hungry for you," Clive whispered, reaching out and stroking her thigh.

Jennifer sighed happily, revelling in Clive's desire for her. His need always stimulated her own. To hell with the food, she thought, wrapping her arms around him and kissing him tenderly. They'd have sex now, then again later, after the food. After all, they had the whole night ahead of them . . .

CHAPTER 17

The Corcrofts lived in a council flat in a purpose-built block in Walthamstow. The outside of the block looked bleak, and graffiti covered the walls of the communal passageways. Vanessa felt as though she'd stepped onto the set of a *film noir* movie. A group of young men wearing hoodies stood around at the entrance to the stairwell, talking and kicking their trainers against the wall, and for a moment Vanessa wondered if she'd made a mistake in coming here. She gave an apologetic smile as they exaggeratedly stood aside to let her through, immediately making sexist comments as soon as she started climbing the stairs.

The stairwell was dark – probably, Vanessa surmised, because the lights had been vandalised. Groping her way upwards, she felt fear for the first time. This was a world she knew nothing about, and suddenly she felt out of her depth. What if these people were as awful as her mother had always maintained? Just because her mother was cheating on her father, it didn't mean that her judgement of other things was impaired. Maybe the Corcrofts would also be angry because her father didn't see them anymore, and they'd order her off the premises. Then, mortified, she'd have to descend the dark stairwell and walk past the hoodies again.

Hesitantly, she knocked on the door of 10 Colchester House. She could hear the blare of a television inside, so she knocked a little harder. Despair filled her. Maybe they were watching their favourite soap opera, and would be angry at being interrupted. And how would she explain why she was there? She could hardly tell them that she hated her mother, and that maybe – just maybe – there was a small element of revenge in what she was doing. She was, in effect, thumbing her nose at her mother. But what if these people turned her away? Told her to go back to her wealthy family and leave them alone? By now, it was getting late, and she was very far from home.

Vanessa knocked again. One of the young men had followed her up the steps and was walking jauntily towards her. She felt a frisson of fear. Presumably he was one of the group who'd been standing downstairs, but she couldn't really tell since they all looked the same, with their faces and bodies hidden within the folds of their hoodie uniforms. The whole area seemed to be populated by young people in hoodies! Her heart was thudding painfully when he stopped right beside her, towering over her as he leaned against the wall.

He muttered something that Vanessa couldn't understand. "Pardon?"

He repeated himself, and although she still couldn't understand him, Vanessa's first feeling was relief that he hadn't mugged her yet.

"I'm looking for the Corcrofts," she told him, hoping that they'd open the door quickly and protect her. On the other hand, it would be better if he'd just go away. The Corcrofts mightn't let her in if they saw her in the company of this uncouth creature, who was clearly a hooligan.

The young man muttered something again, and Vanessa tried to analyse what he'd said. It sounded rather like: "I'm looking for your money."

"I haven't got any money," she said bravely, "Now please go away – I'm waiting for the Corcrofts." She was desperately hoping that the door would open before he knocked her to the ground and made off with her possessions.

Just then, the door of the flat did open, and a woman's head appeared. "Oi, Carl – will you nip round to the chipper for me?"

"Okay." He pointed to Vanessa. "This girl's waiting to see you."

"And who are you?" asked the large woman standing on the doorstep.

"I'm Vanessa Corcroft," she said, not sure whether she should extend her hand.

The large woman beamed. "Well, I never – you must be Benny's girl!"

Vanessa had never heard her father called 'Benny' before. Her mother always used his full name, and insisted others did too. But the name Benny seemed to suit her dad.

"Yes," replied Vanessa.

"Well then, come in, come in!"

As Vanessa stepped across the threshold, the large now-smiling woman pulled her into a hug that nearly suffocated her. She found herself almost buried alive in a gigantic bosom as large fleshy arms enveloped her.

Up to now, all the women in Vanessa's world had been tall and stick-thin, and were always worrying about how they looked and whether or not they'd put on an ounce of weight. By contrast, this woman didn't seem remotely worried about the rolls of flesh encasing her rotund frame.

"I'm Maisie, Benny's sister-in-law," she informed Vanessa, hugging her tightly once again.

Maisie smelled of stale perfume and cigarettes, which was a novel sensation for Vanessa. It was how she assumed women in old black-and-white movies would have smelled, and it made her feel strangely at home, even though it wasn't a smell she'd ever encountered at The Old Vicarage.

The young hoodie had followed them inside, and it suddenly dawned on Vanessa that he might actually live there.

"Oi, Carl," said Maisie, as she released Vanessa from her tight embrace, "I thought I asked you to go for some chips?"

The hoodie grinned. "Okay, Mum – I'm on my way!"

"Better get some extra – we have a guest this evening!"

Saluting, the young man left.

"That's my son Carl," Maisie told Vanessa proudly. "Your first cousin!"

Vanessa was surprised and relieved. Carl certainly looked a lot less dangerous with a smile on his face. Now she realised he hadn't been asking for her money – he'd probably been saying: 'Are you looking for my mother?'

Inside, the flat was small and untidy, and the occupants seemed to have spread themselves and their possessions over every available surface. Ornaments covered the mantelpiece and filled the china cabinet, and Vanessa felt claustrophobic as she surveyed the two large patterned sofas that were also squashed into the tiny space.

"And this is your Uncle Hugh, Vanessa. Your father's brother."

Sitting in front of the large-screen TV was a man who was almost as roly-poly as his wife. On being introduced to Vanessa, he jumped up with surprising agility and clasped her tightly to his beer belly, all the time slapping her on the back affectionately.

"Well, well – Benny's girl!" he kept repeating. "Isn't this a great surprise!"

"You must be starving," Maisie said, looking at her, a worried expression on her face. "Don't worry, Carl will be back soon. He only has to go round the corner to the chippie. In the meanwhile, I'll put on the kettle for a nice cup of tea."

Uncle Hugh grinned. "Maybe she'd prefer a brandy – Vanessa, are you old enough to have a drink?"

"I'm eighteen," Vanessa lied, hoping the make-up she'd applied would hide her blushes, as well as making her look older. While on the train, she'd thickly coated her skin with foundation, adding mascara, eye shadow and eyeliner to complete the effect.

"Eighteen – my goodness!" said Hugh. "Is it really that long since we saw our Benny?"

Maisie's face darkened. "Hrrmmph – it wouldn't surprise me. Once that bitch got her claws into him, she made sure he dropped us!"

Quickly, Hugh threw a warning glance at his wife over his niece's head, but Vanessa didn't care that Maisie had insulted her mother. In her book, her mother deserved it. Apart from cheating on her husband, she'd also denied her two children the pleasure of knowing the Corcrofts. Vanessa wasn't sure if Alan would find pleasure in knowing them, but that wasn't the point. Neither she nor her brother had been given the choice.

"So what brings you here, Vanessa?" asked Uncle Hugh, settling back comfortably in one of the big sofas, and beckoning Vanessa to join him. "Do your father and mother know you're here?"

Vanessa shook her head as she sat down. She'd prepared for this eventuality while on the train.

"No, but now that I'm an adult, I felt that it was time I met the rest of my family."

Hugh nodded. "And we're very glad you did, Vanessa. How is my brother? Is he keeping well?"

Vanessa nodded. And her father would continue to be fine as long as he didn't learn about his wife's affair. Assuming he didn't know already, of course.

"So have you any brothers and sisters, Vanessa?" asked Maisie, still standing in the doorway, and showing no sign of putting on the kettle.

Quickly, Vanessa told them about Alan, but out of loyalty she avoided adding that he was self-centred and a pain. Then she told them about Grey Star, the riding lessons, and the stables where her pony was kept.

Vanessa hoped she didn't sound boastful, since it was obvious that the life of the Walthamstow Corcrofts was very different from her own. On the other hand, she really wanted to share the details of her life with them.

Just then, Carl returned with a large paper bag, leaking with vinegar. Maisie quickly took out the individual chip-bags and put them onto plates, handing one to each person. Vanessa smiled to herself. Her mother would be horrified if she saw her daughter eating with her fingers, and out of a paper bag!

The chips were delicious, and Vanessa ate every single one. No food had ever tasted so wonderful before. She also found herself liking her cousin Carl, who wasn't frightening at all now that he'd removed his hoodie. He had neatly cropped red-blond hair, and Vanessa could see a resemblance to her own father. He was also funny and witty, and soon had her smiling at his jokes and stories.

As they ate, Maisie was fussing around in the background.

"Come on, Vanessa, there are plenty more chips – you look as though you need some proper feeding. You're terribly thin."

Vanessa nodded, realising that Maisie was genuinely enjoying ministering to her newfound guest. Soon, a piping-hot mug full of strong black tea appeared in front of her.

"Milk, sugar, Vanessa?"

Vanessa shook her head.

Maisie tore the large vinegar-soaked chip-bag open, and spread the remaining chips onto a spare plate, which she placed in the centre of the coffee table. Without waiting to be asked, Vanessa helped herself, and Maisie's eye lit up with delight, as though Vanessa had done something quite remarkable.

For the first time in ages, Vanessa felt at peace. No one was making any demands on her, and she felt nurtured by these people whom she hardly knew. She also appreciated that her uncle wasn't pushing her to tell them anything about his brother, other than to query his health. In fact, he hadn't even asked where she lived or where she'd travelled from. He was clearly leaving her to reveal things at her own pace and in her own time.

As she gazed around the cramped flat, Vanessa felt a thrill at being so far from home, and in an environment so unlike her own. She felt really grown-up at having made her way here alone, and she was thrilled at being accepted by these nice people. How on earth could her dad have cut them out of his life?

Later that night, after refusing Carl's offer of his bedroom, Vanessa settled down on one of the sofas in the living room. She lay awake long after Hugh, Maisie and Carl had headed off to their own rooms, unable to sleep because of all the new experiences going round in her head.

It felt strange to be sleeping in someone's living room instead of her own room. Even when she stayed with friends, she was always given the guest room. Here, her backpack was tucked under the sofa. But while it was scary in one way, it was homely in another. Here, everyone treated her like an adult, and was interested in what she had to say. Then she suddenly realised why – they all thought she was eighteen!

She smothered a nervous giggle. By pretending to be eighteen, she'd also turned Alan, aged fifteen, into her younger brother!

Of course, she didn't really want to deceive her relatives. But if she'd told them her real age, they'd probably feel obliged to let her parents know where she was. And just for a little while, she wanted to keep her new family completely to herself.

CHAPTER 18

"C'mon, cuz, I'm taking you shopping – my treat," said Carl, as a sleepy Vanessa awoke on the couch the following morning.

"What?"

"Up you get, sleepyhead – I'm free this morning, so get out of the sack and let's get going!"

"Carl – leave the poor girl alone," Maisie retorted as she bustled in carrying a plate of toast. "She needs a proper breakfast before she can go anywhere!" She turned to Vanessa. "Don't mind him – here, have some toast, dear, and I'll get you a cup of tea right away –"

"Okay, have your breakfast, Vanessa," said Carl cheerfully. "I need to call to a neighbour in the next block, so I'll meet you at the bottom of the steps in ten minutes. Okay?"

Nodding, Vanessa gratefully gobbled down the toast and got dressed, then headed quickly to the bathroom so that she could top up the make-up that would help her to maintain the lie that she was eighteen. She was also intrigued to know what Carl had in mind.

Within minutes, she was ready to go. With Maisie still fussing over her, she kissed her aunt goodbye, left the flat and made her way along the passageway. As she came down the steps, she heard voices below her, and as she reached the bottom of the stairwell, she came upon the three hoodies she'd encountered the day before.

"Well, if it isn't the posh little madam!" said the tallest one, sneering. The others grinned in unison.

"Got any cigarettes, have you?" asked the one in a light-coloured hoodie.

"No," said Vanessa, drawing on all her reserves of bravado, "and you shouldn't be smoking anyway – don't you know it causes cancer?"

"Ooooh – we've got a little Miss Know-it-all here!"

The three hoodies moved menacingly close, and Vanessa felt really frightened. At thirteen, she found any boys difficult to deal with, but aggressive older boys were out of her league altogether.

"Excuse me," she said, trying to push past them, but they weren't willing to let her go. They blocked her way, and jostled her as she tried to go by.

Suddenly, someone shouted down from one of the balconies. "Oi, leave her alone – that's my cousin!"

The hoodies looked briefly defiant as Carl hurried down, then they shuffled away.

"Rozzer, Jack, Leggo – if I catch you being snotty to my cousin again, you'll be sorry!" Carl called after them.

"We were only havin' a laugh!" said one of them sullenly. "Can't she take a joke?"

It was clear to Vanessa that her cousin was held in some regard locally, even it was only by the local layabouts.

"Now fuck off, you lot, or I'll kick your arses down the street," Carl called after them, smiling.

Vanessa was shocked and thrilled all at once. She'd never heard language like that before, and she loved it. At home, even the word 'damn' was frowned on by her mother, although she'd always suspected that her father knew a few choice words himself.

"Don't worry, cuz," said Carl, slipping an arm around her. "They're harmless, really. They only want a bit of respect, you know."

"Well, they certainly don't show any respect to *me*," Vanessa retorted, her relief now turning to anger.

"Look at it from their point of view," said Carl reasonably.

"Everybody treats 'em like shit, so the only way they cope is by trying to act like tough guys."

"But why pick on me?"

Carl grinned. "You're posh, Vanessa – that makes you a threat to them. You remind them how unfair the world is, and what little hope they've got of ever getting anywhere in life."

Vanessa said nothing. How could she be a threat to anyone?

"You working, Vanessa?"

Remembering that she was supposed to be eighteen, Vanessa thought rapidly. "No, I'm starting college soon," she lied, hoping Carl wouldn't ask her for too many details.

"Well, those lads from the estate – they're never going to go to college, maybe will never even have a job."

To thirteen-year-old Vanessa, never having to go to school or work sounded a wonderful prospect, but she was keen to understand her cousin's insights on the situation.

"And what about you, Carl – what do you do all day?"

"I'm a fundraising and development manager with Greenpeace – I finished college two years ago."

Vanessa looked incredulous. "You've been to *university*?"

Then she felt herself turning pink with embarrassment, since she'd assumed that Carl was on the dole.

Her cousin gave her a scathing look. "I've got a Masters in Environmental Science. Just because we live here doesn't mean we're all dossers, y'know. That kind of prejudice pisses people off around here. Especially people like Rozzer, Jack and Leggo, who'd probably love to go to university if they could. They're all bright lads."

"I'm sorry," said Vanessa contritely. "About sounding prejudiced, I mean, but I still don't understand why they can't go to university if they want to?"

Carl sighed. "It's a long story, Vanessa. How many people from council estates do you know who are attending college?"

Vanessa shook her head, feeling that it was acceptable to be ignorant on this matter, since she wasn't supposed to be at university yet.

"Not many," said Carl, answering his own question. "It's not just a matter of brains – there's a lot of prejudice to overcome."

"Like what?" asked Vanessa, keen to learn as much as she could about the world of council-estate inhabitants. "*You've* been to university."

"Yes, but that's because Dad believed in me, and worked hard to support me. The dice is loaded against most people when they come from somewhere like here," he continued with equanimity, "and your accent makes sure that the toffs'll never let you make it to the inner circle of anything."

"Do you think *I'm* a toff?"

Carl grinned. "I suppose so, but you're the nicest one I've ever met!"

"But why can't people change their lives if they really want to?" Vanessa persisted.

Shrugging his shoulders, Carl gave her a smile that told her she'd asked the right question. "We live in a class-ridden society, cuz. The toffs need to maintain an underclass to do their dirty work."

Vanessa felt uncomfortable. She knew that her mother was one of the most prejudiced people she'd ever met, and would abhor Carl and his family. And Rozzer, Jack and Leggo. Listening to Carl, Vanessa found herself almost warming to the three hoodies who'd only recently frightened the life out of her.

As for Carl, well, she was already a little in love with him. Okay, so he was her cousin and she wasn't *really* in love with him, but he gave her a lovely warm woolly feeling that she'd never felt before. He'd protected her when the three hoodies had ridiculed her accent, and he'd seemed proud to tell them that she was his cousin and part of his family.

"But how – ?"

Carl seemed to read her mind. "How are our families so different? I think your father is probably one of those men who always wanted to be a success. And he'd have done anything to get there." He gave a whimsical smile. "My father, on the other hand, is just a worker. A decent man, but not one who'll ever set the world on fire."

Vanessa was annoyed. "Are you saying my father isn't decent? What did you mean when you said he would do anything to be successful?"

Carl grimaced. "Sorry, I didn't mean to cast any aspersions on him – I just assume he's cut corners here and there to get where he wanted. Most rich people do."

"But my father started at the bottom – he was a brickie after he left school – he told me so himself."

"Good for him – he had the brains and the drive to get himself out of the ghetto. All I'm saying is that you don't get to run one of the country's biggest building companies by being a pushover."

Vanessa said nothing. She wanted to rise to her father's defence, but maybe, just maybe, there was a grain of truth in it.

"Come on, Vanessa – you don't believe all that crap we learnt at school about honesty and integrity? They're great ideals in principle, but few successful people have ever adhered to them. Most of the rich in this country have inherited their wealth – because their forebears robbed it from someone else, generations back, or stripped underdeveloped countries of their minerals to fund their lifestyle. As for the rags-to-riches stories – well, you always have to bend a few rules to get to the top."

"So you're saying that your dad decided to stay poor?"

Carl laughed. "Dad wouldn't have the brains to get to the top. And he wouldn't have a clue how to break the rules to get there! He might try to slip a piece of over-ripe fruit into someone's basket from time to time, but that's the height of it. Besides, he enjoys what he does. He loves the banter of the market – in fact, why don't you go with him, and try your hand at selling? Assuming you're staying with us for a few days."

Vanessa nodded. She was enjoying her stay in Walthamstow. It was a world apart from her own life up till now, and she really liked the idea of working on the market stall with her uncle.

By now, they'd arrived at the High Street, and Carl led her into the large and busy shopping mall.

"Where are we going?" Vanessa asked, mystified.

"In here," said Carl as he led her into one of the big fashion stores. Leading her over to a large mirror, he pointed to the clothes she was wearing.

"The jeans are okay, but that dinky little jacket says posh, posh, posh," he said, grinning. "If you're going to stay here for a while, we need to get you into something more suitable!"

"What do you mean?" asked Vanessa, too intrigued to be embarrassed or feel insulted.

"We're getting you a hoodie."

Vanessa was surprised, then pleased, as they looked at the rows of different styles and colours on offer. Finally, they both agreed on a grey one, which Vanessa opted to wear straight away. As Carl paid the shop assistant, Vanessa gazed at herself in the shop mirror. She looked so different, so grown-up!

"You look great, Vanessa – it really suits you," said Carl, smiling.

Vanessa was so overwhelmed by emotion that she had to look away in case she started to cry. Nothing had made her feel quite so accepted as this gesture of Carl's. And she knew, with absolute certainty, that her mother would hate it.

"It's gorgeous, Carl – thank you!" she told her cousin, stretching up on her toes to kiss his cheek. "I'm going to wear it all the time."

"In that case, I think we'd better get you a spare one," said Carl, laughing. "I liked you in the green one – let's get that one as well, okay?"

Vanessa nodded as he paid for the second hoodie. Never had she felt so happy or so cherished.

CHAPTER 19

Zoe's Diary

January 5

I was looking forward to going back to school after Christmas, but four girls from my class have started calling me names. They wait at the crossroads and shout nasty words as I go by. I don't know what I've done to deserve this treatment. They taunt me, laughing at me and saying that my uniform is filthy. It's not true – our clothes are shabby because Mum forgets we need new ones, but I always do my best to wash and iron them. They're also calling Mum horrible names. Why have they suddenly picked on me?

"Zoe Gray's mother's a drunkard!" yelled thirteen-year-old Anne Morgan. Her lip curled with disdain as Zoe walked by, her young shoulders hunched as though warding off a blow. Anne and her friends Emma Durrant, Jennifer Lambe and Fiona Barker all stood sniggering at the crossroads as their timid classmate hurried past. Now that the Christmas holidays were over, they'd made it their mission to taunt the hapless Zoe every day after school.

By her apologetic stance, Zoe almost seemed to invite censure.

And like heat-seeking missiles, the foursome seemed to know that they'd honed in on an easy target for their bullying.

"Her mother made a disgrace of herself at the junior school play!" added Jennifer, loud enough for the retreating Zoe to hear.

"And look at her school uniform – how on earth can she come to school looking like that?" added Fiona maliciously. "She's a disgrace!"

"Her mother lies in bed all day, that's why!" Emma added. And just in case Zoe hadn't heard, she roared again: "Zoe Gray stinks of booze!" and the others began to chant along with her. "Zoe Gray stinks of booze! Zoe Gray stinks of booze!"

Zoe longed to run, but that would add cowardice to the list of offences the bullies had chosen to level against her. Near to tears, she wondered why she'd suddenly become the focus of the girls' ire. She'd done nothing to provoke them, and in class she stayed well away from them. Nevertheless they'd managed to isolate her, and even girls who'd been friendly before were now wary of spending time with her in case they received the same treatment. Right now, she'd only a few loyal friends left.

Zoe longed to cry, but she wouldn't give those horrid girls the satisfaction of knowing they'd upset her. She was well aware that her life wasn't the same as theirs. They all lived in expensive houses, with housekeepers and gardeners to keep everything in order, whereas she and Claire lived in a modest cottage, with shabby furnishings and an overgrown lawn. They tried their best to keep the garden tidy, but the weeds seemed to flourish in spite of their efforts.

Zoe glanced surreptitiously over her shoulder. Thankfully, the bullies hadn't followed her. Now she could cry without fear of being picked on. She often cried as she walked home – like Claire, she missed the happy home they'd had when their father had been there. She remembered his smile, his sense of fun, and she wondered bitterly if she'd ever see him again. She was certain that if her father came back, she wouldn't be a victim of the bullies anymore. They'd no longer have a reason to bully her because her mother would stop drinking, she and Claire would *have new school uniforms, and the cottage would be spotless again.*

Zoe glanced down at her uniform. The bullies were right – it had seen better days. It was years since she'd had a new skirt, blouse or blazer, and each item was now too small, stained and threadbare. Claire's uniform was no better.

Zoe felt a sudden flare of anger towards her mother, who spent so much of the family's money on alcohol. But her anger died just as quickly – after all, her poor mother was ill, and couldn't help the way she was.

Zoe wished there was someone she could turn to for advice, but that would only highlight their mother's shortcomings. She and Claire did their best to hide their mother's excesses from public scrutiny. At weekends, they did their best to keep the house tidy, and in summer they cut the lawn and washed the windows. They tried to make sure that, from the outside at least, the cottage looked well kept, so that none of their neighbours could claim the Gray family were letting down the tone of the village.

As Zoe reached the garden gate, she wiped her tears away and put a smile on her face. She didn't want her mother or Claire to know how much the bullies upset her. Of course, her mother was probably drunk by now, and wouldn't notice anyway. Zoe had little doubt that the constant drinking was gradually destroying her life.

"Hello, I'm home!" she called as she opened the front door, and Claire rushed out of the kitchen to greet her. As she hugged her little sister, Zoe felt a brief moment of contentment. For now, she was safe from her tormentors. And she had a sister who loved her – what could be better than that?

CHAPTER 20

Emma was looking forward to seeing Violet Summers again. She hoped they'd become friends – Violet had made her feel like a competent adult, and they'd had fun together at the reunion. It would be nice to have someone else with whom to go to the movies or the pub. Violet had made her feel good about herself – unlike Anne, Fiona and Jennifer, who always made her feel inferior. Besides, her accounts were in a total mess, and Violet had kindly agreed to sort them out for her.

Emma dialled Hayes, Haddon & Partners and waited patiently as the answering service ran through its list of options. Eventually it gave the number for Reception, and Emma punched it in.

"Hello, Hayes, Haddon & Partners, how may I help you?"

"Good morning," Emma said. "May I speak to Violet Summers, please?"

"What department is she in?"

"Oh – sorry, I don't know."

"Hold on a moment – I'll check the list of extension numbers."

After a few moments, the receptionist was back on the line.

"Sorry, there doesn't seem to be anyone of that name working here."

"There must be," said Emma firmly. "She told me she worked there. Can you check with someone else, please?"

"Okay," said the receptionist, "I'll check with the HR department. Just hang on a moment."

After a few bars of "Greensleeves", the receptionist was back on the line. "I'm sorry, but there's definitely no one of that name working here."

"But she's an accountant –"

"Well, maybe you should try some other accountancy firms," said the receptionist kindly. "You may simply have got the company name mixed up."

"Okay, thank you," said a despondent Emma, replacing the phone. How on earth could she have made such a mistake? But maybe she'd got it wrong because she'd drunk so much wine that day. She'd try some of the other companies, although she could have sworn Violet said Hayes, Haddon & Partners . . .

Her calls to several other major accountancy practices proved fruitless. Then she decided to check the phone book for Violet's home number. Since Violet had said she wasn't married, hopefully her surname would be listed. Although Emma didn't actually know where Violet lived, it seemed safe to assume she lived near the city if she commuted to one of the large accountancy practices.

Quickly, Emma skimmed through the pages of the county phone book, but could find no listing for either Violet or V Summers. Then, just in case Violet might be listed with another letter before her name, such as NV Summers, Emma went through the list of Summers again without success. Then Emma remembered there was another spelling of the name, so she tried everyone listed under Somers, but was equally unsuccessful.

By now Emma was puzzled and disappointed. She'd assumed that contacting Violet would be easy. Nevertheless she was determined to press on with her search, since she really wanted to see her friend again.

Finally, she hit on the idea of ringing one of the organisers of the school reunion. They were bound to have Violet's home address and telephone number!

Digging out the invitation to the reunion – which she'd dumped in her wastepaper bin – Emma found Jane Cartwright's number and dialled it.

"Jane, hello – it's Emma Durrant. I was at the reunion last Wednesday."

"Emma! How lovely to hear from you. Did you enjoy it?"

"Yes, thanks, it was great, and thank you so much for organising it. It was so much fun chatting to all our old school chums." She hesitated. "I was wondering if you could give me a phone number for Violet Summers – we exchanged numbers on Wednesday, but I'm afraid I've mislaid hers."

"Of course – hang on a minute – I'll have to go upstairs and get my list of past pupils."

As Emma waited, she wondered if any other past pupils had renewed friendships at the reunion. She sincerely hoped it had been the starting point for her friendship with Violet.

Soon, Jane Cartwright was back on the phone. "Hmmm, let me see – Violet Summers, ah, yes – here it is."

As Jane called out the number, Emma jotted it down, thanking her old classmate profusely for her time and trouble. With promises to meet up sometime, Emma rang off.

She was surprised to discover that Violet's phone number was in another part of the country. How on earth did she manage to commute to the city? Then it dawned on her that Violet might work as a freelance auditor – that would explain why no one in Hayes, Haddon & Partners knew her.

Feeling a lot happier, she dialled the number Jane Cartwright had given her.

"Hello, Violet?"

"Yes – who's that?"

"It's Emma."

"Emma who?"

"Emma Durrant. Remember we met at the reunion last Wednesday?"

There was a brief pause at the other end of the phone. "I wasn't at the reunion, Emma. I couldn't go because my husband was having a major operation that very week."

"But – you sat beside me at the lunch! We talked about all sorts of thing – you said you'd do my accounts!"

The person at the other end chuckled. "Accounts? I can't add two and two! I think you must have the wrong person, Emma. John's had health problems for months, so the reunion's always been out of the question for me. I guess you just got the name of your accountant friend wrong. Sorry."

Emma found herself unable to speak. She wanted to cry. How could she have got things so wrong?

"Okay, thanks – er, Violet. Hope your husband gets well soon."

Then she rang off and burst into tears. Who on earth was the woman she'd been sitting beside at the reunion? She was positive her name had been Violet Summers! She also remembered Anne, Fiona and Jennifer calling the woman by that name, so she hadn't been imagining it.

Emma was deeply disappointed. Then she brightened. Maybe Violet – or whoever she was – would try to contact her! Then they'd sort out the misunderstanding, have a laugh about it, and take their friendship from there. Then she remembered that she hadn't given Violet – or the woman who called herself Violet – her own address or phone number, and the woman hadn't asked for it. It was almost as though she didn't want to keep in contact.

Emma sighed. In the meantime, she'd have to find someone else to sort out her accounts. Picking up the *Golden Pages*, she opened the section headed '*Accountants*', lifted the phone and began to dial.

CHAPTER 21

Claire felt inordinately pleased with herself. The reunion had worked out so much better than she'd expected. And she'd got all the information she needed.

When she'd first found the invitation for Zoe's class reunion, it had seemed like the most awful trick of fate, a final insult to her poor dead sister. But in fact it had turned out to be a wonderful opportunity.

Attending the reunion had proved the perfect starting-point for getting information about her sister's killers. She conceded that 'killers' was an extreme word to use, but it was how she felt about the four women who'd caused her sister's death. She didn't yet know how she'd make them pay, but now that she'd managed to learn more about their adult lives, she was in a better position to work out a plan.

Guessing that Jane Cartwright's list of past pupils would be more up-to-date than the school's, Claire had rung Jane, asking her to post her a copy. She identified herself as Hazel Bonnington, whom she knew had been Zoe's closest friend at school, but gave her own address. She vaguely implied that she wanted to make advance contact with some of the past pupils, and Jane had been more than happy to comply.

When the list arrived, Claire had been pleased to discover that it had quite a few of the pupils' current addresses on it, and she was surprised at how diverse these locations now were. Therefore, she decided to ring the pupils who now lived farthest away, hoping one of them wouldn't be able to make the long journey back to Trentham-on-Sea. Giving a false name, Claire began to ring names on the list, inferring she was connected with the reunion organising committee, and was checking to see if they'd be attending. Finally, on the eighth call, a woman named Violet Summers informed her that she couldn't possibly attend the reunion because her husband was having a major operation that very week.

"I'm so sorry," Violet informed her. "I've been meaning to send my regrets to the organising committee, but I just haven't got around to it yet."

"Oh dear, Violet, what a pity. Is there absolutely no way you can get there?"

"Not a chance – what with John's surgery, so I couldn't even consider it."

Claire smiled to herself. She'd just found her identity for the reunion.

"Well, maybe we can catch up some time in the future," she said. "And, by the way, don't worry about contacting the organising committee. I'll see that your name is crossed off the list."

"Oh, that's terribly good of you," said Violet gratefully. "I know I should have replied before now, but because of John's health problems, I haven't had much free time –"

"I hope his operation goes well," said Claire soothingly as she rang off.

In the privacy of her own room, Claire punched the air with delight. This was going better than she'd ever hoped. Consulting the past pupils list again, she then dialled Jane Cartwright's number.

"Hello, Jane? It's Violet Summers here. I'd like to book a place at the reunion."

"That's wonderful, Violet! We've been getting a great response, and it looks as though most past pupils will be turning up."

"I'm really looking forward to it," said Claire. "By the way; can I pay you by bank draft? I'm only just back from abroad, and haven't set up a new cheque account yet –"

"Yes, that's fine," said Jane.

Claire sighed with relief. There was no way she could pay for 'Violet' on her own credit card! She hesitated and then said, "One other thing, Jane – will lunch be a buffet or a sit-down meal?"

"We've opted for a wine bar to begin with, followed by a sit-down meal. That seemed the most friendly option to us. And please don't worry, Violet," Jane added kindly, "nearly everyone is coming on their own, since most people have lost contact with their old classmates."

"Does that mean people will just sit where they want?" asked Claire.

"More or less," Jane replied. "We'll be putting out place names for everyone, but if there's someone you particularly want to sit with, you can simply change places with someone else at the table. A few people have booked as a group, so naturally we'll seat them together."

"It sounds as though it'll be a great day, and I'm really looking forward to it," said Claire, genuine enthusiasm in her voice.

"Yes, hopefully, it will. I wonder will any of us recognise each other? Twenty-five years brings a lot of changes, doesn't it?"

Claire smiled at Jane's remark as she rang off. She certainly hoped that none of Zoe's classmates would recognise *her*. Or that any of Violet Summers' old school friends noticed the masquerade.

She was relieved to discover that lunch would be a sit-down affair. On the day of the reunion, she intended to surreptitiously change the place names so that she'd be sitting beside Emma, whom she knew from Zoe's diary to be the most gullible and easily led of the four. Then Emma would hopefully tell her about the other three's lives, careers and marriages.

Fortunately, all four had attended the reunion, so Claire had been able to study them without them even knowing.

Before she'd gone to the reunion, she had made several changes to her appearance. She changed her hair colour and invested in a new dress. After that, everything had been plain sailing. She'd got all the information she could possibly want – in fact, it had been like taking candy from a baby. Now, she was ready to move things along to the next stage . . .

And the first thing she intended to do – now that she knew the four women's addresses, courtesy of talkative Emma – was to drop one of her business cards in each of the four women's letterboxes. There was only a slight possibility that any of them would ever book in for a psychotherapy session. Nevertheless it *was* a possibility, and nothing ventured, nothing gained. Since her name was now Claire Ross, they'd never associate her with Zoe and Claire Gray. And if they did book in, she could quiz them under the guise of professional concern. If not – well, she now had other ideas up her sleeve. She'd avenge Zoe no matter how long it took.

CHAPTER 22

Already, Fiona was growing tired of Jim, the grocer's boy. He was like an exuberant puppy, possessing little finesse and more interested in his own enjoyment than hers. In the beginning, it had been fun teaching him all she knew, but he'd quickly become tiresome in his demands, and was taking far too much for granted.

Somehow, he'd got the idea into his head that she'd be up for it any time he was free, and he expected her to be enthusiastic and willing to leap into bed the minute he arrived at her house. He'd grab her as soon he walked in the door, and Fiona concluded that even his considerable virility wasn't enough to make up for his self-centredness. Also, he'd never brought her so much as a flower or a box of chocolates, and Fiona was beginning to feel used. Didn't he think she deserved even a small token of his esteem for all the tutoring she'd given him? Even a fling had rules of decorum.

He'd also become reckless, arriving at the house too close to the time that Edwin was due home, and expecting her to accommodate him. He might have nothing to lose, but she certainly did. No, Jim would have to go.

Fiona smiled to herself. Besides, there was another young man who was beginning to pique her interest. She'd known him all his life, but suddenly he'd turned from boy to man before her very eyes, and was definitely worth investigating. She suspected he wouldn't be self-centred in the way Jim had been, and with a little of her special tutoring, he'd hopefully become a willing pupil . . .

Briefly, Fiona wondered what her friends would think if they knew she'd been bedding a series of teenage boys. Emma would be appalled, but then most things appalled Emma. Anne would purse her lips in disapproval. Anne didn't believe in rocking any boats, and she didn't like others doing it either. Her own marriage was all that mattered to her, and she was positively obsessive in her devotion to Clive.

Jennifer would probably be amused – Fiona often suspected that Jennifer had her own private agenda. But while Jennifer would be the only one she'd ever be likely to confide in, Fiona also suspected that her friend would always extract a price for her secrecy, and if betrayal offered a greater advantage, she'd drop her in it without a moment's hesitation.

Well, Fiona had no intention in confiding in any of them. Childhood confidences were all very well, but her adult pursuits were another matter altogether. Today, she intended giving Jim the heave-ho and working out a strategy for approaching the cute guy who'd hopefully become her next conquest. Fiona felt positively giddy as she considered her next move.

CHAPTER 23

Zoe's Diary

February 15

Although it was breezy today on the beach, there were lots of people there, so Claire and I were able to make up stories about them. Then we told our own special story again – we never seem to tire of it!

It was a breezy Saturday afternoon as Zoe and Claire strolled along the beach. They usually went there at the weekends, no matter what the weather was like.

All year round, there were people on the beach at Trentham-on-Sea. When the weather was good, people sunbathed and picnicked, and children splashed around in the water or built sandcastles. During the colder months, people walked their dogs and threw sticks and balls into the sea for them. Zoe and Claire were constantly amazed at how the dogs never tired of the repetition, and could spend hours happily running in and out of the water.

Zoe and Claire played their own special game, which gave them endless hours of enjoyment. It cost nothing to dream up fabulous lifestyles and exciting events, and attribute them to the people they saw as they walked along.

"See that woman over there –" murmured Zoe, gesturing to a young woman with long blonde hair, sitting on the beach despite the overcast sky, "– I'll bet you she's an heiress who's run away from her wealthy family because they want her to marry someone she doesn't love."

Claire nodded. "Instead, she's planning to secretly marry the poor man she really loves, but her family are trying to stop them. Look –" She pointed to a man who was running towards the young woman. "That's him, and he's coming to tell her they have to leave immediately, because her family have found out where she's hiding . . ."

As if to confirm their fantasy, the couple left the beach and headed up towards the village. Surprisingly often, people obligingly behaved in ways that seemed to confirm the stories Zoe and Claire invented, adding greatly to their enjoyment.

Just then, an older well-dressed couple walked down to the beach and appeared to be looking around.

"That's her parents!" Claire whispered. "Oh Zoe, I hope the young couple manage to get away!"

Zoe nodded. "If her parents catch them, they'll probably have the poor man put in jail on some trumped-up charge, and they'll keep her at home and never let her see him again." She scanned the road leading to the village. "But don't worry – I think they've escaped."

Zoe always tried to ensure that while their stories were exciting, they also ended happily, because Claire was still very young, and even a made-up story could make her sad. The best thing about stories was that they could be changed at a whim and made to end the way you wanted them to.

"See that boy over there?" said Zoe. "It's his first day of freedom – pirates captured him, and they made him their slave until he was rescued. Now he's able to have fun like everyone else."

"How did anyone know to rescue him?" Claire asked.

Zoe looked out to sea. "He sent a message in a bottle," she

said. "It was washed up on the beach, and the person who found it took it to the police."

Further along the beach, the sisters encountered a young girl coming out of the water. She was shivering, and gave the sisters a rueful smile.

"I'll bet she's a princess in disguise," Claire confided, a conspiratorial grin on her tiny freckled face. "She gets bored with the stuffiness of the palace, so she likes to sneak out and do the things that ordinary people do."

Zoe nodded in agreement. "She has a bodyguard who secretly helps her, and he waits for her while she's having fun, then sneaks her back into the palace."

"He's in love with her too," Claire added solemnly, "but he'll never be able to tell her, because princesses are expected to marry princes."

Both girls were silent. Thinking about unrequited love made them sad. It reminded them too closely of their mother.

"Let's tell our own special story!" said Claire, looking hopefully at her sister. This was the best story of all, because it enabled them to alter their own lives and make them so much better.

Zoe nodded. "Okay. Once upon a time, there were two princesses called Zoe and Claire." She gestured to Claire to continue.

"And they lived in a beautiful palace with their mother and father, the king and queen, who were very happy and very rich," added Claire triumphantly.

"And their mother and father loved each other and they loved their two daughters as well," added Zoe, smiling.

"The girls had everything they could want – and loads of toys and books."

"They often went horse riding in the forest with their father, where they saw all the animals and birds."

Both girls walked along silently, unwilling to take the story to its next level.

Eventually, Claire broke the silence. "Then a bad fairy came to visit, and she was so jealous of how happy the girls and their parents were, that she took their father away."

Zoe took up the story again. "She put a spell on him and locked him in a dungeon, so that he couldn't escape and get back to his wife and daughters."

Claire looked earnestly at Zoe as she continued. "And the queen was so sad that she couldn't rule the kingdom on her own. So the two princesses set out to find their father."

"After months of travelling, they arrived at the bad fairy's castle," said Zoe. "Princess Claire knocked at the door and begged the bad fairy to let her father go."

Claire grinned. "Of course, she wouldn't agree, but the princesses had a plan – while Princess Claire was distracting the bad fairy, Princess Zoe sneaked into the dungeon, found their father and helped him to escape."

"Then they all went back to the palace together, and their mother the queen was thrilled to have them all back safely," said Zoe.

"And they all lived happily ever after," finished Claire.

In silence, the two girls walked along the beach together, each lost in her own thoughts. This story of theirs was a staple, told over and over again, with occasional variants. But at its heart was the story of two young girls who craved a proper family, a mother and father who loved their daughters as well as each other.

As she pondered on the story they'd just told, Zoe wondered if, indeed, some bad fairy, in the guise of another woman, had taken their father away. If so, it was doubtful they'd ever see him again.

As though reading Zoe's thoughts, Claire looked up at her sister. "Do you think Daddy will ever come back?" she asked. She hadn't dared ask their mother again, but the question was still uppermost in her mind.

"I'm sure he will – some day," Zoe said, expressing an optimism she didn't feel.

"Then why doesn't he write to us?" Claire asked. "Do you think he might be dead?"

"Of course not!" said Zoe firmly. "He'll be back, probably when

he's made loads of money, and we'll be so rich that we'll be living like the princesses in our story – you just wait and see. Now come on – it's getting cold, and I've got homework to do for Monday."

"Maybe, when we grow up, we can go and look for him. Like the princesses did in our story," Claire added.

"I'm sure he'll be back before then," said Zoe kindly. "Come on, Claire – I'll race you to that big rock!"

Running on ahead enabled Zoe to hide her tears from her little sister. Why couldn't they have a father like other families?

Claire ran past her sister, thrilled to suddenly be in the lead. But looking back, she stopped when she saw Zoe's blotched face.

"You're crying."

"No, I'm not – I've got sand in my eye!"

Claire nodded, accepting Zoe's explanation. She knew Zoe wouldn't want her to know how badly she, too, was missing their father. In a way, they were conspiring with each other to hide their grief, because if one of them started crying, it would be the undoing of the other.

"Come on, I'll race you to the crossroads," Claire called.

As she ran ahead, she didn't look back. Because if she did, Zoe would see that she was crying too.

CHAPTER 24

Claire was relieved to be finished work for the day. She'd had several emotional clients and one highly charged situation to deal with, all of which left her feeling mentally and physically drained. Right now, all she wanted to do was to go home and put her feet up.

She'd cancelled plans to meet David in town and go to a movie. Luckily, her fiancé hadn't minded, so now she was heading back to her car, intending to have an early night when she got home.

Her thoughts were miles away, so at first she didn't realise that someone was calling her.

"Excuse me, don't I know you?" said a voice.

Claire turned.

"You were at The Gables school reunion. I'm Hazel Bonnington."

"Oh, yes," said Claire, willing herself to slip back into character again. "I'm er, Violet Summers. It's lovely to see you again."

"Great fun, wasn't it? Haven't laughed so much in years. All those toffee-nosed bitches with their BMWs and Mercs, and not a brain between them."

This wasn't the comment Claire had been expecting, but it was one she agreed with wholeheartedly. They *had* been a snobby bunch, except for Emma Durrant, who'd been friendly and kind, and also remorseful over Zoe's death.

Claire was alarmed at being recognised. If this woman saw through her disguise, would others be able to recognise her too?

"Changed your hair since the reunion, haven't you?" barked Hazel, smiling. "This colour suits you much better."

"You obviously have a great eye for detail," said Claire, hoping that flattery might distract her protagonist from any more detailed scrutiny.

"Yes," replied Hazel without even a hint of modesty, "being a journalist trains your eye for the smallest detail. Could mean the difference between getting a good story and getting the sack."

"What newspaper did you say you're with?"

With a flourish, Hazel produced a business card and handed it to Claire.

"Here – keep it, and give me a ring if you ever come across a good story."

"Thanks," said Claire, "I will."

Claire found herself shaking after Hazel had walked off. She'd come so close to disaster! She hadn't actually spoken to Hazel at the reunion, but she'd seen her in the distance, and at one stage she'd watched as Hazel and Anne Ellwood had exchanged angry words. She'd instantly warmed to the woman, since she obviously disliked Anne Ellwood too.

But this near brush with disaster made Claire realise she still needed to be on her guard. What if she bumped into other people from the reunion? Luckily, Hazel had taken her false identity at face value. But if Hazel had challenged her, how would she have explained her way out of that?

CHAPTER 25

The alarm clock went off at 5 a.m. and Vanessa groaned, pulling the duvet over her head. Today she was accompanying her uncle to the market. What had seemed a great idea the previous evening wasn't quite so pleasing now!

"Come on, girl – it's time to get up! I've put on some toast – we'll be leaving in about fifteen minutes."

Uncle Hugh discreetly went back into the kitchen, leaving Vanessa to climb out from under her duvet and dress herself. Half-asleep, she dragged a comb through her hair and slipped into the bathroom to wash her face and pile on her make-up. When she came back to the living room, the sofa looked so inviting that she was tempted to slip back under the duvet again. She thought enviously of Carl and Aunt Maisie, who were both still asleep in their beds.

Uncle Hugh stuck his head round the door. "Toast is ready!" he called cheerfully, and Vanessa reluctantly gave up the idea of sleeping any longer. Besides, Uncle Hugh was introducing her to his world, and out of courtesy she ought to appear enthusiastic about it.

"Why do you start so early?" she asked, gratefully accepting a cup of tea and a slice of toast dripping with melted butter.

"We've got to go to the wholesale market first, love," he explained. "Then when I've bought my stock, we go to the High Street, set up our stall and start selling."

Vanessa shivered as they got into Uncle Hugh's large white van. It was no longer dark outside, but although it was summertime, the inside of the van was freezing and far from comfortable. Vanessa pulled her new green hoodie around her, and wished she'd brought a thicker jacket to London.

As if he'd read her mind, Uncle Hugh gave her a cynical look. "That thing you're wearing isn't going to keep you warm – there's a spare jacket in the back, love."

Leaning into the back of the van, Vanessa found a heavy anorak, which she gratefully slipped on. It was far too big for her, and she could barely see out over the collar, but she felt a lot warmer as she wrapped herself in its folds.

At the wholesalers, Hugh quickly selected trays of cabbage, carrots, aubergines and potatoes and, with Vanessa's help, they were loaded into the van. Then Hugh selected grapefruits, watermelons and oranges from the fruit section, and as they drove back to Walthamstow, Vanessa enjoyed the tangy smell of citrus fruit that now pervaded the van.

Back at the market, Vanessa was delighted to discover that a second breakfast was on the agenda before any work began. It seemed a very long time since she'd eaten that slice of toast!

"C'mon, love, no one can work on an empty stomach," Uncle Hugh told her, taking her arm and guiding her to a greasy spoon café across the street. Inside, it was filled with other traders, all tucking in to bacon, egg, sausage and beans.

With a gesture to the waitress, Hugh appeared to have ordered, because a few minutes later, two large breakfasts appeared in front of them. Vanessa was thrilled at the opportunity to eat all this gorgeous greasy food – at home, her mother wouldn't allow 'unhealthy' meals like these to be served.

Looking around her, Vanessa felt that she'd stepped into another world altogether. The people all spoke exactly like her uncle, and she observed the banter between him and other traders with utter fascination. And she now understood the power of the illicit as she tucked into her fried breakfast – her mother would have a fit if she saw what her daughter was eating!

After setting up his stall and covering the metal frame with a waterproof tarpaulin to protect the produce, Vanessa's uncle handed her a stack of plastic bowls, and it became her job to fill them with produce, the contents of each bowl then being sold for one pound.

"Don't fill the bowls too much – otherwise, I'll make no money!" Uncle Hugh cautioned her with a grin. "And three of those grapefruits are more than enough per bowl!"

Before long, the market was in full swing, and Vanessa found herself enjoying the banter and the jokes being exchanged between stallholders and customers. She even found herself enjoying her uncle's *double entendres* as he urged shoppers to buy his aubergines, hollering at the top of his voice: "Come on, ladies – I've got some lovely big ones 'ere!"

She was also fascinated by the variety of people out shopping – there were people of all colours and ages there, wearing an amazing assortment of clothing, from burqas to mini-skirts. People carted bags and shopping trolleys, everyone jostling along good-humouredly.

Other stallholders added to the enjoyment by exchanging banter with Vanessa and her uncle, and Vanessa was more than happy to take charge of a neighbouring stall while the stallholder took a break.

By late afternoon, most of the fruit and vegetables on her uncle's stall had been cleared, and the remainder would now be sold off cheaply. Although she was exhausted by now, Vanessa enjoyed shouting at the top of her voice that all remaining produce was now half-price.

"That was great fun," said Vanessa, as Uncle Hugh dismantled the stall and began packing away the framework into the back of the van. "Can I come with you again tomorrow?"

"I won't be here tomorrow, love – I have to go to hospital for dialysis."

Vanessa looked puzzled. "What's that?"

Uncle Hugh smiled. "My kidneys don't work properly, Vanessa – and I've got high blood pressure and diabetes as well, so I have to get regular treatment if I'm to keep going." His eyes twinkled. "But you know the old saying: 'It's hard to kill a bad thing'!"

As they drove home from the market, Vanessa pondered on her uncle's illness, and she felt a great weight inside her. She wished there was something she could do to help him – she suspected he could do with extra help at the market, since she'd already noticed how out of breath and tired he'd looked several times during the day.

Later that night, when everyone had gone to bed, Vanessa took out her laptop, inserted her portable modem and connected to the Internet. She quickly found sites explaining dialysis, high blood pressure and diabetes, and came away deeply troubled by what she'd read.

Closing the laptop, Vanessa settled down on the sofa again and pulled the duvet over her. But she couldn't sleep. She'd just found a family – *her* family – and one of them was ill and in need of regular medical attention. Vanessa found herself worrying in case he might die, which would mean that she'd lose him after only just having found him. Then she felt guilty at having such a selfish thought, since Maisie and Carl had an even greater claim on his affections than she had.

The following morning, by the time she woke up, Uncle Hugh had been collected and taken for his dialysis.

"We decided to let you sleep, love," Aunt Maisie told her. "You looked done in – yesterday was a long day for you, especially since you're not used to that kind of work."

"Thanks," said Vanessa, feeling guilty for sleeping so late, "but I would have gone with Uncle Hugh to the hospital. He must get bored, sitting there for such a long time."

"So you know about dialysis, do you?"

Vanessa coloured. "Not really, just what I read about it on the Internet. It said that dialysis takes several hours."

"Yes, it's a nuisance – all that hanging around in hospital, several days a week."

"Will he always have to have it?" asked Vanessa.

Maisie nodded. "Looks like it – unless someone gives him a kidney."

Vanessa found herself brooding on Maisie's words, and decided to discuss the situation with Carl when she got a chance.

Later that evening, Vanessa accompanied Carl to the chip shop around the corner, and she took the opportunity to ask him about his father's kidney problems.

Carl smiled down at her. "Well, if Dad could get a kidney, he wouldn't need the dialysis anymore. Mum and I have both been tested, but neither of us is compatible. We'd gladly give him a kidney if we could, but it just isn't possible."

"How would he get your kidney?" Vanessa asked.

"Well, everyone's got two kidneys, and a healthy person can live perfectly well with one," Carl explained. "So if someone has two bad kidneys – like Dad, and needs regular dialysis – a family member, or someone who's compatible with that person, can give them one of their kidneys. It involves an operation in hospital for both donor and recipient."

Vanessa hesitated for only a second. "Maybe I could be tested," she said, hardly believing what she was saying.

"No, Dad wouldn't dream of it!" Carl said resolutely. "I mean, we hardly know you – it wouldn't be fair to even *think* of letting you do that."

"But I'm family!" shouted Vanessa, stung by his comment and almost in tears. She so desperately wanted to be accepted by them, and now her offer of help had been rejected out of hand.

Seeing how hurt she was, Carl backtracked a little. "Listen, cuz, donating a kidney isn't something you should make a snap decision about."

Vanessa felt a little better. She liked being called 'cuz'.

"But couldn't I at least be tested? How do they do that?"

"A blood group test is the first stage. Mum and I were ruled out immediately."

"Well, I want to do the blood test! Maybe I won't be able to help – but maybe I will. We won't know until I do the first test. *Please*, Carl – I'd really like to be able to help Uncle Hugh."

Carl shook his head resolutely. "Dad wouldn't even hear of

it," he said. "Besides, how would your own family feel about you doing that? Your parents don't even visit us – it would only create more aggravation for everyone. Forget it, Vanessa." He looked closely at her. "Anyway, isn't it time you were going home? Your parents must be worried about you by now."

Vanessa said nothing. She felt as though she'd been dismissed, and suddenly she felt very alone. She'd also noticed that Carl didn't refer to her father as his uncle in the way she called his father Uncle Hugh. Clearly, deep-seated hostilities still existed between the two families.

As they returned to the flat with their fish and chips, the trio of hoodies were standing, as usual, at the entrance to the stairwell. This time, they smiled as Vanessa and Carl approached, and Vanessa felt more comfortable and accepted in her new hoodie.

"Hi, guys," Carl said, saluting them.

"Hello, Miss," one of them said as Vanessa began climbing the stairs, while the other two sniggered.

Vanessa waved back, smiling. At least this was an improvement on her last encounter with them.

"Do they just hang around all the time, doing nothing?" she asked her cousin when the young men were out of earshot.

Carl nodded. "Sometimes I try to get them down to the youth club, but there's not much to do there except play pool or table tennis."

Vanessa felt deeply sorry for the trio. She'd never before encountered people whose lives were so dead-end that they didn't even go to school or foresee a decent future for themselves. In the few days she'd spent in London with her father's family, she'd learnt a lot about poverty and suffering. It just wasn't fair that some people had so much and others had nothing.

Later, Vanessa made another attempt at convincing Carl she might be able to help her uncle. As they ate their fish and chips in front of the television, she whispered in his ear.

"Carl, I really want to be tested – please, will you take me to your dad's hospital?"

Carl shook his head, checking that his parents in the kitchen hadn't overheard. "No, Vanessa, don't even think about it."

"Please, Carl – your dad needn't even know I'm doing the test. I mean, isn't that the best way to donate? If he doesn't know, he'll never feel that he pressured me in any way."

She rushed on with her arguments, hoping that she could convince Carl by her knowledge of the subject. Vanessa imagined herself in the role of her uncle's saviour, thus gaining the lifelong devotion of all the Corcrofts.

"Look, the blood test is only the beginning, Vanessa," Carl said sternly. "Even if your blood group proved compatible, there are lots more tests – and psychological tests – before you'd be considered as a donor."

"Well, at least let me try," begged Vanessa. "If I'm not compatible then there's no harm done."

"But you're only eighteen –"

"That's old enough to be considered," said Vanessa firmly, suddenly wondering what she'd do if she *was* compatible. She'd gladly give him one of her kidneys. Maybe she could get her parents' permission to have the operation . . . She immediately shut out a vision of her mother having hysterics if she even broached the subject. On the other hand, maybe Uncle Hugh could wait for her kidney until she really *was* eighteen. That was only five years away . . .

"Okay," said Carl. "If we can get an appointment I'll take tomorrow afternoon off from work. Okay?"

Vanessa nodded gratefully. Maybe she could even have the operation without telling her parents, she thought, before dismissing the notion. Of course the hospital would need proof she was eighteen . . . Vanessa sighed. At least by doing the test, she felt she was doing something positive for her uncle. She'd worry about the consequences later . . .

CHAPTER 26

Anne stood in the centre of her large kitchen, the sweat running down her brow. Luckily, the day of the garden party was warm and sunny, but the heat was a disadvantage when you were supervising the arrival of the party food in a warm kitchen.

Mrs Hill, the Ellwoods' housekeeper, was fussing as usual. She was alternating between checking the bread she was baking in the oven, and filling vases with the assorted fresh flowers that had just arrived from the local florist.

Anne had ordered the canapés from a small local delicatessen, the meat dishes, quiches and salads from a well-known catering company, and the desserts from her favourite patisserie in the nearest town. She'd used all three companies many times before, and their standards were impeccable. The *pièce de résistance* was Mrs Hill's homemade brown bread, which would initially be served with wild salmon, and again at the end of the party with soup, which always proved an enjoyable late-night going-home snack for the guests.

This was one of the events to which Anne always invited Emma, as well as Jennifer and Fiona and their husbands. Anne felt that nothing too disastrous could happen in the open air, and any misbehaviour on Emma's part wouldn't be quite so obvious when there were a hundred other people milling around. Hopefully, after several glasses of wine, Emma would quietly pass out in the bushes. Maybe she could sideline Fiona or Jennifer to keep an eye on her.

By now, Mrs Hill had done a wonderful job on the flowers, and had distributed the vases throughout the house. Every room was filled with the wonderful scent of carnations, lilies, gardenias and freesias – even the bathrooms were festooned with fresh flowers. Anne always insisted on this, since guests would be coming indoors to use the toilets, and the flowers would add to the elegance and beauty of the house. She had refused to install outside toilets, considering them vulgar and unsightly objects that would reduce the garden party to the status of a teenage rock festival. No way was she having any of those down-market contraptions blighting the landscape at The Grange!

Clive appeared in his dressing gown and was shooed away by both Anne and Mrs Hill.

"Men have no place in a kitchen," said Mrs Hill, clearly not a woman given to feminist views.

"Okay, okay," said Clive good-naturedly, holding up his hands in supplication. "But can I please have some breakfast? I'm starving!"

"I'll bring it to you in the drawing room," Mrs Hill informed him, as she put bread in the toaster.

"Go on, darling – there's no room for you in here," Anne told him, handing him the morning newspapers that had just been delivered.

With a look of resignation, Clive took the papers and left the room, but he was actually relieved to get out of their way. He'd no wish to become embroiled in any of the preparations for the garden party – he always left that in Anne's capable hands. His job of schmoozing wouldn't start until later. There were rumours that an election was pending, so he had lots of groundwork to do. And he had those tiresome South American diplomats arriving – how he wished Anne wasn't quite so keen on keeping his profile high!

In the kitchen, Mrs Hill took the bread out of the oven, and the kitchen was filled with its delicious aroma as she laid out the loaves on wire trays. Then she prepared a breakfast tray and took it into the drawing room to Clive.

Just then, the first of the caterers arrived. As their van drew up, crunching the gravel outside, she rushed out the front door to direct them round the side to the kitchen. Within minutes, the caterers had unloaded their supplies, and the kitchen worktops were covered with a vast array of delicious canapés and finger food.

As Anne lifted the tinfoil covers and surveyed the contents of the stainless-steel trays, she was pleased at how wonderful it all looked. But she wasn't going to compliment the caterers – she preferred to keep people on their toes. Too much praise and they began slacking.

As the morning wore on, another caterer arrived, and once again the kitchen was a hive of activity as trays of delicious desserts were stacked up on the worktops. Mrs Hill was working herself up into a frenzy, claiming there weren't enough dessert forks, and that it would be very bad form to give people full-size ones. Anne calmed her with a cup of tea, and distracted her from the forks by asking her to test the latest batch of creamy desserts that had just arrived. Anne figured that with her mouth full, her housekeeper couldn't create quite so much fuss.

Outside, the gardeners were giving the lawns and flowerbeds a final once-over, to ensure that no weeds had dared to sprout overnight and sully the pristine landscape. The marquee was in place, the stage had been set up beneath the trees, and the three-piece combo had arrived and were doing a sound check. An electrician was checking all the outdoor fairy lights, which were designed to create a romantic atmosphere once dusk arrived.

A bar had been set up in the large conservatory that stretched the entire length of the house at the back. Every conceivable type of drink had been provided, from beer and lager to wines and spirits, juices and cordials, and Anne had even managed to acquire several bottles of the South American diplomats' national drink. It didn't really matter whether they drank it or not, it was merely there for effect. The diplomats would be impressed, and she'd make sure that the politicos knew all about it too. It all helped to highlight what wonderful hosts the Ellwoods were. Anne smiled to herself. She liked to think she'd thought of everything.

Ostensibly, the garden party was being held for the South American diplomats, and she'd had bunting in their national colours hung in the marquee. The combo had learned off their national anthem, and it would be played at some opportune moment when Clive proposed a toast and formally welcomed them to The Grange. But behind the scenes, Clive himself would be doing the real work. Anne knew how critical this event was for him. And with rumours of a general election, it was more important than ever. All the top party and constituency officials had been invited, and two MPs and one minister had sent their acceptances. It promised to be an event that might lead to Clive's ministerial ambitions finally being fulfilled. And, of course, it would cement her own position as the wife of a minister, and perhaps ultimately, wife of the prime minister.

Eventually, the waiting staff from the agency arrived, their pristine uniforms wrapped in polythene and folded over their arms. One of the women arrived slightly behind the others, and came in carrying two large flat boxes.

Anne raised her eyebrows. "What on earth are these?" she asked sharply. "The food has already arrived."

"Sorry, ma'am, but one of the caterers' vans arrived at the gates just as I was starting up the driveway," said the woman apologetically. "They said they'd forgotten to deliver these earlier, and I offered to carry them up, as they were rushing off to make a delivery for another party."

Anne harrumphed, glanced inside the boxes and saw two magnificent latticed quiches smelling of olives and anchovies. They looked gorgeous, and the detail of the piping was delicate and professional. Anne smiled to herself. She'd certainly be happy to serve these magnificent quiches tonight. Dare she claim that she'd made them herself?

Anne nodded her thanks to the woman, who followed Mrs Hill as she directed the hired staff to their changing rooms in the basement. Then, when they'd all changed into their uniforms, they reassembled in the kitchen where Anne explained their individual duties. Some would serve drinks from the bar; others would circulate carrying trays of drinks, and taking orders for any tipples not already on the trays. Some would remain in the kitchen, cutting and preparing individual plates of food, while others would circulate with trays of canapés and finger food. At all times, Anne instructed them, the guests were paramount, and she dangled the prospect of a bonus if the evening was concluded satisfactorily and no breakages were caused by the staff.

Anne sighed with relief as everyone moved off to take up their individual duties. Everything had been taken care of, and now she'd take a quick shower and dress for the event. She'd had her dark-brown hair cut and coloured the week before, so it didn't need any last-minute attention. Luckily, she had good strong hair that held whatever shape she chose to impose on it. She preferred to keep it short, which, she felt, was more befitting her age, and also made it easy to take care of.

She planned to wear a simple grey sheath that looked both pricey and elegant. Of course, it *was* pricey, but that was the whole point. Anne knew that her appearance would be scrutinised by all the party officials. They'd be checking to see if she was an asset to her husband, so it was essential that she looked the part. Today, she was being vetted just as much as Clive was.

CHAPTER 27

The garden party was in full swing, and everyone appeared to be enjoying themselves. Anne was relieved that all was going well, but she knew she wouldn't be able to relax until the last guest had left.

The music provided a pleasant backdrop to the chatter of voices and the clink of glasses, and the staff she'd hired appeared to be taking their responsibilities seriously. Anne watched surreptitiously as they scurried around, offering food and drinks and topping up glasses.

While Anne herself did a certain amount of socialising, much of her time was being spent in the kitchen, which she dubbed 'the command centre' of The Grange. From there, she dished out orders to Mrs Hill and the staff, making occasional forays outdoors to check that everyone had food and drink, and ensuring that she had a brief chat with every guest, so that no one would feel neglected. It would have been so easy to leave everything to Mrs Hill and the hired staff at this point, but who knew what disaster might befall events if she wasn't overseeing things herself? This event was too important to her and Clive to leave anything to chance.

Briefly, she wondered how Fiona, Jennifer and Emma were getting on.

"Betty, I'm slipping out again to check on the guests," she told Mrs Hill. Then she inspected her make-up in the bathroom off the kitchen before heading out to the garden to see if anything or anyone needed attention.

Everything appeared to be fine, and Anne paused to chat with some guests before making her way towards Fiona and Emma, whom she'd spotted standing under one of the trees.

Anne fixed a smile on her face as she approached. Emma was rabbiting on to one of the South American diplomats, and he was nodding his head and smiling, like one of those twee toys that people sometimes stick in the back window of their cars. Clearly, Emma was too drunk to realise that she was boring him to death.

The other was chatting to Fiona, who was smiling and trying to look interested, but Anne could tell that she was just waiting for an opportunity to escape. Earlier, Anne had seen Edwin, Fiona's husband, in the conservatory, topping up his glass for the umpteenth time, and swaying in a state of mild inebriation. At least Edwin was a pleasant drunk, which couldn't be said about Emma, who'd become terribly tiresome as the evening progressed.

Jennifer was nowhere to be seen, but Anne had no doubt that she was off chatting up some man somewhere. Jennifer was a terrible flirt, but Anne didn't blame her – the woman was married to the ghastly and uncouth Benjamin, who was probably, at this very moment, entertaining some of her guests by belching loudly at will – she could only hope that he wasn't doing it in the company of anyone who mattered. She wrinkled her nose in disgust. So who could blame Jennifer if she took a little pleasure elsewhere?

Back in the kitchen, Anne decided that she'd pass off the two anchovy and olive quiches as her own. After all, there was no one around to contradict her and, besides, she'd paid for them anyway. She'd make a point of serving them to Clive's party officials, the two MPs and the minister, since it would look good if she could demonstrate her skills as a competent cook as well as hostess.

She smiled to herself. She'd also enjoy the chance to blow her own trumpet – she was a terrible cook, so it would be nice to receive adulation for a talent she didn't possess!

She unwrapped the quiches, and divided them into sections. She'd bring them outside herself, serving the MPs, minister and party officials first. She'd casually mention she'd made them herself, adding that her tasty cooking was always on offer to visitors to the house. They might drop by more often if they believed there was always good food on offer, thereby increasing Clive's popularity and subsequently his chances of being considered for a ministerial post. It was only a slight possibility, but every opportunity had to be exploited. Besides, the freezer was full of Mrs Hill's delicious pre-cooked meals, which only needing heating in the microwave.

Anne hadn't seen Clive since the party began, but she knew he was out there, working the floor, making contacts and impressing the politicos. She was so proud of him – they made the perfect team, their individual talents complementing the other's. They were like a well-oiled machine, each part working in harmony with the other. Rarely were words needed between them – each instinctively knew what the other was thinking. She'd made a career out of being the perfect politician's wife, and this party would be another stepping-stone on the road to their success.

As Anne brought out the first of the quiches on a tray, she saw Clive chatting to the minister and his parliamentary colleagues, so she headed across the lawn.

The group opened up as she joined them, and one of the party officials immediately offered to take the tray from her.

"Anne, my dear, you shouldn't be carrying all that stuff – your staff should be doing that! You should be relaxing, and chatting with us!"

"Don't worry, Peter," Anne told the minister, wearing her most winning smile, "the staff are attending to everyone else. I just wanted you, George and Harry to be the first to taste my homemade quiche, and give me your honest opinion."

They were happy to oblige, and Anne and her husband

exchanged a knowing smile over their heads as the portions were distributed.

"Delicious!" said the minister as he downed a piece. "My goodness, Anne, you're a woman of many talents – Clive is a lucky man!"

George and Harry nodded in agreement as they munched their way through a slice each.

"Food fit for the Gods!" said Harry fervently, as he eyed a second piece. "Would it be terribly rude of me if I –"

"Of course not," replied Anne, heaping another slice onto his plate. "I'm flattered that you're enjoying it so much."

"This is amazing, Anne," said George, as he followed Harry's example and helped himself to another slice.

"Clive?"

"Just a small piece, darling."

Anne smiled. "There are no small pieces, my love – I've cut them all the same size."

"Oh, all right then," said Clive in mock resignation, taking a piece and popping a fork-load into his mouth. "Mmmm – gorgeous as always, my dear. Maybe I'll have seconds as well?"

Anne almost giggled. Clive was well aware that she couldn't cook at all, but he'd guessed what she was up to.

With one of the quiches eaten, Anne excused herself with a reluctant smile. "Sorry, gentlemen, but I must see to some of the other guests . . ."

"Of course, Anne – wonderful party!" said Harry.

"Amazing!" said George, finishing his second slice of quiche. It wasn't clear whether he was referring to the party or the food, but it was clear that he was enjoying himself immensely.

Next, Anne approached the three South American diplomats, who were clearly the worse for wear. It was obvious they'd consumed a lot of alcohol, and although barely able to stand, they were dancing and singing an out-of-tune version of their national anthem, and drowning out the combo that was playing a jazz number in the background. As they gratefully took the quiche, Anne doubted they'd remember it, let alone the party itself, but at least it might soak up some of the alcohol in their systems!

At which point Anne retired to the kitchen where Mrs Hill was filling the dishwasher yet again, while waiting staff were bringing back pile after pile of used plates.

Suddenly, Anne remembered she'd one more task to carry out. Dusk was approaching, so she turned on the fairy lights in the garden, and everywhere took on a magical appearance as hundreds of tiny bulbs illuminated the grounds. The gardens looked delightful, and Anne was pleased at the effect she'd created. Although judging by the state of some guests, she doubted if they'd even notice the lights. Some of them, like the South Americans, wouldn't remember the party at all, but their hangovers would remind them they'd had a good time!

As the evening progressed, Anne was pleased that the garden party had been a huge success. Groups everywhere were engaged in chat and banter. The food and drink were still flowing, and people were now using the small dance floor to demonstrate their skills. Although most of them were, by now, about as graceful as a herd of elephants. But they were enjoying themselves and that, as far as Anne was concerned, was all that mattered. Clive's party officials would see that the Ellwoods could throw a damn good party.

Anne wondered where Emma, Jennifer and Fiona were. She hadn't seen Jennifer all evening, but she knew her friend would be staying a million miles away from Benjamin, who was now in the conservatory, and waxing eloquent about stocks and shares to anyone who would listen. Anne curled her lip. What on earth would that ignoramus know about a subject like that?

Eventually, she spotted Fiona chatting happily to Jennifer's son Alan, who'd been invited along to help collect the glasses and plates throughout the evening. Anne was relieved that she hadn't needed to invite the boy's sister – thankfully that little madam was staying with her friend for the weekend. Anne always felt that young Vanessa was constantly watching her, and her astute observations always made Anne feel uneasy.

"Have you seen Emma anywhere?" she asked Fiona, who seemed a little distracted, and simply shook her head. Great, Anne thought. I specifically asked you to keep an eye on her. But of course, she couldn't say anything aloud since young Alan was standing beside her.

Feeling very peeved, Anne set off in search of Emma, hoping that she was sleeping off her hangover in some quiet corner of the gardens and not antagonising any of the guests. At times likes this, Anne wondered why she bothered to invite the trio at all. She'd expect her friends and their spouses to be grateful, and to behave themselves at the very least. But both Jennifer and Emma were missing, and Fiona was looking distracted and the worse for wear.

At last, Anne located Emma, who was clinging to a man who appeared to be just as drunk as she was. Neither of them seemed capable of doing anything except, perhaps, falling down and breaking their necks. As long as they did it quietly, Anne was content to leave them to it. She had more important people to attend to.

CHAPTER 28

Anne checked her Cartier watch. It was now 4 a.m. and she could see the first streaks of dawn on the horizon. Surveying the crowd of guests, most of whom were still drinking or dancing, Anne decided it was time to gradually wind things down and bring the evening to a close. She'd arranged for soup, followed by hot ports, to be served towards the end of the party. The soup, served with Mrs Hill's homemade brown bread, would help to soak up the vast amount of alcohol that had been consumed. The hot ports would hopefully serve as a subtle reminder to guests that it might be time to think of going home. Although by now most of them were past subtlety!

As Anne walked across the grass to the house, there appeared to be some sort of commotion in the conservatory, where the bar had been set up. Obviously some idiot was drunk and making a fool of himself – there was always someone who behaved badly. Furious, Anne hurried into the conservatory, to be met by a scene of utter confusion. One of the foreign diplomats was lying prone on a conservatory couch. He'd vomited on the floor, and Anne experienced a brief moment of relief that he'd done it on the stone floor and not on the Axminster carpet in the drawing room. Another of the diplomats was standing helplessly by, while the third made vain attempts to speak to him.

Dear God, thought Anne, how could a career diplomat allow himself to get so drunk? What a horrible thing to happen, just as the party was going so well. Well, this was one person who'd never be invited to The Grange again!

But Anne knew she had to behave with decorum, regardless of her personal feelings of disgust. She hurried over to the man who was, by now, whey-faced, with beads of sweat gathering on his forehead and upper lip.

"José, what on earth is the matter?" she asked, in her most concerned voice. "You poor man, let's make you more comfortable."

Anne directed the other two diplomats to help him to his feet and propel him towards the small TV room off the main reception rooms, where the leather sofa could be wiped clean and the floor was tiled. There was no way he was going anywhere near the Axminster!

Thankfully, only a small number of guests were aware of what happened, and Anne quickly tried to contain the situation. Urging everyone to go on with the party, Anne set off in pursuit of her husband. She didn't want to make any decisions about the diplomat until she'd cleared it with him. After all, the garden party had been held solely to promote Clive's career.

With a fixed smile on her face, Anne brushed aside several attempts by drunken guests to engage her in conversation. She was on a mission, and needed to find Clive urgently. Yet no one seemed to know where he was. He wasn't in the toilets or the bar, and no one could recall seeing him for some time. Anne was livid. Damn it, where *was* the man?

Returning to the TV room, Anne plastered a false smile on her face as she entered.

José wasn't looking any better, and Anne felt nothing but contempt for him. As far as she was concerned, he was simply drunk, but she couldn't risk doing nothing in case it was something more serious. Could he be having a heart attack? She'd never heard of vomiting as a symptom, but whatever it was, the man looked as though he needed a doctor. He wasn't getting any better, and he'd been unable to drink the cup of tea that Mrs Hill had made for him. By now, he was sweating profusely, groaning and clutching his stomach.

Once again, Anne wondered angrily where on earth Clive was. She'd give him a piece of her mind when he finally appeared!

Stepping out into the hall for privacy, Anne quickly dialled the local GP, explaining what had happened. She was aware she should be phoning the locum service, but she didn't want some junior doctor turning up who'd only make things worse. Hopefully, she could depend on the elderly doctor's discretion. Naturally, he wasn't too pleased at being called out at such an hour, but he was well aware of the important role the Ellwoods played in the local community.

"I'll be there in fifteen minutes," he told a very relieved Anne.

Just then, a tired-looking Clive appeared at the door of the TV room, and Anne's relief quickly turned to fear when she saw the expression on his face.

"Anne, George and Harry aren't feeling very well," he told her. "I think they've had too much to drink, because neither of them can tell me exactly what's wrong with them. I've left them sitting on one of the garden benches, but I need to get –"

"Oh God, I don't think it's the drink," said Anne dully.

Turning, Clive suddenly noticed the South American diplomat stretched out on the sofa, groaning and clutching his stomach.

"What on earth is happening here?" he exclaimed.

Anne quickly filled him in on what had happened, just as the local doctor arrived.

After a cursory examination of the diplomat, the doctor stood up and gave his judgement.

"It looks like you've got a case of food poisoning here," he said matter of factly.

"Good God!" Clive exploded. "How on earth could that have happened?"

Just then, another guest hurried into the kitchen. "Excuse me, Clive, George and Harry are both vomiting in the garden, and the minister is looking ill too –"

The elderly GP sighed. "I think you'd better take me to them," he said, taking his bag and following the guest outside.

"Oh Clive!" Anne wailed, wringing her hands in agitation. "What on earth are we going to do?"

"Jesus Christ, if word gets out, I'll never live this down," Clive muttered. "What did you give them to eat?"

"That's right – blame me! All you care about is your own bloody ego! I went to enormous trouble to make this event work for you, so don't even *think* of heaping the blame on me!"

As the exchange became more heated and the hosts' voices became raised, guests began to gravitate towards the TV room. Having eaten and drunk everything the Ellwoods had to offer, they were now ready to enjoy the spectacle of the Ellwoods at war.

As the diplomat writhed in agony on the TV-room sofa, Clive took his wife firmly by the hand and pulled her out into the garden and away from the gathering audience.

"This bloody party is becoming a nightmare," he muttered under his breath, "but we've got to put up a united front, so please stop the bickering."

"*I'm* bickering? Have you heard yourself –"

Just then, the doctor reappeared in the darkness, and Anne stopped in mid-sentence. Clive was right, although she hated him for it. But it was essential they stay calm, and more than anything, they needed to appear concerned about their guests' welfare.

"Doctor, how are George and Harry? And is the minister alright?" Anne called out, trying to inject concern into her voice.

"Three more cases of food poisoning," the doctor confirmed. "I've called an ambulance – it should be here in a few minutes. Now if you'll excuse me, I've been told there's someone else, down by the trees, who needs attention."

As he disappeared, Anne gripped Clive's hand tightly. "An ambulance! Dear God, this is an unmitigated disaster," she whispered. "What are we going to do? It'll be all over the newspapers. I can see the headlines already – I just hope nobody dies."

"Oh, shut up, Anne – things are bad enough without your dramatics. At least let's put on a show of looking concerned."

The following day, things got even worse. The other two South American diplomats also succumbed to food poisoning, and the disastrous garden party made the Monday morning national newspapers. Much as Anne had feared, the headlines ranged from *Food Poisoning at MP Party* to *Minister at MP Party Taken to Hospital*.

Anne railed against the injustice of it all. It wasn't her fault – she'd gone to so much effort to make the event a success, and now Clive was holding her personally responsible for the whole fiasco. Neither of them was speaking to the other, and were only communicating through Mrs Hill.

Anne knew that the source of the contamination would be impossible to find. All of the catering companies had already protested their innocence, and clearly none of them could be held responsible since the food could have been contaminated at any point during the day. Now, Anne wished bitterly that she hadn't lied about making the quiches. What if the guests thought the food she'd cooked had made them sick? No one would ever attend a party at The Grange again – if they ever dared hold one. But the more she thought about it, the more she felt that the quiches were to blame. Every person who'd got sick had eaten the quiche.

At which point, Clive suddenly started feeling unwell, and shortly afterwards, began vomiting. Feeling very sorry for himself, he headed off to bed, leaving Anne feeling thoroughly deserted and alone.

When the phone rang a little later, Anne spoke to the reporter at the other end of the line in *very* un-parliamentary language.

CHAPTER 29

Zoe's Diary

February 22

Today is Claire's birthday, and I've been saving for ages so that I can get her the doll she wants so badly. I asked Mrs Smith to put it by for me, and I've been paying it off at a few pennies a week. Today I'm making the last payment, and bringing the doll home for Claire. I'm so excited!

Having dodged the bullies on her way home from school, Zoe was feeling pleased. They still hadn't figured out her new route across the fields, and it gave her a wonderful sense of achievement to have thwarted them. They'd soon figure it out, she knew, but for now she was enjoying their confusion.

Back at the cottage, Zoe explained to Claire that she'd an errand to run. Claire nodded. Today was her birthday, but she didn't expect any gifts since there was no money available for frivolities like that. Nevertheless, it was her own special day, and she hoped Zoe would make her a card and maybe buy her a Swizzle or Jacko bar if she had the money. She doubted that her mum would remember. But she wasn't really bothered – poor Mum wasn't well and couldn't be expected to remember things like that.

146

Leaving the cottage, Zoe wore a big smile as she walked down to the village shops. Ages ago, Claire had seen a doll in Smith's toyshop window, and she'd fallen in love with it. But there was no way she could ever afford to buy it.

But Zoe had hatched a plan to get it for her sister. Their mother regularly asked Zoe to clear her handbag of all the small change left over from her daily whisky purchases. These discarded coins enabled Zoe to put down a deposit on the doll, and she'd begged Mrs Smith to allow her to pay off a weekly amount until she'd paid for it in full. Now, that day had arrived, and soon she'd have a wonderful surprise for Claire!

As she walked towards the village, Zoe spotted the four bullies in the distance. Ignoring them, she crossed the road to Smith's, but she could feel their eyes boring into her back, so she deliberately walked tall and tried not to let them intimidate her.

In the toyshop, Zoe eyed the doll on the top shelf where Mrs Smith had placed it for safekeeping. Handing over her final payment, Zoe anticipated Claire's joy when she was given the doll that evening. It would be worth all the scrimping and saving just to see Claire so happy.

"Thanks, Mrs Smith," said Zoe, smiling broadly as the woman took down the box containing the doll, and parcelled it up in bright gift-wrap. It looked beautiful, and Zoe was thrilled as she imagined Claire's face when she opened it.

As she left the shop and walked along the road towards the cottage, Zoe suddenly realised that the four bullies were following her. As they reached a bend in the road, where they could no longer be seen from the village, they made their move. Menacingly, they circled around her like sharks going in for the kill.

"What have you got there, Zoe?" Jennifer asked.

"Go on – let's see what you've got!" said Fiona, snatching the parcel from Zoe and tearing off the coloured wrapping paper.

"Aren't you a bit old to be playing with dolls?" said Anne, a sneer on her face, as Fiona revealed the pretty doll in its decorative box.

"It's for my sister," said Zoe defensively.

"Ooh, your sister!" said Jennifer, mocking her accent. "Why

147

would someone like you be buying a doll from Smith's? Dolls aren't for poor people like you!"

"I've saved up for it," said Zoe angrily.

As Zoe tried to take back the doll, Jennifer snatched it from her and tore open the cardboard box that contained it. Then she ripped out the doll and tossed the cardboard onto the ground behind them.

"What a pretty dolly – far too good for any Gray to play with!" Jennifer swung the doll around by one arm while the others stood grinning. With a plop, the doll suddenly landed on the ground.

"Oops, I seem to have dropped it!" shrieked Jennifer in mock horror.

"Oh dear, and I've stood on it – look, the doll's dress has got all dirty!" said Fiona, rubbing her dirty shoe up and down the doll's body, destroying the pretty dress it had been wearing.

"Stop it – stop it at once!" Zoe shouted, angry tears running down her face. "You're ruining my sister's birthday present!"

"That's the general idea," said Anne sarcastically, turning to Emma, who hadn't taken any part in the proceedings so far.

"Emma, pick up the doll and give it back to Zoe," said Anne, giving her a nudge.

Emma was horrified. It was bad enough having to stand on the sidelines, but participating in this orgy of violence was her worst nightmare.

"W-what?"

"Pick up Zoe's doll and give it back to her," Anne repeated, while Fiona and Jennifer's eyes narrowed with pleasure. Anne was making sure that Emma played her part in this event, and was bound to them by being just as culpable as they were.

Fearful of Anne's ridicule, Emma leaned forward gingerly, grabbed the doll by an arm and began lifting it up. At precisely the same moment, Fiona grabbed the other arm and pulled it vigorously. Within seconds, both doll's arms had fallen off.

"Now look what you've done!" screamed Zoe, tears streaming down her face, and not caring who she hit, she lunged forward. At that precise moment, Anne's mother was driving out of the village, and seeing the mêlée, stopped her car and stepped out, just in time to see Zoe lunging at her daughter.

"Good heavens, stop that at once, you little savage!" she screamed, trying to separate the two girls, while the others stood around open-mouthed.

"What on earth is going on?" Anne's mother shrieked.

"Zoe Gray tried to attack me, just because I said her doll was old and raggedy," said Anne, mustering up a tear. "Fiona, Jennifer and Emma will tell you – you saw her hitting me for no reason, didn't you?"

Fiona and Jennifer nodded vigorously, and Jennifer surreptitiously kicked the doll's packaging out of the way so that Mrs Morgan wouldn't see it. Emma said nothing. She was appalled at what had happened and wanted to have a good cry herself. Zoe's doll had been ruined, and she couldn't believe what she'd just witnessed.

Anne's mother stood fuming in front of Zoe. "You Gray girls need to be taught some manners!"

"I didn't do anything – that doll was new –" sobbed Zoe, as she clutched the battered remains of the doll in her arms.

"Stop telling lies this instant!" said Mrs Morgan angrily. "Where on earth would you get the money for a new doll?"

"It was for my sister's birthday –" Zoe sobbed, but Mrs Morgan didn't wait to hear what she was saying. She'd already grabbed her daughter, and was hurrying back to her car.

"Come along with me at once, Anne," she said sternly. "I don't want you hanging around with that dreadful child – Jennifer, Fiona and Emma, do you need a lift home?"

All three girls nodded meekly and, grabbing their schoolbags, they jumped into Mrs Morgan's car, which quickly drove off, leaving a sobbing Zoe beside the torn remnants of Claire's doll.

In the back of her mother's car, Anne dug her nails into Emma's palm, making her wince.

"Really, Emma – you'll have to get more involved if you're going stay friends with us," she muttered crossly, striking fear into Emma's heart.

Jennifer and Fiona grinned at each other, giving each other a discreet thumbs-up. It had been a great afternoon. Zoe Gray might have escaped from them on her way home from school, but they'd more than made up for it later.

Claire couldn't understand what was wrong. She was nine today, and had been feeling very excited and grown-up, but Zoe had returned from her errand with tears streaming down her face. Then she'd rushed into her room and barricaded herself inside. Claire could hear her sobbing through the door, and she wished she could do something – anything – to help her sister. What could have happened to break Zoe's heart? And why did it have to happen today?

Later, Zoe emerged and gave Claire a Swizzle bar. But her nose was bright red and her eyes kept filling with tears, and she kept hugging her little sister so tightly that Claire was afraid she might squeeze the life out of her.

"Someday, I'm going to get you all the toys you've ever wanted," Zoe said through her tears. "We'll buy so many that you won't be able to get in the door of your room!"

Zoe seemed close to hysteria, and Claire was worried. "Look, Zoe – I've all I want, as long as I've got you and Mum. Please don't worry about presents. Seeing you happy would be the best present I could have."

Zoe smiled through her tears. "Of course I'm happy – I've got you for a sister, haven't I? Happy ninth birthday, Claire. There'll be better birthdays ahead – I promise you." Standing up, she took Claire's hand. "Come on – let's remind Mum that it's your birthday. I'm sure she'll want to wish you all the best."

Claire hesitated, reluctant to disturb their mother. Instinctively she knew her poor mother had far more important things to worry about than a birthday. But Zoe insisted, and the two girls entered their mother's darkened room. Inside, Claire looked sadly at their mother as she slept, the empty whiskey bottle beside her. She'd forgotten, as usual.

"Never mind," said Zoe brightly. "There's always next year."

Suddenly, their mother opened her eyes and smiled at them both. "Happy Birthday, Claire," she muttered. Then reaching down by the side of her bed, she produced a large gift-wrapped box. "Here's a present for you," she said.

Claire's face was suddenly wreathed in smiles. Her mother hadn't forgotten! Opening the box and unwrapping the tissue paper, she discovered a beautiful doll inside. She gasped with delight as she felt its rich springy hair and soft velvet dress.

"Look, Zoe," she beamed, "it's like the one I've always wanted!"

Smiling through her tears, Zoe's heart suddenly felt lighter. Maybe there was a reason why she hadn't been able to give Claire the doll – this way, her mother's gift could shine, and being remembered by their mother would mean more to Claire than all the other dolls in the world.

The two girls smiled at each other, and this time Claire had tears in her eyes too. Her mother had remembered – and that was the best birthday present of all.

CHAPTER 30

Claire bit her lip. The Ellwoods' garden party had been a disaster. That was what she'd wanted, wasn't it? Nevertheless, she'd mixed feelings as she looked at all the coverage in the national and local newspapers.

Even before she'd carried out her plan, she'd had moments of doubt, followed by genuine concern for the people who might become ill. After all, it wasn't their fault that Zoe had been bullied and driven to kill herself. But Anne's garden party presented a wonderful opportunity to humiliate one of Zoe's tormentors, and Claire hadn't been able to resist the opportunity.

On Saturday morning, Claire had collected the two quiches she'd ordered from a newly opened French delicatessen in a distant town. It had been easy to bring them to The Grange – she'd simply pretended that one of the catering companies had forgotten to drop them off earlier.

She'd used eggs that she'd found at the back of a kitchen cupboard, that were months past their sell-by date. She'd simply glazed the two quiches with the raw eggs, and hoped that the warm weather would do the rest.

Claire had hoped to serve the quiches to as many VIPs as possible, but was secretly thrilled when Anne's vanity resulted in her passing them off as her own cuisine, and serving the VIPs herself!

And this had been her undoing. Having a minister and two MPs fall ill had been a catastrophe, and would take Anne a long time to live down. Claire felt a momentary stab of guilt for the unfortunate South American diplomats. They'd been unintended casualties. But she'd little sympathy for the politicians . . .

After Emma told 'Violet' about the garden party, Claire had gone to the employment agency closest to the Ellwoods' home and enquired about catering work. She'd mentioned that she knew about the upcoming garden party at the Ellwoods', and was there any hope of a job there? The agency director informed her that those positions had already been filled, but perhaps she'd like to drop in her CV?

Claire managed to look disappointed, but she didn't actually want a job at Anne's party. Just as she was leaving, she turned back as though she'd had an afterthought.

"Oh, by the way, what uniform do your waiting staff wear?"

The director informed her that temporary catering staff were expected to supply their own black trousers and white blouse or shirt. The agency then supplied them with waistcoats bearing the agency logo.

Thanking her, Claire left the building and turned down the lane behind the offices. She'd been there earlier, and had watched as a van delivered rails of freshly dry-cleaned waistcoats to the back door. By a stroke of luck, the back door was open, and the woman who'd just interviewed her was now smoking a cigarette on the doorstep.

Quickly, Claire dialled the phone number of the employment agency, knowing that the woman was the only person in the office. As the phone rang inside, the woman cursed, stubbed out her cigarette and went inside. Instantly, Claire crept into the rear of building and spotted the rail of dry-cleaned waistcoats in their plastic wrapping. Grabbing one of them, she hightailed it out again, hoping that the size she'd grabbed would fit her reasonably well. She certainly wasn't going to hang around to check the sizes! Stuffing the waistcoat in its dry-cleaning wrapper into the large bag she was carrying, she hurried out of the lane and into the street again. Now she *was* ready to attend Anne's garden party.

For her visit to The Grange, Claire wore her long hair in a bun, and used very different make-up than usual. She'd also worn a pair of reading glasses with very low magnification, which helped her to look efficient and dependable.

When she'd gone with the other staff to their changing room, Claire felt confident that the uniform she'd brought would pass any scrutiny. The waistcoat she'd 'temporarily borrowed' was a little large, but the night before she'd pinned it on the inside, and now it fitted reasonably well. She'd also bought a pair of cheap chain-store black trousers and white blouse, neither of which she'd ever wear again after today.

Most of the other waiting staff seemed to know each other, and from time to time they made references or jokes about previous venues, or talked about the rates of pay for different events. While no one was unpleasant to her, no one was overly friendly either, which suited Claire perfectly. She didn't want anyone chatting to her about her non-existent catering career, or enquiring about where she had trained.

The event itself was similar to other garden parties Claire had attended as a guest, in that there were lots of women in pretty dresses, lots of drunken men leering at them, and others were using the occasion for social and political networking. As she flitted among the attendees, offering tasty titbits and smiling inanely, Claire realised that if she'd wanted to know all about the local goings-on, she'd selected the perfect role for information-gathering! Guests treated the waiting staff as though they didn't exist, continuing their most private and informative conversations without any reference to their presence. Claire smiled inwardly as she overheard a variety of intimate revelations. What a pity none of them concerned the Ellwoods or Anne's closest friends!

As the party progressed and people became more and more inebriated, Claire began to doubt if she'd learn anything of value.

At least the quiches would hopefully take effect soon. Food poisoning usually occurred within hours of eating the contaminated food. Even if guests went home before succumbing to illness, the Ellwoods' party would still get the blame . . .

As she'd wandered around, clutching a tray of finger food and smiling pleasantly at everyone she met, her eyes were drawn to Clive Ellwood, who was glancing around furtively. Then, as Claire watched, he appeared to be sneaking off somewhere. Looking around him again, he slipped behind some trees and appeared to be heading for the woods adjoining the Ellwood estate. Dumping her tray, Claire followed him deep into the undergrowth, and was astonished to see him rendezvous with Jennifer behind one of the large oak trees. Claire's heart was thumping so loudly she felt sure they must be able to hear it. But they'd eyes only for each other, and as Claire watched, they proceeded to have urgent and passionate sex. Mesmerised, Claire almost forgot why she was there. But finally she remembered that her mobile phone was in her pocket, so she took it out and photographed them.

Their coupling was rough and urgent, and clearly this wasn't their first time. They were a handsome couple, and Jennifer looked sultry and filled with abandon as she submitted to Clive Ellwood's urgent thrusting. Claire felt that her photograph would almost qualify as artwork, but hopefully it would serve a more useful purpose.

Recovering her tray and sneaking back to the garden party, Claire was hardly able to contain herself. Things were going even better than she could have hoped! She now had evidence she could use to destroy either Anne or Jennifer. Anne's snobbery and Jennifer's deceit showed clearly that these women knew nothing about friendship, and continued to use each other for their own ends. If anything, this reinforced her desire to take them down a peg or two, and make them realise, perhaps for the first time, that life wasn't all about them and their own needs.

As she circled the grounds with a new tray of canapés, Claire kept an eye out for Emma. She was determined to stay well clear of her, since she was the person most likely to identify her.

However, Emma had taken to the wine with gusto, and was downing glass after glass and talking complete gibberish.

Claire had found herself liking Emma. By right, she should hate her for the part she'd played in her sister's death. But Emma had been genuinely remorseful – how could she hate someone who had deep regrets about what they'd done? Besides, Emma had already played a part, albeit unwittingly, in helping Claire to track down Anne, Fiona and Jennifer, who were the ones she really wanted to punish.

Claire could understand why Emma was a best-selling author of children's books – her naïvety and child-like qualities would enable her to immerse herself in the world of the child and brilliantly capture the essence of it.

As she took another tray of canapés around, Claire noticed Fiona talking to Jennifer's fifteen-year-old son Alan, and thought it uncharacteristically nice of her to engage him in conversation. Chatting to a monosyllabic teenager couldn't be much fun. But returning a little later, she noticed that Fiona was now leaning closer to the young boy and was actually flirting with him. Young Alan was obviously enjoying himself, and he looked positively animated for a change. Claire smiled to herself. Obviously Fiona liked male company, and wasn't fussed about what age they were!

Dumping her tray, Claire decided it was time to leave the party. She was anxious to get her phone out safely, now that she'd taken the wonderfully incriminating picture of Clive and Jennifer. So far, there hadn't been any reports of anyone getting sick, but she assumed her efforts would later begin to take effect. Anyway, she didn't want to be around when it happened, in case the temporary staff were expected to mop up after vomiting guests!

Having collected her clothes from the changing room, Claire made her way down the driveway to the gates of the estate. She made sure to turn her face away from the CCTV cameras that were trained on the driveway, and kept in by the trees so that she wouldn't be spotted by the chauffeur waiting in the minister's car.

The two security men employed to keep the hoi polloi out were both, to Claire's relief, sneaking a cigarette behind the gate lodge and were oblivious to her departure. Out on the road at last, Claire made her way to where she'd parked her car, and drove off.

Back home, Claire found herself perversely hoping that nothing bad would happen. Unable to sleep, she spent the night pacing the floor and worrying in case someone became seriously ill. What would she do if an innocent person died? On the other hand, she was probably overreacting, since food poisoning was usually a brief but unpleasant inconvenience. Nevertheless, what had started out as an opportunity to avenge her sister was already giving her nightmares. Bleary-eyed and cold by morning, Claire accepted that she wasn't really cut out for revenge.

CHAPTER 31

As they sat at the breakfast bar on Monday morning, Benjamin looked distastefully at his wife as she read the morning papers. He could see that Jennifer was experiencing *schadenfreude* over the Ellwoods' garden party debacle. There was a gleam in her eye as she read the reports of the food poisoning at The Grange. As she came upon each write-up, she squealed with delight, reading it aloud to Benjamin in case he wasn't fully conversant with the details. How on earth could she consider herself Anne's friend, he wondered, yet derive such pleasure from her humiliation? While Benjamin didn't particularly like Anne, he still believed friends were meant to support each other, not delight in each other's bad luck.

Benjamin considered himself lucky that he'd only experienced a mild stomach upset after the party. And that had been due to his not inconsiderable hangover. He and Edwin had spent most of the evening drinking in the conservatory, and hadn't felt the need for food. Luckily, they hadn't been offered any of the quiches – those had been kept for the elite circle of Clive's political allies. Benjamin was well aware that he didn't belong among Clive's elite, and was only tolerated because he was Jennifer's husband.

Of course, Jennifer never touched food at a party – she was terrified of putting on weight – so there was no chance of her coming down with the bug. As Benjamin looked sourly at his wife, who was now giggling at yet another account of the disastrous garden party, he thought it would serve her right if she'd ended up with a touch of food poisoning herself. Then she mightn't be quite so heartless, and he could have enjoyed a little *schadenfreude* himself.

Suddenly, he felt claustrophobic and needed to get some fresh air.

"I'm off to Clara Court," he told her, but there was no reply.

Jennifer was so engrossed in the newspapers that she either didn't hear him or decided to ignore him.

Later that evening, after the long drive home from the Clara Court development, Benjamin drove through Stonehill village. It was a beautiful evening. The setting sun had turned the sky a glorious orange and the landscape was bathed in its iridescent glow. But today of all days, Benjamin was unable to appreciate it. He had a lot his mind – things weren't going well at Clara Court. The apartments weren't selling the way they used to – previously, they'd all have been sold off plan. He wasn't sure if the error had been in building apartments instead of houses, or if it was caused by the recession, which had descended out of the blue and caught many people napping. Whatever it was, people weren't investing in his properties anymore. He hoped he'd be able to offload the remaining few houses at Bluebell Hill before things got any worse.

On a whim, he suddenly stopped his Land Rover outside the old church in Stonehill village. He wasn't in any hurry home, since Jennifer would be at her golf club, and the kids would be with their friends. He'd been impressed by Georgie Monks' knowledge about the stained-glass windows, and he wanted to have a closer look. Thank goodness she'd pointed out how valuable they were – he'd have destroyed them in his attempts to demolish the old church. Now, hopefully he could sell them and make a tidy profit. He'd looked up Harry Clarke on the Internet, and had been astonished and delighted to discover that the Irishman's stained-glass windows were worth a small fortune.

Benjamin looked around guiltily, expecting a coterie of menacing villagers to suddenly appear and attack him with cudgels. But the village appeared to be its usual sleepy self, and he quietly let himself into the church.

Inside, he gazed up at the windows in awe. They really were quite spectacular. They had a wonderful way of catching the light, and the colours the artist had used were amazingly vivid. Benjamin could imagine the people who'd once sat in these pews being inspired by the beautiful stained-glass images of saints and martyrs.

On the other hand, he'd a more worldly purpose for being there. His intention was to count the windows and list their subject matter, so that he could get a better idea of how much they might be worth on the open market. Later, he'd need an art expert to value them, and ultimately a specialist to remove the windows – he wasn't going to let any of *his* workers near them!

Wandering through the aisles, Benjamin conceded that he'd got a bargain when he purchased the church. Presumably the previous owner hadn't been aware of the valuable windows either, or he'd surely have taken them out and sold them himself.

Standing still, Benjamin watched in wonder as the light created different colours on his skin and clothes. Holding out his hand, he noted it was now blue, then green, then red. He was enjoying the sensation, and moving his hands to catch the different colours, when he heard the door of the church creak open.

First, he saw the red hair, then the elfin face, and knew it was Georgie Monks. Instantly, he felt foolish. Had she seen him catching the light from the windows on his hands?

"You're trespassing!" he barked.

"I see that you're just as ignorant and oafish as the last time we met," she said quietly.

"What the hell are you doing here?" Benjamin roared. "This is *my* property, and neither you nor any of your half-witted friends have any business being here!"

"If anyone's a half-wit, it must be *you*," said Georgie testily. "Only a lunatic would try to destroy priceless art."

"I'm not destroying it, I'm selling it!" he roared back, instantly regretting what he'd just said and wishing he could take it back.

"Selling it? You mean the windows? You bastard!"

"I may be a bastard, but at least the windows are mine to sell!"

"Over my dead body!"

Benjamin laughed harshly. "You said it, sweetheart, not me!"

"Are you threatening me?"

"Do you think I'd waste my time on a pipsqueak like you? I've more important things to do!"

Benjamin stormed out of the building, and for a split second he thought of locking her inside. Momentarily, he relished the thought of her being incarcerated, unable to escape, trapped for hours, maybe even days – and he'd refuse to let her out until she promised not to interfere in his plans anymore . . .

Benjamin was loath to admit it to himself, but Georgie Monks was a pretty little thing. That halo of red hair was amazing, and he longed to grasp it in both hands, and pull her close to him, and . . .

Benjamin wrenched open the door of the Land Rover and climbed inside. If he was honest with himself, he badly wanted to kiss her. But that was never going to happen, because he hated her, and she hated him. And he was married. He'd never been unfaithful to Jennifer, and didn't intend starting now. So he'd just put Georgie Monks' soft lips and gorgeous red hair out of his mind, and keep concentrating on why he hated her . . .

As he drove off, Benjamin felt the tension leaving his body. That little woman had the ability to get him all riled up, and it wasn't good for his blood pressure. Nevertheless, he reluctantly admitted to himself that she fascinated him. He'd really like to see her paintings some day. He imagined they'd be full of vibrant colours – probably similar to Harry Clarke's – since she was such a colourful person herself.

What was it about her that intrigued him so much? Perhaps it was her passion, because that was something he could

161

understand. He felt the same passion for doing business deals and building houses. Jen never expressed any emotions, other than boredom. She glided through life without ever raising her voice, and he resented her for it.

He was surprised to feel more of a kindred spirit with Georgie Monks than he'd ever felt with his wife, yet he and this woman were on opposite sides, for heaven's sake! And for the first time in his life, he felt embarrassed about the direction in which his life had taken him. Georgie Monks' passion was for preserving things, whereas he always seemed hell-bent on destroying them. He cared only about making money, and for what? So that his wife could live her shallow life in even more luxury? He'd spent so much of his life trying to shake off his humble past that he'd lost track of who he really was. He'd become a money-making machine – maybe that was why his wife and children took him so much for granted – machines weren't supposed to have any feelings.

Driving out of the village, Benjamin suddenly wondered if the unlocked church would be safe, because his pride wouldn't let him go back again to lock it. Then he smiled to himself, remembering that he'd left it in the best possible hands . . .

CHAPTER 32

"I'm sorry, Ms Corcroft – your blood group's not compatible with your uncle's."

Several days later, Vanessa sat facing the nephrologist in his office at St Luke's Hospital. On each visit to the hospital, she'd applied lots of make-up to disguise her age, and clearly she'd succeeded in fooling everyone so far.

The doctor smiled sadly at her. "I know it's disappointing, but I'm sure your uncle is very grateful for your willingness to take the test."

Vanessa acknowledged his words with a nod. She felt both relief and disappointment. Relief loomed largest, since it was gradually dawning on her what being a match would actually mean. She now realised that if her blood *had* been compatible, she might have unfairly raised her uncle's hopes, only to cruelly dash them when someone realised she wasn't old enough to actually donate a kidney. Oh, how she wished she really *was* eighteen! It seemed to take ages to grow up . . .

Carl was waiting outside the doctor's office, and when she shook her head, he squeezed her hand affectionately. Suddenly, Vanessa felt like a total fraud. She'd allowed her imagination to carry her along on a wave of euphoria, creating visions of the whole family weeping tears of gratitude as she was wheeled into the operating theatre, and of receiving their adulation and devotion when she later emerged, minus a kidney, having saved her uncle's life. She hadn't given any real thought to the fact that when the chips were down, she wouldn't be able to deliver. At least not for five years, and by then it might be too late. Suddenly, her mind conjured up images of Uncle Hugh lying dead and, overcome by remorse and disappointment, she burst into tears.

Carl slipped his arm around her and hugged her. "Come on, let's get a coffee somewhere," he said, steering her down the corridor and out the main door of the hospital. "There's a nice café just around the corner."

In the café, Carl did his best to cheer Vanessa up. But she was beset by guilt as much as disappointment, yet she couldn't tell Carl without divulging her age.

"I hope your dad finds someone compatible soon," she said at last.

"Look, cuz, it was only a chance that you might be a match," said Carl gently. "Thanks for trying, Vanessa – I'll never forget what you've done."

His kind remarks made Vanessa feel even worse.

CHAPTER 33

"Hi, Dad, it's Vanessa."

"Hello, poppet – how are you?"

"Fine, Dad."

"I miss you. When are you coming back?"

"Er, I'm not sure."

"Well, if Jocelyn's mum can't drop you home, I'll come and collect you myself."

There was a pause. "I'm not at Jocelyn's, Dad – I'm in London, with your brother and his family."

Benjamin nearly dropped the phone. "W-what? Good God!"

"They're really nice, Dad."

"How on earth – I mean, oh Christ!"

"They'd love to see you, Dad. But if you can't collect me, I can get a train back sometime tomorrow."

Benjamin made an immediate and monumental decision. Things had been left to fester for too long.

"No, no – I'll come and collect you. It's been a long time since I've seen them, that's all."

"Thanks, Dad. When will you get here? I know you're very busy and all that –"

"I'll get there tomorrow afternoon. If that's okay with everyone."

"Hang on, Dad, I'll check –"

Within seconds, Vanessa was back on the phone. "That's fine, Dad – see you then."

Benjamin came off the phone wearing an unreadable expression. He wandered back into the dining room where he and Jennifer were eating dinner.

"Who was that?"

"Vanessa."

"When will she be back from Jocelyn's?

"She's not at Jocelyn's – never has been. She's in Walthamstow."

Jennifer looked aghast. "She's *where*?"

"With my family."

"Good God, how on earth –?"

"I don't know, but she seems quite happy there. I said I'd collect her tomorrow."

Jennifer wrinkled her nose disapprovingly. "What on earth possessed her to go there? I mean, she might have been mugged, raped or worse –"

"Jennifer, I know your opinion of my family, but they are *not* muggers or rapists."

Irritated, Jennifer banged her wineglass down on the table. "I didn't mean your family – I meant the area. That part of London isn't exactly safe. I mean, she's only thirteen, for God's sake!"

"Well, if you weren't off playing bridge or golf all the time, maybe you'd have managed to keep an eye on her!"

"You can hardly talk – you're never home!"

"At least I'm out making money – you know, that stuff that buys all the goodies you can't live without!"

Jennifer stormed out, leaving a waft of expensive perfume in her wake. She was furious with Vanessa – how dare she visit those appalling people!

Jennifer had always ensured that Benjamin's awful family didn't intrude into their lives. Imagine having those uncouth and ignorant people turning up at one of their parties – they'd be loud and vulgar, and wouldn't even know what a canapé was.

166

They'd probably think it was something you stood under when it rained!

How on earth had Vanessa found them? Jennifer had always avoided any mention of them and, in deference to her, Benjamin had done the same. After all, her husband was now a highly successful businessman, who had no need of a dubious family history. At her instigation, he'd reinvented himself, giving himself a new family background that had obliterated the Corcroft lunatic fringe.

Of course, sometimes Benjamin couldn't resist dragging up his poor background, and his remarks were usually designed to cause her maximum embarrassment.

But even people who were aware of his lowly background liked his money and the lavish parties he and Jennifer threw at The Old Vicarage. And they admired Jennifer for seeing the shrewd businessman behind the uncouth exterior, and being canny enough to snap him up before someone else did. At least that's what she hoped they were saying, and his money more than made up for the occasional embarrassment he caused her. Besides, Clive Ellwood was all she needed, and she had his love already.

Upstairs in her dressing room, Jennifer stared at her face in the mirror, and didn't like what she saw. There were tension lines around her mouth and eyes, and it was all Vanessa's fault for causing her all this stress.

Even worse, since Benjamin had opted to collect her, he was putting himself in contact with them again. Was there no escaping those ghastly people? No doubt they'd bred copiously, filling the suburb where they lived with yet another generation of uncouth misfits. Well, she wasn't having them to The Old Vicarage, no matter what Benjamin or Vanessa said.

Sitting at her dressing table, Jennifer scrutinised herself thoroughly. Apart from the tension lines, she wasn't looking too bad for her age. She hadn't put on a pound since she'd got married and could still fit into her wedding dress. Her skin was still smooth, and the occasional grey hair was quickly taken care of by a visit to her favourite salon in London.

Loosening her hair from its chignon, she began brushing it fiercely. She was utterly disgusted that Benjamin was crawling back to his loutish family, and Vanessa too was being influenced by their pathetic way of life. Hopefully the novelty would wear off them all soon. If not, she'd have to do something about it.

CHAPTER 34

Zoe's Diary

February 28

Sometimes I hate Dad for leaving, and Mum for letting him go. Then I feel guilty, because I can't possibly understand the world of grown-ups yet. I try to be both mum and dad to Claire, but it's not easy. She needs proper adults who can explain things to her. I'm still trying to learn things myself.

As the two girls sat eating their dinner in the kitchen, each had an ear cocked for the sound of their mother's whiskey bottle hitting the floor. This invariably happened when she passed out and the bottle slipped from her hand. Luckily the bedroom carpet, although threadbare, cushioned the bottle enough to prevent it from breaking.

Crash!

Zoe and Claire nodded at each other. Right on time, their mother was out for the count.

It was heartbreaking, day after day, to watch their mother slip further and further away from them. Both girls felt an overwhelming sense of powerlessness.

"She seems to love drink more than us," said Claire, pushing her plate away.

Zoe shook her head vehemently. "That's not true – she just doesn't realise how it's affecting us. She's ill – she can't help being the way she is."

"But she wasn't ill before," Claire persisted. "She was always happy when Daddy was around."

Zoe nodded sadly. "I think she started drinking to help cope with the loneliness."

"Do you think Daddy knows that Mum is drinking so much?"

"I don't know," said Zoe sadly.

"Do you think Daddy would help us if we could find him and tell him how sick Mum is?" Claire asked, a hopeful expression on her little face.

Zoe shook her head. For all Claire's astuteness, her little sister was also very naïve. Zoe didn't believe there was anything they could do that would bring their father back. They didn't know where he was, he never sent any letters, and their mother refused to talk about him.

"Do you think Mummy knows where he's gone?" Claire persisted.

"I don't know – and don't you dare go asking her again!" Zoe said fiercely. "Remember what happened the last time!"

"Sorry, Zoe," Claire whispered. "I promise I'll never ask again."

In the silence that followed, both girls continued with their homework. Then Claire suddenly looked up from her books. "I know a way we could cheer Mummy up."

Zoe looked interested. "How?"

"We could move the television into her bedroom."

Zoe smiled warmly. "That's a great idea!"

The old television – bought by their father years earlier – was in the drawing room. Claire hoped it might get their mother interested in the outside world, and entertain her while they were at school. It might even distract her from drinking so much.

"Let's move it tomorrow after school!" said Zoe, her eyes sparkling.

Huffing and puffing, the girls carried the old set into their mother's bedroom, and placed it at the foot of her bed.

"*What do you think, Mum?*" said Zoe, turning it on and adjusting the indoor aerial until the reception was reasonable. A quiz programme was on the screen, and her mother's interest was instantly piqued.

"What a marvellous idea – thank you, girls," said their mother, smiling, and the two felt very pleased.

"It was Claire's idea," said Zoe generously. She wasn't going to take the credit for an idea that hadn't been hers.

"Thank you, Claire," said their mother, smiling, and Claire felt ten feet tall.

Every day, when Claire returned from school, she'd hear the drone of the television in their mother's room, and she was happy that she'd come up with such a good idea. Since they'd installed the television, their mother stayed awake later, and watched TV while eating her dinner. Judging by the fewer empty whiskey bottles, she was drinking less too.

One evening, as Zoe was cooking and Claire was preparing the tray for her mother's meal, they heard an angry roar followed by a crash coming from their mother's bedroom. Thinking something dreadful had happened, both girls abandoned what they were doing and rushed into their mother's bedroom.

"Mum, are you alright – oh my God, what's happened?"

The television screen was in smithereens, pieces of shattered grey glass still adhering to the sides of the box, its inside components on view, parts of it still smoking. Their mother was sitting up in bed, a look of fury on her face.

"Oh God, did the television explode? Are you alright?" Zoe screamed.

Claire ran crying to their mother.

"Calm down," said their mother huffily. "There's no need to panic."

Then Zoe spotted an empty whiskey bottle at the base of the television, and it suddenly dawned on her what had happened.

"It was you, Mum – you threw the bottle at the screen!" said Zoe, a look of astonishment on her face. "Why on earth –"

"*I bought him that jacket – I'd recognise it anywhere!*" shouted their mother.

"*Oh God, was Daddy on television?*"

Their mother stared at Zoe venomously. "*I thought we agreed never to mention his name again?*"

Zoe stood her ground. "*But you were the one who –*"

"*Get out, both of you!*" said their mother angrily.

"*Let me at least unplug the TV,*" Zoe begged. "*Otherwise, it might damage the rest of the wiring.*"

Sitting like a sentry in her bed, their mother waited impatiently until Zoe had unplugged the broken set and the two girls shuffled out of the room.

"*Now close the door after you!*" she yelled.

In the kitchen, Zoe and Claire looked anxiously at each other.

"*What was that all about?*" Claire whispered.

"*I don't know – something on the television obviously upset her, and she threw the whiskey bottle at it.*"

Claire smiled whimsically. "*I noticed that the bottle she threw was empty – she wouldn't have risked breaking a full one!*"

Zoe laughed. Her little sister didn't miss much.

"*What was the programme about?*" Claire persisted. "*Was Daddy in it?*"

"*I don't know.*" Zoe shook her head. "*Why would Daddy be on television? Unless it was a programme about engineers, or maybe –*"

Zoe quickly closed her mouth. She'd been about to suggest it might have been an item about men who leave their wives for other women. But Claire was too young to understand these things, and it would destroy her hopes of seeing her father again.

"*Maybe what?*"

"*Oh, nothing.*"

"*If we could find out what programme was on, we might be able to track Daddy down,*" said Claire enthusiastically. In her mind, if they could just find him, he'd magically come home, their mother would stop drinking and they'd be a family again.

Zoe raised her eyebrows.

172

"*If we could get one of those TV magazines,*" Claire added, "*you know, the ones that tell you what programmes are on – we could find out the name of the programme Mum was watching.*"

"*Wow – that's great idea!*" said Zoe, delighted. "*You're a clever girl, Claire! And I know just the person who can help us.*"

During school break-time the following day, having sworn Hazel Bonnington to secrecy, Zoe told her about the demise of the television set, and her certainty that the programme her mother was watching somehow referred to her father.

"*Do you have a listings magazine at home?*" Zoe asked.

Hazel nodded.

"*Great! Mum never buys one, so I need you to check what was on each station yesterday at around six o'clock.*"

"*Okay,*" said Hazel, nodding. "*In fact, I can probably cut out yesterday's page, since it's of no use to anyone now.*"

"*Brilliant! Thanks, Hazel – I'm certain that whatever made Mum angry had something to do with Daddy. Maybe we could track him down through the programme?*"

Hazel looked dubious. "*Is that really a good idea? If your mother hates him so much, why would you want to bring him back into your lives?*"

"*I don't think Mum really hates him,*" said Zoe. "*She's just angry because he left us. If we could find him, and tell him how unwell she is, he might come back.*"

Hazel looked unconvinced.

"*Besides, Claire and I desperately want him back too – then we'd be a family again.*"

The following day, Hazel brought in the page from the TV guide.

"*I don't think this is much help,*" she said, handing it to Zoe during morning break. "*Every station had a news programme on around six o'clock yesterday. There's no way of finding out exactly what your mother was watching, because news stories are changing all the time. By the way,*" she added importantly, "*I've decided I'm going to be a journalist when I grow up.*"

"*You are? Well, I think you'd be very good at it,*" Zoe replied *absentmindedly. She was still scanning the listings page in the hope that Hazel might have missed a listing, but finally she had to accept her friend had been right.*

"*Thanks anyway, Hazel,*" she said. It'd been a long shot. Now she'd have to tell Claire that their dream was just as far away as ever.

CHAPTER 35

Anne and Clive hadn't spoken to each other since the garden party. Their only communication was through words of one syllable. Mrs Hill, tiptoed between them, relaying messages and toning down the insults she was asked to convey.

Having spent two days in bed, claiming to be desperately ill with food poisoning, Clive declared himself thoroughly humiliated by what had happened, and he held Anne personally responsible. "It had to be those bloody quiches of yours – I didn't eat anything else at that damned party!" he roared.

In turn, Anne ignored him, aware that he'd had time to brood, and he'd worked himself into a self-righteous frenzy. The days he'd spent in bed – being looked after by Mrs Hill since Anne refused to go near him – had given him time to dwell on the injustice of it all. It had also been Anne's fault, he reasoned, because she'd been the one who planned the garden party. He hadn't wanted one at all, and had only agreed to it reluctantly since Anne had already sent out the invitations.

Anne treated her husband with icy distain. How dare he criticise her attempts to boost his career! All she'd done was try to create an environment in which he'd be seen at his most affable best. Well, no one could call him affable now.

Anne was seething. While Clive was languishing in bed, claiming to be ill, she'd had to face all the flak from the newspapers. There had even been a TV crew trying to gain access to the grounds in order to show their viewers where the fateful garden party had been held. Anne had the gates quickly locked, but later she spotted someone with a camera trying to climb over the fence between the woods and The Grange. At moments like these, Anne wished she owned a gun. Instead, she rang the local police, and the intruder was quickly dispatched with a flea in his ear.

She'd also been the one who'd had to arrange delivery of bouquets of flowers and baskets of fruit to the guests who'd fallen ill. The minister had been sent an extra-large hamper, in the hopes that he'd make light of the event once he returned to the Commons. Anne shuddered at the thought of the Ellwoods' disastrous garden party being recorded in the minutes of the House and going down in parliamentary history.

Anne also had to play the role of concerned friend, making calls to the victims of food poisoning, expressing regret for what happened and professing sincere concern for their return to good health. By the time Anne had called those who'd fallen ill, she felt drained and angry and ready to throw up. Maybe she should have pretended to have food poisoning herself, and left Clive to make all the calls himself!

Claiming to be only partially recovered, Clive had taken himself off to the living room in his duvet. From there he continued his apoplectic rage, shouting at the top of his voice at anyone who'd listen to him. It wasn't even possible to blame the caterers, he ranted, since Anne had insisted on claiming that she'd made the damned quiches herself.

Anne retaliated with sarcasm. Did Clive expect her to ring up the poisoned guests and tell them she'd lied about making the bloody quiches?

All three catering companies denied supplying the quiches, and Anne had several unpleasant telephone conversations with the proprietors, assuring them that the Ellwoods would never use their services again. But as she put the phone down, Anne admitted to herself that she and Clive were unlikely to risk another social event anyway.

"What am I going to do, Betty?" Anne asked Mrs Hill plaintively.

Anne didn't really need an answer to her question, but it was a relief to be able to talk to someone about what had happened, and especially Mrs Hill, since she'd witnessed the disastrous events at first hand.

The two women were standing in the kitchen, listening to Clive shouting from the living room that he needed someone to bring him a cup of tea and the morning papers.

"Don't worry about him – he'll be okay when he cools down," said Mrs Hill pragmatically. "But you should call your friends and have a meal out with them – there's nothing like your mates for helping to put things in perspective."

Anne nodded. The idea of meeting up with Jennifer, Fiona and Emma sounded like a good idea. Suddenly, she longed for their reassurance that the disastrous garden party would be forgotten before long. They'd have a nice meal in a top restaurant, drink a few bottles of good wine, and before long she'd have forgotten all about it.

"You're a genius, Betty," Anne said happily. It was just the tonic she needed.

Both women pretended to be deaf to Clive's ranting, and ignored his repeated request for tea and the papers. Mrs Hill busied herself filling the dishwasher, while Anne went into the hall and began phoning her friends.

CHAPTER 36

"Dad, I'm sorry – I mean, for pretending I was at Jocelyn's," Vanessa said, rushing to hug her father as he arrived at the Corcrofts' flat.

"I'm sure you had your reasons," Benjamin replied, studying her earnest little face, "I'm just glad you're safe and well."

Benjamin peered closely at his daughter. She looked very grown-up all of a sudden – was that make-up she was wearing?

"I needed to get away."

Benjamin nodded. He didn't see why Vanessa shouldn't be entitled to feel fed up sometimes, too. He often used his job as an excuse to get away. At least she'd had the good sense to come to somewhere that she'd be safe. Even if it meant an embarrassing confrontation for him.

However, there was no opportunity for either embarrassment or confrontation. As soon as Benjamin crossed the threshold of the flat, Hugh was up off the sofa and grasping him in a bear hug.

"Benny, it's great to see you!"

"You too, Hugh!"

As they clutched each other, Benjamin marvelled at the

welcome he'd just received. Then as he and Hugh drew apart, Maisie and Carl embraced him in turn. It was as though he'd just been away on a long holiday, rather than estranged from them by a rift that had festered for more years than he cared to remember.

Instantly, Hugh was urging him to make himself comfortable on one of the large sofas, and within seconds Maisie presented him with a cup of tea.

"Do you still take two sugars, Benny? No? That obviously explains why you're looking so trim!"

Benjamin decided not to mention the fact that Jennifer had weaned him off sugar years before, claiming it was 'so lower class'. As he sat surrounded by his extended family, all of whom were smiling at him, Benjamin felt a strange sense of peace. It hadn't been the awful ordeal he'd feared. All the way up to London in the car, he'd been wondering what would happen when he got there. After all, he was the one who'd cut off his family. He was the one who'd ignored them since his marriage, allowing Jennifer to dictate who was, and who was not, invited to The Old Vicarage. If the situation had been reversed, he doubted if he'd be the one putting out the welcome mat.

Yet as he sat in the Corcrofts' flat, it was as though he'd never been away. Vanessa had already done the groundwork, so he didn't need to fill in any family details. But as everyone chatted, Benjamin was acutely aware that no one had enquired about Jennifer. There seemed to be a tacit agreement that no one would mention her name unless Benjamin himself brought it up. But he, too, carefully avoided any reference to his wife.

As they all began the delicate business of building bridges, Benjamin silently marvelled at how these kind and decent people could put the past behind them and move on without a backward glance. They'd accepted Vanessa when she'd arrived out of the blue on their doorstep. And now, they'd accepted him, even though they were obviously aware that Vanessa's arrival had forced his hand.

He glanced at his daughter, and was overwhelmed with gratitude, since it was her visit that enabled this rift to end. Now that he'd found his brother and his family again, he was never going to let anything – or anyone – destroy that connection again.

After a hugely enjoyable afternoon with his family, Benjamin reluctantly conceded that it was time to start the long drive home.

"Well," said Benjamin, reluctantly rising to his feet, "I'd better get this little minx back." He chanced a reference to Jennifer. "Her mother is having conniptions about her being on her own in the big city." He smiled at Vanessa, tousling her hair. "I don't think she'll be impressed by all that make-up either – isn't thirteen a bit young for all that stuff?"

Maisie looked shocked. "Thirteen? She told us she was eighteen!"

Vanessa went puce as everyone turned to look at her.

"You're only thirteen, Vanessa?" asked Carl, an amused grin on his face.

Vanessa nodded, unable to speak. She was dying inside with embarrassment. She'd managed to fool everyone – in fact, she'd almost *felt* eighteen – and now, just as she was leaving, she'd been humiliated, and by her own father! Why couldn't he have kept his mouth shut, at least until they'd left? Oh God, she'd never be able to hold up her head again!

The tension was broken when Uncle Hugh started to laugh. "Well, you had *me* fooled, girl!" he chuckled. "You can certainly pass for eighteen – and you're as bright as any eighteen-year-old! I think your dad should be very proud of you."

Now with tears in her eyes, Vanessa rushed across the room and hugged her uncle, hiding her embarrassed face in the voluminous folds of his neck.

"I'm sorry," she said , disengaging herself at last. "I just wanted you to think I was old enough to visit without my parents' permission. And then, when I thought I could give you a kidney – well, I had to keep up the deception, didn't I? If I'd been compatible, I'd have told you the truth, and asked my parents if I could do the other tests, then maybe when I was older –"

"What are you talking about?" Benjamin asked, looking bewildered.

Quickly, Hugh told his brother about his illnesses that necessitated a kidney transplant if he was ever to lead a normal life. And he told of Vanessa's generous offer of a kidney, but that her blood hadn't been compatible.

"When she heard about my predicament, she took the test," Hugh told his brother, while smiling gratefully at Vanessa. "But even if she'd been compatible, I'd never have taken a kidney from anyone so young – and by that, I mean eighteen!"

"Well, if you need a kidney, I'll give you one. Tell me where I can be tested," Benjamin replied gruffly.

There was silence for a few seconds, then everyone spoke at once.

"Oh Benny, that's unbelievably decent of you!" said Maisie, looking hopefully at her husband.

"Thanks, Uncle Benny," said Carl.

"Dad, I love you so much!" said Vanessa, surprising herself with her outburst. Her father hugged her tightly, and she was glad she'd briefly let go of her inhibitions. She wanted her dad to know how much he meant to her.

Only Hugh said nothing. He wasn't able, because he was crying quietly in the corner. Tears of joy coursed down his ruddy cheeks and into the rolls of fat around his neck. But he wasn't crying because of the possibility of having his health restored. He was crying because he could hardly believe that the brother he hadn't seen for years could make such a generous offer. Even if Benny was incompatible, it was a wonderful gesture he'd never forget.

Suddenly, Vanessa noticed a strange faraway look on her father's face. He looked as though he wanted to say something, but couldn't. Anxiously she waited, hoping it wasn't anything that would upset the joyful atmosphere in the Corcrofts' flat. After what seemed an eternity, she saw her father brace himself.

"By the way, Hugh, how's Mum?"

For a split second, a frozen look came on Hugh's face. Then he gave a sad smile.

"She's okay, Benny – she's in a nursing home now."

Outrage registered on Benjamin's face. "What on earth is she doing there? Is she sick?"

Hugh pursed his lips. "She's got Alzheimer's, Benny. She's gradually losing her mind."

For a moment, Benjamin looked as though he was about to cry. He swallowed, and Vanessa watched as he clenched his jaw.

"I want to go and see her."

Hugh looked pleased. "Sure, Benny – if you can stay over, we'll go there tomorrow."

"She'll be thrilled to see you, after all these years," said Maisie kindly, unintentionally drawing attention to Benjamin's long-term neglect of his mother.

Carl quickly tried to smooth away his mother's comment by offering his bedroom to his uncle if he was staying. That led on to a discussion that resulted in Benjamin and Vanessa both agreeing to take a couch in the living room each.

Benjamin phoned home to let Jennifer know there had been a change of plan. He'd expected a torrent of abuse, but she was surprisingly accepting of this new arrangement. Then, as he hung up, Benjamin remembered that the following night was her weekly bridge night in London, but she hadn't suggested meeting up so they could all make the trip home together. Benjamin grimaced. Nothing ever got in the way of Jennifer's own plans.

Later that night, Vanessa and her father lay on the sofas in the dark, each of them pretending to be asleep. But they were wide-awake and thinking of their newfound family, who were already impacting on their lives in ways they'd never dreamed of.

Vanessa finally dozed off, dreaming that Rozzer, Jack and Leggo were staying at The Old Vicarage and she was giving them riding lessons on Grey Star. Benjamin, too, drifted off at last, dreaming that Georgie Monks was cross with him for neglecting his mother. But when he told her he was going to visit her the following day, she threw her arms around him. Sighing happily, he snuggled down under the duvet and began to snore.

CHAPTER 37

As they walked down the dingy corridor, Benjamin was appalled at the condition of the nursing home. The windows needed washing, the décor was an institutional grey, and everything else he saw only depressed him even more. As they passed the kitchen, the smell of cabbage was wafting out the door. In the lounge, bored old people were propped up in mismatching armchairs in front of a blaring television that no one was watching. The smell of stale sweat and old age permeated everything, and Benjamin felt like gagging.

"She's down here," said Hugh, guiding his brother down a narrow corridor to the left. As they walked along, past rooms with small grilles in the doors, Benjamin thought sadly how like a prison it was. What an appalling way for old people to end their days! And this was where his poor mother was incarcerated.

Inside the room, an old white-haired woman sat staring into space. Benjamin felt his heart almost break as he stared down at the woman who'd given him birth. He got down on his knees in front of her and took one of her hands in his.

"Hello, Mum," he whispered, tears in his eyes.

"Mum, this is our Benny, come to see you," said Hugh encouragingly.

The old woman continued to look into space, her eyes vacant and uncomprehending. Then she suddenly turned to Benjamin and smiled, and he felt as though his heart was about to burst.

"Mum," he sobbed, "I wish I'd been a better son. I know I've let you down. But I can't blame Jennifer – I went along with her ideas. She said I had to distance myself from you all if I wanted to get ahead." He raised his tear-streaked face to his brother. "Now I'm a millionaire and my own mother doesn't know me! Oh God, what have I done?"

Benjamin's mother held him and patted his head as though he was a wounded child. Although she didn't understand anything he was saying, she knew that whoever this man was, he was in pain and she wanted to ease it.

"Do you think she remembers me?" Benjamin whispered.

Hugh gently patted his shoulder. "Yes, of course she does. See how she's smiling at you."

Benjamin wasn't sure, but he desperately wanted to believe that his brother was right. He'd missed all those years of his mother's life, when he could have made her life more comfortable. Now, she was lost to him forever as she sank gradually into dementia.

"She was always so proud of you," Hugh told him. "It didn't matter that she didn't see you – she was delighted you were so successful. She used to buy all the newspapers and study the society columns. When your picture appeared, she'd show it to all the neighbours. 'That's my son' she'd say, as proud as punch."

But instead of making him feel better, Benjamin only felt worse.

"Didn't that make *you* feel bad?" asked Benjamin as he stood up, suddenly feeling his brother's pain at being the less successful brother. On the other hand, Hugh was the son who didn't need to feel guilty about how he'd treated his mother.

"No, I was proud of you too," Hugh said, hugging him.

As the brothers separated, patting each other awkwardly on the back, Benjamin came to a decision. "We've got to get her out of here," he said quietly. "We can't leave her in this squalid hole."

"I know it's awful, but we couldn't afford anywhere else," said an embarrassed Hugh.

Benjamin opened his mouth, then closed it again. He'd been about to say: Why didn't you contact me? But he knew that his brother and his family had their pride too, and anyway, he was the one who'd let *them* down.

Suddenly, Benjamin realised that once again he was making decisions without even considering his brother's feelings. In business, he was used to making snap decisions on his own, but now he had someone else to consider. Although he doubted that his brother's opinion of the home would vary from his own.

"Hugh, are you happy for us to take her out of here, and for me to pay? I mean, I don't want to intrude on your arrangements –"

"No, no – I agree one hundred per cent," his brother replied. "I hate her being here. But this place is all we were offered, and since neither Carl nor I earn enough to pay for a private home, we had to accept it."

"Okay, so that's settled," said Benjamin, feeling a lot better now that he was doing something. At least he could ensure that his mother would be properly looked after for the rest of her days.

As he turned to look at his mother again, she suddenly gave him a beatific smile. "Benny!" she cried, holding her skinny arms out to him. In that instant, he was both thrilled and humbled. She'd actually recognised him! Tears ran down his face again as he held her bony little body close. Why had he allowed Jennifer to deprive him of all these precious moments?

But he had to admit that he'd been a willing supplicant at the altar of Jennifer's superior knowledge. He'd allowed her to reinvent him and create Brand Corcroft. He'd indulged her because he loved her and hadn't been able to believe his luck when she'd agreed to marry him. He was well aware that she'd never have married him if he'd been penniless, but he'd accepted the situation and been grateful for it.

Now, rage filled his heart. His own family had become strangers to him! It was only through his family's generosity of

185

spirit that he'd been welcomed back, and he was well aware that he didn't deserve their acceptance.

Only for Vanessa's curiosity, he might never have seen his mother again, and she'd have been left mouldering in this awful nursing home. As it was, she was already locked in her own little world, where everything must be confusing and perhaps even threatening. And his brother was condemned to lifelong dialysis, unless he could help him. Even if he couldn't give Hugh a kidney, he intended to get him the best medical treatment possible.

"I love you, Mum," Benjamin whispered in his mother's ear, then suddenly wondered if she'd gone deaf during the intervening years. There were so many things he didn't know, so many reasons to feel guilty. But regardless of whether she could hear him or not, she held him close, patting his back and mumbling to herself.

"She doesn't say much anymore," Hugh informed him. "Sometimes, Alzheimer's robs people of their speech."

And I let Jennifer rob me of my own family, Benjamin thought savagely. Well, it's not going to happen again.

"I'll be back soon, Mum, and we'll get you sorted," Benjamin said, bending down and kissing his mother's wrinkled cheek. He knew that what he was saying was more for himself than for his mother, since it was unlikely she understood anything he said.

"Bye, Mum," said Hugh, as the two brothers left their mother sitting in solitary confinement in her room, just staring into space.

"Jesus!" exploded Benjamin when they were out of earshot. "What an awful place this is!"

"Shhh!" whispered Hugh. "Don't let the staff hear you – we want them to look after her properly until we can find somewhere better!"

"Properly? This place is like a concentration camp!"

As soon as they left the nursing home, Benjamin calmed down, hoping that his disparaging remarks about the home hadn't upset his brother, who'd had no choice but to put their mother there.

Benjamin was silent as Hugh drove them back to Walthamstow in his van. His mind was filled with plans of getting their mother into a cosy, caring environment, where she'd be well looked after and not treated like a piece of garbage. Money was no object, so he could pay for the very best of care. Unlike his poor brother, he thought, giving a sidelong glance at Hugh. The poor fellow could only work three days a week because of his need for regular dialysis. Benjamin considered offering him some cash, then decided against it. His brother had his pride, and Benjamin was learning that not everything could be sorted out with money.

As they pulled up outside the Corcrofts' flat, Benjamin wondered how Alan would feel about meeting his newfound relatives, because he fully intended that his son should meet the other half of his family. Benjamin was worried about Alan – lately, all the boy did was play his guitar and mope around the house. Maybe Carl's drive and commitment would serve as an example to him.

He was pleased that Vanessa and Carl were getting along so well – right now, they were probably playing Scrabble together, or discussing Carl's work with Greenpeace. Benjamin had been astounded to find that his privileged daughter, who didn't need to lift a finger at home, had sold fruit and vegetables in the street and offered his brother a kidney!

He was also beginning to realise how much he owed her. If she hadn't made contact with his family, it was unlikely he'd ever have done so himself. Thanks to Vanessa, he was now realising what he'd missed. Not only had she restored his family to him, she'd also given him back his self-respect.

CHAPTER 38

"Hi, Mum – I'm home!"

Vanessa adopted an outwardly cheerful attitude to camouflage her uneasiness. No doubt she was in for a tongue-lashing from her mother. Not only had she sneaked off to London without telling anyone, she'd made contact with the people her mother reviled.

Her mother came down the stairs wearing impossibly high heels. She was the only woman Vanessa knew who could do that so effortlessly.

"Good God, Vanessa," her mother shrieked, "what's that hideous thing you're wearing?"

"It's a hoodie, Mum."

Jennifer looked angrily at her daughter as she reached the bottom stair. "Well, I've news for you, Vanessa – I forbid you to wear that – that – thing in this house! You look like a vagrant – please take it off immediately!"

Just then, Benjamin appeared, after parking his car in one of the garages. "What's the problem?"

"How could you let your daughter be seen in such a ghastly outfit?" Jennifer shrieked.

"Well, I think it's very nice," said Benjamin mildly, although he was inwardly seething. How dare Jennifer pick on the child before asking if she was safe and well!

Suddenly, he had an idea. He watched Vanessa go upstairs to her bedroom, then he cleared his throat as soon as she was out of earshot.

"Oh, by the way, Jen – I'm bringing my mother to live with us – I hope you don't mind. She's in a nursing home at the moment, but it's pretty dismal, so I thought you could take care of her." Benjamin grimaced. "Since money's tight at the moment, we can't afford any nursing help, so you'll have to manage on your own, at least for a while, anyway."

Jennifer was speechless. The colour drained from her face, leaving two small red patches in the centre of her cheeks. Her mouth dropped open, then she closed it tightly again. This couldn't be happening, she thought angrily. Benjamin had taken leave of his senses. She was filled with fury, and wanted to kill Vanessa for engineering the situation that enabled Benjamin to be reunited with his horrid family.

"I – you can't be serious!"

Benjamin nodded, privately marvelling at his ability to keep a straight face. He could win an Oscar at this rate!

"Look, Jen – we've plenty of room here," he added, looking earnestly at her. "Anyway, she's just an old lady, so she won't need too much attention. Obviously, she'll need a shower daily, and regular meals – oh, and did I say she's also incontinent?"

At this point, Benjamin had to leave the room quickly, since he couldn't keep a straight face any longer. Jennifer looked as though she was about to have a heart attack at the thought of having to care for his mother.

Serve her right, he thought – it's time someone gave her a taste of her own medicine. He'd also enjoy telling her that he intended taking a blood test to see if he was compatible with his brother and, if he was, he'd be taking the next round of tests in order to donate a kidney to him. Benjamin was enjoying himself immensely.

Fuming, Jennifer wondered if it was time to divorce Benjamin.

Over the years she'd groomed him to reach the pinnacle of respectability, but now he was throwing it all away in order to hang out with his hideous relatives once again.

As she sat at her dressing table, furiously brushing her hair, she studied her face in the mirror and conceded that her good looks were wasted on her husband, who had no appreciation of the bargain he'd got when she'd agreed to marry him.

She shuddered as she thought of their friends' reaction if Benjamin produced his dotty mother and the rest of the Corcrofts at their next party. Well, she'd make sure that never happened. The first thing she intended doing was calling off the party she'd been planning for the end of the month. She wasn't having those ne'er-do-wells robbing the silver or embarrassing her in front of her friends. And there was no way she was going to look after his crazy mother either!

She could cheerfully strangle Vanessa for contacting those dreadful people in the first place. Benjamin had even suggested that Alan should meet his cousin Carl – no doubt it wouldn't be long before he'd be adopting the older boy's coarse language and behaviour. Jennifer felt totally let down by her family. After all she had done for them!

Anyway, now that Benjamin was losing so much money on his building projects, he was even less attractive to her than before. Her stupid husband had stretched himself too far, investing in projects that would never now be completed. The Stonegate Farm land was lying idle and would probably never be developed. Benjamin was also in debt to the banks, and she could see penury ahead.

Well, she didn't want any part in his fall from grace. She couldn't bear the thought of people laughing and pointing the finger at her – she'd have to do something to disassociate herself from Benjamin and the shame he was bringing on their family.

God, how she wished she'd met Clive before Anne did! But the clever minx had kept him to herself until the wedding day, ensuring that it was too late for anyone else to make a play for him. But their attraction to each other had been instantaneous, and in her blue bridesmaid dress, Jennifer had fallen in love for the first and only time.

After their initial coupling in the hotel broom closet, she and Clive had resumed their affair as soon as he and Anne returned from their honeymoon in the Seychelles. Jennifer had spent those two weeks in a state of frustration and jealousy, wondering what he was doing with Anne, and longing for him to be doing it to her.

But the minute he returned, he'd phoned her, and within the hour they were making love in the back of his car, unable to keep their hands off each other. And they hadn't stopped ever since. They both acknowledged that theirs would be a lifetime affair, and even Jennifer's marriage to Benjamin hadn't interrupted it.

Jennifer fumed as she continued brushing her hair. It was frustrating to know that Clive would have married her if only the timing had been different. And often over the years, especially after lovemaking, he'd sigh and wish that things could be different. Only the previous week, he'd reiterated his desire to have her as his wife.

"I made the biggest mistake of my life the day I married Anne," he'd whispered, nuzzling her ear. "If only I'd met you before the wedding, my love – well, things would have been a lot different."

Jennifer had raised her head. "Would you have married me instead?"

"Of course."

"Would you still marry me today?"

Clive smiled, loosening her hair and letting it fall around her shoulders. "Of course – you know that. But you have Benjamin and I have Anne, so there's nothing we can do about it. But you'll always be the love of my life."

As she'd lain in his arms, Jennifer had decided that maybe something *could* be done about it. If tiresome Anne wasn't around anymore, she'd leave Benjamin and marry Clive. Then she'd finally be the wife of a cultured man, and the wife of an MP to boot.

Jennifer wondered what it would take for Anne to leave Clive.

Certainly nothing she could think of. Anne was like a limpet, hanging onto her husband for dear life. Her whole identity was tied up in him. Even if Jennifer admitted to Anne that she was having an affair with her husband, Anne would stoically battle on with the marriage, since she'd be nothing without it. The person most affected would be Jennifer herself, since she'd lose Anne's friendship and no doubt Fiona's and Emma's as well. And Clive would be livid with her for telling Anne, and he might stop loving her because she'd been so stupid. Jennifer sighed. Anyway, Anne would make him promise to stop seeing her, and that was something she couldn't bear to think about. No, Anne would never leave the marriage voluntarily. Jennifer knew that she'd have to think of something else.

Each time she lay in Clive's arms, she'd thought how wonderful it would be if Anne could simply disappear off the face of the earth. She smiled to herself as she imagined aliens from outer space carting Anne off in their spaceship. She liked to think of her screaming as she was beamed up by three-legged green monsters who loved the taste of human flesh.

By now, Jennifer's hair was gleaming from the furious brushing she'd given it, and she studied it with something akin to pleasure. Clive loved her long hair, and hated Anne's utilitarian haircuts that made her look like a freshly shorn sheep.

Leaving her dressing table, Jennifer marched downstairs again. Since Benjamin was going to embrace his hideous family again, she wasn't going to hang around. And since he was no longer rich, it was as good a time as any to leave him. Right now, she was going to start making plans for the rest of her life.

CHAPTER 39

Zoe's Diary

March 8

   The bullies are waiting for me outside the school gates every day. I'm glad Claire is in the junior school and doesn't know what's happening to me.

   Mum's cough is very bad, and I'm so afraid the drink is killing her. I sometimes worry that she doesn't care if she dies, but what will happen to Claire and me if that happens?

Having listened to their mother coughing in her sleep for several nights, Zoe was very worried.

"Stop fussing!" her mother said crossly as Zoe pulled back her bedroom curtains on the third morning. Her mother's face glistened with sweat, her throat was hoarse and Zoe felt certain she had a temperature.

"I'm perfectly alright – just a bit of phlegm," her mother added. "I'll be fine in a day or two. Now pass me that bottle please, Zoe. My throat's dry, and the whiskey will ease it a bit."

"Mum, let me get you some tea and toast first," her daughter pleaded.

"Zoe, please – give me that bottle," her mother said stonily.

Exasperated, Zoe passed her mother the bottle of whiskey. "Mum, you're not helping yourself," she said earnestly. *"You don't eat enough, and I'm worried in case you're getting bronchitis or pneumonia –"*

Her mother waved her hand dismissively. "Go and have your own breakfast, love. You can bring me some toast when you're finished."

Her mother smiled at her, and Zoe desperately wanted to throw her arms around her and tell her how precious she was to her daughters, and how worried they were about her health. But Zoe was afraid she might start to cry, so she said nothing.

Back in the kitchen, Claire was eating a bowl of cornflakes. She eyed Zoe as she entered the room but said nothing. She'd heard the raised voices in the bedroom.

"Have you heard Mum coughing at night?" asked Zoe, pouring milk into her own cereal.

Claire nodded. "It's been terrible. Do you think she's going to die?"

"Of course not!" said Zoe hotly. *Yet even as she denied it, the same fear was in the back of her own mind too. Their mother seemed to be on a path to self-destruction. "She probably needs a cough bottle,"* she added. *"I'll call to the surgery on my way to school, and ask Dr Barker if he can call in later today."*

That afternoon, just as Zoe was arriving home from school, Dr Barker arrived at the cottage. With a perfunctory greeting to the girls, he disappeared into their mother's bedroom, then reappeared in the kitchen a short time later.

"I've given your mother a cough bottle for her chest," he said testily. *Then he looked closely at the two girls. "I've seen the whisky bottles, too. Your mother's an alcoholic."*

Zoe bit her lip. She was well aware of her mother's desperate need for alcohol.

"What does that word mean?" Claire asked, looking worried.

"She has an illness that means she can't do without drink. The whisky is her medicine – it helps her to survive."

"She only drinks because Daddy's not here," Claire interjected. "I wish he'd come home again."

"Is that so?" said Dr Barker, smiling unctuously at her before turning to Zoe. "And you, Zoe – would you like to have your father back too?"

"More than anything in the world," said Zoe fervently.

Dr Barker nodded. "I'm sure your father would be delighted to know what fine girls his daughters have become. You're so grown-up Zoe, quite the young lady." He leaned forward and touched Zoe's cheek. "You and your sister are such pretty little things, aren't you?"

Instantly, Zoe recoiled. She disliked Dr Barker, although she couldn't say why. But equally she knew she couldn't afford to be rude to him.

He leaned in closer. "Does your mother look after you and your sister well?"

"Yes, of course!" Zoe lied enthusiastically. "She's a great mother! We manage fine."

"She's the best mum in the world!" Claire added. She'd been listening to the interchange between Zoe and Dr Barker, and she wasn't going to give the doctor any cause to denigrate their mother.

He pursed his lips. "Well, if your mother continues to have these er, bouts of illness, I'd feel duty-bound to let the authorities know. They'd arrange for you girls to be reared in a more suitable environment. There are several good orphanages in the area –"

"No!"

Zoe hadn't meant to sound so vociferous, but she was appalled at the suggestion. She was now regretting calling the doctor, since she'd inadvertently opened up their lives to his scrutiny.

"Well, if you're sure –"

"We're sure," said Zoe firmly.

The doctor picked up his bag, and smirked at the two girls.

"Well, if I ever bump into your father again, I'll tell him how much you're missing him."

Chuckling, he let himself out.

As the door closed, Zoe rushed to her sister and threw her arms around her. "We're never going to let anyone part us!" she swore, tears in her eyes, which she tried to hide by burying her face in Claire's hair.

Claire also felt tears pricking at her eyelids, but she was determined to be brave for Zoe's sake. "I love you, Zoe!" she whispered. "Don't ever leave me, will you?"

"Of course not! Come on, let's go and see how Mum is," said Zoe brightly.

"Do you think Dr Barker might find Daddy for us?" Claire asked, her little face looking earnestly into Zoe's.

Zoe shook her head vehemently. "Dr Barker likes to pretend he's important and that he knows everything that's going on. I'm sure he hasn't got a clue where Daddy is."

Arm in arm, the two girls headed for their mother's bedroom. She'd be well again after taking her cough bottle, but Zoe had understood the doctor's message loud and clear. If their mother became ill again, Dr Barker could have them forcibly taken from her. Zoe felt bowed by the weight of it all. She and Claire would now live in a constant state of fear, hoping their mother wouldn't have any more illnesses that needed medical attention . . .

CHAPTER 40

The four friends were sitting in a very expensive restaurant. Anne felt soothed by the opulent surroundings, the attentive waiters and the low lighting that flattered her complexion. The wine had been opened, and she finally felt at peace as she sipped her first glass. The last week had been hell, but gradually public interest in the Ellwoods' garden party seemed to be dying down as other news took its place.

"It could happen to anyone," said Emma earnestly. "I mean, until those people got ill, it was a really wonderful party."

"Well, I enjoyed the party immensely," said Fiona. "You've got to remember, Anne, that most people *didn't* get sick."

"Yes, but the important ones – sorry, Fiona, I don't mean to offend you – but the people who could help Clive's career are the ones who got sick!"

Fiona raised her eyebrows for a second. "Okay, so we know that you passed off those two quiches as your own – but where on earth did you get them from? Surely you can complain, and maybe ask for a public apology from the company who supplied them?"

Anne chewed her lip. "That's the odd thing – all the catering companies deny knowing anything about them."

"Well, they would, wouldn't they?" reasoned Fiona. "No company wants the finger pointed at them, especially after supplying food to such a high-profile party. They'd be out of business overnight."

Anne wasn't convinced. "No, there's something odd about it, but I can't for the life of me figure out what it is."

"Don't worry, dear, it'll all blow over soon," Jennifer assured Anne. Inwardly, she was delighted at what had happened. While she was concerned for Clive's reputation, anything that could show up Anne as a less than perfect wife was balm to her soul. Clive must realise by now that Anne was a liability rather than an asset. He'd soon see that Jennifer was the one with whom he could reach the pinnacle of success.

"I hope you're right," said Anne fervently as she took another sip of her wine. "Clive is in foul form – we've hardly spoken since the garden party. He thinks I'm responsible for what went wrong."

Jennifer masked her delight with a concerned expression. "You poor love," she said, patting Anne's arm. "Let's drink to the future – none of this will matter in a few months' time."

Hopefully, Jennifer thought, because Clive and I will be together by then. Assuming I can think of some way of getting rid of you.

Suddenly, Emma had an idea. "What about contacting the agency that supplied the waiting staff? Maybe one of them will remember which company dropped off the quiches."

Anne sighed. "I've already contacted them. They claim to have checked with the staff who were on duty that day, and no one seems to know anything. Which is very odd, because I remember one of the women bringing in the quiches. She said a company van had stopped at the gates and asked her to carry them up the driveway."

"Maybe you should ask to speak to her personally?" Emma suggested.

Anne grimaced. "It gets even odder – I've already described her to the woman who runs the agency, and she hasn't a clue who it could be. She says the description I gave her doesn't fit any of their employees."

"Maybe you should interview them all, one by one ?" said

Fiona. "It's probably the only way you're ever going to get the name of the guilty company."

Anne nodded. "That's a good idea, Fiona. I'll get onto the agency right away. It's essential that Clive and I can shift the blame onto the rightful culprits."

Anne looked a lot more cheerful as the starters arrived. Finding the woman who could identify the company van wouldn't change the fact that the Ellwoods' garden party had been a disaster. But if she could get the relevant company to accept liability, it would lessen her own culpability and shift the blame back where it belonged. A public apology from the guilty company – to be published in all the newspapers – would exonerate the Ellwoods of all blame.

Anne grimaced. Okay, so she'd have to admit she hadn't made the quiches herself, but ultimately it would be worth it.

"Hmmm, this is delicious," said Fiona, as she took a mouthful of her *tart tatin*. Then she grinned mischievously at Anne, who'd ordered the same starter. "Were your quiches as nice as this?"

Anne gave her a sour look. "That's not funny," she said.

"Sorry," said Fiona, not looking sorry at all. "I couldn't resist trying to lighten the atmosphere. But I guess you're not in the mood for a joke."

Fiona smiled to herself. She'd got her own back on Anne for the earlier remark about her not being an important guest. It was petty, she knew, but she'd enjoyed Anne's reaction.

Emma poured Anne another glass of wine. "You can't expect Anne to be in the mood for jokes after what she's been through," she scolded.

"That's right," echoed Jennifer. "Anne's been though a very stressful time. We need to look after her."

Anne smiled, feeling pleased at how supportive Emma, Fiona and Jennifer were being. The good food and wine, combined with the pleasant company of good friends, made her feel cherished. To hell with Clive and his bad temper, she thought. Her housekeeper had been right. There were times when nothing mattered more than friendship.

"Let's drink to survival," said Fiona, raising her glass. "We survived the school reunion, so I'm sure you'll get through this too, Anne, with our help."

The other three raised their glasses in unison.

"To survival! To Anne!"

"Did I tell you that the woman I met at the reunion promised to audit my accounts?" asked Emma.

"Yes – a million times," said Fiona, rolling her eyes, "and you couldn't find her when you tried to contact her."

Emma nodded, chastened. She hated when she was caught out repeating herself.

"You've never managed to trace her, have you?" asked Anne.

"No. I spoke on the phone to someone called Violet Summers, but it definitely wasn't her."

"You're probably better off," Anne replied, giving a shudder. "Everyone connected with that reunion was a nightmare. I didn't tell you at the time but I had the misfortune of bumping into that dreadful woman, Hazel Bonnington – do you remember her?"

Three heads nodded.

"Yes, she was the girl in our class who told us we were responsible for Zoe Gray's death," Emma piped up.

There was a sudden silence, as though each woman had been robbed of speech.

They looked from one to the other, horror on every face.

At last, Anne broke the silence. "Emma – I thought we agreed never to mention that name?"

"Oh. Sorry." Emma went puce, grabbed her wineglass and took a swig, as though its contents could fortify her against the disapproval of the others.

Anne looked pointedly at Emma's glass. Really, Emma was such a liability. The silly woman had consumed far too much wine, as usual.

"Come on, let's drink another toast – this time to our friendship," said Fiona hastily.

But no one else seemed interested. It was as though the idea of friendship had suddenly soured.

As the main course was served, everyone found they had little appetite.

CHAPTER 41

Benjamin approached the hospital reception desk and swallowed nervously. He was desperate to help his brother, seeing it as a way of bridging the terrible gap that had separated them for years. He'd driven up to London that morning and, as soon as a sample of his blood was taken, he intended returning to The Old Vicarage. He hadn't told Jennifer where he was going – he saw no point in facing her inquisition unless he knew for certain that he was compatible.

"Hello, my name is Benjamin Corcroft, and I'm here to do a blood test to see if I'm compatible with my brother –"

"And the patient's name?"

"Hugh Corcroft."

The receptionist checked some lists on her computer, then nodded and stood up.

"Okay, Mr Corcroft, come this way, please."

Benjamin followed her down a long corridor to the waiting room of the nephrology department.

He didn't have long to wait before a nurse appeared and took a sample of blood.

"That's fine, Mr Corcroft," she told him as she finished. "The nephrologist will be in touch with you as soon as we get the results."

Benjamin was surprised at how quick and easy it had all been.

"Mr Corcroft? This is Sally, from the Nephrology Department of St Luke's. The doctor would like you to come in and see him, at your convenience."

Benjamin's heart was beating fast. It was only three days since he'd done the test, so a phone call this early sounded positive. "Oh, yes, of course. When would suit?"

"I could give you an appointment for early next week?"

"Yes, that's fine."

Having made the appointment, the doctor's secretary rang off, and Benjamin sat staring into space. He'd been afraid to ask what the results had been, but he suspected they wouldn't tell him over the phone anyway. But it had to be good news for Hugh, hadn't it? He'd hardly have been given an appointment with Hugh's nephrologist so quickly, simply to be told he wasn't compatible. Without realising it, Benjamin had crossed his fingers.

In the nephrologist's office the following week, Benjamin sat nervously waiting. The doctor entered the room, nodded to him, and sat down on his side of the desk facing Benjamin.

To fill the silence, Benjamin began chattering nervously. He didn't know why – perhaps because he was on the threshold of something quite momentous. Within minutes, he'd know if he'd passed the first stage on the road to helping his brother.

"My daughter Vanessa did a test, but she wasn't a match for Hugh," he concluded, "so I'm hoping I'll be able to help him."

Flicking through his notes, the doctor smiled. "I see your daughter's got a fairly uncommon blood group – your wife's obviously A Negative too –"

"No, she's O Positive," Benjamin replied, remembering the time Jennifer's obstetrician had thought a Caesarean might be necessary, and her blood group had been checked just in case.

The doctor looked up, smiling apologetically. "Oh sorry, I didn't realise your daughter was adopted –"

Benjamin looked startled. "She's not – what kind of question is that?"

Momentarily, the doctor looked flustered, but quickly tried to cover it up. "Oh, nothing."

The nervous tension Benjamin had been feeling suddenly erupted into anger. "Come on, man, spit it out. Is there something wrong? Is she ill?"

"No, no –"

"Well, what is it, then?" Benjamin shouted, jumping up and towering over the doctor, his face now red with anger. "Tell me, for Christ's sake!"

The doctor looked as though he'd rather be anywhere else on earth other than in Benjamin's presence.

"Look, I shouldn't have said anything –"

"But you did, and if you don't tell me what's wrong, I swear I'll swing for you!"

The doctor gulped. "Please, Mr Corcroft, calm down. It's just that – since you're also O Positive like your wife, your blood group and your daughter's are – oh God, I'm so sorry."

"What does that mean? Explain it to me, for God's sake – I'm not a bloody doctor!"

The doctor took a deep breath. "It means that you and your daughter are not related."

As Benjamin absorbed this news, his world shifted on its axis and moved into some kind of alternative universe.

"Look, I wouldn't have told you, if you hadn't insisted," the doctor said at last.

Benjamin found that his throat was suddenly constricted, and no words would come out. He felt incoherent and unable to make sense of what he'd just heard. The truth was gradually filtering through to his consciousness. A flicker of pain filled the doctor's eyes before he looked away, and Benjamin realised that he, too, knew what the results meant.

He'd been cuckolded. Vanessa wasn't his; maybe Alan wasn't

either. Now his shock and sorrow was compounded by his wife's infidelity. Probably serial infidelity. As the pain surged through him, Benjamin wondered if he was having a heart attack. At the same time, another part of his brain registered that a hospital was probably the best place to have it.

"I'm sorry," said the doctor, somewhat inadequately.

Benjamin nodded and stumbled to his feet. He wanted to shout and scream, maybe even hit the doctor, but what was the point of shooting the messenger? The one who'd wronged him was his wife. Had she just had affairs, got caught and decided to pass off one or both children as his? Maybe she didn't even know whether they were his or not! Did the children have the same father, or were they by two different men? Benjamin was overwhelmed by emotion. Storming out of the doctor's office and out of the hospital, he headed around the corner to the nearest pub.

There was no one he could talk to. Any of the men he knew could be his children's fathers. And he wasn't going to talk to any of those bitches who were friends of his wife. Besides, their loyalty would be to Jennifer anyway.

As he ordered his first pint, he thought angrily about the wreckage that was his life. When you boiled it all down, he had nothing. At least, nothing worth having. Okay, so he was rich, but what use was that when your heart was breaking? He laughed bitterly. Maybe, if there was a God, he'd done this to make pathetic little Benjamin Corcroft see the error of his ways. Of course, this God was just as likely to be female – at least, that's probably what the likes of Georgie Monks would say.

For a second, Benjamin's fierce expression softened. That was one hell of a feisty lady, and he couldn't help but admire her. But technically, she was his enemy too. In fact, was there anyone in the whole world who cared about him? He supposed his parents had, and his brother too. But he'd been selfish, gone off and made money and disowned his entire family. He'd married Jennifer, thinking her poise and style would be enough. But in his heart, he'd known for a long time that it wasn't. And now, through her infidelity, he'd finally got proof that he'd never possessed more than a part of her. She'd given him the benefit of her class in return for a wealthy lifestyle, but she'd never given him her heart. And his children – she'd robbed him of even that.

By his fifth pint, Benjamin had hoped that his world might seem a little better. But everything still looked bleak. The only difference was that he couldn't see as clearly as before. But his mind was still churning, and his pain no less acute.

Where would he go from here? How would he face Jennifer, and what would he say to his kids, who no doubt weren't really his kids at all? In fact, he was probably living with a group of people to whom he wasn't related at all. He'd been able to accept Jennifer's greed and self-absorption while he'd assumed they were all his family. Now he began to wonder what the future held for them.

Right now, he couldn't face going home. His pain was too raw to deal with the situation. He didn't think he could look at Jennifer's smug face without reacting, and then he'd say things he might regret. And Alan and Vanessa – what would he say to them? Their whole lives would be thrown into disarray. It wasn't fair that they should suffer because of Jennifer's appalling behaviour.

His mind was in turmoil. Was he sterile? Had his wife assumed he'd never find out that Vanessa wasn't his? And what about Alan? Was Jennifer still carrying on with the father, or fathers, of his children? Of course, but for a fluke, he'd never have known. If Vanessa hadn't been so keen to find his relatives, it would have remained a secret. And Jennifer would have continued gliding through life, cushioned by his hard-earned money.

He'd assumed, perhaps naïvely, that she'd cared about him. And when she'd agreed to marry him, he'd been the happiest man in the world. It had never crossed his mind that she'd use him so callously. He'd always been faithful to her, and although his long business hours kept him away from home a lot, he'd always assumed that the comfortable lifestyle he provided was enough to keep his family content.

Right now, he could feel nothing for his wife but contempt. She'd played him like a fool, which he supposed he was. He'd always prided himself on his business acumen – funny how he could spot a dodgy business deal a mile off but somehow he'd never suspected that his wife was playing away.

Pain filled his heart so he ordered another pint. Might as well stay here until closing time. The pub atmosphere was congenial, yet everyone left him alone, which suited him fine. He'd ask the barmaid if they had a room available for the night – he certainly couldn't drive home in his present inebriated state. Besides, he didn't want to go home. He didn't know if he ever wanted to go home again.

CHAPTER 42

Having written up her notes on the last patient for the day, Claire decided it was time to go home. Locking up, she stepped out into the street, and was shocked to find Hazel Bonnington waiting there. It was clear that this was no random encounter, and that Hazel was definitely waiting for her.

"Oh, hello."

"Hello – Claire."

Claire froze, and her heart almost stopped. Hazel Bonnington knew her real name!

Pleased by Claire's shocked reaction, Hazel Bonnington linked arms with her and began propelling her down the street.

"I knew you weren't Violet – but I was curious to know what you were up to."

"Oh God. How did you know?"

"Violet and I were good pals at school, and we still keep in touch – you'd have known that if you'd been in our class. But you weren't, were you?"

"N-no," Claire admitted. She was terrified, since she'd no idea where this interrogation was leading.

"By the way, Violet's husband is fine again – his operation was a great success."

"Oh. I'm glad."

Still leading the way, Hazel paused outside a café and opened the door. "Let's have a cup of coffee and you can tell me what's going on."

The café was fairly empty, for which Claire was grateful. They were served quickly, and once the waitress had placed their coffees in front of them, she retreated behind the counter and left them on their own again.

"So why were you at our school reunion, posing as someone else?" Hazel looked searchingly at her. "You're not with MI5, are you?"

For the first time, Claire smiled. "Definitely not – I wouldn't be very good at my job if you could spot me so easily!"

Hazel continued to stare at her. "So why were you there? You must have had a motive, since no one would voluntarily go to a school reunion. They're god-awful events, even when you've *been* a pupil there!"

Claire took a sip of her coffee. "I *was* a pupil at The Gables, just not in that particular year."

Hazel said nothing, waiting for her to continue.

"It's a long story – but not one you can publish," Claire added hastily.

Hazel grinned. "Sounds intriguing."

"Look, if I tell you – and I suppose I'm going to have to – you've got to promise me that you won't write anything about it."

Hazel laughed. "Why do people always assume journalists think of nothing else but the next story? And that we'd sell our grandmothers to get it?"

"Please, Hazel."

"In that event, you have to tell me this stuff is off the record."

"Okay, this stuff is off the record."

"Fine."

Claire sighed. "Can I really trust you, Hazel? I mean, journalists doorstep people for a good story, go under cover, or wire themselves up –"

Hazel laughed. "You've been watching too many movies, Claire. Anyway, my integrity is important to me. If you say I can't write about it, then I won't. Unless, of course, it's so earth-shattering –"

"Hazel!"

"Only joking – honestly. You have my word."

But Claire wasn't ready to tell her story just yet. "How did you discover my real name, and where I worked?" she asked.

Hazel grinned, pleased at her ingenuity. "Followed you to your car the last time we met. Got your registration number, and asked a copper friend to get me a name and address. Then I looked you up in the phone book. Bingo!"

Claire was amazed, and a little worried, to realise that a person could be traced so easily. But an idea was growing in her mind. Maybe Hazel could prove a useful ally. She'd witnessed Hazel's altercation with Anne at the reunion, and maybe Hazel's dislike of Anne would enable Claire to gain her support. On the other hand, there was always the danger that Hazel would reject the idea of a vendetta, and would try to talk her out of it or interfere in what she planned to do. But she wouldn't know that until she told her story, and Hazel already knew enough to make her a problem.

"You might remember my older sister Zoe – she was four years ahead of me, and in your class at The Gables. She drowned at the age of thirteen."

Hazel whistled. "Wow! I remember that day as though it was yesterday. I really liked Zoe – she was a friend of mine. It was a shocking day for all us kids – it must have been devastating for you."

Even after all this time, Claire could still feel the tears pricking at her eyelids, but she was determined not to cry.

Hazel looked down at her coffee cup to allow Claire time to compose herself. "I did hear a mention of your sister at the reunion – one of the organisers said they'd accidentally sent an invitation to her – is that why you came?"

Claire nodded. It had been part of the reason, but not all of it. Zoe's diary had been the catalyst that made Claire want revenge.

"Bloody thoughtless of them," said Hazel. "But the woman was genuinely upset. Said she'd been given a really old list of class names, which she'd passed on to a niece who'd volunteered to help. The woman never checked the list, and the niece didn't know your sister had died. Poor woman was hoping your family weren't at that address any longer." She looked at Claire. "But someone obviously was."

Claire nodded again. She'd just decided to take another step in her campaign of revenge. She took a deep breath. "I've also got a front-page story for you."

Hazel looked at her, her eyes bright with anticipation.

"But in return, I want you to do something for me."

Hazel nodded. "If I can, I will."

Claire hesitated. She was almost afraid to voice her request, since it was something she wanted so badly. On the other hand, if she got her wish, would her hopes and dreams be dashed forever?

"There's a mystery at the heart of my family," she said. "My father left when Zoe and I were kids, and I don't know what happened to him. Several times, I decided to contact a private detective, but I always got cold feet at the last minute. Zoe died after he left, and I don't even know if he knew what happened. I really want to find him – if he's still alive, that is."

Hazel nodded. "Okay, give me the details. I need his full name, your address when he left, his profession, and anything else you can tell me."

"Thanks, Hazel," said Claire warmly. "Of course, it's also likely that my father's dead, so I'm prepared for the worst. But one way or another, I'd really like to know what happened to him."

"I'll do the best I can," Hazel said kindly, "but don't expect instant results – it may take me a while."

Claire nodded. "No problem. I've waited all my life to find out what happened to him, so I can wait a bit longer. You'll get your front-page story as soon as you get me any information you can on my father."

Hazel looked sceptical. "If this story of yours is as good as you claim it is, how do I know it's going to stay topical for long? Today's news is dead tomorrow, you know."

Claire smiled. "I promise you, Hazel, this story will be worth waiting for."

When Hazel produced the information about her father, Claire intended giving her the photograph of Jennifer and Clive.

CHAPTER 43

He blinked as the beam of a torch shone in his eyes.

"What the hell – oh, for fuck's sake!"

"Oh, sorry – I didn't realise that anyone was here."

"I'm not 'anyone' – I'm the owner of this bloody church! And I have every right to sleep here – undisturbed – if I want to!" Benjamin sat up, red-eyed, and stared malevolently at Georgie Monks. "And you have no business being here – get off my property!"

Georgie was shocked by his appearance. He seemed to have aged overnight. His clothes were crumpled, his hair was standing up in spikes, and his eyes were bloodshot.

"What happened?" she asked him incredulously, ignoring his rude remarks. "You don't look well – can I do anything?"

"If you want to do me a favour, then get lost!" Benjamin replied, snuggling down under the rug he'd brought in from his car to cover himself. It was far from adequate, and he was now shivering from both the cold and the excess of alcohol in his system.

Georgie looked at her watch. It was just after midnight. She'd decided to make a final check on the church before retiring to bed, and had been astonished to find Benjamin Corcroft asleep

212

on one of the pews. He'd obviously parked round the back, because she hadn't noticed his car.

He was still behaving like his old belligerent self, but Georgie's heart went out to him because he seemed so lost. Something bad had obviously happened, but he still couldn't allow her to see his vulnerability.

"Well, goodnight," she said, matter-of-factly, walking out of the church and closing the door.

When she'd gone, Benjamin suddenly wanted to call out her name and beg her to stay. He longed for some company to help him get through the lonely night ahead, but he couldn't ask her because he was the big business tycoon who didn't need anyone, and certainly couldn't ask for help from someone he was supposed to hate. After all, Georgie Monks was just like all the others, trying to undermine what he was trying to do.

On the other hand, he wished he hadn't been so rude to her, but he was hurting and wanted to lash out at everyone. He knew Georgie Monks didn't deserve his wrath since she was only doing what she believed was right. In a way he should be grateful, since she was ensuring that no one would damage the church before he managed to remove the stained-glass windows . . .

Benjamin rolled over, and the thin rug covering him fell to the ground. Cursing, he tried to pull it over him again, but it was pointless. In fact, everything was pointless. He didn't even care about the stained-glass windows anymore. In fact, nothing mattered anymore. Maybe he'd end it all, then Hugh could have both his kidneys. If they were any use to him, that is. Benjamin was furious with himself for not even waiting for the results of his blood test at the hospital. He'd stormed out in a rage when the doctor confirmed that Vanessa wasn't his biological daughter, without even waiting to find out if he could help his brother.

He'd driven to the church late that night. He'd known he wasn't fit to drive, but the pub had no rooms available, and he certainly wasn't going home to face Jennifer yet. He needed time to think about what he was going to do next, and the church had seemed the ideal place to stay while he sorted his head out. He owned it, so he could shut himself away for as long as he wanted to. He intended phoning home tomorrow and saying that he'd be away for a few days due to business commitments. After all, he didn't want to let the children see him in such a state.

He wasn't sure when he was going to tackle the issue with Jennifer, but he wanted to be sure that neither of the children were present when it happened. Nor could he stay married to Jennifer after what he'd found out. He now realised with amazing clarity that she'd never loved him, and he wondered if he'd ever actually loved her. When he analysed things, he realised she'd only helped his career for her own benefit, and he wondered if money was all that mattered to her.

Benjamin fell into a troubled sleep.

As early morning sunlight began trickling through the Harry Clarke windows, Benjamin winced as he tried to turn over, suddenly realising he was sleeping on a hard bench rather than in his own comfortable bed. All the miseries of the previous day began flooding into his memory again, so he closed his eyes and willed them all to go away. He was still in his clothes, he had a dreadful hangover, his mouth was dry, and he longed for some water. But as far as he knew, there wasn't any tap in the church, and even if there was, he felt too ill to go looking for it.

At that moment, he also realised he was covered with several blankets and a quilt, and there was also a pillow beneath his head. Suddenly, he began to cry. He was battered and bruised by his wife's callous disregard for him, but someone he hardly knew had tried to make him comfortable. Georgie Monks had shown him a little kindness, and he was amazed at how much it suddenly meant to him.

And he knew why she'd done it after he'd gone asleep – because he'd have been rude to her again if he'd been awake. She didn't deserve his unpleasantness, and he couldn't even say why he was always rude to her. Maybe it was because she had the ability to make him feel shallow and worthless, so he retaliated with nasty remarks.

But then again, he'd felt shallow and worthless for a long time. He'd spent years trying to justify himself to Jennifer by keeping her in luxury, cutting corners and cheating other people in order to make more money so that she'd never regret marrying him. He'd worked his bollocks off for her, but all the while it was a pointless exercise. A woman like Jennifer would always want more, and he no longer had anything left to give.

And, if he was truthful, there was also the fact that he found Georgie Monks very attractive. Perhaps he'd deliberately distanced himself from her so that he wouldn't have to face up to his feelings. He also admired her. She was a woman of principle, and her views were new and alien to him after living for years with a woman who cared about nothing but herself.

Just then, the door of the church opened, and Georgie Monks walked in carrying a tray. Benjamin could smell the food before he saw it, and he suddenly realised that he was ravenous.

"Good morning," said Georgie, smiling. "I've brought you some breakfast."

She placed the tray on an adjacent pew, and Benjamin eyed the bacon, egg, sausages, beans and buttered toast with undisguised pleasure.

"I didn't know if you took tea or coffee, but I thought tea might be easier on your stomach."

Benjamin nodded. "Thank you," he said sheepishly as she poured tea into a large mug, leaving the teapot beside him in case he needed a refill.

Then she turned and walked towards the door.

"Thanks," he muttered once again.

"No problem," was her noncommittal reply, as she let herself out of the building and closed the door behind her.

Easing himself into an upright position, Benjamin took a mouthful of tea. His head was still thumping, and his stomach felt nauseous, but the food would undoubtedly help. As he picked up a paper napkin on the tray, he discovered that Georgie had stashed a packet of paracetamol tablets beneath it. Once again, he was struck by her thoughtfulness.

Downing two tablets with a mouthful of tea, he then tucked into the fry-up with relish. It tasted delicious, nicer than anything he'd eaten in ages. He didn't care that the butter from the toast ran down his stubbled chin. If it wasn't for his problems, he'd be a contented man.

I must look a sight, he thought suddenly, as he popped the last sausage on the plate into his mouth. He was unwashed, unshaven, and his hair was greasy and unkempt. He couldn't possibly go to any of his sites looking like that!

As if she'd read his mind, the church door opened just as he'd finished and Georgie Monks reappeared.

"If you want to take a shower, you're welcome to use my place," she said. "I think it might be wise to clean up if you're planning to work today."

A retort was already forming on Benjamin's lips, but he bit it back, nodding instead. Old habits died hard, but he'd no reason in the world to be unkind to this woman, who was going out of her way to help him.

"Thank you," he said stiffly, unsure of what to say or do next, and not sure whether saying thanks meant he'd accepted her offer or not.

"Okay then, why don't you come over now? There's plenty of hot water, and feel free to use the shower gel and anything else you need." She surveyed his jaw intently. "I think there might even be a razor there – I hope you won't mind, but it's one I've used myself . . ."

For the first time since his world had overturned, Benjamin was having pleasant thoughts. The idea of using a razor that had glided over Georgie Monks' body was a very pleasing thought.

As they left the church together, Benjamin felt embarrassed at crossing the street to Georgie's cottage – what if any of the other protesters saw them together? But luckily it was so early that few people were about. Besides, Georgie didn't seem to mind. In the comfort of her surprisingly modern home, he stood awkwardly until she directed him to the bathroom, showing him how to turn on the shower and where the toiletries were kept.

It felt wonderful to stand under the scalding water and purge his body of all the stresses of the previous day. But it also felt weird to be doing it in the home of a woman he was at loggerheads with! He sighed contentedly as the heat melted away the aches and pains he'd acquired from sleeping on the church pew. So much had happened since he'd last showered that it felt like aeons ago.

When he stepped out of the shower, he found clean underwear, trousers and an ironed shirt hanging on the back of the door. Just then, Georgie stuck her head round the door, and Benjamin nearly disembowelled himself trying to cover up his genitals.

"I've left you some clean clothes," she told him, smiling at his attempts to cover himself. "By the way, I know what nude men look like," she added, smiling. "I was married for fifteen years."

Benjamin thanked her for the clothes, thinking to himself that there were many things he didn't know about Georgie Monks. And he realised that he wanted to know everything there was to know about her.

Fully dressed in the clothes she'd left for him, he returned to the kitchen, where Georgie was pouring out two mugs of tea. She gestured for him to sit down, and they sat facing each other across the table.

"Are you feeling any better now?" Georgie asked gently.

"Why are you doing this?" Benjamin demanded plaintively. "I mean, we're not exactly the best of friends, are we?"

Georgie blushed, which Benjamin found very appealing.

"Look – even though we disagree over the church, it's obvious that you're suffering," she said softly. "What sort of person would I be if I wouldn't help someone in pain?"

Benjamin felt deflated. Obviously, Georgie was the sort who'd help anyone – she hadn't done it specifically for him.

"Thanks for the clothes," he said self-consciously. They fitted him reasonably well, and he was hoping that by mentioning them, Georgie would be prompted to explain where she'd got them.

"They were my husband's – my late husbands," she said. "I intended taking them to a charity shop ages ago, but I'd completely forgotten they were still in the wardrobe."

"I'm sorry – about your husband, that is."

They looked at each other awkwardly.

"It was a long time ago," Georgie said softly.

Benjamin began standing up. "Well, thanks, I'll get them cleaned and returned to you –"

"No need. Now sit down."

Benjamin was surprised at the steely tone of Georgie's voice. He sat down obediently, not sure what was coming next.

"I hoped you might stop playing the big-shot for five minutes and tell me what's happened," she said. "Sometimes it's good to talk to someone and, despite our differences, I can assure you I'm trustworthy."

Benjamin looked at the floor. "Yes, I suppose you're due an explanation."

"I'm not looking for an explanation," Georgie cut in. "I just want to help. Something's obviously happened to get you into such a state."

Her sympathy opened up something inside Benjamin that had long been closed.

Suddenly, his face crumpled and he was weeping unashamedly.

"I'm a broken man, Georgie," he whispered.

Standing up from the table, she came towards him and opened her arms.

"Come here," she said.

CHAPTER 44

Zoe's Diary

Easter Saturday

Today I met a boy who didn't know that people could have seaweed baths! He was from London, so perhaps city people don't know about these things. I'm going to show him and his brother where the seals are tomorrow. I'm really excited. It's nice to make new friends.

Hazel says if I ignore the bullies, they'll get fed up and start picking on someone else, but I don't think that's true. They seem to have selected me for special punishment, and I've no idea why.

A strong wind was blowing as Zoe made her way down to the beach. She was planning to collect some wrack, and later make a seaweed bath for her mother. It wasn't easy persuading her mother to get in, but she always admitted its relaxing benefits afterwards. Zoe wanted so much to help her mother and at least the seaweed cost nothing.

Zoe breathed the sea air deep into her lungs as she walked along the shore. At least the bullies didn't know about the time she spent on the beach, so she could relax and enjoy her walk. Zoe *felt sorry for the scattering of tourists visiting for the weekend. There was little sun, and the strong wind was preventing children from building sandcastles. Nevertheless, some hardy souls had braved the elements and were swimming in the sea. Zoe watched with amusement as swimmers came out of the water, shivering and blue, then struggled to dry themselves as the wind billowed their towels and threatened to whip them away.*

As she walked along the sand Zoe spotted an amazingly long piece of seaweed and, before it could be carried out to sea again, she grabbed it and hauled it out of the water, running backwards to keep her feet from getting wet. She was so absorbed in what she was doing that she almost bumped into a boy walking in the opposite direction.

"Oops, sorry –"

The boy grunted, stepping out of her way, then stopped to watch what she was doing. His red-blond hair stood up on end, his clothes had seen better days, much like Zoe's own, and she felt an immediate affinity with him.

"What are you doing?" he asked.

"Oh, I'm collecting seaweed for a bath."

"You put that stuff in your bath?" he scoffed.

Zoe grinned. "Yes, it's very relaxing."

"You must be a local, then," he said dismissively.

Even still, Zoe couldn't help liking him.

"Yes, my name is Zoe, and I live just up the road. Are you here on holiday?"

He stuck his hands in his pockets. "I'm here for the weekend with my mum and brother."

"Where's your dad?" Zoe asked. She was always curious about other people's domestic arrangements, and wondered if his dad had left home too.

"He's working – Saturday is his busiest day," the boy replied. "We're from London," he added importantly.

"Where's your brother today?"

"He's sick. He ate so many Easter eggs yesterday that he has a bellyache."

Zoe smiled enviously. Imagine eating enough chocolate to make you sick – heavenly!

"Why don't you bring your brother here tomorrow?" Zoe suggested. "If he's feeling better, we could play rounders on the beach."

"We don't usually play with girls," was the gruff reply.

"Well, I can show you the best places to swim," Zoe said earnestly. For some reason, she didn't want him to leave. "And there's a place where you can see the seals basking – but not many people know about that."

The boy was looking decidedly interested now. "How close can you get to the seals?"

"Fairly close – there's a ledge on one of the rocks which brings you right up beside them."

"Don't they mind people being near?"

"Not if you're quiet," Zoe replied. "I could also show you the whirlpools out along the rocks – if you throw in a pebble or a stick, you can watch it swirl around for ages before it's sucked in and disappears."

Zoe didn't know why she wanted to see this boy again, but for the first time in her life, she had a funny feeling in her tummy – rather like butterflies – and she wondered what it meant. Was this the feeling older girls in school talked about, when they had crushes on boys?

"Are there really whirlpools?"

Zoe laughed. "Yes, of course – did you think I was making them up?"

The boy shrugged his shoulders. "Okay, I'll bring my brother here tomorrow morning around nine. Can you be here by then?"

Zoe nodded. She didn't mention her younger sister to him, but she figured that Claire would like to come along too. They'd almost be like The Famous Five, minus Timmy the dog, and hopefully they'd have lots of adventures together.

The following morning, Zoe called her sister early. "Come on, lazybones – it's Easter, and we're off to the beach!"

She didn't tell Claire about the boys they were meeting because she felt shy and slightly vulnerable. She'd never liked a boy this much before, and she didn't want Claire teasing her.

Claire was surprised at being called so early, but said nothing and obligingly got dressed.

After taking in tea and toast to their mother – and wishing her a Happy Easter – Zoe and Claire set off for the beach. Zoe was also clutching a small bag containing her mother's discarded coins – she didn't want Claire to feel left out if the boys had money for sweets. Zoe had worn her best dress, although it wasn't really suitable for climbing over rocks. But she wanted to look nice, although she didn't really know why.

By the time they reached the beach, the wind was blowing fiercely, and Zoe's dress was billowing all around her. Angry with herself, she wondered why on earth she hadn't worn sensible trousers like Claire had.

Zoe's heart sank even further as she scanned the beach and cliffs. There was no sign of the boys anywhere, although it was now after nine. Suggesting to Claire that they collect shells, the girls walked the length of the beach, and all the while Zoe kept watching for the boys in case they were late. Claire chatted happily, oblivious to Zoe's distress. She was enjoying this unexpected outing, and excited at the thought of being bought an Easter treat in Leonard's shop.

"Let's go out to the rocks," Zoe said brusquely.

Claire nodded. It was gradually dawning on her that Zoe's mood was changing, and she wished she could take away whatever problem was bothering her.

Like someone possessed, Zoe now headed for the rocks, determined to check in case the boys decided to try getting there on their own. She knew they'd never manage to find her special place, but she still had to be sure.

When she and Claire arrived at the rocky outcrop, there was no one there except several basking seals. They continued climbing out along the rocks leading to the whirlpools, but there was no one there either.

Zoe was so disappointed that she wanted to cry. She'd been so looking forward to today! She'd lain awake half the night, filled with excitement as she thought about the day ahead. And since she'd expected to be away from home all day, she'd even prepared a meal for their mother, and left it wrapped in tinfoil beside her bed. Now it had all come to nothing, and they'd be home before lunchtime anyway.

"Are you alright, Zoe?" Claire asked, studying her sister's face.

"Of course – I'm fine," Zoe lied.

"Then why were we rushing from place to place so quickly? Were you looking for something?"

"No, er, I just – well, I thought –"

Zoe felt defeated. She couldn't think of any plausible explanation.

"Don't worry," said Claire, smiling impishly. "It was a great game. Maybe we can go round even faster the next time? We could time ourselves, and try to beat our own record."

Zoe looked closely at her sister. If she hadn't known that Claire didn't understand sarcasm yet, she might have believed her sister was having a go at her. But Claire's innocent little face was a picture of openness and honesty.

Zoe leaned down and kissed her forehead. "You're a little darling, do you know that?" she said, smiling. "Come on, let's see if we have enough money to buy you an Easter egg."

Clutching the bag of coins, Zoe led them from the beach up to Leonard's store. She was trying her best to hide her disappointment from Claire, but the boy had represented more to her than just a new friend – she'd already cast him in the role of hero, feeling certain that if she told him about the bullies, he'd warn them off and let them know he was her protector.

Zoe sighed. She hadn't even asked him his name.

CHAPTER 45

Benjamin awoke to find a naked Georgie leaning on one elbow and smiling down at him. They were in Georgie's bed, where they'd just made love before falling asleep. Benjamin could hardly believe what had happened, yet it also felt like the most natural thing in the world.

"Your hangover seems a lot better," said Georgie mischievously, planting a kiss on his lips.

"Oh, Georgie . . ." he whispered, and suddenly they were making love again.

After he'd broken down earlier, Georgie had held him while he cried. Then he'd told her everything, and she'd been incensed that Jennifer could be so cruel, but her concern, like his, was for the children.

"Vanessa's still your daughter, always will be," Georgie said quietly. "As long as she's happy and healthy, you've no need to let her or Alan know." She smiled. "Besides, she's found your family in Walthamstow, and she's made them *her* family now." Then, as they sat across from each other at the kitchen table, she'd leaned across and taken both his hands in hers. "Most people have secrets, Benjamin – yours isn't the worst kind. You're simply the keeper of your daughter's and your son's happiness. That's an important trust to keep."

Benjamin nodded. Georgie's words were kind, but also true. He *was* the custodian of Vanessa and Alan's happiness, and even if Alan wasn't his child either he'd honour that trust until the day he died. And he'd be the best father he could possibly be.

The air had already been raw with emotion as they sat holding hands, and it only took a glance between them to ignite a groundswell of feelings. Georgie leaned across the table to plant a sympathetic kiss on his cheek, and suddenly that brief physical contact had ignited a spark between them. Benjamin felt an overwhelming and primitive desire to possess her. Suddenly, he was fulfilling all his fantasies as he grasped her glorious red hair and pulled her face to his. Their lips met, and a rush of desire overcame them both.

Now, many hours later, Benjamin sat up in bed and looked sheepishly at a contented and satiated Georgie.

"I ought to be making a move," he said hesitantly, hoping she'd disagree. He suddenly wanted to spend more time with Georgie Monks, and he hoped that this afternoon hadn't been just a casual fling for her.

Georgie smiled lazily. "I don't want you to go, but I know you've got things to do."

They both began to get dressed, Benjamin getting back into the clothes Georgie had given him earlier.

As he attempted to speak, Benjamin's throat felt constricted, and he was suddenly so nervous that it came out as a growl. "Can I see you again?" He held his breath, no longer caring about the church or the stained-glass windows. If the church vanished into outer space, it didn't matter a damn to him.

"Of course," she said, and Benjamin's heart soared.

As he was leaving the cottage, he turned back and kissed her, an impish smile on his face. "I'll be staying in the church again tonight. Will you bring me another breakfast tomorrow morning?"

Georgie smiled back. "You'll only get breakfast if you stay here tonight."

Benjamin turned puce with pleasure. He'd genuinely been

asking for nothing more than a breakfast – now he was being offered a warm bed, a loving companion and breakfast as well!

"What will the other protesters say, if they find out you've been sleeping with the enemy?" he asked, worried in case he was jeopardising her position in the village.

She gave him a radiant smile. "I don't care," she said.

Suddenly, his world seemed bright again, and he was filled with a delicious sense of anticipation.

"Okay, I'll be back later," he said, grinning from ear to ear.

Twenty-four hours ago, he'd felt destroyed. Now, he was filled with hope for the future. He had two children whom he loved deeply, and he wasn't going to let the question of their parentage interfere with anything. He was their father in all the ways that mattered. And now, he was beginning to hope that something special might develop with Georgie too.

He'd already made up his mind to divorce Jennifer, because there was no way he could live with her now that he knew what she'd done. But he'd wait until the time was right – he'd pick a time when the children weren't around – then he'd tell her that their marriage was over. And he'd contact the hospital nephrology department and get the results of his test. Hopefully, he'd be able to help his brother.

Benjamin was smiling as he drove away. He felt good. In fact, he hadn't felt so good in a very long time.

CHAPTER 46

"I think it's a great idea," said David enthusiastically. "You must often have wondered what happened to him."

Claire nodded. She was relieved that David was pleased she'd asked Hazel to look for her father.

"It would be nice for you to have a parent around – especially since you've recently lost your mother," David added. "He'd also be able to answer those questions that have plagued you all your life."

Claire was cooking dinner in David's apartment. She enjoyed cooking, and found it restful after a day dealing with all aspects of human misery.

"I'm a bit scared, I suppose," she admitted. "I mean, if he's alive, why has he stayed away all this time? Does he know what happened to my sister?"

"Well, if you find him, you can ask him," David replied. "I suppose it *is* a bit odd that he's never been in touch. Of course, he may be dead. I presume you've considered that possibility?"

Claire nodded. "It's the most logical explanation, isn't it? Maybe he was killed in a plane crash, got cancer, or had a heart attack. He'd be too young to die of old age, since he'd only be in his sixties now."

Claire served up two portions of paella and carried them to the table.

"Wow! This is great!" David said, tucking into his portion with gusto. "You really can concoct the most amazing meals! I'm a lucky man!"

Claire laughed. "Don't you dare expect me to cook every evening when we're married!" she said. "You're going to share the cooking, even if I have to teach you myself!"

Claire smiled to herself. When she didn't do the cooking, David lived on tinned and frozen food, and meals in the university canteen, and she often wondered how he managed to look so well and stay so healthy. She intended remedying that situation when they got married, by ensuring he had good-quality food every day. In fact, she didn't mind doing the cooking at all, she simply wanted to make certain that if their circumstances changed – if hopefully they had children – David could take over responsibility for the kitchen when needed. How wonderful it would be if they could become parents!

After the meal, David filled the dishwasher, then they settled down to watch a totally forgettable film on the television. Claire wasn't paying much attention to it, but she was enjoying holding David as they snuggled up together on the sofa.

Later, when they went to bed, they made love tenderly, then David quickly fell asleep. Claire lay awake listening to his gentle snoring, and wondering if she was wise to be searching for her father. Surely David was enough for her? Why did she need to pursue a will-o'-the wisp, a man who'd walked out of her life more than thirty years earlier? And despite David's words of encouragement, did she really need someone who'd never even sent a birthday card?

Claire was assailed by feelings of uncertainty. What would her father be like today? Since he wasn't that old, they'd have years in which to get to know each other. She tried to envisage him – hopefully he'd still be the warm, gentle and kind man she remembered from her childhood. He held the key to many of the mysteries that had stalked her all her life, and at last she might discover why he'd left, and why their mother drank so much. Did he know about Zoe's death? Or had he been abroad, and knew nothing about what had happened? Why had her father stayed away all those years? Didn't he want to know what had happened to his family?

Then it occurred to Claire that her father might have another family by now. Which would mean she might have half-brothers and sisters. And these new relatives – if they existed – would they want to know her? Was she inadvertently stirring up a hornet's nest?

As she tossed and turned, Claire wondered if she should simply ring Hazel and tell her to forget looking for her father. She was now experiencing the same fears she'd felt each time she'd considered employing a private detective to search for him. She was afraid of being disappointed, since she'd built her father up to be such an exciting and mysterious person.

Claire snuggled up against David's back, and felt the comforting heat of his body. Hazel would think her a fool if she rang back. Anyway, she was worrying unnecessarily. Maybe Hazel wouldn't be able to find him, or she'd discover than he'd died years earlier. There was no point in worrying about what might happen until it happened. And even if Hazel found out where he lived, it didn't mean she had to contact him. On the other hand, if he was out there somewhere, she really did want to find him again . . .

Eventually, she fell into a troubled sleep.

CHAPTER 47

Jennifer didn't like it when Benjamin talked about money problems. Since he'd returned from his business trip, he'd talked about nothing else. Now he was telling her that, since money was tight, she'd have to close her account at Harrods.

Jennifer was apoplectic. Sitting at the table in the kitchen, pushing her evening meal around on her plate, she threw down her fork and stared balefully at her husband.

"If we're so badly off, then at least you can sell those church windows – you've been saying for ages how valuable they are," she told him.

"I'm not selling them. They're staying where they are."

"What?" Jennifer shrieked. "You told me all those village in-breds were getting in your way, and you were going to show them who was boss –"

"I've changed my mind," said Benjamin curtly. He continued to shovel great fork-loads of food into his mouth, and Jennifer curled her lip in distaste as she watched him. His appetite certainly wasn't affected by their financial problems!

Shrugging her shoulders, Jennifer left the table. When Benjamin got an idea into his head, there was no way of changing it. Arguing with him would only make him dig in his heels even further. Besides, she wasn't someone who saw much benefit in arguing. She'd take matters into her own hands and check out the windows herself.

Jennifer went upstairs to the bedroom she now regarded as hers. When he'd returned from the business trip, Benjamin had moved into the spare room, claiming he needed to work late on his computer, and that he'd be less likely to disturb her if he slept there as well. This suited Jennifer's own plans perfectly. Now she was able to dream about her future with Clive, uninterrupted by her husband's snoring at night.

In her bedroom, Jennifer took her make-up off and began applying her new night cream. Studying her reflection in the mirror, she was pleased that it seemed to be working, because she definitely had fewer lines around her mouth than before.

But as her thoughts turned to her husband, her expression darkened. Benjamin was still planning to bring his brain-dead mother to The Old Vicarage. If he did so, it would be over her dead body! He'd also got the results of some blood test, which showed he was compatible with his ghastly brother – now he was planning to take a raft of additional tests to see if he could offer him one of his kidneys.

Jennifer set her mouth in a tight line. His selfish action could put the whole family's future at risk! With only one kidney, his health might deteriorate, and he'd no longer be able to earn the kind of money they needed to maintain their current standard of living. She certainly didn't intend being lumbered with a disabled husband if the operation went wrong!

The Clara Court apartments weren't selling either. Everything seemed to point to the fact that she was making the right decision in planning to leave him.

She smiled to herself. The church windows would make a nice little dowry for her new life with Clive. Before she told Benjamin she was divorcing him, she'd have the windows taken out and sold – and the money in her account – before he realised what was happening.

Jennifer knew that Benjamin didn't like being humiliated, so when he discovered what she'd done, he'd pretend, at least in public, that he'd known all about it. Dear old Benjamin would never go to court – his pride wouldn't allow it – so the windows were already as good as hers.

Besides, she'd need the money to run The Old Vicarage. It was clear in her mind that Benjamin would be the one to go, leaving her the house and the children. Then, with Anne gone, she'd sell The Old Vicarage and she and the children would move into The Grange, which was a lot bigger. Of course, she and Clive might pool their resources and buy something much more spectacular. Maybe a stately home like Chequers – something befitting a minister and, hopefully one day, a prime minister.

And as a gift to Clive – possibly a wedding gift – she'd finally reveal that he was the father of both her children. He'd be thrilled, especially since Anne had never managed to produce any offspring. Finally she, Clive and the children would live happily ever after. She'd eventually tell the children that Clive was their father – it would only be fair since they'd all be living together. She felt sure Alan and Vanessa would understand. In fact, they'd probably be pleased to have such an important man as their father!

Jennifer smirked to herself. She'd never told anyone about her children's parentage – not even her closest friends – since she always suspected it could be used to destroy her. But how could anyone think she'd want Benjamin's spawn? She'd only ever wanted children with the man she loved, children from good breeding stock, who'd naturally be drawn to all the proper country pursuits. Already, Vanessa was showing promise at riding and dressage – hopefully she'd be taking part in the Badminton Horse Trials in another few years.

Jennifer sighed. If only she could get rid of Anne! Then she could step into her shoes and support Clive through his upcoming election bid. Then Benjamin could take a hike. How dare he expect her to look after his mother, and nurse him too, if his operation went wrong! That was typical of Benjamin – only thinking of himself.

Jennifer pursed her lips. It was definitely time for change.

CHAPTER 48

Benjamin felt glum as he stood outside his latest development. Only two of the apartments at Clara Court had been sold, and he'd had to pay the stamp duty as an incentive to offload them. This time last year, his development at Heathfield Park had been sold out. Everywhere, people were losing their jobs, and at this rate, he might have to let workers go himself.

Luckily, he wasn't as badly off as many people were. He'd money stashed away in overseas accounts, and would be well able to weather the storm. But in order to wind Jennifer up, he'd let her believe they were almost on the breadline. It was only fair that he got some revenge for what she'd done to him.

He hadn't yet raised the subject of divorce – he'd do it when *he* was ready. And he'd tell her nothing about the overseas money. He'd give her the house and a monthly allowance, so she'd do extremely well. In the meantime, he was enjoying watching her squirm, especially since he'd kept up the pretence of bringing his mother to live with them.

As if he'd subject his poor mother to Jennifer's ministrations! No, she'd be better off in a decent nursing home. He and Hugh had already checked out several homes, but hadn't yet reached a final decision. They'd agreed to pick a nursing home that was convenient for both of them to visit. Benjamin was determined that, from now on, he'd see his mother regularly and make sure she had the very best of everything. He'd a lot to make up for, and he intended doing his very best.

He was also proud of his kids. Alan was just as keen as Vanessa to meet his father's family. He and Carl had already chatted on the phone and had hit it off straight away, and Carl was planning to take him to a few music gigs in London, and maybe get Alan's band a try-out with an agent he knew. Alan was in seventh heaven, and so what if he didn't go up to Cambridge? He might make more money in the music business. Even better, he might find a career he loved, which was more important than anything else. Of course, Jennifer was having conniptions, and threatening to disown her son if he didn't stop these 'silly notions' right away. But Alan knew he had his father's support, so his mother's threats had fallen on deaf ears.

Benjamin chuckled to himself. The tables had suddenly turned, and Jennifer was being marginalised as the odd one out in the family. The children might be hers biologically, but they were more like him in many ways.

And then there was Georgie. Benjamin's mood lifted every time he thought of her. To hell with the Clara Court development – he'd survive even if most of the remaining apartments stayed empty. Anyway, he could always tart them up and rent them out if things got really bad. Nevertheless, he had a good feeling that everything was going to be all right.

"I'm leaving Benjamin."

Clive went pale. "Good God. Why?"

"Well," said Jennifer, unfurling herself from the sofa in Clive's Westminster apartment, "he's insisting the children socialise with that ghastly family of his, he's being tested in order to give his awful brother one of his kidneys, so I could end up looking after an invalid if the operation goes wrong." She pursed her lips. "He's also planning to bring his brain-dead mother to live with us – can you believe it? And he's expecting me to look after her, since he can no longer afford to put her in a nursing home!"

It crossed Clive's mind that looking after Benjamin's mother might be a fair exchange for all Benjamin had done for Jennifer over the years, but he forbore to say so. He'd already heard from Anne, who'd heard it from Jennifer that the recession had caught up with Benjamin and his latest building project at Stonegate was on hold, probably costing him millions.

Jennifer glared at him. "I don't know what's got into Benjamin. He's been behaving like a lunatic ever since he's been in contact with those awful people again. He's not thinking of anyone but himself!"

Clive put down his glass of champagne. Suddenly, it seemed to have lost its sparkle.

"Anyway, you're always saying how much you want us to be together," Jennifer went on. "Well, now we can. Since I'm going to divorce Benjamin, I'll be a free woman soon. If you divorce Anne, we can be a couple at last."

Clive was shocked, and suddenly very worried. Jennifer was sounding like a loose cannon! He was the nearest he'd ever been to a ministerial post, and he didn't want anything getting in the way.

By now, his colour had returned and he tried to adopt an air of reason.

"Look, darling, this isn't a good time. You know you mean the world to me, but there's a general election coming up soon – and for that, regrettably, I need Anne by my side. Anyway, it's going to take a while before your divorce comes through – let's wait and talk about it then. When the election is over, we'll start making plans."

Jennifer was far from satisfied with Clive's reaction. She'd expected a warmer and more enthusiastic response to her news. But she could appreciate his dilemma – he was stuck with Anne, and divorce proceedings could turn the electorate against him.

On the other hand, being widowed might win him a lot of sympathy votes. Maybe it was time she started helping things along herself.

CHAPTER 49

Having checked Benjamin's schedule and satisfied herself that he wouldn't be anywhere near the church, Jennifer drove into Stonehill village. She'd taken her Maserati today, intending to rub those country bumpkins' noses in it.

Parking in what she assumed was the main street, she wrinkled her nose in disgust – what a hick little place! There wasn't even a decent teashop or shopping centre. What on earth did these dreadful people do all day?

Nevertheless, there *was* something of interest to Jennifer there. As she walked up the street, wearing her Gucci jeans and jacket, she spotted the church at the top of an incline. It was an imposing building, and Jennifer wondered how such beautiful architecture had been created in an awful place like Stonehill.

But when she reached the gate and walked into the church grounds, she could see at once why Benjamin had bought it. Behind the church, the landscape swept across to Stonegate Farm. Once demolished, the church land would provide the perfect entrance to Benjamin's new building project.

Of course it was now doubtful if the Stonegate project would ever get started, so it was odd that he'd decided against selling the windows. But as far as Jennifer was concerned, that decision would now work to her advantage.

Circling the building, Jennifer noted the ornate gargoyles at each corner, and the pretty bell tower with its louvered windows at the top. Returning to the front entrance, she produced the key she'd taken from Benjamin's pocket. Letting herself in, she gazed up in wonder at the magnificent windows, and was charmed by their vivid colours. They really were spectacular.

Suddenly, Jennifer had an idea. She'd ask Anne to take a look at them. Anne had studied fine arts at college, and had actually taken a course in stained-glass appreciation. She'd surely know what they were worth. Of course, she wouldn't tell Anne what she intended doing with the windows – she'd pretend she simply wanted them valued for insurance purposes.

Jennifer was very impressed by the church. She wandered around inside, studying the ornate carvings on the decorative arches and pews, and thinking to herself that some hotel or salvage merchant would pay handsomely for them.

At the back of the church, she discovered a door that led up a flight of circular stone steps. Mindful of her Gucci jeans and jacket, she took care not to brush against the walls as she went up. Above was a floor where the ropes from the belfry hung down and, finding a straight staircase against one of the walls, she headed up the next flight.

Stepping out onto another floor, she stared in awe at the enormous bells that sat in their giant frame. They were magnificent, and clearly worth a lot of money. Pound signs were flashing in Jennifer's brain. This little church was a goldmine! Above the bells were the louvered windows designed to carry the sound of the bells out across the parish, and beside one of the louvered windows, Jennifer spotted another staircase, presumably leading up to the rooftop.

Jennifer smiled. Maybe there were more treasures to be found on the bell-tower roof. At the very least, she could look down and check the condition of the roof on the main part of the church. The slates would be worth good money, and maybe there was even copper and lead piping still in place. She knew that many old churches had been built and maintained with the best of materials. Hopefully, vandals hadn't already helped themselves to what she now felt was rightly hers.

Opening the small trapdoor at the top of the steps, she stepped out into bright sunshine. After the dark interior, the sunlight was almost blinding at first, but her eyes quickly adjusted to the light, and she gazed in awe at the views all around her. She could see for miles across the beautiful countryside, with its muted shades of grey, green and blue.

But when she looked over the parapet, she felt dizzy. It was a very lengthy drop – anyone falling over would plunge to their death.

Suddenly, Jennifer's heart started racing. She'd just had the most brilliant idea – this could be the way to get rid of Anne! Jennifer was so pleased with her idea that she didn't bother checking the slates or the lead piping. Instead, she left the rooftop, closing the trapdoor and hurrying down the stairway. There was no time to lose.

She already had the perfect reason for inviting Anne to the church – and when she got her there, she'd invite up to the top of the tower to enjoy the view. Then Anne would be quickly dispatched over the side to her death.

Jennifer experienced a brief moment of regret – she'd miss Anne, despite her bossiness and dictatorial commands. Anne had been the one who'd held the four of them together, and lunch with the girls would never be the same again. On the other hand, she'd probably drop Fiona and Emma anyway, since they'd serve no useful purpose when she was the wife of an MP.

As she let herself out of the church, Jennifer noticed a small woman with red hair walking through the grounds. The woman reached the church gate ahead of her, and stood there with her arms folded as though preparing for a confrontation.

What on earth did the tiresome woman want? She was clearly making a nuisance of herself, and Jennifer felt very annoyed. Why was she staring at her? Maybe, Jennifer thought condescendingly, the woman had never seen anyone wearing designer clothes before.

Suddenly, the red-haired woman spoke. "This church is private property – perhaps you didn't realise you were trespassing?"

Jennifer was incensed by the woman's attitude. She'd soon bring her down to size – which wouldn't be difficult, since she was only knee-high to a grasshopper!

"Excuse me?" Jennifer said in her most haughty voice. On occasions like this, her height was an added bonus, and she often used it to intimidate people. Especially cheeky people like this little madam.

"I said the church is private property," Georgie repeated.

"Well, I'd like to inform *you* that I'm the owner of this church, and *you're* the one trespassing."

Much to Jennifer's chagrin, the woman didn't seem in the slightest bit intimidated.

"So you must be Benjamin's wife," she said.

"Which is none of your business either!" said Jennifer, striding out the gate angrily, and banging it closed behind her.

Jennifer fumed as she hurried towards her car. What a hideous creature that woman was! For once she had to agree with Benjamin – these yokels were overstepping their authority. The sooner she got the church stripped the better. And how dare that woman refer to her husband as 'Benjamin'! Really, her husband was allowing these people to be far too familiar with him.

As she drove home through the countryside, Jennifer felt herself gradually relaxing. To hell with that tiresome woman, she had more important fish to fry. On her next visit to the church, there would be a terrible accident. And her dear friend Anne would be no more. Briefly, Jennifer was assailed by guilt, but she quickly stifled it. Since she wanted Clive, there was no room for Anne in her life anymore.

CHAPTER 50

Zoe's Diary

April 3

For months now, I've been dreading the hours after school, but today was the worst I've ever experienced. I'm so upset I can't even write about it. The bullies have found out I'm bleeding, and I know they're planning to use it against me somehow. Why oh why can't they leave me alone?

Arriving home after school, Zoe seemed in quite a state. She looked flustered and frightened, and Claire was worried. Her sister looked as though she'd run all the way home, with a herd of wild elephants in pursuit.

"Zoe, are you okay?"

"Yes, I'm fine," Zoe said tersely, disappearing into the bathroom.

Once inside, she locked the door. There was blood in her panties, and she was frightened. Quickly, she slipped them off and put on a clean pair.

While in the bathroom, she took the packet of detergent from under the sink, and tackled the stain in cold water. She knew that blood needed to be washed in this way, so that it didn't have time to set. Relieved, she watched the pink water slurp down the plughole as the stain disappeared. She couldn't afford to lose a pair of panties – she had few pairs enough already.

Plastering a false smile on her face, she returned to the kitchen.

The following morning, Zoe awoke to find blood on the sheet. How could she possibly go to school like this? She wished she could ask her mother's advice, but it was too late for that. Nevertheless Claire had to be got ready for school, so reluctantly she climbed out of bed, whipped the stained sheet off her bed and hid it in a cupboard. She'd wash it later when she got home from school. Shoving a large handkerchief into her panties, she could only hope the blood would stop soon.

In the kitchen, Zoe tried to maintain a pleasant demeanour in front of Claire, since she didn't want to frighten her sister, but her insides were churning with fear and embarrassment. What if she had a leak in class? The bullies would love that! They'd laugh at her and turn her into a spectacle for everyone's amusement.

She thought briefly of asking Dr Barker's advice, but daren't risk it because of his threat to send her and Claire to an orphanage. She'd already discovered to her cost that asking anything of Dr Barker was a big mistake.

"Are you okay, Zoe?" Claire asked, a quizzical look on her face. "You should go back to bed – you don't look well."

Oh God, Zoe thought, was it even obvious to a nine-year-old girl that there was something wrong? If so, how could she hope to avoid the bullies' attention? On the other hand, if she went back to bed, her mother would want to know why. And staying home from school might bring her to the attention of the school-attendance inspectors, and all those other authorities who could intervene and break up their little family. No, Zoe decided, she'd brave the day at school.

Waving goodbye to Claire as she headed off to the junior school, Zoe crossed the road and began walking gingerly towards the *senior school at the other end of the village. Since she'd left the cottage, she'd been keeping her knees close together, in order to keep the handkerchief in place, and Claire had been amused at the strange way she was walking.*

Spotting Emma Durrant in the distance, Zoe quickly changed direction. Going as fast as her knock-kneed gait would allow, she hurried past the bicycle shed, ignoring Emma who was now close behind. The last person she wanted to meet in her present situation was one of the bullies.

"Zoe!"

Pretending not to hear, Zoe continued walking.

"Zoe, stop! Have you seen the back of your skirt?"

Reluctantly, Zoe turned around, expecting to be the butt of some rude comment or nasty remark.

"There's blood on it," Emma said. "You can't go into class like that."

Zoe stifled a groan. Clearly the handkerchief wasn't absorbent enough.

Reaching into her schoolbag, Emma took out the sanitary towel she always carried in case her first period started.

"Here – use this," she said, handing the soft cotton pad to an embarrassed Zoe, who gratefully took it, surprised at this gesture of support.

"Thanks," Zoe said, her face puce with embarrassment.

It looked to Emma as though Zoe was having her monthly period. Emma knew all about periods, because her mother had told her all about the bodily changes occurring at puberty. But Zoe didn't seem to have any idea what was going on.

"Don't you know what's happening to you?" Emma asked, then wished she'd kept her mouth shut. It was none of her business what Zoe Gray did or thought. If Jennifer, Anne or Fiona saw her talking to Zoe, she might as well be dead, since they'd drop her instantly and turn their malevolent attention on her instead.

When Zoe merely grimaced, Emma shrugged her shoulders. It wasn't her job to explain the facts of life to her. Besides, since she'd *never had a period herself she could be mistaken, and then she'd end up looking like a fool. And that was something Emma couldn't bear to contemplate. Her dignity was very important to her.*

As Emma walked off, Zoe ducked into the school cloakroom, which was mercifully empty, removed the sodden handkerchief, slipped it into a pocket of her schoolbag and inserted the sanitary towel into her panties. Slipping off her school skirt, she went to one of the basins and held the stained part of her skirt under running water, rubbing the bloodstained patch until the water ran clear. She'd have to sit in damp panties and skirt for the rest of the day, but the dark material of the skirt hid the damp stain, and thanks to Emma she'd be able to contain the bleeding for a while.

At mid-morning, all the seniors assembled in the schoolyard, to chat or play games while the teachers took their tea break. Zoe was quick to head for the only bench in the yard – hopefully sitting down would minimise the risk of any blood leaking out. Zoe had been pleasantly surprised at Emma's kindness earlier that morning. When she wasn't being influenced by the other three, Emma seemed to be a nice person.

On the other side of the schoolyard, Jennifer, Emma, Anne and Fiona were leaning against the school wall, looking bored and making sneering comments about the other pupils. At which point it was decided that Emma should go to the tuck shop for sweets, and she happily hurried off to do their bidding. The trio had come to regard her as their personal servant, and she was pathetically grateful and willing to do their bidding.

Emma hadn't been able to believe her luck when the others had befriended her. She was well aware that it was safer to be with them than against them. And now that she had powerful friends, she'd do whatever it took to keep them.

"Here you are –" said Emma, arriving back with an armful of goodies from the tuck shop, a glow of pleasure on her face. She was happy to be useful to her friends. It was good to feel wanted.

"Didn't they have any Swizzle bars?" asked Fiona, curling her lip in annoyance.

Emma's eyes clouded over. "I'm afraid not – Mrs Hanly sold the last one just before I arrived."

"Who did she sell it to?" Fiona asked slyly. She hated being thwarted.

Emma blushed. She knew that if she told, that pupil would be hassled for no reason other than that they'd unwittingly deprived Fiona of her favourite toffee bar.

"I don't know – I didn't see them."

"Wake up, Durrant – did you leave your brains at home today?" said Jennifer nastily.

Anne gave an exaggerated sigh. "Poor Fiona – I think, Emma, you should give her your Jacko bar as compensation," she said authoritatively.

"Of course," said Emma, now empty-handed but grateful she'd got off so lightly. It wasn't easy staying on her toes all the time, but when she got something right and her friends praised her, it was like manna from heaven. And she'd do anything to bask in the warmth of their approval.

Right now, she was feeling the weight of their disapproval. She'd disappointed her friends, and she didn't like the way that made her feel. She needed to redeem herself by providing them with some juicy titbit of gossip. They always praised her when she did, and it made her feel so important.

Glancing around, her eyes alighted on Zoe Gray, who was sitting alone on the bench and writing in her diary.

"Zoe Gray is having her first period!" Emma confided.

"How do you know?" asked Jennifer, gazing across the playground to Zoe's forlorn figure.

Emma bit her lip. This was the tricky bit. She could hardly tell them she'd helped Zoe earlier!

"I – um, I noticed a bloodstain on her skirt earlier," she said. "She doesn't seem to have any sanitary towels."

"I'm not surprised," said Anne acerbically. "That drunken mother of hers wouldn't have money to spare for practical things like that – booze is all that matters to her."

"So what's she using?" asked Fiona rhetorically, a nasty glint

in her eye. "How dare she subject the rest of us to her messy monthlies! I'm certainly not going near that bench ever again!"

Fiona had never had a period herself, but she still liked to consider herself an authority on the subject.

"Actually, I don't think she knows what's happening to her," Emma added. Briefly, she felt genuine empathy with poor Zoe Gray. How awful to be so neglected and ill-informed. But her guilt at betraying Zoe's ignorance was outweighed by the reward of seeing her friends' interest piqued.

"Really?" said Anne, her eyebrows arching. "Surely nobody in this day and age can be so ignorant?"

"How do you know this, Emma?" asked Jennifer, her beady eyes staring down at her smaller companion. "You haven't been talking to her, have you?"

Emma gave a theatrical shudder. "God, no!"

"Then why do you think she doesn't know about periods?" Anne persisted.

Emma was thinking fast. "Well, it stands to reason, doesn't it? If she's so neglected, her mother would hardly have told her about them, would she? You said it yourself, Anne – all the woman thinks about is drink!"

Anne nodded, then turned and grinned malevolently at the others. "If that's the case, I think we can have a bit of fun," she said. "Fiona, you have a job to do."

Late that night, while her parents were asleep, Fiona left her bed and sneaked downstairs to her father's library, where she spent ages poring over his medical books. At all times, she kept an eye on the door, since she was acutely aware that if her father found her there, there'd be hell to pay. He'd been at his club, and on these nights he limited his activities to violence. In the early hours after he'd come home, she'd heard her mother being battered for some minor infringement of a rule that only her father was aware of. Now he was snoring and would hopefully sleep until morning. Fiona didn't relish a demonstration of her father's violent temper, but she was prepared to take the risk for the glory that would soon be hers. Her friends would be in awe when she came up with a horrendous disease to scare the living daylights out of Zoe Gray!

Eventually, as dawn began to filter through the library, Fiona turned off the desk lamp and headed upstairs to bed. She was exhausted, but exhilarated at the thought of all the fun she and the others would have at Zoe Gray's expense.

After school the next day, the bullies were waiting in their usual place at the crossroads. But today they replaced their insults with a new line of attack.

"Oh God, look at Zoe Gray – there's blood running down her legs!" Jennifer shouted as Zoe walked by.

Horrified and embarrassed, Zoe looked down, but could thankfully see nothing. However, she could hear the others sniggering in the background.

"Zoe Gray's got a prolapsed womb!" Fiona stage-whispered.

Zoe was suddenly frightened. She knew she was meant to hear the comments, and since Fiona's father was a doctor, it stood to reason that she knew more than most people about medical matters.

"Is it true that if she doesn't get to hospital soon, she could die?" Anne asked spitefully, pleased at the look of terror her comment had registered on Zoe's face.

Still in a stage whisper, Fiona answered: "Yes, without treatment her womb will fall out onto the ground. Then she'll never be able to get it back in again, and she'll die in agony!"

Zoe desperately wanted to cry. She suspected Fiona was right, but not for the reason the bullies assumed. She had a vision of her womb – which she imagined might resemble a hollow chocolate Easter egg – dropping out between her legs and dangling from her body by a few viscous threads of mucus. It was a terrifying thought, and Zoe felt she might faint.

Zoe and Emma exchanged a brief glance, and Zoe felt a flash of gratitude for her kindness. Emma had been waiting outside the school toilets earlier that afternoon, and had whispered about the plan to frighten her. She'd also assured Zoe that a monthly blood flow was a normal occurrence, but begged her to keep up the pretence of being frightened so the others wouldn't suspect she'd spoken to her.

Zoe quickly glanced at Emma again – no doubt her newfound ally assumed she was playing along, but Zoe didn't need to pretend. She was genuinely terrified. Tears filled her eyes at the sheer malevolence of her tormentors, and she began running away as quickly as she could, not even caring if blood was dripping onto the road.

"Zoe really did look upset," Emma ventured timidly, eager to ingratiate herself now that Zoe had gone. "I think you really scared her, Fiona."

Anne was looking thoughtful. "Emma's right – Zoe Gray is very frightened. There's something different about her – haven't any of you noticed?"

Jennifer nodded cheerfully. "I'm not surprised! Assuming she believes us, she must be terrified!"

Zoe made her way down to the shore, unable to cope with her tormentors any longer but unwilling to go home until she'd managed to stop crying. As the wind blew fiercely, she pulled her thread-worn cardigan around her.

Zoe was deeply grateful to Emma. As she'd listened to Emma's embarrassed explanations about puberty, she'd kept up the pretence of knowing nothing about periods. But in fact, she knew all about them. Her mum might be drunk most of the time, but she hadn't forgotten to tell her daughter all about the bodily changes that occurred when a girl became a woman.

Zoe sighed. She'd been having periods for months now, and she'd just finished a period the week before. For that reason, she couldn't ask her mother for money for more sanitary towels, because she'd want to know why Zoe was bleeding again so soon, and Zoe didn't dare tell her.

If only there was someone she could talk to! But Zoe was afraid to speak to anyone in authority, since they might visit her *home, see all the empty whiskey bottles and discover the conditions under which she and her sister lived. Nor could she allow the authorities to heap blame on her poor mother, who was only doing the best she could.*

Zoe bit her lip. Maybe Fiona was right, and she did need to go to hospital. She'd wait another day or two, and if the bleeding hadn't stopped by then, she'd definitely have to get help.

CHAPTER 51

Turning the key in the front door, Vanessa let herself into the hall of The Old Vicarage. She listened, but it was clear that no one else was at home.

Grinning, she slipped off her shoes. She loved sliding across the tiles – but of course her mother didn't approve, and if caught, she'd find herself in big trouble. According to her mother, young ladies should never behave in such a crude and exuberant manner. Vanessa always found it annoying that she could be regarded as 'a young lady' when it suited her mother, but at other times she was merely 'a child', typically when she wanted to do something interesting or go somewhere exciting. Anyway, she'd soon be grown up, and then her mother wouldn't be able to disapprove of everything she did.

Having tired of sliding up and down the hall floor, Vanessa put on her shoes again and made her way into the kitchen. She was suddenly hungry, so she made herself a large cheese sandwich, boiled the kettle and made a cup of tea. Since it was a sunny afternoon, she decided to take her food outside and sit at the garden table. A vixen and her cubs sometimes visited the garden, so maybe she'd see them today.

In the garden, Vanessa settled herself comfortably at the

garden table. Turning her face up to the sun, she revelled in its warmth. It seemed to augur well for the summer – and nearly two whole months' holidays . . .

As she took a bite of her sandwich, Vanessa scanned the gardens in the hope of spotting the vixen. But suddenly her eyes were drawn to the row of garages set back from the house among the trees. There was some kind of vapour coming out from under one of the doors. She craned forward to get a better view. Could one of the family cars be on fire? Suddenly, her heart almost stopping, she jumped up and began running down the lawn. Something wasn't right, but she had no idea what it was, or what she could do about it.

Outside the garage door, Vanessa stood helplessly, unsure of what to do. She needed to prise the door open, but it was locked. Looking around, she found a spade leaning against the building, and tried to open the garage door with it. But it was no use, she simply didn't have the strength to force it open. Then she remembered there was an old door at the back of the garage – she and Alan used to play pirates in that garage when they were young. The back door was never used – maybe it hadn't been locked, or the lock might be broken?

Racing round to the back, Vanessa found the door overgrown with ivy and assorted weeds. She pulled at the ivy in vain, then raced around to the front of the garage, grabbed the spade and returned with it, then tried to use it to lever open the door. But it wouldn't budge. Then Vanessa began stabbing at the ivy roots with the edge of the spade. The ivy was strong, but she kept hacking at it, and within seconds she'd cut through the main tendrils that were holding the door closed. Her hands now bleeding, Vanessa yanked open the door, breaking her nails and barely able to see through the smoke inside.

In the dim light of the garage, she could make out the outline of a car – was there someone inside it? Pulling open the car door, Vanessa's heart almost stopped. Alan was in there, and he was unconscious!

"Oh, God – wake up, Alan!" Vanessa screamed, coughing from the fumes that were filling the garage. Realising that the ignition was on, Vanessa leaned across and turned it off. Then she grabbed Alan around the waist and tried to haul him out of the car. He seemed to weigh a ton, and she wasn't able to lift him, but she knew that it was essential to get him out into the fresh air if there was any hope of him surviving. Instead, she dragged him out of the car by pulling at his clothes, holding his head while she slid him onto the ground. Then she walked backwards, tugging him after her. She desperately wished that someone else was on hand to help, and she cursed the fact that she was so far from a phone.

At last she succeeded in dragging Alan out the back door of the garage. Leaving him lying in the grass, she rushed up to the house, grabbed the phone and dialled the emergency services.

"My brother – I've just pulled him out of the car – it was full of smoke – oh, please help us, quickly!"

Patiently, the operator asked the location of the house, who their parents were, and all sorts of information that seemed irrelevant to Vanessa. She tried to answer them as succinctly as she could, but every question she was asked seemed to be delaying help for Alan.

"Please!" she begged the operator. "Can you get us help quickly? I don't know if he's still alive –"

"Don't worry, I've already dispatched an ambulance to your house," the operator assured her. "It should be with you in minutes. In the meantime, do you know how to do CPR? If not, don't worry – just try to get your brother awake, if you can. Talk to him, and try to get him to respond."

"Thanks, I'll go back to him now," Vanessa said, ringing off and racing back to Alan who was still lying motionless on the grass behind the garage.

Her heart was pounding as she gazed at her brother, who looked lifeless and pale. Tears scalded her cheeks as she thought bitterly of all the times they'd hardly spoken to each other or been rude to each other. How could it all have come to this?

"Oh God, Alan – please wake up," she sobbed, feeling small and useless. She began compressing his chest, as she'd seen it done in movies, but she doubted if it was having any effect. She kept pounding, because to do nothing was worse.

Just then, she heard a faint groan, and her brother began to vomit. Quickly, she pushed him over onto his side so that he wouldn't choke, and watched impotently as the vomit dripped down his face and onto the grass. Then his eyes opened, and Vanessa burst into tears of relief. She knew it was no guarantee that he was going to be okay, but at least he was conscious.

Alan groaned and tried to sit up.

"Take it easy, there's help on the way," Vanessa told him, smiling through her tears. "Don't try to sit up."

Taking off her jacket, she placed it behind his head.

"Oh God, I've a splitting headache," her brother whispered. "I thought – what happened?"

"You tried to top yourself," said Vanessa. "What the hell got into you, Alan?"

Her brother looked embarrassed, and his pale cheeks turned red. For ages he said nothing, and Vanessa began to wonder if his brain had been damaged by the fumes in the car.

"I just couldn't cope anymore," he mumbled at last. "She said she was finished with me, and that it was over –"

"Mum? Mum said that?"

"No, not Mum – Fiona."

"Fiona? Mum's friend Fiona? Alan, you're not making sense."

Alan sighed, his head lolling to one side. "I thought she really cared about me – but it was just an amusing game to her."

"You did this because of – of – something Fiona said to you?" Vanessa screamed incredulously. "You tried to kill yourself because of some remark she made?"

Alan shook his head wearily. "No – well yes, in a way. She dumped me. She said she never really cared for me – but I really loved her – I always will!"

"Hold on – I don't understand anything you're saying," Vanessa said. "The Fiona we know is old, and she's married – are you talking about some other Fiona?"

Shaking his head, Alan closed his eyes, and Vanessa could see tears spilling out from under his tightly closed eyelids. She'd never seen her brother cry before, and her heart was breaking for him. Yet nothing he was saying made any sense. Perhaps that was because he was disoriented from the exhaust fumes in the car?

Alan tried to sit up, but Vanessa urged him to lie down again. "Take it easy, Alan – there's help on the way," she whispered.

"I really love her – but I was just a kid to her. I thought I was the only one – I didn't know she liked other boys, and that I was nothing special."

"But, is this Mum's friend Fiona that you're talking about?" Vanessa asked again in astonishment.

Alan nodded. Then great gulping sobs wracked his body, and Vanessa held him tightly in her arms. It was almost impossible to believe that Fiona had propositioned her brother, he'd fallen in love with her, and then she'd dumped him.

"You mean – you've had sex with Mum's friend?" she asked incredulously.

Alan nodded, turning his face away from his sister as though he couldn't look at her as he spoke.

"When? I mean, how long has this been going on?"

Alan stared into space, as though trying to detach himself from what he was saying.

"It's been going on since the Ellwoods' garden party," he said at last. "We were in love – at least I was, and she told me I was special to her. Then I discovered she'd been having it off with the grocer's van boy and some other lad from the stables. When I accused her, she didn't even deny it! She said it was only just a bit of fun for her, and that it was time we finished anyway!"

Suddenly, he was weeping again, and Vanessa threw her arms around him.

"It's okay, Alan," she whispered, not really knowing if those words had any value. But by holding him close, he'd hopefully know that she'd support him through his painful ordeal. First love – especially unrequited first love – was clearly a horrendous experience, and Vanessa was relieved that she'd never felt this way about anyone – yet. She was also furious with Fiona – how could she do this to her brother?

In the distance, they could hear an ambulance siren, and it gradually got louder as it approached The Old Vicarage. Eventually, it turned in the gate, and within seconds several paramedics had disgorged themselves and were attending to Alan. Vanessa stepped back, suddenly feeling light-headed. At least she didn't have to worry about Alan anymore, since he was now in good hands.

"Are you okay?" one of the paramedics asked Vanessa. "You don't look too good. Maybe you should come in the ambulance with us."

"No, I'm fine," Vanessa assured him, then promptly fainted into his arms.

CHAPTER 52

Fiona drove out the gates of Bloomfield House and through the sleepy village of Chillingham where she and Edwin lived. She was planning to get to The Old Vicarage before Jennifer returned from her weekly bridge night in London.

It was a sunny day, and the trees cast dappled light across the country roads as Fiona drove along. She glanced down at her new Jimmy Choos – she'd been so bored the day before that she'd gone into town on a shopping spree and bought three pairs. Luckily, Edwin never seemed to mind how much money she spent.

Sometimes, though, she wished she'd married someone more exciting than Edwin. On the other hand, he'd represented a chance to escape from her father's abuse. Dr Barker had always been held in high regard in Trentham-on-Sea where she'd grown up. But the locals hadn't known what a different man he was in the privacy of his own home. When she or her mother sported an occasional black eye or a broken wrist, it was always passed off as an unfortunate accident: a too exuberant daughter who'd crashed into a wall on her bike; a silly wife who'd been trying to hang the new curtains without help.

To an outsider, Fiona led a charmed life. Being the doctor's

255

daughter gave her an edge over the other children, which she'd used ruthlessly to full effect. But that made her contrasting home life all the more awful. Behind closed doors, she counted for nothing. No one knew that the charming Dr Barker became a monster when he closed the door of the surgery and returned to the bosom of his family. She and her mother had lived in a constant state of fear. One wrong word could promote a violent outburst, or worse, a beating.

But even worse was when she turned ten, and her father started visiting her bedroom at night. Her initial reluctance had been quickly overcome by a severe beating.

Her only comfort had been her friendship with Anne, Jennifer and Emma. Their combined role as the four most feared girls in the school had allowed her to feel that she was striking back at the unfairness of life. While she couldn't direct her anger at her father, she could direct it at others, particularly Zoe Gray.

Her father's behaviour had later dictated the kind of men she was attracted to. In contrast to her father's heavy brooding presence, Fiona had always been drawn to slightly built, boyish men, probably because they represented safety from the kind of harm her father represented. Edwin had been such a man, and his agreeable temperament and the comfortable lifestyle he offered had soothed her fears and provided her with all the material things she needed. Bloomfield, with its magnificent gardens, was a home anyone could be proud of.

Of course, the kind of men who offered safety and security were rarely sexually adventurous, so Fiona found it necessary to take her pleasures elsewhere. But the fear of violence never left her, so she came on to younger men, usually boys just embarking on a sexual life, who signified no danger to her. In these instances it was she who made the first move, a situation that also helped her to feel in control. After all those childhood years of living in fear, Fiona liked to be the one in charge. She also found it thrilling to introduce a young man to sex, and to be the first woman to give him pleasure.

Fiona smiled as she drove along the road. Most young men

were pathetically grateful for her interest, and were more than willing to do her bidding. In many primitive tribes, it was older women who introduced young men to the pleasures of sex, so what she was doing had an established historical precedent.

All of the boys accepted the conditions of these brief liaisons and were grateful for Fiona's tutoring. Later, they moved on to girls of their own age, remembering her, Fiona hoped, with gratitude and affection. At least that's how it had always been until Alan Corcroft did the unthinkable, and added emotion to the equation.

At first, introducing Jennifer's son to sex had been a bit of fun. She'd enjoyed the sneaking round, the liaisons in the back of her car, in her kitchen, or in her bedroom while Edwin was at work. Alan's initial timidity had been a big turn-on, but gradually he'd become tiresome, professing undying devotion to her, and somehow he'd got the notion they were going to be together forever some day. Fiona had been amused at the ability of the young and inexperienced to make heavy drama out of light relief. Did he really think she was going to leave Edwin for him? How did he expect Fiona to maintain her comfortable lifestyle, or had he even thought that far ahead?

The previous week, she'd had to nip the situation in the bud. She'd explained to Alan that he was taking it far too seriously, and that it was just a bit of fun as far as she was concerned. She'd tried telling him he'd soon forget her but, of course, he hadn't been willing to believe that. He'd also been upset to discover he wasn't the only young man she'd ever had a relationship with, and it was gradually dawning on her that the situation could become a lot more awkward than she'd ever envisaged.

As she neared The Old Vicarage, Fiona glanced at her watch. Hopefully, young Vanessa would have left for the stables by the time she got there. It was also Mrs Quick's day off, so there'd be no housekeeper lurking about while she tried to talk some sense into Alan. Fiona didn't want him moping around all summer and drawing unwanted attention to their little liaison. A lovesick teenager was a complication she didn't need. He had to understand the rules of the game – for game was all it was – and she'd remind him of the immense benefits her tutoring would have when he started dating girls of his own age.

Sweeping in the main gate of The Old Vicarage, Fiona parked her car and stepped out onto the gravel, realising too late that she should have worn more sensible footwear than her new Jimmy Choos. But Fiona always liked to look her best when dealing with young men, even ones she was in the process of dumping. She was aware that no one but Alan was likely to be home, but she had a story prepared, just in case.

She went to the front door, rang the bell several times and waited. No one answered. She rang again. Nothing.

"Cooeee! Anyone home?" Circling the house on foot, Fiona called up to the open windows of Alan's bedroom on the second floor, but there was no reply and she was annoyed. She really needed to see him. If he wouldn't see sense, she'd have to consider being unpleasant to him, in the hope that such a drastic tactic might have the desired effect.

As she prepared to leave, Fiona noticed a cold cup of tea and a half-eaten cheese sandwich on the garden table. Someone must have left in a hurry, or forgotten to tidy up after themselves.

Puzzled, Fiona looked around again, but it was clear that no one was at home. Disappointed, she climbed back into her car and drove away.

CHAPTER 53

Jennifer was furious as she drove towards the hospital. Benjamin had been in a state when he'd contacted her, shouting over the phone that Alan had tried to kill himself. According to him, Fiona had been having sex with their son, Alan had fallen in love with her, then she'd dumped him. Benjamin had been apoplectic when he'd phoned, and Jennifer had tried to calm him, all to no avail. He'd been screaming blue murder, and promising to put Fiona behind bars for interfering with a minor.

Jennifer had been on the train when Benjamin phoned. She'd been returning from her Wednesday night stay-over at Clive's Westminster apartment, but of course Benjamin thought she'd been playing bridge at her club.

Jennifer was puzzled. She couldn't understand why Alan was making such a fuss – she'd thought that young men were always up for it, especially when it was freely on offer. Alan had merely been experiencing a bout of overactive teenage hormones.

As for falling for Fiona – why, that was preposterous! At his age, Alan should be experimenting behind the school bicycle-shed with girls of his own age from wealthy families. Surely Benjamin had got it all wrong? Whatever the situation, she felt certain that he was making a mountain out of a molehill, and encouraging Alan to turn a small incident into a major drama.

Anyway, why couldn't Alan have just enjoyed the sex bit, and left his emotions out of it? Mind you, she was annoyed with Fiona for creeping around behind her back. She'd always been aware of Fiona's liking for young men, but she never expected her friend to turn her beady eye onto Alan!

Jennifer shivered. It almost felt like incest to have her son fancying his mother's friend. The silly boy had obviously confused lust with his emotions. Jennifer didn't really 'do' emotions and, subsequently, she didn't always understand them in other people. She loved her children with a fierce maternal love – after all, they were her own flesh and blood – and an extension of her union with Clive, the only man she truly loved, and with whom she soon hoped to spend the rest of her life. But turning a first fling into love? Now that was something she didn't understand.

Having arrived home, she'd dumped her overnight bag, showered and changed, then got in her car and set out for the hospital. Dear God, what a mess, Jennifer thought, as she drove round a corner too quickly. Had Benjamin no sense of decorum in pursuing this matter? Didn't he know that people with class usually dealt with these matters in their own quiet way? They didn't go in for public shouting matches, in courts of law, with reporters lurking everywhere. If this got into the newspapers – which it surely would if Benjamin maintained his present frame of mind – how on earth were they going to hold their heads up? And had Alan any idea what he was doing to the family when he'd locked himself in the garage and let the car fill with exhaust fumes?

Jennifer bit her lip. She loved her son dearly, but she didn't understand him at all. He'd been all set for Cambridge in a few years' time until he'd started hanging out with a group of local kids who aspired to be musicians. Now, he'd taken up the guitar and was writing his own songs, for heaven's sake! And, of course, Benjamin had been encouraging him, and Alan now had notions of becoming a famous rock star. Jennifer could visualise her son homeless and on the streets before he was twenty.

Jennifer slowed down, realising that she was driving far too fast. What a pity it wasn't Anne who'd pursued him, she thought sourly. I'd have made certain Clive knew all about *that*. Then he'd definitely have had to divorce her, since such a scandal would ruin his chances of a ministerial post.

Jennifer sighed. She'd need to have a serious talk with Alan when he was released from hospital. He had to understand that families needed to keep their problems within their own four walls, instead of shouting about them from the rooftops. Anyway, weren't schools supposed to deal with this kind of thing? What was the point of paying for an expensive education, if the children weren't taught how to deal with a variety of situations?

It was all simply a storm in a teacup, she decided. But she needed to get to the hospital quickly, before Benjamin went off half-cocked about things, and started ringing solicitors. There were far better ways to handle a situation like this. She'd quietly ensure that Fiona and her husband were ostracised from local society, and that would be a far greater punishment that anything some grubby little reporter could write about. Besides, it was clearly time she dispensed with some of her childhood friendships.

Turning into the hospital gate, Jennifer was relieved to find a vacant car space straight away. Quickly, she parked her Maserati and headed towards the main hospital building. The sooner she talked to Alan and Benjamin, the sooner this nasty little incident could be consigned to oblivion.

"We are *not* going to ignore what's happened!" Benjamin roared. "Alan is a minor, and he was abused by that woman – as far as I'm concerned, we're going to court!"

"Benjamin, please keep your voice down!" Jennifer hissed. "There are other people in this hospital, and I don't want our business becoming common knowledge!" A sympathetic look on her face, she turned to her son, who was lying prone in his hospital bed. "Darling, I don't think washing your dirty linen in public is the best way forward," she soothed. "Think of –"

"*His* dirty linen? If anyone's guilty of having dirty linen, it's bloody Fiona!" Benjamin shouted. "If I ever see that woman again, so help me –"

"Benjamin – please!"

Eventually, Benjamin calmed down, but Jennifer knew it wouldn't take much to get him going again. And she was right. He began pacing the room, muttering angrily and shaking his head incredulously.

As he paced up and down, Benjamin glanced at his wife and felt nothing but contempt for her. He longed to scream at her that he knew she'd been playing away, but that wouldn't help poor Alan, who was slouching in his bed and staring into space as though he wasn't part of this scenario at all. Benjamin longed to assure him that he could still have a wonderful future, and that there were millions of girls his own age who'd love to go out with him, but the boy wasn't responding to anything. Yet all Jennifer cared about was preventing the incident from going public. Personally, he didn't care what she thought – all he wanted was to avenge poor Alan.

"Benjamin, really – we've got to discuss this matter logically –"

"Alan tried to kill himself, and all you can do is think of yourself! Anyway, why the fuck weren't *you* at home?" he shouted. "Because you were off playing bloody bridge in London, or whatever else you get up to there! Instead of looking after your children, who –"

"How dare you! You can't afford to speak – you're never around when you're needed! I've raised these children single-handed!"

"I might have known you'd turn the situation around, and use it to show how wonderful you are! Don't you realise that Alan would have died, if it wasn't for Vanessa? She saved her brother's life – and I'm going to buy that girl anything she wants!"

"Yes, that's your answer to everything – buy people off with money, but don't give them any of your time!"

Benjamin glared at her angrily. "I've never heard *you* complaining!"

"Mum, Dad – please stop!" Alan implored them. "It's all my fault, and I'm sorry! Please stop fighting –" His young face was sad and blotchy, and there was a stubble of soft baby hairs on his chin. "Neither of you understand – I love her! She didn't abuse me – she dumped me! I wanted to spend my life with her –"

Alan began to weep, and both parents were suddenly silent.

CHAPTER 54

While Claire was in mid-session, her phone rang, and she smiled apologetically at her client as she reached for it. She knew the call must be important, otherwise Teresa would never interrupt a consultation.

"Yes, Teresa?"

"Claire, a woman called Hazel Bonnington is on the line. She says she needs to talk to you urgently."

"Okay, put her through."

"Excuse me," Claire said, turning to her patient. "I won't be a minute – this appears to be an urgent call."

As Hazel came on the line, Claire tried to maintain a professional demeanour in front of her patient. She didn't want the man thinking that she'd interrupt his consultation for something trivial.

"Hello?"

"Claire, you're not going to believe this – I've found your father, and he's alive and well!"

Claire felt something akin to an electric shock run through her. Was it possible? Finding her father had been her dream for most of her life.

"Oh God." Claire felt weak. "Look, Hazel – I'm with someone at the moment. Can I ring you back?"

"'Fraid not," Hazel told her. "Right now, I'm on my way to do an interview – you'll never guess what a certain actress and a married law lord have been doing together – anyway, I just wanted to let you know immediately. I'll phone you at home this evening and fill you in."

"Okay, thank you so much."

Claire didn't know if she could wait till that evening to find out all the details, but she needed to behave professionally while her clients were paying for her time and expertise. She tried not to let her agitation show as her current client told her about his disintegrating marriage, and she managed to mask her eagerness to get rid of him when the session ended.

Claire couldn't stop thinking about Hazel's phone call throughout the rest of the day. How amazing that Hazel had managed to track down her father! After a lifetime of fearing that he was dead, a clever journalist had been able to use her sources to find him so quickly!

Later that evening, Hazel phoned with an address for Claire's father. He didn't live very far away from where Claire had her professional rooms, and she wondered if she'd even passed him in the street without knowing.

"How did you manage to find him?"

"I forwarded your father's details to several contacts of mine, including a friend who works for a credit-rating agency. Jim was the first one to come back to me, and he was able to give me your father's current address – I'm sorry it's only an address, Claire, but that's the only personal information credit agencies hold. At least you'll be able to make contact with him now."

"Thanks, Hazel – this is a wonderful surprise. I really expected you to tell me he was dead. I wonder why he never got in touch?"

"Well, you can ask him that when you meet him," said Hazel briskly. "I presume you'll write to him, and arrange a meeting?"

Claire smiled. "You try and stop me! Thanks again, Hazel – I'll never be able to thank you enough."

"Just remember, he mightn't answer your letter," Hazel warned. "It's been a long time – maybe he has another family now."

"I know – I've given that one a lot of thought. But even if he has, I can see no reason why we can't still meet. I've no problem with meeting new brothers and sisters. In fact, it might be fun."

"Well, I hope it all works out for you, Claire. Just be prepared to be disappointed."

Nevertheless, Claire had a really good feeling.

"Now, you said you had a front-page story for me?" said Hazel.

"I have indeed," said Claire, smiling. "I'll download the photograph to your computer immediately."

"A photograph?" Hazel sounded disappointed.

"It's not just any photograph," said Claire, "Believe me, you're going to love it."

While she waited for David to arrive at her apartment that evening, Claire sat down and wrote to her father at the address Hazel had given her. When David arrived, he was astonished to find her in a state of euphoria, and even more astonished when she revealed the reason why.

"I'm so thrilled!" she squealed, jumping up and down like an excited child.

David was pleased for her. Claire always seemed such a loner, and finding her father would give her the sense of family that had been missing from her life. He smiled to himself. Until they started their own family, of course . . .

That evening at the theatre, Claire was unable to concentrate on the play, despite it being one she'd wanted to see for ages. She'd posted the letter to her father on the way there. She'd decided to write immediately, rather than taking time to deliberate on what she was going to say. She knew that if she did that, she'd never get it written! She'd keep changing it in the hope of making it sound better, and time would be lost, valuable time she could be spending with her father.

As she anticipated their first meeting, she was filled with equal measures of dread and excitement. There would be so much to talk about, so much information for each to impart to the other.

Suddenly, Claire thought of another exciting possibility – perhaps he could walk her down the aisle on her wedding day?

Of course, she might never get an answer to her letter. Her father mightn't want to see her. After all, why had he never got in touch before now?

David squeezed her hand, catapulting Claire back to reality. The curtain was closing for the interval of the play, and Claire hadn't consciously watched any of the first half!

"Enjoying it?"

"Yes, it's great!" Claire lied enthusiastically as she and David left their seats and headed for the theatre bar.

After fifteen minutes of inane chatter with other theatregoers they vaguely knew, Claire was delighted when the lights began to dim again and patrons made their way back to their seats. She couldn't wait for the second half to start, because then she could continue daydreaming about meeting her father. In the dark of the theatre, she crossed her fingers. There was so much she wanted to know about her past, and hopefully, the man who could tell her would soon become part of her future.

CHAPTER 55

Fiona was bereft. Young Alan Corcroft had tried to kill himself! She'd never thought she was harming anyone – it had just been a bit of fun, with both people gaining from the experience. But now that she viewed the situation objectively, she was shocked, ashamed and disgusted by her own behaviour. She'd forgotten that sex was something new and amazing for a young person. Instead, she'd toyed with a young boy's feelings, and her rejection had pushed him over the edge. Worst of all, her guilty little secret had been exposed, and Edwin would undoubtedly file for divorce.

She could hardly bear to look at Edwin since he'd received the phone call that evening from Benjamin Corcroft. She heard Benjamin blustering in the background as he told Edwin what happened, and she overheard the word 'court' which sent shivers down her spine. Edwin contributed little to the conversation, but when he'd come off the phone, his face had been white, and he'd simply stared at her with loathing, and she'd felt reduced to the level of an insect he might crush underfoot.

"Edwin, I –"

The words had stuck in her throat, and she'd been unable to say anything as her husband walked off in disgust. And in that one fateful moment, mild, gentle, harmless Edwin had had his life and his marriage overturned.

As Edwin went upstairs, Fiona dissolved into tears. She didn't blame Benjamin for phoning – after all, he was angry, and only protecting his son. Why had she only seen the harm she'd done with the clarity of hindsight? No doubt Jennifer would also feel her friend had broken a sacred trust, as indeed she had. Had she expected Alan to be an automaton? Perhaps it was because she'd always felt unlovable herself that she'd never believed someone could actually fall for her.

"I'm off."

Coming out of her reverie, Fiona stared at Edwin, who was now standing in front of her, suitcase in one hand and his laptop case over his shoulder. For a split second she thought he was leaving for good, then she remembered he'd been leaving today anyway, for a two-week business trip to Scotland on behalf of a client. It had been planned long before Benjamin's phone call had altered both their lives.

Fiona used her sleeve to wipe her eyes. "Oh, sorry – I'd forgotten about your trip."

As she spoke the words, she suspected that Edwin was thinking bitterly of how often he'd heard her use the word 'forgot' before. She'd been so busy catering for her own needs, and coping with her past, that she hadn't given any thought to Edwin's needs. He'd always been a safe haven for her painful insecurities, but she'd never once considered his own feelings, and now it was too late.

Edwin gave her a searching look, then, without saying another word, walked out the door. Within seconds, she heard the engine of his car starting. And she remembered how, in the early days of their marriage, she'd be standing at the door and waving each time he went away. Now, she could hear him driving off, and soon he'd no longer be a part of her life at all. Suddenly, she was filled with a desire to run to the door and call after him, but it was pointless now, since it was too late for everything.

Fiona sat back in an armchair and wept. Why did the past never go away? Why did its evil continue to leach into every aspect of life, even after you thought it had been consigned to the earth and given a decent burial?

In her desolation, Fiona's thoughts turned once again to her late father, the once-revered Dr Barker. As a child, she'd longed to tell her three friends what was happening behind closed doors in the Barker household, but her fear of being ostracised from the group was greater than her need to share her pain. She needed her friends desperately because, in a way, they were the only real family she had, and Fiona had no intention of being a victim twice over.

Their treatment of Zoe Gray confirmed Fiona's worst fears. As they all ganged up on the unfortunate Zoe, she herself became the most vociferous of bullies. Her anger might have been displaced, but victimising others helped her to regain some power and control over her own life.

Fiona wiped away a tear. In retrospect, she realised how cruel her behaviour to Zoe Gray had been. And now she'd broken Edwin's heart, and all for nothing, really. She should have gone for psychotherapy years ago, but she'd managed to keep a tight lid on all the memories of her father, never allowing any to escape. Up until now, she hadn't realised that they still affected every single thing she did.

She'd even denied poor Edwin a family. Irrationally, she'd been terrified that any child she had would grow up to be abused like her – if not by Edwin, by some stranger. As a child, and even as an adult, she'd felt that these men were everywhere. So she'd considered it safer to have no children. She'd pretended to Edwin that she was keen for a family, but she'd secretly taken the pill, and while poor Edwin consoled and supported her in her barrenness, he'd never realised that all the time she was fooling him.

I'm a despicable person, she told herself, tears streaming down her face. Edwin would never molest any child, and I've deprived him of any hope of being a father. Even now, if she wanted to, it was probably too late to conceive, since she was almost forty-two. Anyway, Edwin no longer wanted anything to do with her. Too late, she realised how much he meant to her.

CHAPTER 56

As Jennifer drove her Maserati towards the church, Anne gazed out of the passenger window as the countryside flew by. Jennifer was driving too fast, but Anne didn't dare say anything. Jennifer was in a strange mood, and Anne felt that any comment would only be seen as criticism of Jennifer's driving. At least she wouldn't be responsible if Jennifer was stopped and given a ticket!

She and Jennifer hadn't really spoken about what had happened to young Alan, and Anne wasn't sure how to broach the subject. Jennifer appeared distracted and didn't seem to want any conversation.

"How is Alan?" Anne asked tentatively.

"Fine," said Jennifer. "Storm in a teacup, if you ask me. Now, tell me again about these windows."

Anne had been surprised when Jennifer had asked her to check out the stained-glass windows in the church. She rarely had an opportunity to flaunt the knowledge she'd acquired at university, and these windows – if indeed they were Harry Clarke windows – would be amazing to see.

Anne secretly hoped that the windows weren't genuine, and she longed for the chance to put Jennifer in her place. She'd refreshed her knowledge of Harry Clarke on the Internet and at the library, and felt confident she could distinguish the Irish artist's work from that of other less important stained-glass artists.

But when they entered the church, Anne knew immediately that the windows were indeed Harry Clarke's work. Her heart sank. Why on earth was Jennifer so lucky? Everything fell into her lap – now she and the dreadful Benjamin had become the owners of a priceless art collection. It just wasn't fair.

Nevertheless, Anne felt she might as well use the opportunity to display her knowledge. She began explaining Harry Clarke's background in Dublin, his training in England and his preference for certain colours, but suddenly realised that Jennifer wasn't paying any attention.

Anne felt decidedly peeved since she'd expected a more favourable reaction. It was all very odd, but maybe Jennifer was more concerned about her son than she was letting on. In fact, Anne conceded, Jennifer's eyes weren't on the stained-glass windows at all. She kept looking everywhere except at the windows.

"Jennifer, are you alright?" Anne asked her. "You seem a little off colour today."

"No, no – I'm fine," Jennifer assured her. "How much do you think the windows are worth?"

"You'll need an art expert for that, but I expect you'll need to insure them for several hundred thousand."

Yet strangely, the woman whose biggest turn-on in life was money seemed surprisingly uninterested in Anne's pronouncement, and clearly preoccupied by something else.

"Jennifer, don't you want to know about the windows?" Anne asked, exasperated. "When you asked me to come here, I did some research, and I can tell you that these windows are a very rare, hitherto undiscovered collection of Harry Clarke's work – it's always been assumed that all his work was already known and catalogued."

"Marvellous," said Jennifer, quickly glancing at the windows. "I'm grateful for your help, Anne – now come upstairs with me, and let me show you the wonderful views from the top of the tower."

Anne shrugged her shoulders. Jennifer was behaving so oddly! She'd locked the church door from the inside after they'd entered, and left the key in the lock so that no one could open the door from the outside. When Anne had asked why, Jennifer informed her it was to prevent any of the locals interfering. Apparently, Jennifer had recently had an encounter with some nasty local woman.

Nevertheless, Anne felt that something very strange was going on. Jennifer had been acting weirdly all morning, and chattering inanely, which was totally out of character. She seemed slightly feverish, and Anne glanced at her surreptitiously, wondering if she might be running a temperature.

"Did you know that Harry Clarke was only forty-two when he died?" she said, hoping to stimulate some interest in the man she'd spent hours reading about.

"No, I didn't."

Anne couldn't see her friend's face but Jennifer was smiling to herself and thinking: You'll be around the same age when *you* die, Anne . . .

Anne was exhausted by the time she and Jennifer reached the top of the tower. She was still peeved at Jennifer's lack of interest in the windows, and was determined to pay her back by showing no interest in the view, no matter how spectacular it was.

Since Jennifer seemed so edgy, Anne wondered briefly if she was intending to confide in her. Could Jennifer be having difficulties in her marriage? Anne wouldn't be at all surprised. She didn't know how Jennifer endured Benjamin Corcroft's advances. Anne felt ill at the mere thought of that uncouth man touching her.

As she followed Jennifer through the trapdoor and out onto the roof, Anne was becoming more and more annoyed.

"Is this what you've been fussing about?" Anne said, looking disdainfully around her. The view was, in fact, stunning.

They were very high up, and Anne wondered briefly if the tower was safe. But of course it had to be – it was housing bells that weighed several tons. All the same, the edging along the tower wall didn't look very safe. The wall seemed to be crumbling in parts, and Anne felt decidedly uncomfortable at being so exposed to the elements. She couldn't see any reason why they needed to linger up there any longer. Even though it was summer, a cold wind was blowing, and it was turning Anne's hands blue.

"Jennifer, I think it's time we went back inside –"

"In a minute, Anne. Come over here and see the view from this side!"

Reluctantly, Anne treaded gingerly across the floor to where Jennifer was standing, thinking that the flagstones didn't look very safe either. There was definitely a crack in the wall where Jennifer was standing . . .

Suddenly, Jennifer knocked against her and Anne felt herself pitch forward. A scream rose to her lips as for a split second she thought she was going to fall over the side, and she grabbed one of the ornate bricks for support. Her immediate thought was that Jennifer had slipped and accidentally fallen against her, but when she turned and saw the malevolent expression on Jennifer's face, her brain seemed to stop functioning and she was unable to comprehend what was happening.

"*Aaaagh!*" Anne screamed as she turned over on her ankle. The shock and pain left her winded and, as she pulled herself up, she felt weak and disoriented. Suddenly Jennifer was dragging her towards the edge, and Anne felt under some strange hypnotic spell. She had to stop Jennifer, who'd clearly taken leave of her senses.

Suddenly, there was a loud cracking noise, followed by a piercing scream as part of the wall crumbled and fell away, and Anne found herself looking at a gap where the wall had been only seconds before. Where was Jennifer? Everything in her world seemed to be moving in slow motion . . .

Gradually, Anne's brain registered that it was Jennifer who'd fallen screaming through the gap in the wall. But, somehow, she couldn't even summon the energy to look down. Every part of her body felt like lead, as though she was in a submersion tank. With her head throbbing painfully, she summoned up the courage to crawl over to where the parapet had been. She felt dizzy when she looked over and saw Jennifer's crumpled body lying in the grass below. Jennifer's limbs were at odd angles, like a discarded rag doll, and she wasn't moving. It was obvious that she was dead. Anne felt an overwhelming urge to vomit, and she hurriedly stepped back from the edge, scared in case her dizziness might cause her to lose her balance and plummet over the edge too.

Later, she didn't remember how she'd got down the three flights of stairs and unlocked the door, or how she'd managed to call the emergency services on her mobile. Before long, an ambulance and paramedics arrived at the church, although a shocked and shivering Anne was unable to tell them anything.

As one of the paramedics wrapped a blanket round her shoulders, then took her blood pressure, Anne felt detached, as though she was watching some drama unfolding on television. This wasn't real. It couldn't be real. In a few minutes, she'd wake up and everything would be as it was. Jennifer would appear at her side, making some nasty comment about Benjamin, and all would be right again in her world.

Suddenly, Anne's teeth were chattering. Had she imagined it, or had Jennifer just tried to kill her? No, it couldn't be true – it was just the shock that was confusing her thoughts. Her friend would never do that. On the other hand, what other explanation could there be? After all, Jennifer had orchestrated this visit to the church, and she'd been overly keen to get Anne up to the top of the bell tower.

No, she was being ridiculous. What possible reason could Jennifer have for wanting her out of the way? They'd been friends since schooldays – there was no way Jennifer would try to kill her. It had just been a horrible tragedy.

Suddenly, Anne recalled another horrible tragedy thirty years earlier, when Zoe Gray had ended her own life because of their bullying. Anne began to shiver violently as her mind filled with unbidden images of her and her three friends taunting the hapless Zoe. After a lifetime of suppressing these images, there was suddenly no escape. Anne broke down and began to weep.

CHAPTER 57

Zoe's Diary

April 14

Although the bleeding has thankfully stopped, the bullies are still taunting me about being unclean. Today, they tried to get me into trouble at Leonard's store. Why are they so vindictive? I've never done anything to deserve their nastiness.

As she walked home from school, Zoe was delighted to find a twenty-pence piece near the crossroads. Despite all the stress she was coping with, it seemed like a wonderful piece of serendipity, and she headed to Leonard's Stores in the centre of the village.

Today had been a good day in other ways too. She'd managed to sneak past the bullies by crossing one of the fields behind the school, thereby avoiding the crossroads where they were usually waiting. She knew it wouldn't be long before they discovered her new route, but she felt pleased at getting one over on them for today at least.

"Hello, Mr Leonard," Zoe said to the owner as she entered the shop.

"Hello, Zoe," Mr Leonard replied. "In the money today, are we?"

Zoe nodded, smiling. "I found a twenty-pence piece on my way home, and I'm going to get Claire a Swizzle bar and myself a Jacko bar. Or maybe Claire would prefer some bonbons – I can't make up my mind!"

Mr Leonard smiled. "Take your time, Zoe – there's a big selection to choose from!"

She gazed at all the assorted confectionary, and thought how wonderful it would be to try them all. Lost in thought, she gazed at the tubes of sweets, packets of sherbet, liquorice shoelaces and sticks of holiday rock with Trentham-on-Sea running through them.

Preoccupied with so many possibilities, Zoe didn't notice that the four bullies had silently entered the shop. As she made her way along the aisle where all the sweets were displayed, the bullies suddenly pushed past her, sniggering and looking back as she stared after them. Her heart sank. What on earth were they up to now?

Having finally decided on her original choice, Zoe approached the counter where Mr Leonard was adding up his till receipts.

"I've decided on these," she said, smiling as she placed a Jacko bar and a Swizzle bar on the counter, along with the twenty-pence piece.

"Good choice, Zoe," said Mr Leonard, smiling back.

Just at the moment, the four bullies also approached the counter, crowding in behind Zoe, while one of them aimed a kick at her shin. As Zoe tried to leave, they grabbed her and hauled her back.

"Mr Leonard, I think you need to search Zoe Gray's pockets," said Jennifer, grinning spitefully.

"Yes," said Anne authoritatively. "I saw her put a chocolate bar in her pocket, and she hasn't paid for it!"

"Look, here it is!" said Fiona, triumphantly pulling a bar of expensive chocolate out of the back pocket of Zoe's school skirt.

The colour drained from Zoe's face. "I didn't take it, Mr Leonard!" she cried, almost in tears. "I'd never do anything like that!"

"We saw her," said Anne. "Didn't we, girls?"

Jennifer, Fiona and Emma all nodded.

As Zoe stood silent and shivering, Mr Leonard looked at the excited faces of Zoe's four accusers as they anticipated her humiliation. He leaned forward conspiratorially.

"Follow me – all of you," he whispered to the five girls, and he led them to the back of the shop. Zoe trailed behind the others, unsure of what humiliation or punishment might be waiting for her there.

"Look up there," said Mr Leonard, pointing to the ceiling, "There are several hidden cameras up on the ceiling, which I can watch from behind the counter."

He smiled at their incredulous faces.

"You can't see them, can you? That's because they're so well hidden. But I can see everything that goes on in my store."

He looked around him, studying each girl in turn.

"I saw exactly what happened," he said, wagging a finger at Anne, Fiona, Jennifer and Emma, "So I know young Zoe didn't put that chocolate bar in her pocket. One of you four did it, and I know which of you it was."

He looked sternly from one to the other, and each of the four girls flushed crimson. He didn't actually know who'd done it, but they were all equally to blame as far as he was concerned.

"Now, I suggest you four leave here at once, while I decide whether to tell your parents or not."

He chuckled to himself as the four left the shop, their heads bowed and looking dejected and chastened. There were no hidden cameras, but he could spot a sting a mile away. Anyway, it would be helpful if word got out that there were cameras in his store, since it might cut down on pilferage by the local schoolchildren.

Concerned, he looked at the eldest Gray child. "Are you alright, Zoe?"

She nodded. She'd been crying with shock, but some colour was now returning to her cheeks.

"Thanks, Mr Leonard, I'm so glad you believed me. I'd never take anything –"

"I know that, Zoe. But you've got some powerful enemies there – what have you done that's made that lot so vindictive?"

Zoe shook her head. "I don't know, Mr Leonard. They've been picking on me for ages. Sometimes I wonder how long I can . . ."

Zoe's voice trailed off with a sigh, and Mr Leonard felt a surge of anger towards the four girls who were making this poor child's life a misery.

"Here, you might as well keep the chocolate bar," said Mr Leonard kindly, handing the supposedly stolen bar to Zoe.

"Oh but I couldn't, Mr Leonard –"

"Take it, Zoe," he said good-naturedly. "Make the most of it while I'm feeling generous!"

"Well, thanks, Mr Leonard, if you're really sure –"

As Zoe left the store, Mr Leonard gazed after her. It was funny how the nice ones always got picked on. Those two Gray children had a difficult life, and he didn't know how they coped with that alcoholic mother and absent father. He wished he could bar the other four girls from his store permanently, but their families brought a lot of business his way, and one of them was the doctor's daughter, so he could be opening up a can of worms for himself if he did . . .

He sighed as he began to make up the weekly orders for delivery. He'd throw in a few extra tomatoes and a cauliflower with the Grays' order next week. And maybe a few Jacko and Swizzle bars for those poor girls . . .

In the street, the four bullies were seething with rage. Their little plan to get Zoe into trouble had backfired. Each longed to blame the others for their humiliation, but they'd all been willing participants in the plan.

"I'll never go into that shop again!" said Anne, her face red with fury at being caught out. "Whose idea was this anyway?"

"Yours, actually," said Fiona, pleased she hadn't been the one to think it up. "You thought Mr Leonard would believe us because we're from better-off families than Zoe Gray, but he didn't, did he? He saw through our plan, because it was stupid!"

"You were fully in agreement earlier!" said Anne, furious at Fiona's attack.

"Do you think he'll really contact our families?" Emma asked, looking worried. *"If my mother hears about this, I'll be grounded!"*

"I doubt it," said Jennifer authoritatively. *"He's only a shopkeeper, after all. He needs our families' custom – I wish I'd thought of reminding him of that."*

"Look – there's Zoe Gray!" said Fiona suddenly, *"Come on – let's make her pay!"*

But Zoe had seen them as she'd left Mr Leonard's store, and had dodged into the bakery next door, where she waited patiently inside until the baker was leaving to make a delivery to the hotel. Since he was driving past the cottage, he was happy to drop her off on his way.

From the far side of the village square, the four bullies watched Zoe get into the baker's van.

"Watch out, Zoe Gray," Jennifer muttered under her breath. *"We'll get you when you're least expecting it."*

The others nodded in agreement. As far as they were concerned, they were only beginning their campaign. Zoe Gray might have won a minor victory, but they intended to win the war.

Back home, Zoe felt crushed by the weight of all that had happened to her. But she put on a bright smile as she presented Claire with the Swizzle bar, and told her about finding the twenty-pence piece.

"Then why is your face looking all funny?" Claire asked astutely. *"I know you've been crying – your eyes look red and watery."*

"Oh, I – well, I fell and hurt my arm when I was walking home. But it's okay now."

Claire said nothing, but she knew Zoe was lying.

"And I've got a bar of chocolate for us to share after dinner!" added Zoe, smiling brightly.

"How did you get it?" Claire asked, closely watching Zoe's

face. Chocolate bars were expensive, and Claire knew Zoe didn't have the money for anything like that.

"Mr Leonard gave it to me."

"Why would he do that?"

"I think he was just in a good mood."

Claire looked dubious. "Come on, Zoe – tell me the truth," she said, hands on her hips, trying to look stern.

Zoe was amused at Claire's stance, and she grabbed her little sister and twirled her around, then the two sisters dissolved into a fit of giggling and tickling. But despite the laughter, Claire knew that Zoe's gaiety was contrived. And she was worried, because Zoe always looked so sad lately. Claire would notice a far-away look on her face, but Zoe would instantly brighten when she realised her sister was watching her.

Could Zoe be worried about her schoolwork? Or all the responsibility at home? Instantly, Claire decided to help more around the house, to keep her room tidier and to wash her own school blouse at the weekends. Now that she'd turned nine, it wasn't fair to expect Zoe to do it all the time. Claire was willing to do anything to see her sister happy again.

CHAPTER 58

Clive sat in his rooms in the Commons and stared at the old portraits on the walls without actually seeing them. His mind was elsewhere, and he couldn't concentrate on anything. He'd asked his PA to divert all calls, since he wasn't in the mood to speak to anyone. He couldn't believe that Jennifer was dead. In his own way, he'd loved her, and it was heartbreaking to think he'd never see her again. They'd spent so many fun-filled and exciting times together.

But another part of him was actually relieved. Jennifer had been talking of leaving Benjamin, and worse still, she'd been prompting him to leave Anne. Which was never going to happen. While Jennifer had provided excitement and fun, Anne was the solid base on which his career as a politician was built. If it had come to a confrontation with Jennifer, he'd have had to tell her he couldn't leave Anne, and then who knows what she'd have done? As long as they'd both been married, everything had been fine, since each had as much to lose as the other. But the scales had tipped dangerously when Jennifer informed him she was going to divorce Benjamin, and she expected a greater commitment from him in return. A commitment he could never make to her.

Clive had always known that Jennifer married Benjamin on the rebound from his own marriage to Anne. Often, over the years, he'd wondered how different his life might have been if he'd met Jennifer first. But this way, he'd had the best of both worlds. He'd had a wife who adored him, and a lover who'd excited him and had been prepared to take risks to keep their sexual relationship always on the boil. Fondly, he now recalled the only enjoyable aspect of the garden party, when he and Jennifer had slipped away and made love in the woods. The risk of being caught had always been an added fillip for both of them.

But lately he'd seen a side of Jennifer that he hadn't liked. While he was aware that Benjamin wasn't exactly top-drawer, the man was likeable nonetheless. Yet Jennifer had been prepared to dump him simply because he'd lost some of his wealth and had reconnected with his family whom she despised.

For a brief while, Clive had been deeply worried. He hadn't wanted the well-oiled machinery of his life to be dismantled, yet that was precisely what Jennifer had been demanding. She'd wanted him to leave Anne and eventually marry her, which would have created a messy situation all round. If that had happened, he'd certainly have had to kiss goodbye to any hopes of heading a ministry.

Clive shuddered. That disastrous garden party had almost finished his career, but luckily, the Conservatives needed him as much as he needed them, and the press had been quietly asked to play down the story. The Tories had enough media friends in high places to ensure that the story quickly died, and the few who'd got food poisoning were warned to keep quiet about their suffering. So the fallout hadn't been as bad as might have been expected.

Clive bit his lip. Poor Anne was also very shaken by Jennifer's death. The experience of being present when the wall broke away and carried Jennifer to her death would stay with her for a long time. Maybe he'd take her abroad for a holiday to lift her spirits. The Commons was already in recess for the summer, so he'd take her somewhere nice, maybe back to the Seychelles where they'd honeymooned all those years ago. A second honeymoon would cement their relationship again, and he could assure her – this time, truthfully – that she was the only woman in his life. After all, he was going to need Anne's support in the next election, which was likely to be held in the next six months.

Clive lifted the phone, rang his PA and asked her to check availability to the Seychelles later that month. Might as well get it organised now and surprise Anne with the tickets.

As he sat staring at the walls again, Clive felt a momentary pang of loss. Jennifer had been such fun, and always eager to satisfy him. He doubted he'd ever replace her. There might be an occasional dalliance here or there, but a long-term relationship would be rather tricky when he was a minister. Clive felt a great sense of relief that Anne never found out about his relationship with Jennifer, and now that Jennifer was dead, she never would.

Suddenly, Clive felt almost cheerful as he contemplated the holiday ahead. One part of his life had ended, but another had just begun.

CHAPTER 59

Benjamin stood staring out the kitchen window. It was hard to believe that Jennifer was dead. Even though he'd been planning to divorce her, he wished her life hadn't ended so tragically. He also hoped he was up to the job of caring for the children and helping them through their grief.

The kitchen door creaked open, and he knew immediately that Vanessa had entered the room. Her face was tear-stained, and Benjamin knew she'd been crying again.

"Hello, pet – are you okay?"

"Fine, Dad – can I talk to you about Mum's funeral?"

"Of course, love. But you don't have to worry, I'll organise everything –"

"Dad – could we have an environmentally friendly coffin for Mum? You know, one of those wicker ones? Willow is a local, sustainable wood."

Benjamin looked at her solemn young face and was overwhelmed by the desire to hug her and never let her go.

"Of course, pet – that's a really nice idea. I'm sure you mother would like that."

Benjamin had to stifle a smile until Vanessa had gone. Jennifer would have hated the idea – if Gucci made coffins, then Jennifer would have wanted one! As for the environment, she'd never given a damn about it during her lifetime – all she'd wanted was to keep her own expensive lifestyle on track. Now, Benjamin got a perverse delight at the thought of Jennifer going to her final resting place in a cheap wicker basket!

Of course, he had to face the fact that he hadn't been a great supporter of the environment himself. But since Vanessa came back from Walthamstow, she'd been quizzing him about the viability of building environmentally friendly houses in future. He grinned. Between his daughter and Georgie, he was surrounded by very strong and opinionated women!

Hugh, Maisie and Carl were subdued as they arrived at The Old Vicarage in Hugh's big white van. Since Hugh still needed regular dialysis at the local hospital, their visit would be brief, but he wanted to support his brother at this difficult time. He and Maisie were in awe of the opulent surroundings, and unsure of how they should behave.

"Sorry for your trouble, Benny," said Hugh, grasping his brother's hand, clearly embarrassed and at a loss to know what to say. He'd only met Jennifer a few times, he hadn't liked her at all, and now that made him feel guilty.

Maisie hugged Benjamin. "Sorry, love – you must be in a terrible state. Look, I've baked some apple pies for the funeral afters – I'll go put them in the fridge."

Benjamin was deeply moved, and hadn't the heart to tell her that the afters for the funeral were being held in one of the hotels in the nearest town. He hadn't wanted the hassle of having the house full of hangers-on, so the easiest option was to book the best local hotel and provide lunch for anyone who came to the funeral.

Vanessa came hurrying into the hall, hugging each of them in turn. Carl took a card from his pocket and handed it to her.

With trembling fingers, Vanessa opened the envelope and extracted the condolences card. It said: 'Vanessa – sorry about your mum.' It was signed by Rozzer, Jack and Leggo.

Vanessa dissolved into floods of tears, and Carl held her as she sobbed. She was deeply touched by the three young men's efforts to reach out to her. She suspected that Carl was the instigator, but that didn't lessen the impact of their effort.

Alan, who'd been upstairs playing mournful tunes on his guitar, came downstairs and finally met his family from Walthamstow. He, too, was in a highly emotional state, although he tried to hide it. Carl, understanding how he felt, distracted him by asking questions about his band.

In the kitchen, Vanessa filled the kettle and turned it on to boil. It was Mrs Quick's day off, although she'd offered to come in and help in any way she could. But Benjamin had declined, feeling that right now, he, Vanessa and Alan needed to be alone. Of course, Maisie, Hugh and Carl were family, so their presence was both welcome and comforting.

"Oh dear, everything in this house is so perfect," said Maisie nervously, as Vanessa asked her to take down some mugs from a high shelf. "I'm afraid to touch anything in case I damage it!"

"Don't worry, Aunt Maisie – honestly," Vanessa reassured her. "Please make yourself at home. Mum –"

It had been on the tip of Vanessa's tongue to say that her mother would have wanted them to feel comfortable, but she knew that wasn't true. Jennifer would have been appalled to think that these people whom she'd hated were now coming to her funeral. So it's just as well she'll never know, Vanessa thought. While alive, her mother had tried to keep a tight control over everything. In death, she'd finally lost her grip.

"I'm sure you miss your mum terribly," said Maisie kindly, "but you've got us now, so don't be lonely – we're here to support you, in any way we can."

Vanessa nodded. It was good to have family around her. She'd never realised the importance of kin before now.

Since her mother's tragic death, Vanessa had tried to keep busy. All the activity kept her from thinking, because that meant examining her feelings. On the one hand, she'd loved her mother deeply, and wept in private for the woman who'd raised her, and who'd often been kind and caring. On the other hand, she'd loathed her mother's snobbery, and was racked with guilt because she'd hated her for having an affair and risking the family's happiness.

Vanessa wondered if Clive Ellwood would be at the funeral. No doubt he and Anne would be at the church, basking in their role as community benefactors as well as personal friends. How she wished she could wipe the smug look off their faces by telling them what she knew! She wondered briefly how Clive Ellwood was feeling. Had he actually cared for her mother? Or had it just been a fling that was now conveniently over?

Vanessa also wondered how her poor brother was coping. Alan didn't show his feelings but she knew he'd loved their mother as much as she had. At least his grieving could be straightforward and uncomplicated, since he wasn't burdened with the knowledge of their mother's affair.

Of course, her poor brother would soon have his own demons to face when his court case was scheduled but, luckily, as a minor, he wouldn't be named publicly. Vanessa had always doubted the wisdom of contacting the police. What was the point? Fiona had sex with a minor, but Alan had been a willing participant. Alan had tried to kill himself because she rejected him, not because she seduced him, and his pain was what needed to be addressed. Sometimes, she thought, their father had a tendency to act before thinking things through . . .

When Vanessa returned to the kitchen, everyone had finished their tea, and Benjamin and Uncle Hugh had gone out to the van to bring in the suitcases. There were an awful lot of them, Vanessa noticed. She suspected that Aunt Maisie had been unable to decide what was suitable attire for a 'posh' funeral, so she'd brought everything she possessed just in case.

"Are you okay, cuz?" Carl asked her, as Aunt Maisie poured her another cup of tea.

She nodded, not trusting herself to speak. When anyone expressed concern, she invariably dissolved into tears, and it was very embarrassing.

"If you ever want to talk," he added, "just let me know."

Vanessa nodded. Her pain was still raw and she hadn't yet come to terms with it. But if she needed to talk to anyone, Carl would definitely be someone she'd confide in.

But there was someone else who always understood, and in whom she'd confided many secrets over the years. Slipping on a jacket, Vanessa collected her bicycle and rode the half-mile to the stables. Grey Star was waiting for her, and he whinnied softly with pleasure as she approached.

Untying a bale of hay, Vanessa carried it into his stable, hugged him and dug into her pocket for the sugar treats he loved so much. As she felt his warm breath on her face, Vanessa finally let go and cried unashamedly. In Grey Star's company, at last she could be herself. The gentle pony knew something was wrong, and he nuzzled her, whinnying softly to comfort her as she wept.

CHAPTER 60

On the morning of the funeral, all the Corcrofts assembled for breakfast in the kitchen of The Old Vicarage. It was a solemn affair, and when Hugh started telling a joke, he was quickly cut short by his wife, who feared that any frivolity might upset Alan and Vanessa.

"It's okay, Maisie," Benjamin said, leaning over and patting her hand. "A joke might be what we need to liven things up a bit. I know it's a sad day, but being miserable won't make it any easier for us."

Benjamin himself felt a strange ambivalence about Jennifer's death. For so long, she'd been a part of his life, and initially a major player in his financial success. He had many bittersweet memories of their years together, but her betrayal had overshadowed everything else. She'd robbed him of his right to parenthood – certainly of one child, possibly two – and he'd never forgive her for that. At least now he didn't need to tell them he'd been planning to divorce her.

Briefly, he thought of Georgie, and a smile crept unbidden across his face. Then he felt a pang of guilt – he was fortunate to have someone waiting for him, whereas Jennifer was irreplaceable to the children.

Shortly after breakfast, Jennifer's family arrived, and Benjamin felt deeply sorry for her mother. No parent should ever have to see their child die – it went against the natural order of things. Normally a glamorous and elegant woman, Mrs Lambe now looked as though she'd aged a decade overnight. As Benjamin hugged her, she felt like a bag of crumbling bones, and he suspected that the shock of Jennifer's death might soon hasten her own demise.

Despite introductions to Hugh, Maisie and Carl, the Lambes sat huddled together as they drank the teas and coffees Vanessa and Alan placed in front of them. The cousins, who were younger than Alan and Vanessa, sat quietly by their parents' side, and Benjamin wondered with amusement what they'd been told about the common-as-muck Corcrofts.

Eventually, it was time to leave for the church. The funeral cars had arrived and were parked outside on the gravel, the drivers in their dark suits with subdued and deferential expressions on their faces.

As he sat in the back of the stretch limousine with Vanessa and Alan, Benjamin wondered what Jennifer had been doing at the church that day. According to Anne, she'd been interested in the value of the windows for insurance purposes. Even more surprising was that she'd also been there the day before, because Georgie told him they'd exchanged a few terse words.

Georgie had promised to attend the funeral, but they'd agreed not to make a point of acknowledging each other. Nevertheless, her presence would give him moral support, and he could be strong for the children just knowing she was there.

When they'd talked on the phone the previous evening, he'd told her how much he longed to spend the following night with her.

"Don't even think of it – you've two children who'll need all your support after the funeral," she'd told him firmly. "Besides, we'll have all the time in the world later."

He'd been secretly thrilled by her words, because they seemed to indicate she was thinking of a future with him, too.

As the cars turned into the old churchyard, Benjamin surveyed the assembled crowds. Anne and Clive were to the forefront of the crowd. Benjamin had never liked Anne, but he genuinely hoped she wasn't too traumatised after witnessing Jennifer's death. According to Clive, she'd been in quite a state for days afterwards, and had been babbling incessantly about some incident that took place during her schooldays. No doubt Clive would also be using the funeral to promote his bid for a ministerial post by pressing the flesh at every opportunity.

Benjamin grunted to himself. For every genuine person who'd be attending today, there'd be at least as many hangers-on and people using the occasion for their own benefit. No doubt all the old dears of the parish would be lining up for their free lunch at the hotel. Well, so what, he thought. He didn't care. After today, he was finished with all these people. They might have mattered to Jennifer, but he didn't give a toss about any of them. While she was alive, he'd allowed her to dictate who his friends were and how he lived his life, and she'd made a mockery of him at every opportunity. From now on, he was going to do things *his* way.

As Benjamin stepped out of the limousine, Clive greeted him warmly, no longer needing to feel guilty since his affair with Jennifer was now conveniently consigned to history.

As Anne stepped forward to hug him, Benjamin was shocked by her appearance. Her eyes were hollow and her skin had an unnatural hue. In fact, Benjamin thought she'd the distinct look of a corpse herself. Jennifer's death had obviously affected her badly, so maybe he'd underestimated their fondness for each other.

It felt odd not having Fiona and Edwin present. Benjamin knew that Edwin was away on business – he'd sent Benjamin a condolence card from Scotland, signed on behalf of both himself and Fiona. Benjamin liked Edwin, and deeply regretted that they could no longer be friends. He felt ambivalent about Fiona – he felt sorry for her as Jennifer's friend, but he hated her for the harm she'd done to Alan. Glancing at his son, he wondered what painful emotions were running through the boy's head today. In a sense, Alan was grieving for two women – the mother he'd just lost, and the woman who'd been his first love.

Suddenly, Benjamin recalled an Easter weekend he'd spent in Trentham-on-Sea as a kid, and the girl he'd met collecting seaweed on the beach. He'd been looking forward to seeing her again the next day, but there'd been an unfortunate change of plan . . .

Emma was weeping loudly and copiously, and generally creating a scene. Most people assumed she was Jennifer's sister or at least some close relative, and she was lapping up all the attention. Benjamin wondered for the umpteenth time what on earth could have drawn this odd collection of women together.

After the service, the vicar led the prayers as the coffin was wheeled out into the sunlight by the funeral parlour staff. Benjamin, Vanessa and Alan followed it, with Jennifer's family close behind. Hugh, Maisie and Carl followed them, and with his children on either side, linking arms, Benjamin pressed them tightly to him as they walked down the cemetery path to Jennifer's final resting place. Today was a defining moment in their young lives, and he wanted to ensure that they knew he was there for them one hundred per cent.

Everyone was subdued as the funeral cortege reached the freshly dug grave, and Benjamin knew that this would be the hardest part for the children. They'd have to say their final goodbyes to their mother, and hear the thud of clay on her coffin as she was consigned to the earth.

In the crowd surrounding the grave, Benjamin noticed his foreman from the Stonegate Farm project, his architects, and most of his brickies and site clearance workers, and Mrs Quick their housekeeper. Georgie was there too, looking demure in a dark suit. He also recognised several of the protesters from Stonehill village, but it was obvious they hadn't come to gloat, but to sympathise, and Benjamin was deeply touched by their ability to set aside their differences and give support when it was needed.

As the vicar intoned the final blessing, Benjamin leaned

forward, and dropped a red rose onto Jennifer's coffin. When Georgie had suggested he make this final gesture, he'd felt it would be hypocritical. But she'd made him realise he'd be doing it for his children. Vanessa and Alan would find strength in believing that their parents had been happy together.

Watching her father drop the rose onto the coffin, Vanessa was moved by his gesture, but not for the reason her father intended. She was watching a man who'd been cheated on, and she gave his hand an affectionate squeeze. She'd hoped to get through the day without crying, but as she looked down at her mother's willow coffin in the deep grave, her eyes filled with tears, and a lump in her throat threatened to overwhelm her. Goodbye, Mum, she whispered, I love you and miss you so much . . .

Alan seemed in a catatonic state, moving like an automaton as though he wasn't part of the ceremony at all. Vanessa felt a stab of pity for her brother. He was so ill-equipped to deal with all the things that had happened to him. Right now, Vanessa felt like an older sister. Gently, she squeezed his hand, and felt him squeeze hers back. She didn't dare look at him, since she knew they were both crying. But she felt reassured by his response. Even without their mother, they were still a family, and somehow they'd all get through this together.

CHAPTER 61

Alone in her kitchen, Fiona stared out across the lawns of Bloomfield House. Never had she felt so isolated. She hadn't dared go to Jennifer's funeral the previous day, although she'd longed to pay her respects to her old friend. Under different circumstances, she, Anne and Emma would have been supporting each other through this tragedy. Now she was a pariah and no one was phoning anymore.

When she'd read about Jennifer's death in the newspapers, she'd felt as though her whole world had come crashing down around her. Hot bitter tears had trickled down her cheeks, and she'd wished with all her heart that she'd been on better terms with Jennifer before her fatal accident. But her treatment of young Alan had already severed that bond between them.

Looking around the large kitchen, she eyed the beautiful streamlined units, the latest hob and oven, the huge American-style fridge-freezer. They'd all been bought in the last year, and paid for by Edwin, in an attempt to make her happy. But they hadn't made her happy, and she'd treated her husband appallingly despite his generosity. A new kitchen couldn't fix what was wrong with her. She doubted if anything could. Anyway, she'd soon have to forsake the sweeping lawns and majestic flowerbeds of

Bloomfield and find herself a bedsitter somewhere, which was all she deserved.

Suddenly, the phone rang. At first, Fiona ignored it, but its insistent ringing began to get on her nerves. Reluctantly she got up and lifted the receiver. She could always bang it down again if it was someone who wanted to hurl insults at her.

"Fiona?"

Relief flooded through her as she recognised the voice, but was just as quickly replaced by fear. Was Emma going to yell at her, tell her what an appalling human being she was?

"Y-yes."

"Are you okay? I heard what happened. I couldn't believe it, I mean, why would you –"

"Look, if you've rung to give me a lecture –"

"No, no I haven't – sorry, I only rang to see if you're alright."

Tears filled Fiona's eyes. It seemed that Emma was the only one who wasn't prepared to judge her. Anne had clearly sided with Jennifer and Benjamin. She couldn't blame Anne for avoiding her – she'd done a terrible thing, and a boy had nearly ended his life because of her behaviour.

"Thanks, Ems – it's good of you to call. If you want the truth, I feel like shit. Benjamin rang Edwin and told him everything. Anyway, Edwin's away on a business trip right now, and being apart is probably a good thing."

"Look, I'll come round," said Emma decisively. "You shouldn't be on your own at a time like this."

"I'm not very good company right now –"

"I'm not coming round for scintillating conversation. I'm your friend, and I want to help you, if I can."

After they'd hung up, Fiona felt a little better, if it was possible to feel better in her present situation. Why had she been so stupid, only realising what she had when she was about to lose it? And for what? For a tawdry little grope with boys less than half her age, and all because she couldn't cope with sex with a real man. Now she'd almost destroyed a young man's life, because she'd been so self-centred and forgotten how painful rejection could be.

By the time Emma arrived an hour later, Fiona had taken a shower and dressed. Her eyes were still red from crying, but she felt better for having made the effort.

Emma made a point of hugging Fiona, prompting more tears as the two women clung together.

"Emma, I'm thoroughly ashamed of myself," Fiona said, looking earnestly at her friend. "I know you're shocked that I've been unfaithful to Edwin, and that I've been amusing myself with young boys – I'm shocked at my own behaviour. Instead of dealing with my problems years ago, I've allowed them to fester. And now I've destroyed my marriage, and let down Edwin, the most decent man I ever met."

Fiona's speech brought on another bout of crying, and Emma patted her back awkwardly.

Emma felt strange being the one in control – it was usually she who was the insecure one in the group, the one looking for approval from the others. Of course, now that she thought about it, there was no group anymore. Despite all the years of shared friendship, it had fragmented and splintered in an instant.

"Do you think you're afraid of men?" Emma asked, as they walked into the kitchen, and Fiona was startled by her friend's perception. Before she could answer, Emma was talking again.

"That's my problem too – I can only chat up a man when I've had a few glasses of wine," Emma confided. "But by then I'm pissed, and I behave stupidly, so I ruin any chance I might've had. I think I deliberately sabotage my chances, because I'm afraid to take things any further."

Fiona nodded, squeezing Emma's hand in sympathy. Over the years, she and the others had often speculated as to whether or not Emma was still a virgin. Now Fiona thought guiltily of all the times in school when she, Anne and Jennifer had made Emma into their scapegoat. On other occasions, they'd made her do things she clearly didn't want to do, just to prove to themselves that they could make her do them. Tears of guilt filled Fiona's eyes. Even after all those indignities and mistreatment, Emma was the only friend who'd come to give her support.

Emma gave a lopsided smile. "I think maybe I write children's books because I've never really grown up myself. It might help you to know that – you're not the only one who's screwed up their life."

"Oh Ems!"

Suddenly, the two women were hugging each other again.

This time, Fiona didn't even bother to wipe away her tears. Why hadn't they confided in each other before? In fact, none of their group had ever shared any real confidences. If they had, maybe she and Emma might have made a better go of their lives to date. Fiona wondered why it took a shameful revelation like hers to bring them closer than they'd ever been before.

When the women broke apart, Fiona crossed to the kitchen worktop. "I haven't even made you a cup of tea yet," she said, turning on the electric kettle, and taking down two mugs for tea. "It's also time I told you why I've been behaving this way. I'm tired of secrets, Emma. They have a way of stopping you from being yourself. Secrets mean you always have to be on your guard, even with the people you care about." She gave a sad smile. "In fact, it's mostly with the people you care about, because you don't want them to know the kind of person you really are."

"You're a good person, Fiona," Emma said stoutly. "You've always been a good friend to me."

Fiona felt the tears gathering behind her eyelids. And she remembered again the cruel way she and the others had treated Emma during their schooldays. And for the second time since Emma's arrival, Fiona felt her face burn with shame.

When the tea was made, Fiona brought the cups to the table and the two women sat in companionable silence.

"I wish I could have gone to Jennifer's funeral," Fiona said at last.

Emma nodded. "I wish you could've been there too. Those two kids were so dignified – I was the one who was crying and making a show of myself."

"And Benjamin?"

"He seemed okay. He was gracious and pleasant to everyone.

Needless to say, Clive was playing his 'I'm an MP' role as usual. Did you know Benjamin supplied lunch for everyone at the Hayfield Hotel?"

Fiona raised her eyebrows, although she wasn't really surprised. Benjamin had always been a generous man.

"I just can't believe Jennifer's gone," she whispered, as the tears began again.

Emma's eyes also filled up. "I keep remembering the things we did, the places we went together. Nothing will ever be the same again, will it?"

Lost in their own thoughts, the tea in both women's cups grew cold.

CHAPTER 62

Claire was shocked to hear of Jennifer's death. As she sat at her desk, reading the morning newspapers before her first client arrived, all of them carried variations of the headline '*MP's Wife Witnesses Death Plunge*'. The small print told how the two friends were admiring the view from the tower of the old church in Stonehill, owned by Jennifer and her wealthy developer husband, when part of the tower wall gave way, and Jennifer fell to her death. Claire now felt guilty that she'd ever wished the dead woman harm.

She was also filled with regret that she'd given the photo of Jennifer and Clive to Hazel – maybe Hazel wouldn't use it now that Jennifer was dead? On the other hand, she'd traded the photo for information on her father, so now it was Hazel's to use as she chose.

When Claire received a letter from her father, she was ecstatic. He was willing to meet her! After almost thirty years of wondering what had happened to him, she'd soon have the answers she craved. But she was also nervous, and unsure of how this initial meeting might go. Would they like each other? Would there be awkward gaps in conversation? Was the time gap too great to be bridged?

Claire arrived at David's apartment that evening, clutching the letter, a wide grin on her face. All evening she chattered about the proposed meeting, what she'd wear, where the meeting would take place, and David was pleased for her.

"You'll come with me when I meet him, won't you, love?" Claire begged David, as they ate dinner at the large table in David's kitchen. "I'm scared about seeing him for the first time, and I'd really like you there for moral support."

"You'll be fine on your own," said David, in between mouthfuls of casserole.

"But what if it doesn't work out, and I want to get away?"

David grinned. "I'm sure you and your dad will have so much to talk about that I'll be superfluous!"

"Please, darling – it might be a disaster," Claire wheedled. "I might need you there to keep the conversation going, or extricate me from any awkward situations."

"Okay, if you insist," he said, smiling. "But I'm sure you're both going to get along fine. He is your dad, after all. You knew and loved him all those years ago, why wouldn't you feel the same about him now?"

Claire nodded. "I suppose so. But there's so much I need to know. I mean, what kept him away for thirty years? Does he know about Zoe's death? Why did he and Mum break up? I'm hoping he can give me some answers."

CHAPTER 63

In the days immediately following Jennifer's funeral, many people called to The Old Vicarage, either to pay their respects, bring cooked meals, or invite the family to their homes for a meal. Benjamin was deeply touched by people's generosity and kindness, but he knew that before long this sentiment would dry up, and they'd be left to face life as a family of just three.

In fact, they were doing fine as a family already. Breakfast time at The Old Vicarage had become a sleepy affair. Neither Vanessa, Alan or Benjamin were morning people, and now that Jennifer wasn't there to shriek about their bad manners, they could give way to their natural inclinations and munch their breakfasts in silence without anyone else being offended.

Benjamin was also pleased to see the close bond that had developed between Alan and Vanessa. Alan seemed to be coping well with the loss of his mother and his first devastating experience of love. He was attending weekly counselling sessions at the hospital, and they appeared to be providing a beneficial outlet for all Alan's pain.

The boy was also realising he now had the freedom to think for himself and to do what he wanted. Benjamin knew he'd felt stifled by Jennifer's insistence that Cambridge was the only route he could follow. Now he was finding solace in his music, and Benjamin often heard him singing in his bedroom, and was amazed that such a powerful voice was coming from a fifteen-year-old boy.

But this particular morning, Benjamin was more alert than usual.

"Kids, I need to talk to you about something."

Alan lifted his head from his cereal bowl, and Vanessa suspended her slice of toast midway between the plate and her mouth.

"Yesterday, I got the results of my final test back from the hospital, and I'm fully compatible with your Uncle Hugh. So I'm going to give him one of my kidneys, if that's okay with both of you."

Both children nodded.

"I'll be in hospital for about six days, so I'll arrange for Mrs Quick to stay here and look after you." He paused. "Or you could stay with Maisie and Carl instead. You'd be on your own a lot because they'll be at the hospital too, but –"

"Maisie and Carl!" said the two children in unison.

Benjamin smiled. He was pleased his kids liked his family, and he was relieved they hadn't objected to his decision to donate a kidney. Although there was risk attached to any surgical procedure, this one was straightforward from his point of view. It was Hugh's body that would have the job of accepting the new kidney and adapting to a new way of life.

"Will Jocelyn look after Grey Star?" he asked, and Vanessa nodded.

"And you, Alan – I presume you'll bring your guitar to Walthamstow?"

Alan nodded, and Benjamin was surprised at how bright and interested both children suddenly looked. Gone was the usual morning lethargy!

"Carl said he'd take me to some gigs in London," Alan confirmed, and Benjamin was pleased that his son was taking an interest in life again.

Since Alan left hospital, neither he nor Benjamin had mentioned the court case. For Benjamin, notifying the police had been about finding closure for Alan, but it seemed his son had other plans.

When Vanessa left the kitchen, he approached his father, looking furtive and embarrassed.

"Dad, look – I really don't want this – this – well, I don't want to go to court. I mean –" He hopped from one foot to the other, his face red with embarrassment. "If the police contact you, just tell them I won't be making any statement. The matter with Fiona is over as far as I'm concerned." He looked earnestly at Benjamin. "I'm fine now, Dad – besides, if the band becomes successful, it wouldn't help our image if this kind of thing got into the newspapers."

Benjamin nodded. He could see Alan's point of view and, in a way, he was also relieved. By now, he'd come round to thinking there was little to be gained from a court case other than further trauma for everyone.

"Okay, son – if that's what you want."

Alan nodded, giving an embarrassed smile.

"Can I tell Edwin?" Benjamin asked.

Alan nodded again. "Yeah, I guess it's only fair."

Benjamin grimaced to himself. If he was honest, he'd like Fiona to sweat for just a bit longer, but Edwin's professional reputation was also at stake, and he didn't want him to suffer. He felt a surge of pity for poor, inoffensive Edwin, and for the empty shell of a marriage he'd be coming home to. Hopefully, in time, relations between him and Edwin would mellow, but right now he was still angry about what had happened to Alan.

CHAPTER 64

Fiona was on edge. Edwin was due back from his business trip that night, and she wasn't sure what was going to happen. Would they speak to each other? Should she prepare a meal for him? Would Edwin prefer if she stayed out of his sight?

Fiona went upstairs and made up the bed in the spare room. She'd no longer go near the bedroom where she and Edwin had slept for most of their married life. That was Edwin's room now. Anyway, she'd soon be moving out and finding a bedsit somewhere. And although she was probably entitled to fifty per cent of their assets, she felt that in all fairness she didn't deserve anything. She'd led a charmed life, playing golf and shopping, but had never fully appreciated the value of what she'd had.

Besides, she couldn't expect Edwin to give up everything he'd paid for, when she'd been the one to destroy their marriage. Perhaps he'd agree to give her a small allowance? She'd some money left over from the sale of her late parents' house, but it wasn't enough to see her through old age. Nor had she been in paid employment since she and Edwin married, and with the leaps technology had taken since then, she'd hardly even be qualified to take charge of a chicken run.

The threat of the court case filled Fiona with fear and guilt.

She owed it to Edwin to leave as soon as possible, and save him the humiliation of seeing his wife in court. It certainly wouldn't look good for the local solicitor's wife to be up on a charge of perverting a minor, or whatever the charge might be called. Presumably she could go to prison for what she'd done, so it would be better for Edwin if they'd gone their separate ways before then.

Before retiring to bed, Fiona prepared a dish of cold meat and salad in case Edwin was hungry, and placed it in the fridge. Then she headed for the spare room. As she climbed into the cold double bed, she felt the tears starting once again. She'd always taken Edwin's warm body for granted. There had been comfort and security in hearing him snore, and soon she'd never hear him again.

Eventually, Fiona fell into a restless sleep, in which she dreamed of standing naked in front of all the people who'd once been her friends, while they called her names and shouted abuse at her. She felt frightened and vulnerable until Zoe Gray appeared, and told them all to leave Fiona alone. Then she offered Fiona her cardigan to cover her nakedness, and Fiona woke up crying, filled with guilt for what she'd done to Zoe, Alan and Edwin.

Just then, she heard Edwin's car drive up, and she listened to the sounds of the car door being locked and the front door being opened. No doubt he was relieved that she'd chosen to stay out of his way. She wondered if he felt that in some way she was responsible for Jennifer's death too. Right now, she felt responsible for everything bad that had happened.

Having dozed off again, Fiona didn't know what time it was when the door of the bedroom opened, the light came on and Edwin stood on the threshold. He was still wearing his business suit, and looked tired and drawn. Fiona noticed for the first time the little tufts of grey in his sideburns. She was overwhelmed with guilt that she might have caused his grey hairs. Before, she'd never thought of his feelings. It hadn't mattered to her whether he was happy or sad, as long as she had money in her bank account. She'd never asked him about his clients, or shown any interest in his successes or failures. She'd never even questioned how hard he'd had to work to give her all that she had.

"Are you okay?" he said, still standing in the doorway.

Fiona nodded. "Yes, thanks," she mumbled.

"Then why are you sleeping in here?"

"I – I thought it would be better for both of us."

Edwin seemed to be weighing her words carefully, as though looking for some hidden meaning in them. Then he sighed. "Well, if that's what you want, Fiona. I presume you didn't go to Jennifer's funeral?"

Fiona shivered. "No. Benjamin would've taken a shotgun to me if I'd turned up."

Edwin hesitated. "I wish it hadn't happened like this – I mean, you two not being friends before she died."

"Thanks," Fiona said, feeling tears forming behind her eyelids.

"I'm sorry I wasn't here for the funeral either, but I posted a condolence card to Benjamin from both of us."

"Thanks," said Fiona again.

"I've also some good news for you," Edwin added. "There won't be any court case. Benjamin rang earlier today and told me."

Fiona felt weak with relief. The public part of her nightmare was over.

"Oh," Fiona said again, not trusting herself to say anything else.

Suddenly, Edwin strode across the room, and in Fiona's mind he became her father, and she flinched, expecting a violent outburst. Instead, he stopped at the edge of the bed and stared at her.

"Why did you flinch like that?" he demanded.

"Oh God, I'm sorry – it's just that – well, I thought you were going to hit me."

Edwin gave her a look of disgust. "I've never hit anyone in my life, Fiona – do you think so little of me?"

"No, no – it's just that –"

"I'm still trying to figure out why you needed to seduce that young boy. Wasn't I enough for you?" he said angrily.

Fiona buried her head in the pillow with shame. This decent man hadn't deserved to be humiliated in this way.

"Why, Fiona, why?"

"I don't know, Edwin," she said, turning back to face him, "But none of it is your fault, and I don't deserve you. I should have dealt with my past long ago, but –"

"Your past? What do you mean by 'your past'?"

For a moment Fiona didn't speak, then she started to cry. "I've hidden from it for years. I never told you anything about the beatings and the sexual abuse. I wanted you to think I was normal – I wanted to *be* normal! But one thing this – this recent – episode has taught me is that you have to deal with the past or you'll never be free of it."

Edwin looked horrified. "My God, Fiona, I'd have helped you – I'd have done anything for you!"

Fiona's lower lip trembled. "Nothing I've done has been fair to you, Edwin. I even married you because you were gentle and kind, and wouldn't make me feel afraid. But I should never have married you, Edwin – you don't deserve someone who's a mess like me."

Edwin glowered down at her. "Why couldn't you tell me what was wrong?" Still holding her gaze, he began to undress. "I've been gentle and understanding because I thought that was what you wanted," he said grimly, "but maybe you need something very different."

Naked now, he climbed in beside her, bruising her lips with the strength of his kiss. Then he took her in anger, and she found herself shocked and sexually excited by his masterful approach. In fact, it was the first time she'd ever been carried away on a wave of passion for her own husband. Edwin was a frenzied lover, and on a tide of emotion, she had the most amazing orgasm. Then another, as he relentlessly possessed her body again.

As she lay spent in his arms afterwards, she faced a surprising truth. She'd just experienced the most amazing sex, with the man she'd been married to for fifteen years! It had been like making love with a stranger, yet at the same time with someone whose body she knew so well. Now, she felt heartbreaking regret that it would be the first and last time she'd ever experience such passion.

The following morning, when Fiona awoke, Edwin was still sleeping beside her in the spare room. Turning towards him, she stared at him in awe. She was looking at a man whom she'd never guessed was so experienced in the ways of love, a man she hardly knew. She'd thought him timid and weak, and she'd selected him on that basis, to satisfy her own needs rather than his. Now she felt a deep sadness that she'd been so shallow and so cruel.

Tentatively, she touched the sprouting hairs on his chest that were suddenly so dear to her, especially now that she was about to lose him.

Suddenly, Edwin opened one eye and looked at her. She blushed, feeling guilty for touching his body, to which she no longer had any right.

"I'm sorry for everything," Fiona said humbly. "I realise you made love to me last night to show me what I could have had, if only I'd treated you with the respect you deserved."

Edwin sat up on one elbow and looked into her face. "Is that what you think? When will you ever learn, Fiona? I did it to show you how much I love you, and to let you know that I won't be treated like garbage anymore. Things have got to change – if you want us to stay married, that is. *I* do. But you're going to have to learn to trust me. And we need to get you professional help."

Fiona nodded, unable to speak because of the large lump in her throat. She was totally overwhelmed by Edwin's decency and generosity of spirit. She'd embarrassed him publicly and disgraced herself, yet he was still willing to give her his support.

"I don't deserve you," she said humbly, a fresh bout of tears running down her cheeks.

"Is that a yes?" Edwin asked gently. "We can get through this, Fi."

Perhaps it was the use of her pet name that broke the ice surrounding her heart for so long. She threw herself into his arms, sobbing uncontrollably. She suddenly felt as though all the bad experiences of her past were being cleansed by his forgiveness.

When eventually her tears were spent, she looked earnestly at him through red and swollen eyes.

"I love you, Edwin," she whispered.

Edwin smiled, hugging her. "I love you too."

Fiona felt safe and comforted in his arms. It would be an uphill battle, but she'd get there. And today she'd take the first step. She owed it to Edwin as much as to herself. Now, she had someone on her side who had faith in her. She'd do her best to be the kind of wife he needed – and she'd immediately get rid of the contraceptive pills in her bedside locker.

CHAPTER 65

In the ward at St Luke's Hospital, Benjamin lay resting after his operation. He felt as though he'd gone several rounds with Muhammad Ali, but he felt pleased with himself, and grateful that the transplant had been a success for Hugh.

Long before the operation, he'd been put through a barrage of hospital tests, and had been thoroughly fed up with all the procedures he'd had to endure. As far as he was concerned, the soul-searching and psychological testing were unnecessary, since he was already committed to giving his brother a kidney. On the other hand, he reluctantly conceded they had a value in ensuring that donors made an informed decision.

Maisie and Carl had been in to see him straight after the operation, and much to Benjamin's embarrassment, Maisie had been weeping with gratitude, constantly dabbing her eyes and calling him a saint. Seeing his embarrassment, Carl had promptly whisked his mother out of the room so that Benjamin could get some much-needed sleep.

"Hello, Benjamin?"

He must have dozed off again, because when he opened his eyes, Georgie Monks was sitting beside his bed.

Delighted, he reached out his hand and clasped hers. At that precise moment, Vanessa and Alan also entered the room. Vanessa's eyes instantly darted to the two joined hands, and a half-smile registered on her face.

"You must be Vanessa – and you're Alan," said Georgie, standing up and shaking their hands. "It's so nice to meet you – I'm Georgie Monks."

As the children shook hands, their eyes met over her head in a brief almost imperceptible nod. Was something going on here? If so, Dad wasn't wasting any time! It was only a few weeks since their mother had died, and both children had assumed it would be months, or even years, before they had to deal with this kind of situation.

Nevertheless, Vanessa immediately liked Georgie Monks. She was everything her mother wasn't, and the clothes she wore certainly weren't designer labels. Designer wear had been her mother's yardstick for assessing someone's worthiness, so by Jennifer's standards Georgie Monks wouldn't have rated very highly. But Vanessa immediately saw through Georgie's clothes. She was wearing jeans, a T-shirt and casual jacket, and it was clear she dressed for comfort rather than to impress. And Vanessa liked that.

Alan blushed as he and Georgie shook hands, and Vanessa could see he liked her too, despite being wary now around women of a certain age.

Vanessa wondered if this woman and her father had been having an affair before her mother died. If so, she couldn't find it in her heart to condemn them – after all, her mother had been having an affair with Clive Ellwood! Sometimes, Vanessa thought, it was safer not to delve too far below the surface of things. You might discover things you didn't need to know.

"Hey, I thought you all came to see me?" Benjamin grunted from his bed. "I need a bit of attention here!"

Everyone laughed, and the two children rushed to their father's bed to hug him.

"Easy on – I've just had a great chunk taken out of me!" he howled, fending off his children's fierce embraces. But he was enjoying the attention, and the rare opportunity to feel good about himself.

Fleetingly, he recalled Jennifer's appalled reaction to his kidney-donor plan. "I don't want to be stuck with an invalid on my hands!" she'd shrieked, spoiling his joy at being able to give something back to his brother. It was strange that the people she'd hated so much were now part of his life again, yet she was gone forever.

Benjamin glanced over his children's heads to where Georgie was looking on and smiling. He was thrilled she'd visited him in hospital, although they still had to resolve the question of the church, which was now being repaired by one of his construction crews.

As far as he was concerned, there was no longer any question of demolishing it. Since Jennifer died there, he felt it would be disrespectful to her memory, and to the children's feelings, to destroy it. Anyway, he suspected he'd actually been using the threat of demolition to see more of Georgie Monks.

But he didn't want to tell Georgie about his decision just yet. It was silly, he knew, but he wanted to string out the delicious feeling of anticipation. He was relishing the thought of her incredulous expression when he told her. And, if he was honest, he needed to know she wasn't just stringing him along in order to get him to change his mind. He wanted to be sure that when he next gave his heart, he'd be loved for himself, not for his possessions or wealth.

"I'll go and get a coffee in the café, and leave you kids to chat with your dad," said Georgie, standing up. "Can I bring back food or drinks for anyone?"

All three shook their heads, and Vanessa mentally awarded Georgie top marks for thoughtfulness as she left the room.

"Okay, Dad – so who exactly is Georgie?" asked Vanessa immediately, adopting the role of interrogator. "Ve haf vays of making you tok!"

Benjamin grinned, looking from one child to the other. "She's a very nice woman who's been protesting over the church in

Stonehill," he explained. "She thinks it should be preserved as a historical monument, but I've been planning to demolish it."

"But you're not going to destroy it now, are you?" Vanessa asked sharply. "I mean, Mum –"

"No," Benjamin confirmed, "I'll never demolish it now. But please don't tell that to Georgie. I want to tell her in my own time, okay? Let that be our little secret for now."

Alan and Vanessa nodded in agreement. They liked sharing a secret with their father.

"But why is she here at the hospital, Dad – if she's, I mean, if you're –" Alan looked confused.

"We saw you holding hands," Vanessa added, grinning. "A strange way to treat your enemy, don't you think, Dad?"

Benjamin's neck suffused with red. "Well, it's like this – I – well, we – I mean, we also like each other – a lot." He looked from Alan to Vanessa, his eyes earnestly on them both. "I hope you two don't feel – I mean, that I'm jumping the gun and upsetting you by –"

"It's okay, Dad," said Alan, blushing to the roots of his hair.

"It's fine, Dad," said Vanessa, smiling. "We just want you to be happy."

"But I want you both to be happy too!" Benjamin said earnestly. "If I thought for one moment that you felt I was dishonouring your mother's memory –"

He didn't get a chance to finish his sentence, because both Alan and Vanessa had lunged at him, throwing their arms around him and hugging him tightly. This time, he didn't bother to mention the pain in his side. He could endure it, because he was a very lucky man.

As they left the ward, Vanessa turned to her brother, grinning.

"Dad's testing her," she said. "I guess he doesn't want to make another mistake."

"What do you mean?"

Vanessa shrugged. "I don't think Mum ever cared for him enough," she said. "I think he's the kind of man who needs an awful lot of loving."

"Well, *we* can give him that!" replied Alan enthusiastically.

Vanessa gave him a scathing look. "I don't think so, dear brother. Not *that* kind of love."

Alan nodded, blushed and shoved his hands in his pockets. At the moment, he hated being reminded about *that* kind of love.

After enduring another of Maisie's visits, and more tearful gratitude, Benjamin was feeling in need of a respite. Carl could see that Benjamin was tired, and was doing his best to chivvy his mother out of the room.

Georgie had thoughtfully remained outside the ward after returning from the cafeteria, assuming Benjamin might want to chat privately to Maisie and Carl. But Benjamin knew she was somewhere out there, and he was longing to hold her hand again. As Carl and Maisie rose to leave, Benjamin cleared his throat.

"Carl, if you see Georgie Monks, can you ask her to come back in?"

Carl's expression was blank, and Benjamin realised they mightn't have met.

"She's a little woman, very pretty, with amazing red hair?"

Suddenly, a look of recognition crossed Carl's face. "Ah, yes – the woman who was in the waiting room while you were having your operation?" He grinned. "She was in a right old state over you, Uncle Benny."

Maisie turned back, smiling. "Yes, we spoke a bit while you were being operated on, and she seemed really worried about you. She said she was a friend of yours, but I didn't like to ask anymore." She gave Benjamin a knowing smile. "Is she someone special, Benny?"

Embarrassed, Benjamin pretended to have dozed off, but as Carl and Maisie left, his heart was soaring with joy. Without realising it, his nephew and sister-in-law had confirmed that Georgie cared for him.

As she entered his hospital room again, Benjamin's heart was beating so fast that he wondered if he might die on the spot. What a way to go! But no, he wasn't ready to die yet. Right now, all he wanted was to get well for his kids and his extended family, and, of course, for Georgie.

Immediately, she kissed him, and sat beside his bed, holding his hand.

"Am I in heaven?" he whispered.

"Thank goodness you're not – that's what I was worried about while you were in the operating theatre!"

"But if I'd died, I wouldn't be able to demolish the church," he said mischievously. "Then you could save it for the local community."

"Don't say things like that!" said Georgie angrily. "Honestly, I haven't thought about the damn church for ages – all I could think of was that you mightn't come through the operation."

"Really?"

Georgie nodded. "It was amazingly generous of you to donate a kidney to your brother, but if anything had gone wrong, I think I'd have killed him with my bare hands!"

Benjamin looked at her earnestly. "But what about us – I mean, is there an 'us' when I get out of here?"

Georgie looked at him impishly. "I don't see why not, as long as you don't expect me to stop organising the protests!"

Benjamin's face relaxed into a grin. "Well, if we're an 'us', you won't have time to spare for protests. You'll be spending all your time making love to me!"

Georgie had stopped smiling. "Seriously, Benjamin, if only for your children's sake, I'm hoping you'll see sense about the church."

Benjamin squeezed her hand. "My dear woman, I'm not going to demolish the church – or take out the windows."

Georgie looked astonished.

"I'm going to make a gift of it to the people of Stonehill, on condition that it's kept intact as a heritage site, properly insured and secured against vandals."

"Like you?" Georgie couldn't resist a last jibe.

"No, I'm a philistine – at least, that's what you told me I was!"

"Well, right now I think you're the most amazing man in the world!" she whispered, hugging him.

Benjamin grinned. "So you like me – just a little bit?"

Georgie blushed. "Heaven help me, I even fancied you that first time we met, the night you started dancing on my placard!" Then, suddenly, she looked serious. "But please, Benjamin – let's keep things low-key because of your kids. It's too soon for them to see you with another woman – it's only a short time since they lost their mother."

Benjamin smiled. "But the kids like you already."

Georgie looked at him earnestly. "I'm serious, Benjamin – those kids don't need any more surprises just yet."

She smiled as she stood up to leave.

"And right now, dear man, you need to concentrate on getting well again. There are lots of people who have a vested interest in seeing you healthy again."

After she'd gone, Benjamin lay back in his bed and contemplated his future. It was going to be a very different life from the one he'd envisaged only a short time ago. Back then, he'd felt annihilated. Now, he had everything to look forward to.

CHAPTER 66

Zoe's Diary

May 13

I'm looking forward to having dinner at Hazel's house tomorrow. It means the bullies won't dare have a go at me while Hazel's with me. Her parents are really nice, and they never ask me awkward questions about Mum. I just hope Claire will be able to keep an eye on her while I'm gone.

"Can you come to my house for an early dinner tomorrow after school?" Hazel asked Zoe. They'll pick us up in the car."

Zoe nodded, pleased to be asked. Lately, she had few reasons to enjoy herself.

"Will your sister be able to cope with your mother?"

"Yes, of course she will – Mum's fine!"

Zoe felt an intense loyalty to her mother, and even though Hazel was a friend and hadn't meant anything disparaging by her remark, Zoe felt it necessary to rise to her mother's defence.

Hazel's invitation had been casually extended, but to Zoe it was as exciting as an invitation to Buckingham Palace. As she and Hazel parted company at the crossroads, there was no sign *of the bullies, so she walked along the road with a spring in her step. Even when the bullies eventually cornered her near Leonard's store, their taunts and nasty comments couldn't dampen her good spirits.*

Back at the cottage, Zoe immediately sought Claire's help, and her little sister was thrilled at being given the opportunity of taking charge the following evening. It made her feel really grown up.

"Will you be able to bring Mum a cup of tea if she needs one?" Claire nodded. "Of course."

"I'll leave a salad ready for you and Mum, so all you'll have to do is take it out of the fridge," Zoe added.

"Stop fussing!" said Claire, "Everything will be fine."

"I just want to be sure you can manage."

Zoe was enjoying herself at the Bonningtons' house. It allowed her to forget, for a little while at least, the problems she was facing. Mr Bonnington was a pleasant, easy-going man who sat reading his newspaper and intermittently telling jokes, while Mrs Bonnington was cooking up a storm in the kitchen. Delicious aromas wafted out the door, and Zoe's stomach rumbled in joyful anticipation.

Hazel's younger brother tried unsuccessfully to impress the girls with his prowess at riding his bicycle round the lawn, then tried to involve them in card games that he knew he could win. Hazel good-naturedly dismissed him as a pest, and took Zoe upstairs to her bedroom, which was a mass of pink curtains, bedspread and valance.

Zoe gazed around her in wonder. She'd never seen a more beautiful room. Her own room at home contrasted poorly against this riot of colour and luxury, but she didn't feel a single pang of jealousy. She was delighted that her friend had such a lovely room.

The girls had just started on their homework when Mrs Bonnington called them downstairs.

Thrilled, Zoe joined the Bonningtons at the dinner table, hardly able to believe how much food was on their plates! There was melon for starters, followed by steak, vegetables and potatoes for the main course. Mrs Bonnington was clearly delighted that Zoe ate everything she was given, and when pudding was served she shyly accepted a second portion of homemade apple pie.

"I always bake several pies at a time, so why don't you take one home for your Mum and sister?" Mrs Bonnington suggested.

In between mouthfuls, Zoe nodded her thanks. It would be a lovely treat for her mother and Claire. Zoe liked Mr and Mrs Bonnington very much, and briefly, she allowed herself to daydream about being part of a normal family like theirs, but then she felt a pang of guilt at even thinking such a thing.

Earlier that day, as Claire walked home from school, she couldn't stop smiling. She was in charge of everything while Zoe was at Hazel's house.

Claire liked the idea of having time alone with her mother. Of course, she knew that by the time she got home, her mother would have retired to bed, having drunk the best part of a bottle of whiskey. Nevertheless, Claire planned on bringing her a cup of tea as soon as she got home, and maybe miraculously her mother would be sober, and they'd have a lovely chat, like they used to do in the old days.

Claire was pleased for Zoe. Not many people invited the Grays anywhere, so this was a rare occasion for her sister. If anyone deserved a treat it was Zoe, who always put everyone else before herself. She knew that something was bothering Zoe, although she always denied it. Claire longed for something exciting to happen that would lift her sister out of her depression. Hopefully the trip to Hazel's house might be the first of many visits.

As she approached the cottage, Claire was filled with a delicious sense of anticipation. By being left in charge, she felt as though she'd taken a major step on the road to adulthood. Assuming all went well today, Zoe could leave her in charge more often, which would give Zoe more freedom and enable Claire to feel less of a burden. It felt good to be growing up – before long, they could stop worrying about social services intervening. And when they'd got careers and incomes of their *own, they'd be able to get their mother the help she needed. They'd become the glamorous Gray sisters, the ones everyone envied. And they'd turn up their noses at all the people in Trentham-on-Sea who'd scorned them in the past.*

Claire was still smiling as she slipped her key into the front door lock and turned it. But the door wouldn't open. Beset by a moment of panic, she took the key out and tried it again. Maybe the lock was rusty, or she wasn't turning it properly? It still wouldn't open, and now she was feeling frightened. What if she couldn't get in to look after her mother? And why oh why did it have to happen today of all days?

Suddenly, Claire brightened. Maybe a window or door at the back was open. Rushing around, she found the back door unlocked, and relief flooded through her. As soon as she checked on her mother, she'd find out what was causing the problem with the front door. If she could solve the problem on her own, that would be one less for Zoe to have to deal with.

Claire's little heart almost stopped when she opened her mother's bedroom door and discovered she wasn't there. Nor was she in the bathroom or the kitchen.

Now worried, Claire rushed into the hall, only to find her mother's inert body lying on the floor and leaning against the front door. Which meant that each time Claire had pushed from outside, she'd been pushing against her poor mother!

Tears scalded Claire's eyes. Was her mother dead?

"Mummy! Mummy!" she screamed. "Please say something!"

Not sure what she should do, Claire knelt down and pressed her face close to her mother's, and managed to detect a faint breath. She recoiled from the smell of vomit, and was afraid her mother might choke, so she tried to move her onto her side. But her mother was a dead weight, and her attempts at moving her proved futile.

What was she supposed to do now? Having felt so grown up a few minutes before, Claire was now feeling frightened and insecure. She needed to get help, but that created a dilemma. After their earlier episode with Dr Barker, Zoe had warned her never to contact him again in case he referred the family to social services.

LINDA KAVANAGH

Claire wiped her tears away with the back of her hand. If her mother didn't get help, she might die, and then they'd be put in an orphanage anyway. She sucked her thumb, something she hadn't done since she was a baby. She needed to make a decision quickly – otherwise, her mother might pass away while she was still trying to make up her mind!

Although she was loath to do it, there was only one thing to do – get Zoe. She dreaded spoiling Zoe's visit to Hazel's house, but what other choice did she have? Every second might count if their mother was to be saved.

As the children played rounders in Hazel's front garden after dinner, some sixth sense made Zoe look up to see Claire running towards her as fast as her little legs would carry her. Abandoning the game, Zoe rushed out to meet her.

"It's Mum!" Claire shouted. "I can't lift her up, and she's lying on the floor!"

Calling to Hazel, Zoe explained she had to leave urgently. Then the two sisters ran down the road, past the crossroads and down the lane, until they arrived panting at the cottage.

Racing through the back door and into the hall, they found their mother still lying on the floor. But by now she was snoring loudly, and both daughters gave a huge sigh of relief. At least she was still alive. Now they had the problem of getting her off the floor and safely into bed.

"Come on, Mum!" Zoe urged her, her mouth close to her mother's ear. "We need to get you into bed."

Their mother groaned, rolling over into her own vomit and opening her eyes. "I don't feel well," she mumbled.

"That's why we want to get you into bed," Zoe urged her. "Come on, Mum – try to stand up."

Now grumbling loudly, their mother made an attempt to stand, but her knees buckled and she fell back again. Cursing, she made another attempt, and this time, with her daughters' help, she was finally upright. Frogmarching her into the bedroom, the girls sat her on the bed. She felt loose and floppy, like a puppet whose strings were no longer attached. Working in unison, the two girls managed to raise her arms and remove her smelly clothing. Then Zoe wiped her with a warm soap-laden flannel, and between them they managed to slide a clean nightdress over her head. Then they lifted her feet and levered her around until she was lying prone on the bed. Covering her with a duvet, they looked at each other in relief.

In the kitchen, they were confronted with a bizarre array of vegetables strewn across the worktops and uncooked potatoes in a pot of water on the stove. A bottle of cooking oil lay spilt on the floor. There was also a large slab of uncooked meat lying in brown paper on the draining board, with several flies buzzing around it. Zoe quickly wrapped the meat up again and tossed it into the bin.

"What's been going on here?" Claire asked, bewildered.

Zoe sighed. "I don't know, Claire. But come on, let's tidy this mess up – then we can have a nice cup of tea."

Later that evening, Mrs Bonnington and Hazel walked through the village and took the turn that led to the Gray's cottage. Outside, Mrs Bonnington scanned the windows for a sign that might indicate anything was wrong inside, but everything seemed peaceful and quiet.

"Don't you think we should call?" Mrs Bonnington asked her daughter. "Just to make sure that everything's alright?"

"No," said Hazel firmly. "Zoe and Claire are well able to manage."

Zoe had confided her fear of the social services to Hazel, so there was no way she was allowing her mother to stick her nose – however well-meaning – into the Grays' life. Besides, Hazel couldn't be sure her mother wouldn't think it in the children's best interests to contact the authorities herself. But Hazel knew that Zoe and her little sister could deal with most crises on their own. Adults just never gave children credit for anything.

"Do you think we should offer them some money?" asked Mrs Bonnington, biting her lip. "Those girls seem to have such a hard life."

"Definitely not, Mum," said Hazel firmly. "They're not

actually short of money, it's just that their mother tends to get her priorities a bit mixed up."

"Well, if you're sure –" said Mrs Bonnington, looking unhappily at her daughter, "– but I thought Zoe looked tired and worried today – she's not a happy and confident girl, like someone her age should be."

Hazel said nothing, because she'd have to agree with her mother.

Mrs Bonnington opened her shopping bag, took out a parcel and placed it on the Gray's doorstep. "Well, at least I can leave poor Zoe the apple pie I promised her."

Zoe had seen Mrs Bonnington leave the pie outside the front door. She felt bad at not being able to acknowledge their presence and invite them in, but she daren't let Mrs Bonnington see the state of the cottage.

Zoe bit her lip. If only she could confide in kind Mrs Bonnington. But it was out of the question. Besides, it was probably too late for anyone to help her now.

The following morning, Zoe and Claire were exhausted. The previous evening they'd spent hours tidying up the kitchen, mopping up the oil on the kitchen floor and the vomit in the hall.

"Good morning!" their mother said cheerfully as a bleary-eyed Claire entered her room, followed by Zoe carrying her mother's tea and toast. "How are my wonderful daughters today?"

Zoe and Claire each managed to muster up a tired smile.

"I hope you enjoyed your dinner last night," their mother added. "I thought you both deserved a nice surprise."

Claire's mouth fell open and she gazed uncomprehendingly at their mother. But Zoe had already guessed what the previous evening's array of food had meant. Their mother had forgotten that she was going to the Bonningtons for dinner, and intended making dinner herself, but she'd passed out at some point before managing to cook it. Now she'd no recollection of what had happened.

Claire was astounded. "But you didn't – ow!"

Zoe had kicked her on the shin.

"The meal was lovely, Mum," Zoe said, a look of mock delight on her face. "It was the nicest meal we've had in ages, wasn't it, Claire?"

Taking her cue from Zoe, Claire nodded. She didn't like lying to her mother, but Zoe seemed to feel it was the right thing to do.

"It was brilliant, Mum," she said. "I've never tasted anything so delicious!" If she was going to lie, she might as well give the meal a superlative endorsement.

"Thanks, Mum, we really appreciated it – but we've got to leave for school soon," said Zoe. "Will you be okay?"

"Never felt better!" said their mother as she drank her tea.

After saying goodbye, Zoe grabbed Claire's hand and quickly ushered her out of the room.

"There's no point in reminding her about what really happened," Zoe whispered, as they collected their schoolbags and left the cottage. "Let her believe she cooked dinner, because it makes her happy to think she's looking after us."

"But why doesn't she remember?"

"It's called amnesia, and it can happen when people drink a lot of alcohol," Zoe explained. "I read about it in a library book – people like Mum can appear to function normally, but afterwards they've no recollection of anything."

Claire looked at her sister earnestly. "I'm sorry I had to mess up your visit to Hazel's yesterday."

"Don't worry – there wasn't anything else you could do. Thank goodness Mum is okay."

Claire waved to her sister as she headed off to the junior school. "At least tonight we have Mrs Bonnington's apple pie to look forward to!" she said.

Nodding, Zoe waved back. But as soon as Claire was out of sight, Zoe's face darkened. She had more torment to endure before she saw her sister again.

CHAPTER 67

Anne felt a changed woman. She'd expected to shake off the trauma of events in the church tower, but somehow she couldn't. Everyone kept saying she didn't look well, and she only had to look in the mirror to confirm it. Clive had booked them a holiday in the Seychelles, but she couldn't even summon up the enthusiasm to go. The dear man was simply trying to cheer her up, and she really appreciated his concern. She could only hope she'd feel better by the time their departure date arrived.

Sitting alone in her kitchen, Anne gazed across the manicured lawns. The more she thought about what happened on top of the church tower, the more certain she was that Jennifer had tried to kill her. But why? Hadn't their years of friendship meant anything? What on earth did Jennifer stand to gain by her death?

Anne bit her lip in anguish. Had Jennifer been ill? She'd certainly seemed in a peculiar mood that day. Could some sort of fever have led to a brief bout of madness? Anne had been paralysed with shock and disbelief as she and Jennifer had struggled, unable to accept what her friend was doing. But now that she'd had time to reflect, she remembered Jennifer's malevolent face, and felt certain her friend had been planning her demise.

Anne wished there was someone she could confide in. But who? If she told Clive, he'd simply tell her to pull herself together and stop being ridiculous. Nor could she confide in Fiona, since she'd been responsible for Jennifer's son's attempted suicide. Clive had advised giving Fiona a wide berth until they saw how the matter was going to pan out. As a result, Anne now checked the caller display on the landline and mobile phone before answering. Besides, now that Jennifer was gone – Anne still couldn't bring herself to say "dead" – they didn't know if Benjamin was going to push ahead with the court case. Maybe it would all be hushed up, and in time she'd be able to talk to Fiona again. At this rate, she'd soon have no friends left!

At least, she could still talk to Emma. On the other hand, Emma was hard to keep under control, and couldn't be depended upon to keep her mouth shut, especially after a few glasses of wine.

Maybe she should consider having a session with a psychologist or psychotherapist? In private, of course, and she'd never let anyone else know. It might be good to talk things through with someone neutral and unbiased. She needed to clear her head, and there was no one else to whom she could talk freely. There were too many agendas and too many uncertainties with people she knew.

Something suddenly clicked in her brain. Hadn't she received a card through the letterbox recently, from some psychotherapist, offering counselling sessions? With professional help, she could talk through all her thoughts about what happened, in a private and confidential environment.

Anne stood up and began searching the kitchen shelves and drawers. She knew she hadn't thrown out the card – where on earth had she put it? A trawl through her personal documents failed to produce it, but at last she found it on the drawing-room mantelpiece, behind the clock. Anne eyed it with undisguised relief. Yes, the psychotherapist offered counselling sessions and assorted therapies. She'd ring and make an appointment as soon as possible.

Since Jennifer's death, she'd also been plagued by thoughts of Zoe Gray. It was as though the shock of one tragedy brought back memories of the other, opening up her own personal Pandora's Box, and releasing all the demons she'd previously managed to keep under control.

With amazing clarity, it had all come back to her as though it was only yesterday. When she, Fiona, Jennifer and Emma had taunted Zoe Gray, they'd been punishing her for something over which she'd had no control. Anne herself had wanted to hit out, and Zoe had been an easy target.

Right now, Anne felt ashamed. For thirty years, they'd managed to suppress their guilt about what happened to Zoe. Through their meanness and cruelty, they'd driven the poor girl to suicide.

She looked once again at the psychotherapist's card. Maybe it was time to unburden herself. With a psychologist's help, she could voice her belief that Jennifer tried to kill her. And she could also rid herself of the guilt she still felt, all these years later, over Zoe Gray's suicide. Once all that stress and worry was out in the open, she could look forward to her holiday with Clive. After which she'd be refreshed, and ready for the general election. Suddenly, Anne felt a lot better.

CHAPTER 68

The atmosphere was hot and stuffy at London's newest music club, but the packed audience were willing to put up with the inconvenience. They were there to hear the latest band from the United States, who were on a UK whistle-stop tour, and were being hailed as the next big thing.

Alan, along with his band members Jerry, Tony and Doug, sat in the wings, occasionally peeping out at the audience who were still taking their seats. Thanks to Carl, they were the supporting act. Carl knew the guy who ran the club, and at the last minute he'd been let down by the support band. Carl had said his cousin was in a band, there'd been frantic phone calls to Alan and his friends, a hurried train trip to London, and suddenly it was all happening! The night before, they'd all slept on the floor of the Corcrofts' flat in Walthamstow, and today they were all aching from lying on the hard wooden boards.

Earlier that afternoon, they'd set up their equipment and done the necessary sound checks. Now, all they had to do was wait until they were called on stage. Much to their relief, the American band hadn't arrived yet, since they'd feel too intimidated to play if the others were listening to them. As it was, they were scared out of their wits. What if the audience booed them? What if their songs were crap?

"Listen, guys – this is the best chance we've ever had!" Alan whispered. "We've got to do our best!"

Jerry glared at him. "Aw, shut up – I'm petrified! I swear I'm going to piss myself!"

Tony said nothing, but his incessant gum-chewing was getting on Alan's nerves, and Doug was cracking his knuckles in time to some tune playing in his head.

"Okay lads – you're on!" whispered the club manager, and feeling scared, the three guitarists went out and picked up their instruments, while Tony took his place behind the drums. Fear rippled through them as they faced the audience, and for one ghastly moment, Alan wondered if they'd be capable of performing at all.

The audience gave them lukewarm applause. Yet something amazing happened when they started to play. All shyness and nerves disappeared, and as they began their first number a change came over the audience. People began tapping their feet in time to the rhythm, leaning forward in their seats, and wondering if *this* was the band on the threshold of something big.

Sitting beside Carl in the audience, Vanessa too was filled with nerves. If things went well tonight, her brother might be starting a new and exciting life, doing what he most wanted to do. Sitting on Vanessa's other side were Rozzer, Jack and Leggo, whom Carl had also invited to the gig. As she glanced in their direction, she saw that they, too, were tapping their feet in time to the music.

For their final number, Alan took the microphone and spoke for the first time. "Our final number is about first love –" He reddened. "It's an experience everyone remembers, but it's hell when you've been rejected –"

His face and neck got all red, and Vanessa turned away, because she knew that if she looked at him, she'd burst into tears. He was the best brother any girl could have. And to think she'd nearly lost him. If she could strangle Fiona this very minute, she'd do it.

As the band began to play again, Vanessa was thrilled at how good they sounded. And when Alan sang, she was amazed by the lyrics. If he could write other songs as good as this one, she felt certain the band could go far.

Leaving the stage to tumultuous applause, they discovered that the American band had arrived and were applauding them from the wings. Alan and his band were then invited to replace the support band for the rest of their tour.

"Well, what do you think, guys?" Alan asked his bandmates, grinning. "Are we going?"

"You bet!"

"Definitely!"

"Try and stop us!"

While the American band was on stage, Jerry, Tony and Doug phoned home to make sure they'd be allowed go on tour. All were relieved to get the go-ahead. Alan didn't need to ring his father in hospital – he knew his dad would be pleased for him. And hopefully, he'd soon be well enough to come to one of their gigs.

Later, they all headed back to Walthamstow for another uncomfortable night on the Corcrofts' floor. Carl drove Uncle Hugh's white van, with Vanessa beside him, while Alan and friends crowded into the back, along with Rozzer, Jack and Leggo. Alan couldn't stop smiling, and every time he caught someone else's eye they were smiling too.

Then he suddenly thought of his mother, and the sudden pain of loss threatened to wipe out his happiness. He missed her terribly – always would – and he could feel his eyes filling with tears. Surreptitiously, he wiped them away, embarrassed in case anyone else noticed. But everyone was chatting animatedly, oblivious to his pain. He wished he could share his success with his mum, but he was also well aware that the tour wouldn't be happening if she was still alive.

Be happy for me, Mum, he begged her silently. This is what I've always wanted to do, and I swear I'll make you proud of me.

Then he had a wonderful idea. He'd write a song about his mother! He'd sing it at every gig, then she'd be with him always. Already, he could hear the tune forming in his head, and he began humming it softly. Suddenly, he felt happy again, and in the dark of the van he began composing the words.

CHAPTER 69

As the day of the meeting with her father approached, Claire became increasingly apprehensive. She'd arranged to meet him in a restaurant close to where she worked, and she and David met outside her office when she'd finished up for the day.

"I'm scared," she told him, as he greeted her on the steps of the building.

"Everything will be fine," he promised her, planting a kiss on her forehead. "I'll be beside you all the way."

Claire gripped David's arm tightly as they made their way to the restaurant. She'd decided that an early evening meal was the most appropriate venue in which to meet the man she hadn't seen since childhood. Now she wasn't so sure. Maybe a noisy pub would have helped to mask any awkward silences!

As they entered the restaurant, Claire was a little disappointed when she saw a stooped, elderly man getting up from his table to greet her. But when he smiled, she could see that he was still her own dear father, the man she remembered from all those years ago, and she rushed into his arms.

"My dear Claire!"

"Daddy!"

As they hugged, Claire felt the years roll back and she was a little girl again. Now that she'd found him again, they'd hopefully make up for all the time they'd lost.

Having introduced David to her father, the three of them sat down and were handed menus by a waiter. As they studied the list of starters and main courses, Claire and her father kept darting happy glances at each other, as though unable to believe the other was really there. After the waiter took their orders, they continued smiling, thrilled at being in each other's company at last.

"I've missed you so much," Claire whispered.

"I've missed you, too," her father said ruefully. "I wish I hadn't lost out on all those years of your childhood."

Claire hesitated. "Mum died a few months ago. I presume you also know about Zoe?"

Her father looked sad, bowing his head as though to ward off the painful memory. "Yes, I heard – what a tragic thing to happen. Can you imagine how I felt? I was thousands of miles away, and couldn't get back to pay my respects to my eldest daughter."

"Where were you?"

"In Australia. There was always plenty of work for engineers there."

Claire took a deep breath. There was a question she needed to ask, one she'd waited thirty years to have answered.

"Dad, why did you leave us?"

Her father looked incredibly sad. "I didn't do it from choice, Claire. When your mother and I broke up, she refused to let me see either you or Zoe. Since your mother owned the house, there was little I could do about it. I stayed in the area for a while, but eventually I decided to leave. I worked in Australia until two years ago, when I felt the urge to come home again." He smiled. "And now I'm glad I did," he said, patting her hand.

Claire was incensed. How dare her mother deprive her and Zoe of their father! Not only had her mother been a drunkard, she'd cruelly sent their father away!

Her father grimaced. "Look, Claire, I don't want to speak ill of the dead, but your mother . . ." His voice tailed off. "It doesn't matter."

"It does, Dad – go on, what were you going to say?"

Realising the momentousness of what her father might be about to say, David squeezed Claire's hand supportively. But she seemed almost oblivious to his touch.

Her father took a deep breath. "Your mother's family were wealthy, and we lived comfortably on her inheritance and my earnings. But – well, her family were also a little, er, mentally unstable. Your mother was violent, but I put up with it because of you and Zoe – but one day, while you were both at school, she stabbed me with a kitchen knife and ordered me out of the house for good. I knew she'd never hurt you children, so I left."

Claire's eyes filled with tears. What an awful life he'd had with her mother! She'd mistakenly believed they'd been a contented couple – how flawed one's memories could be! Then she suddenly remembered the incident with the television set, when her mother had smashed the screen with an empty whiskey bottle, and it seemed to confirm everything her father had been saying.

After their starters arrived, Claire's eyes searched her father's face. "Who let you know about Zoe's death?"

Her father hesitated. "Dennis Barker wrote to me."

Claire nodded. So all those years ago, the late Dr Barker had known where their father was, although he'd never let on when she and Zoe had expressed their longing to see him again. On the other hand, she couldn't fault his conduct after Zoe's death – as their family doctor, he'd let her father know the tragic news. She well remembered that he'd been the one who had signed the death certificate when Zoe's body was retrieved from the sea. But even his professional courtesy still couldn't make her warm to him. She'd never liked the man.

She wished she could tell her father about her quest for revenge, but she hadn't told David either and they might both be disappointed in her. It would also mean she'd have to tell her father about Zoe's diary and that her sister had taken her own life, and that would hurt him even more.

"Oh, Dad – I'm sorry we missed all those years together," she said, her eyes filling with tears. Reaching across the table, she took his hand. "But you never tried to get in touch – or even sent a birthday card . . ."

Her father looked astonished. "I did – I sent you a birthday card every year!" His expression was now bitter. "I thought you got them all, but I suppose your mother must have kept them from you. I'm so sorry, Claire – I wanted you to know I was always thinking of you."

Claire wanted to cry. Why had her mother been so cruel?

David was the only one at the table who was eating – the other two starters remained untouched. Silently, David nudged Claire, indicating the food, and she began moving it around on her plate. But she was oblivious to anything except her need to uncover her family history.

"But you must have been lonely," she said to her father. "Did you marry again?"

Grimacing, he shook his head. "No, I never got over losing my family. No one else could ever come close."

Claire was overwhelmed with sadness for this poor man who'd lost so much all those years ago. And furious with her mother for depriving her daughters of both parents. Because once their father left, their mother's heavy drinking had ensured they'd no real parent left.

"Is your accommodation comfortable, Dad?"

Her father looked embarrassed. "I'm renting a small flat at the moment – my pension took a nosedive when I transferred it back to the UK."

"Why don't you stay at our old home in Trentham-on-Sea, Dad?" Claire said impulsively. "Mum left the cottage to me, and I intend selling it eventually. But you could stay there for as long as you like."

David made a gasping sound, and Claire realised that she'd been totally neglecting him. She darted a glance in his direction, and his unguarded expression was one of naked disapproval. What on earth for? He probably wasn't happy that she'd invited her father to stay at the cottage.

However, her father's eyes had lit up. "Why, Claire, that's very decent of you. Your mother and I had many years of happiness there – before everything started going wrong." He looked at her gratefully. "Yes, I'd like to see the old place. Don't suppose I'll know anyone in the village anymore. I heard that Dennis Barker died some years ago. Cancer, I believe."

At yet another mention of Fiona's father, Claire's expression darkened, but her father didn't need to know that she'd never liked the man so she tried to look suitably sympathetic.

"The cottage is much the same as it was thirty years ago," she said apologetically. "Mum never updated it, so conditions are fairly primitive."

Her father laughed. "Don't worry – it'll be nice to be back in the village. I have some great memories of my time there."

Claire was gradually becoming aware that David had said nothing so far. In fact, at times she'd almost forgotten he was there.

"David, are you okay?"

Her fiancé, who was still silently nibbling his starter, looked up. "Gosh, yes – I'm fine, love. Just leaving you and your father to catch up."

"I hope you don't feel we're excluding you –"

David smiled. "This is your day – yours and your father's."

Nevertheless, Claire detected something edgy in David's manner, something she couldn't put a finger on. It felt like an undercurrent she could barely sense, but it was there nonetheless. Whatever it was, she fully intended to find out later. But right now, she wasn't going to allow his mood to spoil her time with her father.

The rest of the evening passed pleasantly, and as Claire and David parted company with her father outside the restaurant, she felt happy and relieved at how well their meeting had gone. She'd promised to collect him and his luggage from his flat the following weekend, and drive him down to Trentham-on-Sea.

As David drove back to her apartment, Claire was chatty and voluble, unable to stop talking about her father, and expressing her joy that he was now back in her life. Yet David was still surprisingly silent, just making occasional grunts to signify that he was listening to her. Claire was annoyed. He didn't seemed too thrilled about the meeting with her father, but she didn't feel she needed to pander to his bruised ego, if indeed that was his problem. Surely he couldn't be jealous because she was enjoying time with her father?

"What's the matter?" she asked him sharply.

"Oh, nothing."

"You're not upset because I've found my dad?"

"No, no – of course not."

"Then what's wrong?"

"Oh, nothing. I'm just tired."

"You don't seem very happy that *I'm* happy. I thought you'd want the best for me."

David smiled as he pulled up outside her apartment. "Darling, I'm just tired. I've a lot on my plate right now at the university. But I do want you to be happy – honestly."

With that, she had to be content. But she knew something was definitely bothering him. Perhaps the upcoming appointment of a new chancellor was preying on his mind.

Claire climbed out of David's car and began walking towards the main door of the complex. But David didn't seem to be following her as planned. Earlier, he'd agreed to stay over, so that they could dissect the meeting with her father, and exchange opinions on what had transpired before heading to bed.

"Aren't you coming?" Claire called, looking back at David, who hadn't moved from the car.

"If you don't mind, I'll head on home," David said apologetically. "I didn't realise how much paperwork I need to catch up on. End of term and all that."

"Well, I *do* mind!" Claire said stubbornly. "You promised you'd stay."

Reluctantly, David got out of the car. "Oh, alright. If you really want me to."

"Of course I want you to! But if you're going to be miserable, then you might as well go home."

After a few seconds' stand-off, David locked the car door and followed Claire up to her apartment on the second floor.

Inside, Claire opened a bottle of red wine and filled two glasses. As she and David sat down beside each other on one of the couches, he seemed to relax a little. He raised his glass and looked earnestly at her.

"I really do wish you well, Claire – you know that. It's just –"

Claire could feel her hackles rising. "You don't like my father, do you? I thought you were on my side, but it looks as though you can't bear for me to have someone else in my life!"

Finally goaded, David retaliated. "That's not true – but haven't you noticed that all your father does is talk about himself? Everything is interpreted by the way it's affected him. He strikes me as a very selfish old man."

"You're just jealous!" said Claire angrily. "Of course he's going to talk about the way things affected him – Zoe was his eldest daughter, so why wouldn't he talk about his pain? He knows I share the same pain myself!"

Angrily, they sat in silence.

Eventually, Claire spoke. "Aren't you going to say anything?"

"No. You're turning everything I say into an argument."

"*You're* the one picking the arguments! Just because my father –"

Resolutely, David stood up. "Look, I'm going to go home. There's little point in staying if we're just going to argue."

"You're right. Goodnight."

Claire held the door open, and David left without saying goodnight or kissing her. Livid, she slammed the door behind him, went back inside and topped up her wineglass. Then she sank back into the couch, furious with David and furious with herself.

She hoped her father's reappearance wasn't going to drive a wedge between her and David. She'd assumed the two men would get on well, and she'd allowed her mind to run riot, envisaging the patter of tiny feet and a doting grandfather baby-sitting. If she'd to choose one man over the other, who would it be? Claire didn't want to think about it, because she genuinely didn't know. Her father was the magical figure from her childhood, who was now giving her the chance to relive the past, but David was the caring, solid rock on which she now depended. Anyway, why should she have to choose? David was simply being awkward, and he'd soon come round. Okay, her father might have some foibles. But didn't we all? Everything would be fine when they got to know each other.

CHAPTER 70

Benjamin sat drinking his morning cuppa in the kitchen while reading the newspaper. He was now fully recovered from his operation, and had nothing to show for it except a tiny scar. Georgie thought it was cute, and insisted on kissing it every chance she got. Benjamin was also relieved that his brother's new kidney was working well, and Hugh was experiencing a new lease of life.

His mother, too, had been moved to a quality nursing home, chosen by both brothers and paid for by Benjamin. The atmosphere in this new home was delightful – there were vases of fresh flowers in all the rooms, the surroundings were spotlessly clean, and pleasant staff in crisp uniforms actually seemed to enjoy their work. Benjamin felt he'd done his best for his mother, even though he knew it could never make up for all the years he'd neglected her.

The kitchen was quiet, and he missed Alan's presence. But he wasn't worried about his son anymore – the boy had come through a lot in the past few weeks, and he seemed to have matured a great deal as a result. Touring with the band had given him a new lease of life, and he, Doug, Jerry and Tony were currently somewhere in Wales.

Benjamin had even taken to reading the music columns of the newspapers and, since the tour started, the columns had increasingly mentioned Alan's band. There were rumours of a deal with a record company, but Benjamin knew that as minors they'd all require parental permission to sign. Which would ensure that the contract was fully checked out by lawyers before anything happened. He was pleased for Alan. This was what he wanted to do, and if it meant no Cambridge degree, or putting his degree on hold, then that was fine by him.

Benjamin poured himself another cup of tea. Right now, he was supremely contented with his life, and happier than he could've imagined possible several months ago. Although he and the kids were less well-off than before – in common with millions of other people – he didn't care too much right now. The market would swing back eventually, and people always needed houses.

A sleepy-eyed Vanessa appeared at the breakfast bar, and without speaking Benjamin poured her a cup of tea. Silently, she hugged him, then padded off to put some bread in the toaster. As always, Benjamin was overwhelmed by love for this child. She, too, had undergone a metamorphosis. Jennifer's death had been a terrible blow to both her and Alan, and he knew it had changed them in ways he couldn't fully comprehend. Not surprisingly, Jennifer's death had also brought the three of them closer, and made them all more aware of each other's needs.

Georgie's regular visits to The Old Vicarage were an added bonus, but she never tried to make the children like her, or force herself into their lives. Anyway, Alan and Vanessa claimed to like her a lot, and they seemed genuinely happy for their father to have a new woman in his life.

As Vanessa joined him at the breakfast bar, he decided it was time to acquaint her with the realities of the recession, and its potential effect on their lives.

"Love, I need to talk to you. Things aren't going too well financially for us. Clara Court isn't selling, so we may have to cut back on what we're spending."

Vanessa looked alarmed. "Are you saying Grey Star has to go?"

"God, no," said Benjamin hastily. "I just meant that we can't spend money as freely as we used to. But we're not the only ones having to cut back – everyone is being affected by this bloody recession."

Vanessa gave him a scathing look. "And who caused the recession, Dad? Greedy bankers and speculators, who didn't give a damn about anyone but themselves!"

While Vanessa's assessment was somewhat simplistic, Benjamin was surprised at a thirteen-year-old's grasp of the situation.

"Bankers weren't the only ones who were greedy," Benjamin pointed out.

Vanessa bit into a piece of toast. "I know, Dad – it's capitalism itself that's at fault. It's based on greed, and it allows people to be greedy until they destroy the very things they're trying to exploit." Vanessa was warming to her theme. "Taking shortcuts to make more money is what causes so many of the world's problems. You've been doing that, Dad – building cheap houses and cutting corners anywhere you can. That's not fair – people pay their hard-earned money to buy a home."

Benjamin bowed his head. Vanessa was right. He'd taken shortcuts anywhere he could, just to make more money. And for what? Mainly to keep Jennifer happy. Which he didn't need to do anymore.

He was also hugely proud of his daughter's powers of deduction, and of her ability to evaluate the current situation. Carl and his work for Greenpeace had clearly been a big influence on her, and Benjamin got a kick out of knowing that a member of his own family had been a factor in counteracting Jennifer's self-centred views.

But Vanessa wasn't finished yet. "Intensive farming is another way for the greedy to make money – animals are living creatures, Dad, not an industrial product. By stopping them from living a natural life, we create diseases, for them and us. And what about the greedy businesses that take shortcuts like letting their waste leach into rivers and streams? And the rainforests, Dad – we're destroying them for short-term gain. We need them to absorb carbon dioxide, or global warming will get even worse!" She glared balefully at her father. "What use is money, Dad, if we've destroyed the planet? There'll be nothing left to buy!"

Benjamin was mesmerised by his daughter's eloquence. He could mentally fast-forward ten or twenty years, and imagine her on a platform somewhere, espousing her views and rallying the public to her cause. He looked at her impassioned little face and vowed there and then that he'd make changes in his own life. He was guilty of having destroyed so many beauty spots, and God knows how many creatures' habitats. He'd make restitution, and Vanessa would show him how.

In fact, the more Benjamin thought about it, the more he liked the idea of becoming the foremost builder of eco-friendly homes in the country. He'd employ architects to design a variety of homes using sustainable energy, and all would have solar panels, water-butts and composting facilities included. He'd only use indigenous woods, and reject materials made using dangerous chemicals. He'd become the industry leader in his field. Already, he could envisage himself being awarded a knighthood . . .

Benjamin smiled to himself. He'd just worked out that a person could actually become rich by doing the right thing.

CHAPTER 71

As she picked up the pile of morning newspapers the delivery boy had just dropped off, Anne glanced at the top one on the pile. Her face drained of colour. The headline declared that the newspaper had a photograph of The Right Hon Clive Ellwood *in flagrante delicto*, and challenged him to deny it.

Bursting into Clive's study, Anne threw down the newspapers in front of him as though they were contaminated with bubonic plague.

"Clive – look at this!" Anne was livid. "How dare they! Really, you must sue this rag immediately – how dare they drag your good name through the mud, and just months before the election! The opposition's dirty-tricks brigade is at it again!"

There was silence.

"Clive, are you listening to me? We can't let them get away with this – this – scurrilous accusation!"

Clive sighed as he glanced at the headline. His worst nightmare had finally come true. He thought he'd got away with it – he and Jennifer had always been so careful, but obviously they hadn't been clever enough. Well, it looked like the game was up, and just as he was intending to behave himself, too. There was a certain irony in that, he supposed. Hopefully Anne would forgive him. He'd need her support to have any hope of hanging onto his seat. He could probably kiss goodbye to a ministerial post at this point, but maybe, after a few years, when the electorate had forgotten about it . . .

"Anne, I need to talk to you."

Anne's heart almost stopped. Clive's expression told her all she needed to know. She desperately wanted to freeze that moment in time, to stop herself from hearing what was coming next.

Clive grimaced. "Sorry, Anne, we never meant to hurt you –"

Paralysed with shock, Anne's brain suddenly began to analyse the 'we' Clive had just referred to. Which had to mean his lover was someone they both knew. Suddenly, with amazing clarity, a picture of Jennifer forced its way into her brain. Now, at last, she realised why her friend had tried to kill her – she'd wanted Clive for herself!

Anne spoke at last. "So it was Jennifer?"

Ashamed, Clive nodded his head.

Anne's mind was already absorbing and re-evaluating all those occasions when Clive hadn't been where he was supposed to be. There were years of excuses, when she'd thought he was using these occasions to advance his political career, whereas instead the advances were being made to one of her best friends.

Anne glanced again at the newspaper title, and suddenly felt weak. Wasn't that the sleazy rag Hazel Bonnington wrote for? Snatching up the paper, Anne's eyes blazed with fury as she read the by-line. Hazel Bonnington had also written the story! Seething with rage and impotence, Anne flung down the newspaper. The bitch would be gloating, as would everyone else who'd been at The Gables School for Girls. As for all their present-day friends and acquaintances – how would she ever hold her head up again?

Anne headed for the door. She didn't intend staying with Clive for one minute longer. He could take a hike, and if the party dropped him, so be it, she didn't give two hoots what happened to him.

"Anne, please!" Clive pleaded. "You and I will need to present a united front when the press arrive at the door –"

Anne kept on walking.

"Look, when this all blows over, we can still take that trip to the Seychelles –"

Anne turned back, her eyes blazing. "Go to hell, you bastard!"

Clive looked worried. "But you love the Seychelles!"

He sighed resignedly as Anne slammed the door behind her. That holiday had cost him an arm and a leg. He doubted if the insurance company would reimburse him, since he could hardly cite his affair as the cause for not travelling. As far as he knew, they only reimbursed people if they were too sick to travel. Well, he certainly felt sick right now.

Pacing the floor, Clive cursed his bad luck. He'd assumed the chances of his affair being uncovered had ended with Jennifer's death. Who on earth had found out? The newspaper claimed to have a photograph of him and a woman having sex, but they'd always been so careful . . .

Suddenly, he remembered – oh damn, the garden party! While he and Jennifer had been at it in the woods, he now recalled seeing one of the waitresses walking nearby. She was very pretty, and at the time he'd thought he'd like to give her one, too. That must have been it – she'd been a reporter in disguise!

Pacing the floor, Clive hoped that Anne wasn't too upset – after all, she wanted to be a minister's wife as much as he wanted to be a minister. At least he hoped that was still the case. What a pity they'd never had kids – they might have kept her more grounded, and less likely to dump him because of a stupid little affair. Okay, a stupid big affair. He'd have liked kids himself, but it wasn't very likely now. Unless, of course, Anne *did* divorce him, and he found himself a much younger wife . . .

Clive gritted his teeth. Nice idea, but just pie in the sky and not very practical. Hopefully, Anne would soon come round, because otherwise, he could see all his political dreams disintegrating . . .

CHAPTER 72

The day after Hazel Bonnington's newspaper broke the news of Clive's affair, every other newspaper in the country had taken up the story. The Grange was overrun by reporters and photographers, speculation was rife, and no corner of Clive Ellwood's life was left unscrutinised.

Clive had admitted the affair, but refused to name the woman, begging the media to 'respect his and his wife's privacy'. But the press weren't prepared to do anything of the sort, and pictures of Anne leaving and re-entering the house appeared in all the newspapers.

Since no other newspaper had the photograph, Hazel's newspaper continued to hold the advantage. But since Jennifer was now dead, the newspaper had no intention of releasing her name and, as Clive remained tight-lipped, the media were forced to speculate on every female politician, personal assistant and intern of his acquaintance.

Additionally, reporters digging through their files on the Ellwoods came upon stories about the recent disastrous garden party, so the fiasco got a second airing.

As Claire studied the newspapers and watched the news on TV, she felt both elation and regret. This was what she'd wanted, wasn't it? She was doing this for Zoe. Yet watching Anne's tight-lipped expression as she dodged reporters on her doorstep filled Claire with guilt. She was the reason this was happening to Anne. Okay, so Clive Ellwood was the one who'd actually had the affair. But it might never have come to light if Claire hadn't given the photo to Hazel. Suddenly, it felt a hollow victory, and she wondered if Zoe would have approved of her actions.

But by the time Hazel phoned, she was feeling in a more positive mood.

"Well, what did you think of it?"

Claire smiled. "It was a remarkable scoop – you must have impeccable sources!"

"Thanks to you, I'll also have a few nice follow-up features. I'm dying to see what'll happen next – will Anne divorce him? Will he lose his seat at the next election? I doubt he'll get that ministry now."

"I'm glad it's worked out well for you," said Claire.

"By the way, have you met your father yet?" Hazel asked.

"Yes, and it was great," Claire told her enthusiastically. "He's really nice, and we'd lots to chat about."

"Will you be seeing him again?"

"Oh, yes! He's moving into the cottage in Trentham-on-Sea for a while, and –"

"Is that wise?" Hazel cut in.

"Wise?" Claire was annoyed. She owed Hazel a lot, but now she was being as difficult as David. "Why not? He's my dad, and it was his home originally, before he went to Australia."

"Australia, you say? Hmmm. Has David met him yet?"

"Yes."

"What does he think of him?"

Claire hesitated. "We had a row over Dad – I think he's jealous."

"I see. What gave you that impression?"

"Well, when we met my father, David never said a word all night. He thinks Dad's a selfish old man, and he's annoyed with me for inviting him to stay in the cottage."

"Sometimes it's wise to be cautious, Claire. I mean, how well do you know your father?"

"He's not an impostor, if that's what you mean," Claire said hastily. "He's definitely the father I knew as a child."

"That's not what I meant – oh, what the hell, it's not my business to interfere. I'm glad you've made contact, and I hope you get things sorted out with David."

"Thanks, Hazel," said Claire, smiling again.

CHAPTER 73

Anne was astonished to see Emma on her doorstep. This was the first time ever Emma had initiated contact. Normally it fell to one of the others to contact her after arrangements had already been made. Emma was always an afterthought.

Of course, everything had changed, Anne thought angrily as she stared down at her friend. Jennifer was dead, Fiona was in disgrace and her own life was disintegrating around her. She'd been betrayed by both husband and friend, and while Jennifer had been betraying her with Clive, Fiona had been betraying Jennifer with young Alan. It had been a right old merry-go-round of betrayal.

The only one who wasn't involved in betrayal – at least none that Anne knew of – was now standing on her doorstep, looking determined and belligerent.

"Anne, we need to talk," said Emma, stepping across the threshold without waiting for an invitation.

Anne raised her eyebrows but set her reservations aside. Emma's unusual behaviour had to be a portent of something equally unusual.

Emma led the way into the Ellwoods' kitchen. Then she pointed to the kettle and smiled.

"I'd love a cup of tea, Anne," she said but, since Anne seemed unable to move, she proceeded to fill the kettle without waiting for permission or approval.

Anne was too surprised to say anything, and sat in a daze at the kitchen table while Emma filled two mugs with boiling water, dropped in the tea bags and placed one in front of her.

"What do you want to talk about? I'm not exactly in the mood for chitchat after all the publicity over Clive's affair," said Anne grumpily.

She was tired and angry. Whatever Emma had to say had better be important enough to justify her ill-mannered intrusion. Maybe she wanted to apologise for her bad behaviour at the garden party, but if so, it would be the very first time! Besides, Anne thought bitterly, Emma's behaviour at the garden party was of little significance in the overall scheme of things. The whole event had been a disaster, and the beginning of the end for her and Clive.

"Well, first of all, I want to say how sorry I am to hear about you and Clive," Emma said. "It must be awful for you."

Anne shrugged. She wasn't used to having people feel sorry for her, and feeling like a victim didn't sit well with her. Briefly, she felt defensive, then she finally shrugged her shoulders. Might as well get it over with.

"Do you know who Clive was shagging?"

Emma looked vague. "Some aide or PA in his office?"

Anne pursed her lips. "No," she said at last. "It was our dear departed friend Jennifer."

Emma looked aghast. Her jaw dropped, and for a moment she was speechless. Then she brightened. "Oh well, at least it's over now. I mean, with Jennifer gone, it's not going to continue –" She gulped, abruptly closing her mouth. She was only trying to cheer Anne up, but somehow it hadn't come out quite the way she'd meant it to.

"Yes, it's difficult to conduct an affair when you're dead," Anne said acerbically. She wanted to strangle Emma. Would the woman ever learn tact?

"So what are you going to do now?" Emma ventured at last. "I presume you and Clive will patch things up?"

Anne's face darkened. "If you think I'm staying with Clive, you're very much mistaken. Please don't mention that man's name again. Now, was there something else you wanted to say to me?"

Emma grimaced. She was still flabbergasted at Jennifer's duplicity, but for now she needed to deal with the problems of the living rather than the dead.

"Well, I also want to talk to you about Fiona," said Emma.

Anne waved her arm as though swatting a fly. "What on earth is there to talk about? For heaven's sake, the woman's a fruitcake!"

"Well, she's *our* fruitcake," said Emma, matter-of-factly. "I know what she did was wrong, but she's had problems in her past that drove her to behave stupidly."

Anne's eyebrows rose at the mention of problems in Fiona's past. She'd always believed that Fiona led a charmed life as the doctor's daughter.

"So what are you saying, Emma?"

"I'm saying that Fiona is our friend – has been since schooldays – and it's not fair to ignore her now. You've got to contact her, Anne. Just because she made one mistake doesn't mean we should treat her like a pariah. We've all shared too much for that."

"Oh yes, we've all shared a lot!" Anne exclaimed bitterly, feeling bile rising in her throat. "Jennifer had no qualms about sharing my husband, had she? What sort of a friend does that?"

Emma winced beneath Anne's ferocious glare. She'd no answer to Anne's question. Jennifer's behaviour had been reprehensible. But that made it all the more important that the remaining three friends stick together.

"Look, I think you should talk to Fiona," Emma entreated her. "She and Edwin are breaking up, you and Clive are breaking up, and you both need each other at a time like this."

Anne said nothing, her lips set in a tight line. But she was beginning to see the merits of what Emma was saying. And since

Fiona's offence was so embarrassing, Anne could appear magnanimous in deigning to contact with her.

"You've seen her?"

Emma nodded.

"How is she?" Anne tried to inject some concern into her voice, coupled with a modicum of steely reserve. She wasn't prepared to capitulate just yet.

"Not surprisingly, she's in quite a state. She's realised all that she stands to lose – and I don't mean just in a material sense – she now knows how much Edwin means to her, but of course, it's too late to salvage anything there."

Anne nodded. Things did seem a mess. "What on earth made her set her cap at Jennifer's son?" she asked, "I mean, surely she'd have realised that the gullible boy might fall for her? You feel everything so intensely at that age."

Anne felt a sudden pang of guilt, remembering the intensity of her own rage all those years ago. She'd been the one who'd orchestrated the hate campaign against Zoe Gray, leaving the poor child to take the brunt of all her anger. Since the target of her hatred was out of reach, Zoe Gray had served as the next best thing.

Emma grimaced. "I should really let Fiona tell you all this, but maybe she'd find it too stressful and embarrassing . . ."

Anne raised her eyebrows.

"Well, you *are* rather intimidating, Anne," said Emma with a rueful smile.

Anne was astonished at how the tables had turned in recent weeks. Previously, she'd been the one to call all the shots, and the other three had fallen in line without question. Now, everything was out of her control. Even timid Emma was pointing the finger at her!

"Well," Emma went on, "Fiona's always had a thing for young men."

"Always?"

"Yes, she told me the only way she can feel in control is by selecting young inexperienced ones."

"Hmmm, I see what you mean. Edwin's a weedy little specimen, isn't he?"

"I'm scared of relationships, too," said Emma plaintively. "Why do you think I never married?" She gave a painful smile. "I'm still a virgin, Anne – can you believe that – at forty-two?"

Anne reached for Emma's hand. "Yes, I must admit I did sometimes wonder . . . oh dear, it's all such a mess, isn't it?"

Emma nodded.

As Anne sat silently holding Emma's hand, she felt as though a burden was gradually being lifted from her own shoulders. She wasn't the only one who had problems with life and relationships. And here and now, she, too, was being offered an opportunity to let out all the hurt she'd held inside for too long. Confession could be good for the soul.

Anne broke the silence. "I've never been able to have children, Emma."

Emma's mouth opened, then closed quickly as she swallowed.

Anne pursed her lips. "I've never told anyone what happened, not even Clive. And I'm certainly not going to tell him now!"

A silence grew between them, until Emma ventured another question.

"Would you have liked children, Anne?"

"Of course I bloody wanted children!" Anne shouted. "I wanted them more than anything in the world!"

Suddenly, she was sobbing, and Emma leapt up from her chair and threw her arms around her friend. As Anne continued to sob, Emma strained to hear what she was saying. Her breath was coming in jagged gasps, and her words, between sobs, sounded like a tiny animal in pain.

"Poor Zoe Gray," Anne whispered. "She wasn't to blame for what happened, but it was all my fault that we killed her –"

A shaken Emma wondered if any of them were immune from their past. Dear God, she thought, it all comes back to Zoe Gray. Will we ever escape from what we did?

CHAPTER 74

Zoe's Diary

May 28

I've tried to hide my problems from Claire, but she knows something's wrong. I hate shutting her out, but I can't possibly tell her what's been happening to me. I lie awake at night, worrying, then I'm exhausted the next day. I'm sometimes short-tempered with Claire when she asks questions in that direct way of hers, but I have to protect her at all costs.

Walking along the beach, Zoe seemed to have retreated into a world of her own, and Claire glanced at her worriedly. Usually they had fun together, but lately Zoe seemed like someone possessed. Now she was striding ahead, and Claire had to run to keep up with her.

"Let's tell our special story again," said Claire. That was usually guaranteed to bring a smile to Zoe's face, and it always made them feel close.

"No," said Zoe abruptly. "Not today."

"Why not?" Claire persisted.

"Because."

"Because what?"

"Because I'm not in the mood."

"But you always enjoy it when we tell it together –"

"Oh, for goodness sake, Claire, leave me alone!"

Zoe began heading for the rocks. Claire followed her, longing to find some way of cheering her sister up.

"Come on, Zoe – it'll be fun!" Claire urged. "Once upon a time, there were two princesses called Zoe and Claire –"

"For God's sake, stop!"

Claire was startled, and instantly contrite. "Sorry, Zoe – I didn't mean to upset you."

"Look, it's just a stupid childish game – we're both too old to be playing it anymore."

"But it's fun," said Claire, surprised and disappointed. Their make-believe story had always brightened their darkest hours, and given them hope that things might get better some day. Maybe Zoe didn't want to look to the future anymore. "And you're always happy when we find Daddy and bring him home again, and we all live happily ever after –" Claire glanced at her sister. "Zoe – what's wrong?" she whispered, a look of alarm on her little face. She hadn't meant to upset her sister – she'd only been trying to make her smile.

"That 'happy ever after' crap isn't going to happen!" Zoe shouted. "Now please, Claire, stop going on about it, with your stupid stories about – about –"

Claire had never seen her sister so upset, and she threw her arms around her, holding her while she sobbed. She wished she could take back every word of that silly story she'd insisted on telling.

Eventually Zoe broke away. "I'm sorry, Claire," she said gruffly, wiping her tears, "I'm just in a bad mood today."

Claire nodded, feeling totally bewildered. Why had their story made Zoe happy before, but today it made her cry?

The two girls continued down the beach in silence. The wind was blowing, and there were few people around, but Claire still *found enough people to populate the stories she silently created in her mind. She imagined the old man walking his dog was a prince who'd been placed under a spell and, when the princess found him, she'd kiss him and he'd be transformed back into a young prince again. And the girl collecting shells on the beach was searching for a magic key that would release her family from the prison where they'd been trapped by an evil witch.*

Finally, Claire tried to relive their own special story, about the two princesses called Claire and Zoe, and how they set out to rescue their father and make their mother happy again, but somehow she couldn't muster up enough enthusiasm. It just wasn't the same if she couldn't share it with Zoe.

Glancing at her sister again, Claire bit her lip. She and Zoe used to share everything, but she was beginning to feel that her sister was slipping away from her. Zoe seemed to have something major on her mind that she didn't want to share with her. It felt like a loosening of the ties that bound them to each other, and Claire desperately wished she could grow up faster so that she could be Zoe's confidante.

For reassurance, Claire squeezed her sister's hand, and Zoe absentmindedly squeezed back. For now, Claire felt comforted by her sister's love, but something told her their future mightn't have the happy ending their special story always foretold. Claire shivered, and Zoe slipped her arm around her. But the frightening thought of losing Zoe just wouldn't go away.

CHAPTER 75

Sitting in the dining room of the Clara Valley Hotel, Benjamin waited eagerly for his breakfast to be served. This time tomorrow, he thought, I'll be having breakfast at Georgie's place . . .

Since the Clara Court development was a two-hour drive from home, Benjamin had been staying at the hotel for the previous three nights. He'd needed to be on site by seven each morning, and Mrs Quick was staying at The Old Vicarage to look after Vanessa.

He'd been supervising the upgrading of all unsold apartments at Clara Court, and they were now tiled, carpeted and furnished to a high standard as an added incentive to buyers. He needed to get them sold as quickly as possible, because the market had dried up much sooner than he'd expected. Luckily, he'd successfully tendered for a school refurbishment programme in Trentham-on-Sea that would keep the company ticking over while he waited for his architects to draw up plans for his eco-housing project.

Opening the morning newspaper, Benjamin was amused to see that Clive's affair was still making the headlines. He felt genuinely sorry for Anne, and wondered if their marriage could survive all the publicity. If Jennifer hadn't died, his own marriage would have ended in divorce, but Anne was a different kettle of fish. She'd made a career out of being The Right Honourable Clive Ellwood's wife.

He was also curious about the identity of the woman for whom Clive had risked his career and his marriage. Probably some constituency secretary or PA. Maybe he should ring The Grange and offer some sort of support – after all, Anne and Clive had both attended Jennifer's funeral. But to sympathise with one would surely alienate the other. In the end, Benjamin shrugged. He'd worry about it later. Right now, his breakfast was arriving, and besides, he'd more pressing matters on his mind.

Benjamin's most pressing problem was Georgie. He was tired of having to make baby-sitting arrangements with Mrs Quick every time he wanted to spend the night with her. He'd suggested she move into The Old Vicarage, but she'd refused because she was worried about the children's feelings. He tried to assure her that his kids wouldn't mind, but Georgie insisted it was far too soon after their mother's death. They needed time, she felt, to adjust to a new woman in their father's life.

Before breakfast, Benjamin had tried Georgie's phone number, but she wasn't answering. He'd tried unsuccessfully to contact her several times during the previous few days, but could never get a reply. But he wasn't worried – they were both busy people. She was preparing for an exhibition at a major city gallery, and he knew she was feeling under pressure right now. She was probably working flat out in her studio at the back of the house, and answering the phone would only be a distraction.

Just thinking about her brought a smile to his face. Benjamin still couldn't quite believe she was part of his life – and while he understood her reluctance to impose herself on the children, he honestly believed Alan and Vanessa were happy for him.

After he'd finished his breakfast and paid his hotel bill, Benjamin began the two-hour drive back to The Old Vicarage. He was looking forward to seeing Vanessa, then later he intended heading over to Georgie's, since Mrs Quick had agreed to stay for an extra night with Vanessa. He and Georgie would catch up on all of each other's news . . . He felt himself become aroused at the mere thought of making love to her later that evening.

When he arrived home, Vanessa rushed to greet him, and

Benjamin secretly marvelled at how close they'd all become. The change in their family dynamic had happened since Vanessa made contact with his family in Walthamstow, and the children had benefited greatly from knowing Hugh, Maisie and Carl. It had given them both a new perspective on life, and an appreciation of what they had, rather than an assumption that they were entitled to it. Jennifer's death had also been a major factor in drawing them closer to each other, and in enabling contact with the Walthamstow Corcrofts to continue. As Jennifer's materialistic influence on the children gradually waned, Benjamin felt confident that over time they'd become strong, well-balanced adults who didn't need to be surrounded by wealth in order to feel worthwhile.

After a tasty lunch, which Vanessa had cooked with Mrs Quick's help, Benjamin left the kitchen and rang Alan. The tour was going fine, his son told him. The band was currently in the midlands, and audiences seemed to love their music. Benjamin was pleased that everything was turning out well, and he rang off with a smile on his face.

Now, it was time to call Georgie. He felt a sudden thrill as he dialled her number and waited to hear her voice. He felt like a teenager with a crush, and his heart was pounding as he waited for her to answer.

There was no reply, so he dialled her number again, just in case he'd dialled a wrong digit. Still no reply. Perhaps she was out? They hadn't made any definite arrangements for tonight, but she knew he was due back from Clara Court that afternoon. Maybe she'd gone to check out the venue for her exhibition? He was disappointed, but then Georgie was an independent woman, with a life of her own. Hopefully she'd contact him later.

But there was no call from Georgie, and his own calls went unanswered. Throughout the afternoon, as he worked at home on his computer, he'd stopped intermittently to phone her, but there was never any reply. Eventually, a disgruntled Benjamin headed for the kitchen. He'd better let Mrs Quick know that she wouldn't be needed tonight. It looked as though he and Vanessa were going to have a quiet night in.

CHAPTER 76

On Saturday morning, before driving her father down to the cottage in Trentham-on-Sea, Claire spent an enjoyable hour in a large department store. She selected cushions, a throw, a table lamp, sheets and a duvet, a new set of pots and pans and a kettle. Then she went to a grocery store and stocked up on a selection of food items, so that her father would have at least a modicum of home comforts in the otherwise primitive cottage. Based on his comments about his pension, she suspected he didn't have much money, so she was looking forward to spoiling him, albeit discreetly, and looking after him as he got older. If he wanted to remain in the cottage long-term, she'd have it modernised so that he could live out his days there in comfort. Claire felt really excited at being part of a family at last.

Since they'd spent so many years apart, Claire was determined to make up for lost time by spending as much time as she could in his company. Her father, in turn, seemed pleased to be spending time with her too, and after their first meeting in the restaurant they'd agreed to stay in regular contact.

Her father was now waiting on the steps of the block of flats where he'd been staying, his luggage beside him as she arrived to pick him up.

"Hello, darling!" he said, beaming as she drew up outside.

"Hi, Daddy, it's great to see you," said Claire happily, jumping out and helping to load his suitcases into the boot of her car.

Claire eyed the well-worn suitcases, thinking that her poor father hadn't fared too well financially over the years.

As though reading her mind, her father looked at her ruefully. "Unfortunately, I had to leave my furniture and possessions in Australia. I thought about shipping it all home, but there seemed little point, since I didn't know where I was going to live, and besides, it would cost a fortune to get it here. So I donated all of it to one of the orphanages there. Hopefully they made a bit of money from selling it."

Claire smiled happily as she helped him into the car. No wonder she loved him all over again – what a kind, thoughtful person he was!

When they arrived at the cottage, Claire helped her father carry his cases in, then made them both a cup of tea, using the new kettle she'd bought. Then, while her father familiarised himself with the old homestead, she made up the bed in the main bedroom, replacing the old bed linen with pristine sheets, new duvet and cover. She felt happy that she could help her father, and pleased that she hadn't yet put the cottage on the market. As far as she was concerned, the cottage was his for as long as he wanted it. Hadn't it originally been his home, anyway?

Her father seemed pleased to be back in the village, and talked incessantly about this person and that person who'd once lived there.

"They're all gone now, Dad," said Claire. "Many of them are dead, others have moved on. I doubt if there's anyone here who'll know you."

"Never mind," he said sadly. "I suppose it's inevitable at my age. But it's nice to be back."

As he spoke, Claire thought sadly of how her mother had denied her any contact with her father. Well, Mum, she thought angrily, at least I've found him now. And he's back in the house that you evicted him from.

"Are any of Dennis Barker's family still living in his house?"

Claire shook her head. "No, Dad, that house was sold about five years ago, when Dr Barker died." Her father didn't need to know that his friend's daughter Fiona had been instrumental in Zoe's death.

Her father sighed. "Ah, those were the days. I wish your mother hadn't been so vindictive." He brightened. "But, I'm back again now, thanks to you, love. I can't tell you how glad I am to be home."

Claire hadn't seen David since the night of her first meeting with her father. Nor had he telephoned. Well, he can take a hike, Claire thought angrily, as she drove back from Trentham-on-Sea, it's clear that he's not interested in my happiness. I thought he'd be pleased I'd found my father, but I was wrong. He hasn't even rung to apologise for marching off in a huff that night.

David was obviously sulking, which wasn't really like him at all. Claire was puzzled, wondering what it was about the evening that had upset him. Had she or her father said something that offended him? How she wished David would simply say what was on his mind, instead of pretending nothing was wrong! That first meeting with her father was so clearly imprinted in her mind, and Claire went over it bit by bit, analysing what had been said in case David could have misinterpreted anything. But she could find nothing in any of their exchanges that could have upset him.

It must be jealousy, she concluded. Maybe he felt displaced by her father, since previously he'd been the most important man – in fact, the only man – in her life. In fact, he'd become her entire family, and maybe he suddenly felt usurped in that role.

By the time she'd reached her apartment, Claire had cooled down, and decided to ring her fiancé and try to sort things out. After all, she reasoned, if he was feeling insecure, she really should do her best to reassure him. In a way, his insecurity was endearing, since it meant he obviously cared for her. She should be looking on it as a good sign, rather than getting annoyed about it.

Smiling, she lifted the phone. "David? Hi, it's me."

"Hello, Me."

Claire was relieved that he sounded his usual pleasant and humorous self.

"Fancy coming over for a bite to eat? I'm making a chilli – your favourite."

"Yummy! I'll be there in fifteen minutes!"

Claire busied herself happily in the kitchen, preparing the ingredients for the chilli, and looking forward to seeing David again. Hopefully, their little spat had been no more than a hiccup in their relationship. With hindsight, she realised she'd no right to pressure him into saying he liked her father – hopefully it would happen over time, but meanwhile she had to allow him to make that decision on his own. As she lightly fried the meat, Claire wondered how anyone could dislike her father. He was a lovely man, and she was looking forward to many happy years of being his daughter.

She was pleased that her father was now settled back in the home where they'd all once been a family. Having him there would enable her to relive the happy parts of her childhood, and remove the loneliness that had dogged her all her life.

Of course, David was the one with whom she'd be building a future. There'd hopefully be children, and what could be nicer than having a kind and loving grandfather to visit? Would they call him 'Granddad' or 'Grandpa'? Claire delighted in thinking about the new and happy dimension that had been added to her future.

By the time David arrived, delicious aromas were emanating from Claire's kitchen.

"Hmmm – smells wonderful!" he said appreciatively as he kissed her. "Thank goodness I'm marrying a woman with such wonderful culinary skills!"

Claire smiled, relieved that their row was behind them. She'd suspected she'd been right in thinking he'd suffered a brief bout of jealousy, and now that she'd taken steps to reassure him, their little spat was over. Hopefully it would be plain sailing from here on in. She was also pleased that David had again confirmed his intention of marrying her!

"Speaking of getting married –" said Claire as she spooned out two rice and chilli portions, "– I've asked my Dad to give me away on our wedding day."

"You've *what*?" David's expression was one of incredulity.

"I've asked him to walk me down the aisle. He's my father, after all."

"But you hardly know him – anyway, don't I get a say in any of this?"

"No, you don't!" said Claire angrily. "If he'd been around since you met me, you wouldn't be putting up this opposition now."

"Claire, are you losing your marbles? You've only just met the man – don't you think you should wait a bit longer before bringing him into our lives? I mean, you know nothing about where –"

"He's always been my father, whether you like it or not. But you haven't always been my fiancé," she added spitefully, "and at this rate, it doesn't look like you'll ever be my husband!"

"Jesus, I'm not putting up with this crap any longer," David said angrily. "If you don't want to marry me, just say so. But ever since you met the man, you've been trying to turn everything into a competition between your father and me!"

"You don't like him, do you?"

"No, I don't!"

"Well, in that event, you'd better leave."

"Too right I will!"

David stormed out of the apartment, leaving Claire staring at two uneaten plates of chilli and rice. They smelled delicious, but suddenly Claire found she had no appetite. With a sigh, she carried both plates over to the bin and tipped them in.

CHAPTER 77

When Fiona heard about Clive's affair on the news, she'd longed to lift the phone and call Anne to offer support. But she didn't dare. Anne hadn't been in touch since Alan Corcroft was taken to hospital. She didn't blame Anne for cutting her off – her behaviour had been inexcusable. If Alan hadn't been found by his sister, there might have been two Corcroft funerals instead of one.

Fiona felt deeply sorry for Anne, who'd suffered so much lately – firstly, the garden party incident, then she'd been present when Jennifer died, and now, Emma told her, she'd discovered that Clive had been sleeping with Jennifer.

Fiona dabbed her eyes. All their lives had come unstuck. She was lucky that Edwin was willing to stick by her and help her through her problems.

Suddenly, the phone rang. Fiona stared at it for a few seconds, then picked it up gingerly. There weren't many people she wanted to talk to, and probably fewer still who wanted to talk to her.

"Fiona?"

"Oh." She hesitated. "Anne, hello."

"How are you feeling?"

There was a pause. "Not great, I'm afraid. But then, you've got troubles of your own – I'm so sorry about you and Clive. So much has gone wrong for us all lately, hasn't it?"

Anne sighed. "Yes, it has."

Fiona blew her nose. "I'm lucky Edwin's forgiven me, and is prepared to help me sort out the mess I created. I've agreed to go for psychotherapy, and I'm relieved that there isn't going to be a court case either."

Anne was a little peeved that Fiona's problems had sorted themselves out so easily. Despite humiliating Edwin, he'd been willing to take her back. On the other hand, she'd never be able to accept Clive's betrayal.

"I missed seeing you at Jennifer's funeral," Anne said.

"You could hardly expect me to go – not after what happened!" Fiona said angrily, "Now, if you're just ringing to have a go at me –"

"No, no, sorry, I didn't mean to imply anything – I just missed you being there. I mean, we were all once so close –"

"Anne, are you living in cloud-cuckoo-land?" Fiona asked. "We haven't been close for years! You tell us what to do, and we all fall in line. It's been a long time since any of us really talked about our feelings, or our past. And now, it looks like I've got few friends left."

"Well, you have me," said Anne firmly, ignoring Fiona's outburst. "And Emma, too. Now that Jennifer's gone, I think we three remaining friends should stick together. You're not the only one who's made mistakes."

"Obviously Emma's been talking to you."

"Er, yes." Anne felt annoyed that Fiona guessed she'd needed prompting and hadn't rung of her own volition.

"She's been a really good friend," said Fiona warmly. "I don't know what I'd have done if she hadn't come round. She's made me realise that I have to put this episode behind me, and get on with my life." She grimaced. "You've no idea how guilty I feel about Alan Corcroft, Anne. I wish I could take back the things I said to him –" She blew her nose. "I was angry that he brought emotions into something that was just meant to be a bit of fun. How could I have been so cruel? But I've been emotionally dead for so long myself that I've learnt to despise feelings in other people."

Anne felt a surge of affection for her old friend that she hadn't felt in a long time. Suddenly, it felt good to care, to be needed, and to have friends who weren't perfect, since it allowed her to be less than perfect, too.

"Young Alan will soon move on with his life," Anne said supportively. "He's young and resilient. You have to forgive yourself too, Fiona."

During the few moments of silence that followed, Anne could hear a tearful Fiona blowing her nose again, and knew her friend was fighting to regain her composure.

"So what's happening with you and Clive?" Fiona asked at last.

"There's no me and Clive anymore," Anne said curtly. "I presume you know it was Jennifer he was cheating with?"

"Yes, Emma told me. But I assumed it would all blow over . . ."

"Then neither of you really know me," Anne replied angrily. "Maybe none of us really know each other anymore. You're right, Fiona – it's been a long time since any of us talked about important things like our feelings."

"So you're really going to leave Clive?"

"Yes," said Anne firmly. "I'm not one of those pathetic little political wives who'll take back the cheating husband for the sake of his career. I have a degree in fine arts, so I'll probably find a job easily enough – anyway, I'll make sure Clive pays substantial maintenance. I've already engaged the best divorce lawyer in the country."

"Well, good for you!"

Anne and Clive were still living together in The Grange, but Anne was refusing to have anything to do with him. She found his wheedling and begging for forgiveness quite nauseating.

"As far as I'm concerned, Clive is the one who's leaving," she said determinedly, "You know, Fiona, that damned garden party was the beginning of all our troubles. How dare Clive blame me for everything that went wrong, while at the same time shagging one of my closest friends! What a hypocrite!"

Anne was still fuming at the injustice of being held responsible for Clive's political allies getting sick. It was unfortunate that she'd claimed the quiches as her own, but Clive had been agreeable to the subterfuge at the time. It was only afterwards that he'd decided to hold her accountable. Nor was it her fault that the agency couldn't locate the woman who'd taken delivery of the quiches.

"You're a brave woman, Anne," Fiona told her. "I don't know how you've managed to cope so well with all the publicity. But you've come through it all with your head held high and your dignity intact."

"Well, it might look that way – but the truth is I'm devastated, Fiona," Anne admitted. "I'm tired of holding my head up high and pretending that Clive's behaviour hasn't upset me. And I'm scared because I don't know what the future's going to hold."

She immediately felt better for having spoken the truth and the sky hadn't fallen when she'd done so.

"Maybe you should consider taking him back?"

Anne didn't hesitate for even a second. "Definitely not! The idyllic life Clive and I had was all a lie anyway – the only one having an idyllic life was Clive, with a wife and a mistress both catering to his needs. Well, now he has no one."

In the silence that followed, Anne was the first to speak again.

"Fiona, we've got to put all this behind us. Let's get together for lunch soon – all three of us," she said determinedly.

A lump had formed in her throat, because she was realising just how much these other women meant to her. And suddenly, it didn't matter if the others knew she was frightened and confused, and that she was no longer the leader they'd all once looked to for decisions. People had to be allowed to change, and strong friendships could always accommodate that.

"Yes, I'd love to have lunch with you and Emma," said Fiona. "Thank goodness you're still both my friends." She sighed. "If only we could turn back the clock . . ."

As the two women ended their call, Anne suddenly remembered the card from the psychotherapist. She'd planned to get help after Jennifer's death, but then Clive's affair and all the media coverage had relegated it far down her list of priorities. But now, at last, she was going to ring and make an appointment.

CHAPTER 78

Claire was in a rotten mood. She hadn't heard from David, but she was determined she wasn't going to be the one to phone. But by lunchtime, she'd begun to worry. In all the time they'd been together they'd never argued, but now, within a short space of time, they'd had two major rows. And regrettably, they'd both been about her father.

During lunch hour, she phoned her father, who appeared to have settled in well in Trentham-on-Sea. She felt sorry he had so little money after a lifetime of working abroad. But in the current economic climate, many people had lost heavily on investments and pensions that had been ploughed into risky schemes, leaving them the losers while the risk-takers seemed to walk away scot-free. She hoped that the new bed linen and the other items she'd bought had brightened up the house and made him feel at home. She felt good at being able to provide him with somewhere to live, since she suspected his flat had been little more than basic.

"Do you need anything, Dad?"

"No, everything's fine, love," he told her cheerfully, and it made her feel on top of the world to hear her dear old dad's voice again. She still hadn't got over the novelty of having found him again, and she silently thanked Hazel for keeping her end of the bargain.

"Okay, Dad, I'll see you at the weekend?"

"Great – I'll look forward to seeing my little girl again. How's David?"

"Oh, er – he's fine," Claire lied. She wasn't going to tell her father that they weren't speaking to each other because of him!

When she'd rung off, Claire felt irrationally angry at her fiancé. He was spoiling her happiness by his petty behaviour, and she could see difficulties and embarrassment ahead if she had to make excuses to her father for David's absence.

Since Teresa was on her lunch break, Claire was answering any calls to the office. She'd bought a sandwich and was eating it at her desk while flicking through a professional journal when a call came through to her phone. She hoped it might be David – since he knew her schedule, this would be the time he'd phone.

"Hello, Claire Ross's office –"

She almost dropped the phone when the caller announced her name as Anne Ellwood, and requested an appointment. For one terrifying moment, Claire wondered if Anne had discovered who she was, and was phoning to have a go at her.

"You, er, want to book a consultation?"

"Yes, of course," Anne replied tersely. "Why else would I be ringing?"

"Yes, sorry, I – when do you want to make the appointment for?"

"As soon as possible," Anne replied.

Having made an appointment for the following week, Anne rang off, leaving Claire shocked and worried. She felt wrong-footed by Anne's abrasiveness, and she wondered what would happen when Anne arrived. On the other hand, hadn't she been the one who'd delivered her business cards to the four women, in the hope that one or more of them might make an appointment? Up until now, she'd forgotten all about her original little ploy.

Claire spent the rest of her lunch break worrying. Could Anne know about her attendance at the Ellwoods' garden party? Or on arrival, would Anne recognise her as one of the waiting staff? Or might she remember her from the reunion? Hazel Bonnington had recognised her despite her new hair colour. She could only hope that Anne wasn't quite so observant. Or could Anne somehow have discovered she was the one who'd given the incriminating photo of Clive and Jennifer to Hazel? Was this appointment simply an opportunity to confront her? Claire felt sick. Anne's arrival could only spell disaster.

She sighed. And David still hadn't phoned.

CHAPTER 79

At the breakfast table, Benjamin was reading the morning newspaper and following up on the latest stories about Clive Ellwood's affair while Vanessa munched her cereal. Father and daughter enjoyed their silent but companionable breakfasts, with neither of them feeling the need to make conversation.

Benjamin was in a good mood, because he was expecting to see Georgie that evening. He'd been annoyed at not seeing her the night before, but now, tonight's reunion would be all the more exciting!

Vanessa gave him a smile, rinsed her cereal bowl, then left for the stables. Finishing his tea, Benjamin rose to his feet. He hadn't time to hang about either. He was expected at the Stonegate Farm site shortly, to meet his team of architects. He had decisions to make about the viability of the site, now that the recession had truly bitten, and he was giving serious consideration to Vanessa's lecture about saving the planet. He was going to re-apply for planning permission to build ecologically sound houses. Instead of the thousands of soulless boxes he'd intended squashing onto the site, he was now planning to substantially lower the housing density, and establish large parkland areas and public amenities. What was the point of building houses without creating an infrastructure that would enable the residents to create a community?

As he arrived at the Stonegate Farm site, Benjamin's mood was upbeat. He was enjoying the idea of making a complete turnaround in his business practices. In the site office, he studied the range of house designs his architects had produced, and was extremely pleased. The designs incorporated numerous features like thermostats, indoor water-filters, solar panels, outside water-butts, composting facilities and reed-bed sewage treatment. The houses would also be built of indigenous materials and local woods, and there would be several different designs and sizes for buyers to choose from. And before the site was prepared, Benjamin intended to seek the advice of the RSPB and the Wildlife Trust with regard to preserving animal and bird habitats. Since the animals had been there first, Benjamin felt that their homes deserved consideration too. Besides, being ecological meant being at one with nature, didn't it?

Feeling happy and righteous, he left his architects with instructions to draw up new plans for submission to the local council. He spent the rest of the day in meetings at the Stonegate site, the most important of which involved showing senior officials from the bank the proposed layout for the new eco-development. It amused him to see them plodding after him through the mud in their business suits!

As his business day concluded, and since he was already on the outskirts of Stonehill village, Benjamin decided he'd call to Georgie's house on his way home. Then, having made arrangements with her, he'd return home to see Vanessa, collect Mrs Quick who'd agreed to stay overnight at The Old Vicarage, and come back to spend the night with Georgie.

Whistling cheerfully, Benjamin parked outside Georgie's house, got out and knocked on the door. But there was no answer. The house looked forlorn, and her car wasn't in the driveway either. For one terrifying moment, he wondered if she'd packed up and left the village. His mind ran riot as he considered that he might have put too much pressure on her to move into The Old Vicarage.

He shook his head vehemently. Georgie would never run away without telling him. No, something must be wrong. Maybe she'd received bad news – perhaps a relative had died – and she'd had to leave in a hurry. Maybe, at this very minute, there was a message from her waiting on his answer phone at home?

Before he left Georgie's house, Benjamin circled the perimeter of the building, peering in through the downstairs windows. All the rooms were in darkness, and there wasn't a sound to be heard, so he concluded there was no one there.

Back home, there was no message on his answer phone either, and Benjamin's heart plummeted. Where on earth was Georgie? Had he found love, only to lose it again? No, she'd never treat him like that. Or would she?

Suddenly, he felt a cold weight in the pit of his stomach as he recalled how just before he'd left for the Clara Court apartments, he'd signed over the church and its stained-glass windows to the Stonehill community. Maybe that was all Georgie had wanted and, now that she'd achieved her aim, she'd left the village. Maybe she was a professional agitator who communities hired to do their dirty work. Perhaps at this very minute she was settling into some new community and being brought up to date on their plans. Being petite and pretty, Georgie could always use seduction as her modus operandi. Get the old fool on the opposing side to fall in love with her. Job done. Time to move on again.

Benjamin roared aloud in anger and heartache. He'd been fooled again. He'd let another woman walk all over him. How could he have been so stupid? Jennifer had treated him like dirt, and now Georgie seemed to have done it too. Did he look like a victim? Did he have the word '*Idiot*' tattooed across his forehead?

He strode into the kitchen and put the kettle on. Then having made himself a cup of tea, he sat in front of it, staring into space and leaving it to go cold. The act of making tea had simply been a brief distraction, because he didn't really want anything to drink. Except maybe a bottle of brandy, assuming his fears about Georgie were correct.

He buried his head in his hands. It was now four days since he'd heard from her. There was no reply from her phone, nor had she answered the door when he'd called. Her car was gone. What on earth was he supposed to think? He was overcome by panic. All he wanted was Georgie, to fill the gaping hole that now existed inside him. He tried not to think of her impish face, her gorgeous red hair that felt so soft in his hands. But he had to face the truth – she'd deceived him brilliantly. She'd even pretended to be concerned about his kids and how they'd react to another woman in their father's life. No wonder she hadn't wanted to move in – she'd no intention of sticking around!

He wondered if she'd left him a note at the cottage. If so, she'd probably put it in the flowerpot where she sometimes hid her spare keys, and it would say: 'Ha ha! Gotcha!' Well, he'd go round there again later, since he might as well know the truth. Besides, he didn't want anyone else finding proof that he'd been made a fool of yet again.

Furious, he paced the kitchen, unsure of what to do. He certainly wasn't going to take this treatment lying down. Suddenly, he had an idea, and he laughed harshly at the thought.

When he was upset, Benjamin was incapable of sitting around and doing nothing. Georgie's deceitfulness had hurt him to the core, and he needed to do something to ease the pain that was raging inside him. She'd taken him for a sucker, which he clearly was. She'd made him fall in love with her, and now she'd thrown his love back in his face. All she'd cared about was the preservation of Stonegate church, and as soon as she'd got her way, she'd upped and left him.

Benjamin growled. Well, he wasn't going to take this treatment lying down. He'd show Georgie Monks exactly what he thought of her deceitful behaviour!

CHAPTER 80

Angry and hurt, Benjamin left the house and climbed into his car. He'd conceived a brilliant plan of action, which he intended to carry out straight away. He was definitely going to make his feelings known. No woman was ever going to mess with his heart again! He was relieved that Vanessa was out at the stables. If she'd been at home, she'd have detected his mood and refused to let him leave until he'd explained what was wrong. And by then his anger might have dissipated. Right now, he *wanted* to feel angry and hard-done-by.

Still fuelled by his anger and sense of injustice, he drove to the site at Stonegate Farm. With a cursory nod to the night watchman who opened the site gate, Benjamin drove up to the Stonegate Farm buildings, and around to the back where the industrial plant and building supplies were stored. Searching through one of the portacabins, Benjamin found what he wanted, and emerged a while later with a paint tin, a large brush, and a smirk on his face. Pleased, he got into his car, signalled to the watchman to open the gate again, and drove off.

As he drove towards Georgie's house, Benjamin's anger was reaching boiling point again, and mentally he listed her offences in order to justify what he was about to do. It was quite possible she wasn't even an artist either, and had simply created that persona as a cover for her real career as saboteur. He'd allowed himself to fall for that little redheaded minx, and she'd thrown his love back in his face!

When he reached Georgie's cottage, Benjamin experienced his first moment of uncertainty. What on earth was he doing? Vanessa would be appalled if she knew what her father was contemplating. On the other hand, Georgie had given him no other choice.

Benjamin intended parking on the grass, leaving the driveway clear for his own artwork, but as he drove through the gate at an angle, he hit one of the pillars and clipped the side of his Land Rover. This made him even more furious, and he considered Georgie responsible for that too. It was all her fault that he was here anyway.

In a temper, he yanked open the boot of the car, opened the tin of white paint and armed himself with the brush. Now, he'd show her what he thought of her behaviour! He wanted to see the horror on Georgie's face – if she ever came back, that is – when she saw what he'd written. Because right now, he was going to let her know – in large white letters across her driveway – what he thought of her duplicity. He hadn't yet decided whether he'd write *Liar* or *Cheat*, or maybe even *Why Did You Deceive Me?* His anger would tell him what to do when he started painting. Georgie Monks might have got her way over the church, but now it was payback time!

He was stirring the paint when the front door opened, and a pale face, surrounded by a mass of tousled red hair, appeared like an apparition.

"Benjamin! What on earth are you doing?"

Like a schoolboy caught robbing an orchard, Benjamin could feel himself turning the colour of Georgie's hair.

"I – er, I –"

"And what are you doing with that tin of paint?"

"Oh er –" he thought desperately for a few nanoseconds, "– I was going to edge your driveway in white, er, to make it easier for you to see it at night."

"That might be useful if I was arriving by helicopter," Georgie observed wryly, "but my car hasn't managed to make it off the ground yet."

Wrong-footed, Benjamin decided to go on the attack. "You've been ignoring my phone calls!" he shouted at her angrily. "You could've just told me honestly you didn't want to be with me. You didn't have to resort to –"

"For Christ's sake, I've been trying to stay away from you, because I don't want to pass on this flu!" Georgie said angrily.

In view of his anger, she'd been about to query his true plan for the white paint, but suddenly she had to run back inside and, as Benjamin followed her, he heard her throwing up in the bathroom.

"Georgie, will I send for the doctor?" he called, suddenly worried.

Looking exhausted, she nodded as she reappeared in the hall again. "Okay, thanks. I thought I could sleep my way through it, but I just can't seem to shake this bug. I'm sick of feeling unwell, and I can't keep any food down."

She padded back to the bedroom and got into bed.

As soon as he'd telephoned the doctor, Benjamin followed Georgie into her bedroom.

"I was desperately worried when I didn't hear from you," he said, tenderly pulling the covers over her. He avoided mentioning his earlier irrational belief that she'd left him. "I called to the house, but there was no answer. And there was no answer from your mobile phone."

Georgie grimaced. "The battery was flat – sorry, I forgot to charge it," she said apologetically. "Honestly, these last few days I've been too unwell to do anything." She tried briefly to sit up, then decided against it and flopped back on her pillows again. "Was that you who called by earlier today? I thought I heard someone at the back of the house, but I didn't have the energy to get up. I've been sleeping most of the time. When I'm up, all I seem to do is get sick."

"Where's your car?"

"Oh, Christ, I'd forgotten all about it!" Georgie moaned. "It's in for a service at the garage beside the library – would you be a dear and collect it for me?"

Benjamin nodded, relief flooding his face.

"So you haven't been trying to get rid of me?"

"For Christ's sake, Benjamin – everything isn't all about you!" Georgie said angrily. "Just because I'm ill doesn't mean I've finished with you. If you're going to freak out every time I get flu, we're going to have a very stormy relationship!"

"But think of all the making-up!" Benjamin said, suddenly smiling as he leaned forward to kiss her. He'd been a silly emotional fool, and he deserved Georgie's anger. Thank goodness she didn't realise what he'd been planning to do!

As he was about to kiss her, Georgie turned her face away.

"Please, Benjamin – I don't want you catching this dose, and bringing it home to Vanessa –"

"Don't worry," said Benjamin soothingly. "The doctor will be here soon, and he'll give you something to make you feel better." He held her hand tightly. "If it's contagious, I'm sure he'll prescribe something for Vanessa and me. Anyway, I don't mind sharing diseases with you. After all, I'm hoping to share my life with you!"

Half an hour later, the local doctor arrived, and Benjamin left him and Georgie alone while he strolled around the garden. How could he have doubted her? How could he have been such a fool? In fact, as soon as Georgie was better, he was going to ask her to marry him. That way, there would be no more uncertainties.

As he re-entered the hallway, the doctor was just leaving Georgie's bedroom.

"Well, doctor – have you given her something for the flu?" Benjamin demanded.

The doctor smiled. "She doesn't have the flu," he replied.

Benjamin's brow furrowed. "Then what wrong with her? I mean, she's feeling awful –"

"There's nothing *wrong* with her," said the doctor. "But I'll let her tell you all about it herself."

Smiling, the doctor let himself out the front door, but Benjamin didn't notice. He was already hurrying down the corridor to Georgie's bedroom.

"Georgie, are you okay?" Benjamin whispered, overcome by emotion as he surveyed her pale elfin face. "Tell me what's wrong with you – the doctor said you don't have flu."

"No, I'm pregnant," said Georgie, so softly that Benjamin hardly heard her.

"W-what?"

"I'm pregnant. We're expecting a baby."

Benjamin's heart did a somersault of joy. "But I thought you couldn't –"

"So did I. Since it never happened during all the years I was married, I assumed –"

"It just shows we're meant for each other," said Benjamin, kissing her excitedly.

He was overcome with joy and relief. Clearly, he wasn't sterile either. This would be his third child, possibly his first biological one. But he wouldn't love this child any more than he loved Alan and Vanessa. They were all his children and he'd move heaven and earth for them if he had to.

"I love you," he whispered, patting the soft mound of her belly. "When are we due?"

"In seven months' time," said Georgie.

"Well, that means you'll have to move into The Old Vicarage," Benjamin said, smiling. "And you'll have to marry me, too."

Georgie smiled at him. "Is that a proposal?"

Nodding, Benjamin affirmed it with a kiss.

"Let's put the wedding on hold until after the baby's born – it'll give Alan and Vanessa time to adjust to the new arrival," Georgie said. "Next summer sounds perfect – what do you think?"

Benjamin nodded. An hour earlier he'd thought his heart was broken – now he was having a baby and getting married! He couldn't wait to tell Alan and Vanessa the news.

Georgie smiled impishly, her eyes twinkling. "Oh, by the way, since I'm moving into The Old Vicarage, you needn't bother painting the edges of my driveway anymore. It was a nice thought, but not a lot of use without a helicopter."

"You want a helicopter? I'll buy you one for a wedding present!" said Benjamin enthusiastically.

"I don't need one," said Georgie, smiling. "I'm floating on air already."

CHAPTER 81

After several sleepless nights, Claire finally arose to face the day of Anne's appointment. She felt apprehensive, and dog-tired from not sleeping. She certainly wouldn't be giving Anne her best professional attention today! She also made a point of wearing her hair in a different style to the way she'd worn it at the reunion and the garden party – she was keen to make as many changes as possible to prevent Anne recognising her. She'd applied darker make-up than usual, and had been rewarded by a strange look from Teresa when she'd arrived at the office.

David still hadn't rung, and Claire was beginning to feel frightened. Had she pushed him too far? On the other hand, why couldn't he be happy for her? She'd met *his* parents several times, yet she hadn't insulted *him* by saying they were selfish and egotistical! Well, right now, Claire felt that she'd more to worry about than David's tantrums. Anne was her last appointment of the day, and she was dreading it.

What on earth would Anne want to talk about? She'd need to stay on her toes in case Anne started talking about things Claire already knew. She'd need to resist making any input that might alert Anne to the fact that she knew more than she should. Oh God, what a day this was going to be! Claire had a full morning ahead, so luckily there'd be little time to brood on Anne's impending arrival.

During lunch break, Claire was so nervous she wasn't able to eat anything. In the local café she left her food almost untouched. One bite and a drink of tea was all she could manage, and she hoped her stomach wouldn't start grumbling during her session with Anne.

Later that afternoon, when Anne swept into Claire's consulting rooms, she clearly expected Claire to know who she was.

"You can hardly be surprised that I'm here," Anne said acerbically, "unless you've been living under a rock for the last few weeks. All the newspapers have covered the story about my husband's affair. The other woman hasn't been mentioned, but I know who she is. I mean, was."

She removed her jacket and placed it on the coat-rack before sitting down facing Claire.

"You look familiar," she said abruptly. "Have we met before?"

Claire gave a nervous smile. "I don't think so – I seem to have one of those faces that people always think they recognise."

Anne seemed to accept Claire's explanation, and settled back in her chair. Relieved, Claire hoped that Anne's preoccupation with her own problems would protect her from further scrutiny.

"I presume everything I say here is completely confidential?"

"Yes, of course."

"Well, Clive's affair isn't specifically why I'm here –"

Claire held her breath, fearful that Anne was going to unmask her . . .

"– I've been intending to make an appointment anyway, because lots of things have gone wrong lately. I've been having flashbacks, due to a recent traumatic event."

Claire was surprised, and a little scared, that this event – whatever it was – might somehow rebound on her. She'd been stupid to distribute her business cards to the people she wanted to hurt, and now she was being drawn into their lives in a way she didn't want. But she was a qualified psychotherapist, so at the very least she needed to behave in a normal professional manner.

"Do you want to begin by discussing your husband's affair?" Claire asked.

Anne waved a hand imperiously. "There's nothing to discuss," she said. "I've no intention of staying with a man who was shagging one of my closest friends for years. Her name's been kept out of the papers – probably in deference to the fact that she's now dead – but that doesn't make any difference to how I feel. Everything I thought I had with Clive was a lie." She looked down at her hands, which were now in her lap. "Suddenly, everything's changed," she said abruptly, "My traitorous friend Jennifer is now dead, and another friend has been carrying on with young boys. There's very little left of the life I had."

Claire was surprised to feel a sudden wave of sympathy for Anne. She knew what it was like to lose people you loved. She also admired Anne's bravery in refusing to continue with a marriage that was clearly a sham. And she felt guilty that she'd been the one who'd given the photo of Clive and Jennifer to Hazel Bonnington.

"Of course, I'm going to take him for everything I can get," Anne added, with malicious glee. "He's not going to get away without a fight. I've already engaged one of the country's best lawyers to look after my interests."

Silently, Claire applauded her. If anything so humiliating ever happened to her, she hoped she'd feel the same sense of injustice that Anne did. In a way, wasn't it the same kind of redress she was seeking for Zoe?

Anne hesitated. "I'm having a lot of nightmares since the – since my friend – my so-called friend Jennifer – tried to kill me."

Claire turned a gasp into a cough. So Jennifer tried to kill her own friend, and died herself in the attempt! Jennifer's death had been reported in the newspapers as a tragic accident.

"That's perfectly understandable – you're bound to be suffering a lot of stress," Claire said hastily. "Has this matter been referred to the police?"

Anne shook her head. "No one but me knows what happened that day. But it's as though what happened on top of the church

384

tower has opened up the past as well. I'm having flashbacks to my childhood, and they're very distressing."

Claire's heart did an uncomfortable somersault. "Do you want to tell me about them?"

Anne said nothing for a while, and the silence between them grew. However, Claire was used to these silences, since clients often needed time before they could articulate their worries and bring them out into the open.

At last, Anne spoke. "When I was thirteen, my friends and I did something terrible that's haunted us all ever since. And lately I can't stop thinking about it. It's taken over my mind, and I need to resolve it, since I'm going to need all my wits to cope with Clive and the divorce."

Claire felt sick with apprehension. Was she at last going to learn the truth about her sister?

"What did you do that was so awful?"

"My friends and I used to pick on one particular girl in our class. We'd call her names, and shout insults at her."

Suddenly, Claire felt unable to breathe and for a brief moment she thought she might pass out from shock. But although she was shaking, she knew she had to remain professional, no matter how hard she was finding it. One slip and everything could change.

"Why did you all taunt this girl?" Claire asked, trying to keep her voice as normal as possible.

Anne hesitated. "I was the ringleader, you know," she said at last. "The other three always did what I suggested, and it was me who decided we'd pick on Zoe Gray."

Claire gulped. At last, her sister had been mentioned by name!

"Well, why did you decide that this Zoe Gray should be picked on?"

Anne looked sadly at Claire. "I was a very unhappy child back then."

"But why this particular girl?" Claire tried to keep the hysteria out of her voice.

Suddenly, Anne began to weep, her initial tears turning into big gulping sobs. She cried as though she was never going to stop, and Claire wondered fearfully what could be causing her so much pain.

Claire rested her hand lightly on Anne's shoulder, so that she'd know she wasn't alone. Gradually, Anne's tears subsided, and Claire handed her a box of tissues so that she could wipe her red and swollen eyes.

"Take your time – just tell me when you're ready," she said.

Trembling, Anne took a deep breath. "When I was thirteen, in the village where we lived, he . . . it was just before Christmas . . . a man I knew saw me taking a shortcut home through the fields . . . he followed me and raped me."

Claire was shocked, and surprised at what seemed like a change in direction, but she went with it, hoping they'd return to the subject of her sister later.

"Did you tell a teacher, your parents or the police?"

"No." Anne shrugged her shoulders. "I wouldn't have known what to say. It was frightening to find yourself attractive to an old man, and I suppose I felt ashamed that I could arouse someone like that. I felt sure he must have seen something bad in me – why else would he have picked me? I didn't know anything about sexual attraction. I just felt that somehow I'd be blamed if I told anyone." She suddenly gave a mirthless laugh. "It's odd, isn't it, that I considered him old? Back then, he was probably younger than we are now!" She wiped her eyes. "I bled for a while from what he did, but I let my mother and my friends assume I was having my first period."

Claire was horrified. "You must have felt awful."

Anne's voice trembled. "I felt dirty, powerless and used. How could I go to anyone for help? Besides, Mr Gray knew I'd be too afraid to tell anyone. That's how people like him keep kids in their power."

Anne wiped her eyes, unaware that Claire's world was collapsing around her.

Anne had just spoken about *her father*! Claire was in a state of shock, and felt that she was going to have a heart attack.

"You mean Zoe's father was the one who raped you?" she said at last, trying to conceal the tremble in her voice.

Anne nodded. "He'd already abandoned his family and wasn't living in the village anymore, so taunting Zoe was the only form of revenge I could get. I encouraged the others to join me in shouting abuse at her. Of course, they didn't know why I wanted to do it – it just seemed like good fun to them, and they were happy to join in. I suppose I felt that in some way Zoe had to be like him, and that by punishing her I was somehow getting back at him."

Claire was so appalled she couldn't speak. So this was why her father left home – their mother must have evicted him, which would also explain why that poor, sad woman drank so much! She suddenly felt weak, and thought for a few fleeting seconds that she might faint.

Anne looked at the floor. "My friend Fiona, the doctor's daughter, was also abused by her father, but neither of us knew about each other's problems back then. It's only since Jennifer's death that we've opened up to each other. Each of us kept our history a secret – I suppose bullying that poor girl helped us to feel we'd some control over our lives."

Claire felt deeply sorry for Anne and Fiona, two young girls who'd each endured horrific abuse. And she thought of her poor sister, who'd done nothing wrong, but who'd been branded evil because their father had been evil.

"Poor Zoe," said Anne, looking shamefaced. "We were so unkind to her. Another day she came to school with blood on her skirt. She didn't seem to know what a period was, so to frighten her we told her she was suffering from a fatal illness, and needed to go to hospital immediately. We enjoyed frightening her, and even after the bleeding stopped, we still kept taunting her about being unclean. We said some horrible things – and then one day, she drowned. We knew – and all the other girls at school knew – that she'd killed herself because of what we'd done to her."

Allowing her heartbeat time to get back to normal, Claire moved the questioning on. She was desperate to know as much as possible about her sister. "So you only hated Zoe because of her father?"

Anne gave a hollow laugh. "Zoe Gray was a perfectly nice girl – but of course I couldn't see that back then. She didn't have many friends left – only a few other girls stuck by her – but that was our fault too, since we ganged up on anyone who tried to befriend her. I think her diary became her friend, because during break times, she was always writing in it."

Claire heart was beating faster. Zoe's diary had finally been mentioned! Maybe Anne knew something about the missing pages . . .

"Did you ever read her diary?"

Anne's lower lip quivered as she spoke. "We were always trying to grab it from her, but we never succeeded until the day before she drowned. Then Jennifer crept up on her in the playground while she was writing in it, and managed to rip out the middle pages. Zoe was very upset, and Jennifer kept dancing around her, and waving the torn pages in front of her, to tease her."

"What happened to those pages?"

"Why do you want to know every little detail?" asked Anne sharply.

"Oh, it sometimes helps people to deal with their past," said Claire hastily. "We've got to work though as much detail as possible, so you can finally lay the past to rest."

She took a deep breath. "Now relax, Anne," she said, trying to sound professional and uninvolved, "and please try to remember what Jennifer did with the pages from Zoe's diary."

Anne concentrated this time. "She told Zoe she'd give them back after she'd read them."

"Did she read them?" Claire asked sharply.

"No, there wasn't time –"

"Why?"

"We were called for hockey practice. Jennifer took the pages with her to the sports pavilion, and stuffed them behind her locker while we were changing into our sports gear."

"Did any of you read them later?"

Anne shook her head. "We all went back to Jennifer's locker after hockey practice, intending to read what Zoe had written, but unfortunately Jennifer had pushed the pages in too far, and they fell down the back of the locker. We tried poking pencils and sticks in behind the locker, but we couldn't reach them." Her expression darkened. "Then when Zoe drowned the next day, we didn't dare to go near anything that linked us to her." She looked directly at Claire, an impassioned and vulnerable look on her face. "If I could take back what we did to that girl, I would," she whispered. "All our lives have been defined by it. I know she had a younger sister – I wish I could face her, and say I'm sorry –"

She looked at the floor, and when she looked up again, there were tears in her eyes. To Claire, that was as near to an apology as she could ever expect for Zoe, and it surprisingly soothed her soul.

"I'm sure Zoe – and her sister – have forgiven you," she said.

Claire was trembling herself, although she desperately tried to maintain a professional exterior. But an unspeakably awful thought was pushing its way into her mind . . .

Anne seemed to sense it too, because she looked piercingly at Claire. "I wonder if Zoe was raped too? It never crossed my mind until now – maybe the blood we taunted her about wasn't really a period after all . . ."

In the silence that followed, the two women looked at each other. Claire found it almost impossible to mask her own inner turmoil, so she snatched up a tissue and pretended to stifle a sneeze. This brief respite enabled her to compose herself, and appear calm before Anne once again.

"Hopefully you're feeling a little better now?" Claire asked gently, and was shocked by Anne's response.

"No!" said Anne, her face suddenly contorted with anger and emotion. "I'll never be alright because of what that man did to me!" She gripped the arms of her chair until her knuckles were white. "During my teens and early twenties, I was plagued with urinary tract infections, so eventually I was referred to a specialist – and he discovered I'd suffered from untreated chlamydia for years." She looked directly at Claire. "Since I'd never allowed another man near me, I knew I'd got it from Mr Gray." She began to weep again. "It made me infertile – I've never been able to have children because of that evil man!"

Claire found it hard not to weep along with her. Her own eyes filled up with tears and she had to brush them aside surreptitiously. She could hardly believe it – her father had destroyed Anne's future simply for his own brief gratification, and Anne's anger and pain had resulted in Zoe's victimisation.

Claire took Anne's hand in hers and held it for a long time. There was nothing she could say. "I'm so sorry," she whispered at last.

This time Claire was the one apologising – for her father's cruel treatment of Anne and for her own vindictiveness – but of course Anne didn't realise her meaning, and Claire didn't dare tell her.

After a bout of silence on both sides, the session came to a natural end. Anne rose from her chair and shook Claire's hand. "Thank you," she said stiffly. "Before I came, I wasn't sure about the value of therapy, but now I can see that a trained person can make you face your demons, deal with them, and hopefully heal."

By tacit agreement, neither woman made any arrangement for a further session.

Claire followed Anne to the reception desk and, as Anne was taking out her credit card, she spoke to Teresa.

"There's no charge for Mrs Ellwood," she said.

"What?" Anne looked startled.

"We never charge for a one-off consultation," Claire lied, as Teresa stared open-mouthed at her, wondering if her employer had briefly lost her mind.

The two women shook hands again.

"Well, thank you – for everything," said Anne, smiling. "By the way, I'm not Mrs Ellwood anymore, just plain old Anne Morgan."

"Well, good luck in your new life," said Claire, surprised to realise she genuinely meant it.

After Anne had gone, Claire returned to her room, sat at her desk and stared at the wall, feeling sick and empty inside. She now realised how easy it was to hurt people who were labelled 'the enemy', but when you got to know them, it became a lot harder. She'd set out to harm people who were already damaged, and now she deeply regretted it.

She didn't dare think about her father, the man she'd idolised all her life, and who was a traitor to human decency. Right now, she wouldn't think about him. He didn't deserve any space in her thoughts. David had been right about him all along. How had her fiancé detected something in her father that she hadn't seen? Perhaps her delight at meeting him again had blinded her to the things David had picked up on. She owed David a sincere apology. She just hoped she hadn't left it too late . . .

As she closed up the office and left for home, Claire's mind was working overtime. An idea was beginning to form in her brain, because by now she was no longer convinced that the four bullies had driven Zoe to suicide. And thanks to Anne, she'd discovered the one place that might reveal what had really happened to Zoe . . .

CHAPTER 82

Zoe's Diary

June 16

There's a saying: 'Be careful what you wish for', and I know to my cost what it means now. When your dream comes true, you may be sorry you wished for it in the first place. I certainly am. But I'm keeping Claire safe, and that's all that matters . . .

Zoe sat in her favourite place on the beach. She liked watching the tide coming in and going out, and seeing how the seascape changed in the space of a few hours. It helped her to accept that nothing would be forever – eventually, she'd be free and able to live the life she longed for. But for now, she'd no choice but to put up with the situation in order to keep Claire safe.

Zoe felt tears pricking her eyelids. She was deeply grateful for what her mother had done for her and Claire. Before either of her daughters was old enough to know what was happening, their mother had protected them from their sexually abusive father. But Zoe had misinterpreted her mother's anger, thinking it meant she wanted her husband back, and in her own mind her father became the magical figure whose return would solve all *their problems. As a result, her own life was now spiralling out of control.*

Her present ordeal had brought back all the memories her brain had earlier suppressed, and Zoe had finally remembered what happened all those years ago. And she recalled those evenings when, as a little child, her father had slipped into her bedroom. He'd always called her his special little girl, and she'd loved her daddy so much that she'd have done anything to please him. He'd ask her to do strange things that she didn't understand, but he said only special girls were allowed to do that, and that it was their special secret. She'd been sworn to secrecy, and she'd enjoyed sharing a special secret that no one else in the family knew about.

But as she'd got older, she'd hadn't liked the way he'd started touching her. But he'd said that was part of their secret, so she'd accepted it, knowing it made Daddy happy. But one day Mummy had seen what he was doing, and had immediately ordered him out of the house. The subject had never been mentioned again, and Zoe never knew where Daddy went. In time, she'd suppressed the memories of what had happened and, like Claire, she'd come to miss him terribly.

Then a few months ago, she'd spotted him coming through the woods.

"Hello, darling," he'd said, "I've come to see you because Dr Barker said you were missing me. He said you were so grown up now, and I can see he was telling the truth!"

When he'd opened his arms, she'd run to him. It was good to feel his warmth and strength. She'd missed him so much.

That day by the stream, Daddy had been especially friendly and caring.

"You're old enough now for me to show you a very special kind of love," he'd whispered, and it was as though all her birthdays had come together at once. She'd gone willingly with him to his car. Daddy had seemed, to her inexperienced and childish eyes, to be the parent most in control. Besides, her daddy was the only one who'd ever shown he cared about her. Her mother was drunk and incoherent most of the time.

In the car, he'd kissed her forehead gently, but gradually his kisses stopped being the affectionate kind that parents bestowed on their children.

"Stop, Daddy – please!" she whispered, but he didn't seem to hear her anymore. She became frightened as he pulled her knickers off, and suddenly she wanted more than anything to be home with her mother and sister.

Why was Daddy hurting her so much? It was pain like she'd never experienced before. But her father kept grunting and saying, "Don't worry, it's going to be okay." So how could she doubt him? He was her daddy, after all. He loved her, didn't he, so why would he hurt her, unless it was for her own good?

When he'd finished, he'd smirked as she stumbled, crying, from the car.

"You'd better be here at the same time next week," he muttered. "If not, or if you tell anyone, I'll get Dennis Barker to ring the authorities and get you and your sister taken away."

As a trickle of blood ran down her leg, Zoe was terrified. Oh God, she wondered, what's Daddy done? But when she turned back to speak to him, he'd already turned on the ignition and driven off.

That day had just been the start of it. She'd had no choice but to do as he wanted, because Daddy constantly reminded her that if she disobeyed him, he'd make sure she and Claire were sent to separate orphanages, so they'd never see each other again.

He also told her that if she wasn't cooperative, he'd seek out Claire to take her place.

Tears ran down Zoe's cheeks as she walked along the beach. At least she could ensure that Claire never became a victim. To save Claire, she was prepared to do anything Daddy wanted.

CHAPTER 83

Claire felt overwhelmed by all she'd discovered about her father, her mother and Zoe. As she made her way home from work after her session with Anne, she felt as though she was walking through treacle, and it was an effort to take even the smallest step. Her whole world had been turned on its head, yet she felt certain there was more she didn't yet know. And she was determined to find it out, no matter what the cost.

She felt increasingly guilty about the way she'd treated David when he'd expressed reservations about her father, even though he'd only done so after she'd goaded him into voicing his opinion! But she knew he wasn't the kind of man to gloat – instead, he'd be deeply disappointed that her father hadn't been the man she'd longed him to be. On the other hand, she was lucky to have a wonderful man like David – assuming she hadn't pushed him so far that he didn't want her anymore.

As soon as she'd got home, she dialled David's number.

"David? It's me."

"Hello, love, I've been meaning to call, but – well, I thought I'd give you space for a while. All we seem to do lately is argue."

"Oh, David –"

"Are you okay? You sound stressed."

Claire burst into tears. "You were right all along! I've just found out that my father's an evil paedophile who's done so much harm!"

"You poor love, I'll come over right away –"

"No, please – if you don't mind, I really need to be alone right now," Claire said, drying her eyes.

Briefly, she explained how she'd found out about her father, feeling sick as she described some of the things he'd done.

"But how did *you* spot something weird about my father, and I didn't?" she demanded.

"I don't know," said David truthfully. "I suppose I just had a bad feeling about him – call it a sixth sense – but, Claire, you don't have to tackle this all on your own. When you feel up to it, I'll go with you to Trentham-on-Sea to face your father. You have me to support you – never forget that."

Claire smiled through her tears. "I know, and you're the most wonderful man in the world! Just be patient with me – there's something I need to do first. Then it'll all be over."

David sounded alarmed. "I don't like the sound of that, Claire – you're not to even *think* of tackling your father on your own –"

"Don't worry, I'm not going to deal with him yet," Claire said. "I really appreciate your support, love – but I won't be going anywhere for a while. I've got clients every hour for the next few days, so I'm going to be very busy. I'll let you know when I'm free to go down to the cottage – maybe at the weekend?"

"Okay," David said reluctantly. "Ring me anytime – day or night – and remember I love you, won't you? Are you sure you don't want me to come over right away?"

"No, I'm fine, and I love you too," said Claire.

That much was true, but everything else she'd told him was a lie.

Arriving for work the following morning, Claire felt like a zombie. Teresa looked at her oddly, noting her pallor and the fact that she was too preoccupied to even say 'good morning'.

Claire had a genuinely busy day ahead, and for once she was

grateful for it. It would hopefully stop her from thinking about her father, the man she'd invited to live in her mother's cottage – the paedophile who preyed on young children. She'd ask him to leave the cottage as soon as she had time to confront him, but there was something she urgently needed to do first.

That afternoon, as Claire waited for her last appointment to arrive, she rang The Gables School for Girls. She'd put off ringing all day, not sure what she was going to say. She'd tried to think of something that would sound plausible, but in the end, she decided to tell the truth. Or at least as much of it as was feasible.

"How can I help you?" asked the pleasant woman's voice at the other end.

"Hello, I'm an old pupil of the school," Claire told her, "and I was wondering if it would be possible to take a look around the old buildings? I've such wonderful memories of my days there –"

She'd hated her days at The Gables, but praising the school seemed the safest approach to take. They'd be unlikely to let her look around if she claimed to hate the place!

"Oh, dear," said the woman apologetically, "under normal circumstances, there wouldn't be any problem, but we're undertaking a big refurbishment programme this summer. As I'm sure you're aware, the school is closed for the summer, so maybe you'd like to visit when the new buildings are finished –"

"W-what?" shrieked Claire. "What sort of refurbishment?"

The woman seemed startled by Claire's shocked interjection. "Well, we've just had a new science block built on the site of the old refectory. The next phase will replace the old sports pavilion and dressing rooms –"

By now, Claire had broken out in a sweat. "Do you think I could just see the place for one last time?" she whispered. Otherwise, her last chance of finding the pages of Zoe's diary would be lost . . .

"Oh dear, sorry, I'm afraid not," the woman replied, sounding disappointed she couldn't oblige. "The school's been boarded up, and there are hoardings all round, so the public can't gain access. But enrolments are still possible over the Internet. If you'd like the school's email address . . .?"

Claire wanted to scream. She was so close to an answer, yet suddenly all hope was being snatched away from her.

"No, that's okay, thank you," she said dully, ringing off.

By the time Claire ushered in her last client of the day, she'd come to a decision. She couldn't afford to waste any time, so she intended setting out for The Gables School for Girls that very evening. Maybe she could bribe the night watchman to let her in, or she'd search for an opening in the hoarding and try to break in.

She'd try not to think that her father was now living less than a mile from the school, but she'd deal with him another day. Right now, this was her only chance of finding the missing pages from Zoe's diary. Hopefully, they'd provide the last link in the chain that would reveal how and why Zoe died.

It was a three-hour drive to Trentham-on-Sea, and a lifetime since she'd been a pupil at the school. Claire hoped to arrive by nightfall. Dressed in jeans and a hooded anorak, she'd brought a torch and tools in case she needed to break through the hoarding. Claire hadn't even considered that she'd be guilty of trespass and that, if caught, she could end up in a police cell for the night. Right now, nothing was going to get in her way.

When she arrived in Trentham-on-Sea, Claire drove slowly past the school. There were hoardings all around it, and a large sign announcing the names of the architects and – Claire's heart skipped a beat – Corcroft Construction was listed as the company doing the building work!

At first glance there appeared to be no way of getting in. Then, as Claire slowed down her car, a tall man stepped out from a door set into the wooden hoarding. He was well dressed and didn't look like a watchman or a workman. As he walked off into the dark Claire parked her car in a nearby laneway, put the tools and torch in her pocket and began walking back towards the school. This time there was no one around, so she quickly located the door in the wooden structure and was relieved to find the man hadn't locked it after him.

Stepping through, Claire found herself transported back to her childhood. The old school buildings were even more oppressive than she'd remembered, and she experienced a frisson of fear as she felt the ghosts of the past swirling around her.

After a few minutes, Claire's eyes had adjusted to the dark, and she began to get a sense of where she was. She remembered that the changing rooms were down to the left, facing the playing fields, so she inched her way down a narrow pathway between two buildings. Although it was a warm evening, Claire pulled up the hood of her anorak. She was shivering at the thought of what she intended to do, and what the results could mean for her.

At last in the damp and empty sports pavilion, Claire moved from one room to another. Debris and abandoned newspapers lay on the floor and, cursing, she slipped several times. In the dark, she fell over an upended bench, hurting her shin, but she was trying not to use her torch for fear it might alert someone to her presence. Wincing, she carried on, tears of frustration clouding her vision. Damn oh damn, where were the old lockers the students used? As she searched, everything felt unreal, except the reason she was there. This was her only chance of finding Zoe's last written words, and she was prepared to take any risk to find them.

As she hurried through the building, her nerves fraught with tension, she found the line of metal lockers at last. They were still standing where she'd remembered them, and she shone her torch along the row. But which one had been Jennifer's? Hundreds of girls had passed through the school since Jennifer had been there. Tears filled Claire's eyes. What had she been thinking of? It would take her all night to unscrew each locker off the wall.

Suddenly, she recalled her conversation with Anne, and remembered that she'd said Jennifer hid the pages *behind* her locker. Looking at the row of lockers now, she realised that would only be possible if it had been an end one . . .

"What the fuck –?"

Claire's heart almost stopped as a man's silhouette appeared in the doorway.

As he walked menacingly towards her, blinding her with the light of his torch, Claire felt very afraid. She'd just realised the predicament she was in – she was alone with this man in a derelict building, and no one else knew where she was . . .

As he reached her, Claire flinched. He towered over her, and for a split second, she was afraid he was going to hit her . . .

Suddenly, his face broke into an incredulous grin. "Good god – you're a woman! What on earth are you doing here? All the teaching staff left hours ago . . ." Then he noticed her pockets were bulging with tools. "If you're a burglar, you're wasting your time – anything valuable is locked up in our stores."

Suddenly Claire realised he was the man who'd left the building just before she arrived and, close up, she recognised him from the garden party. It was Benjamin Corcroft!

"I'm sorry about your wife," she said without thinking. "She went to school here too, didn't she?"

Puzzled, Benjamin looked down at her. "How do you know that? Who the hell are you?"

Claire took a deep breath. She'd nothing to lose by telling him why she was there. He could throw her out – but she'd a feeling he might actually help her. Instinct told her that beneath the gruff exterior, there could be someone kind and caring.

Quickly, without going into detail about the bullies, she explained about the diary pages and how important they were to her, and that they might explain what had happened to her late sister.

"Look, if there'd been time, I'd have contacted your company directly," Claire implored him, "but I couldn't take the chance that someone would stop me –"

Benjamin grinned. "You were just being proactive – I can understand that – I tend to be a bit hot-headed myself." He still felt embarrassed when he thought of what he'd nearly done to Georgie's driveway. He rubbed his chin. "You said your sister's name was Zoe – that name rings a bell – funny how you never forget things from your childhood, isn't it? I came to Trentham-on-Sea for a weekend with my mother and brother when we were kids." He grimaced. "I'll never forget it because my father died and we had to go home early. But I met a girl on the beach – she said her name was Zoe – and she was collecting seaweed for a bath!"

Claire smiled sadly. "Yes, that was definitely my sister. She used to make seaweed baths for our mum."

Benjamin raised his eyebrows. "You say she drowned?"

"I always thought that was what happened, but now I'm not so sure. Finding these pages might help me discover the truth." She looked expectantly at Benjamin Corcroft. "Will you help me – please?"

Benjamin didn't hesitate. "Of course. But I'd better get some proper tools – yours don't look capable of doing much." He smiled. "Anyway, you've got me intrigued – I want to know what happened to Zoe, too."

As Claire waited, excited and fearful at the same time, Benjamin returned a few minutes later with a crowbar and an assortment of other professional tools.

"It has to be one of the end lockers," Claire told him. It felt weird asking him to pull out the locker his own late wife had used at school, and to know that it was Jennifer who'd put the pages here. But she wouldn't tell him that – he was probably grieving and it wouldn't be fair to sully his late wife's reputation.

As Benjamin began unscrewing the first of the two end lockers, Claire began to wonder if, indeed, the pages could still be there. The lockers could have been replaced years ago, and the pages found by someone else, and discarded as rubbish at any time during the previous thirty years. All her efforts would probably be fruitless . . .

As Benjamin prised the first locker away from the wall, it crashed to the ground, raising clouds of dust. Eagerly, Claire began combing through the debris, but there was nothing there. Disappointed, she watched as Benjamin prised off the other end locker and, as it fell, she saw several pieces of paper flutter to the ground.

"Oh my God!"

Fumbling among the dirt on the floor, and choking as the dust filled her lungs, Claire managed to grab the crumpled pages, clutching them to her chest as though they were priceless works of literature. Even in the dark, she was sure she could recognise Zoe's writing.

"I've found them!" she called to Benjamin.

He shone his torch on the pages, and they both stared at them. They looked so inconspicuous, yet Claire had high hopes they might ultimately reveal so much.

"Thank you so much for you help!" she said, her eyes shining. "I'll never forget what you've done."

Benjamin wiped the dust from his face. "Glad to be of service. You were in luck this evening – if the regular watchman had been here instead of me, he'd probably have sent you packing."

"Yes, I wondered why you were here. I mean, you're the boss –"

Benjamin nodded. "The site manager's on holiday, so I'm staying at the Trentham Arms Hotel and overseeing the project until he gets back." He smiled. "It's not a big job, but during the recession, we need all the work we can get. When the night watchman's wife went into labour earlier tonight, it made sense for me to cover for him since the hotel's only a few hundred yards from the school." He grinned at her. "I was pissed off at having to leave the comfortable hotel bar, but I wouldn't have missed this for anything!"

Claire smiled. She was glad Benjamin had been here. She shuddered to think how she'd have coped otherwise.

Together, Claire and Benjamin left the sports building and began walking back towards the door in the hoarding.

Benjamin cleared his throat. "Er, did you know Jennifer well?"

"No, she was in my sister's class."

Benjamin smiled to himself. He'd guessed this woman wouldn't be the type Jennifer would befriend anyway – she wasn't the sort who'd wear designer labels, play golf or travel to London for bridge every week. He wondered if Jennifer had known Zoe, but decided not to ask.

He glanced at Claire. He longed to tell her he'd already put

Jennifer's death behind him and found someone new. But Georgie had warned him not to broadcast their relationship or the pregnancy yet. It was too early, she said, and tongues would start wagging. But he was so happy he wanted the whole world to know!

As he opened the door in the hoarding to let her out, Claire reached up and hugged him. "Thank you, thank you, thank you," she said, her eyes filling with tears.

"No problem. Let me know what you find out, won't you?" he asked, pleased and embarrassed at the same time. Then he took out one of his business cards and handed it to her.

"I will," Claire promised, placing the card in her pocket.

As she walked back to her car, Claire felt over the moon. She was covered in dust, she had a three-hour drive ahead of her but she didn't care. Soon, her sister's words would reveal the end of her story. Claire desperately wanted to know what had been in Zoe's mind before she'd walked into the sea . . . or had she?

But she wouldn't read the pages until she got home – they were grubby and crumpled, and she'd need proper lighting and space to examine them. She was also terrified of what she might find out, and wanted to be in a safe environment when she uncovered the truth.

Claire turned on the ignition and headed for home. When she had all the answers, she'd be able to get on with her own life, and marry David the following spring. And when she'd solved the mystery of Zoe's death, she'd ring that nice man Benjamin Corcroft and tell him everything.

CHAPTER 84

As the waiter opened the bottle of white wine and filled three glasses, Anne, Emma and Fiona waited expectantly. They were having lunch in a local bistro, and all three women were edgy because it was quite a while since they'd seen each other, and it was their first get-together since Jennifer's death and Fiona's incident with Alan Corcroft. Their friendship had taken a battering, but the events that had almost destroyed their friendship had also been instrumental in bringing them back together again.

As soon as the waiter had taken their orders and left, the three women raised their glasses and took a sip. Fiona was looking radiant and Anne observed her with a sour expression. Despite having wronged her husband, Edwin had taken her back, and Anne felt decidedly peeved. Trust Fiona to have such luck! She certainly wasn't going to take back her own errant spouse, not after all the public humiliation she'd endured. Clive had already moved into his apartment in Westminster, but he was making noises about selling The Grange. As far as Anne was concerned, it would be over her dead body, and fortunately her solicitor was fully in agreement with her.

Emma looked anxiously from Anne to Fiona. "Do you think –" she said tentatively, "we should drink a toast in memory of our late friend Jennifer? I know, Anne, that she and Clive –" Emma's voice trailed off as she decided that maybe, once again, she'd said the wrong thing.

"If you do, I'm leaving," said Anne contemptuously. "Jennifer wasn't just an adulterer, you know –" She looked from one woman to the other and took a deep breath. "I can see it's time I told you both the truth." Turning to Emma, she looked at her sternly. "And you, madam, had better zip your lip, because what I'm going to tell you is for you and Fiona only."

Emma blushed, only too aware of her propensity to talk out of turn after a few glasses of wine.

Briefly, Anne told them what had really happened on top of the church tower.

"I couldn't fathom why she'd want to throw me off," she added angrily. "I thought I was imagining things, I mean, what reason had I to think my friend would try to kill me? It was only later – when Clive admitted the affair and said that Jennifer wanted him to divorce me and marry her – that I realised why. If I was out of the way, she'd have Clive all to herself."

Emma reached for her wineglass. She really needed a drink right now. "Even after all the years we've been friends, we didn't really know her at all," she whispered, gulping down a large mouthful of wine.

Anne shrugged her shoulders. "Maybe, given certain circumstances, we'd all behave in ways we'd never expect."

"Well, let's drink to the three of us instead," said Fiona, and they raised their glasses in unison.

"To us!" they said, just as the first course arrived.

Anne cast another surreptitious glance at Fiona. There was definitely something different about her today, an underlying excitement that Anne couldn't quite decipher. Fiona's mood reminded her a little of the feverishness Jennifer had exhibited just before she'd tried to throw her off the church tower. Hopefully, Anne thought, Fiona wasn't intending to dispatch her with her luncheon knife!

"Fiona, are you all right?" Anne asked warily. "You seem a little, er, hyper today."

Fiona smiled. "I've a lot to be happy about – not that long ago, I felt like a pariah, and I never expected to be sitting here with you two today. Alan Corcroft has thankfully put that er, incident behind him, and Edwin and I have talked about everything. I've told him about what happened to me during my childhood –"

Anne's eyebrows shot up. "You've told him about your father?"

Fiona nodded. "I should have told him years ago. I should have told *you*, my dearest friends, as well. If you and I had shared what happened to us back then, Anne, we might have been able to support each other." She smiled. "I've agreed to go for psychotherapy. Edwin thinks that I need to face the past if I'm serious about our future together."

Normally, Anne would have said nothing about her own experience of psychotherapy, but in the spirit of openness, she took a deep breath. "I've recently had psychotherapy myself," she announced. "I had just one session, but it was a great help. I feel differently now about a lot of things."

"Good for you," said Fiona, smiling. "I got a card through the letterbox ages ago – I'm thinking of making an appointment with this person soon."

Anne raised her eyebrows. "Was the name Claire Ross, by any chance?"

Fiona reached for her handbag, extracted a card and handed it to Anne.

"Yes, that's the woman I went to," said Anne. "I can thoroughly recommend her."

"I got one of those cards through the letterbox, too!" Emma squealed, delighted that she hadn't been left out. "When you go, Fiona – if you agree with Anne that she's good, I might consider going too –"

"She helped me to work through what we did to Zoe Gray," said Anne, and the other two were astonished to hear her freely using the name that had previously been taboo. "It was all displaced hatred, because the one I really wanted to hurt was Mr Gray. I really felt –" she paused, "– that just by talking to her, I was forgiven."

"You were both far too young to cope with what happened to

you," Emma said sadly. "Yet I'll bet each of you thought you were the only one. That's what paedophiles do, isn't it? They isolate their victims so they've no one to turn to."

She turned to Fiona. "I know your dad's been dead for several years, but I wonder whatever happened to that horrible Mr Gray?"

"Well, it's all in the past now, thank goodness," Fiona said firmly. "Now I want to tell you the good news." She smiled radiantly, looking from one woman to the other. "I'm pregnant! Can you believe it? After all these years, Edwin and I are having a baby!"

Although Fiona's joy brought back all the pain of her own barrenness, Anne had the good grace to raise her glass and smile at her friend.

"Congratulations, Fiona," she said.

By now Emma had leapt up from her chair and was hugging Fiona.

"How far gone are you?" Anne asked.

"Only six weeks," said Fiona, "so it's early days yet. I won't be telling anyone else for a while, but I wanted to share it with my two dearest friends. Edwin and I are thrilled – it's a dream come true for both of us."

Anne did a quick calculation and was relieved. At only six weeks, there was no way Fiona could be pregnant by young Alan Corcroft.

Emma looked thoughtful as she returned to her chair and sat down again. "It's funny, isn't it? Although we've all been friends for years, it's only recently that we've all opened up, and discovered so much more about each other." She looked from one to the other earnestly. "And we're still friends, despite everything. In my book, that counts for something. Something very important."

Anne and Fiona nodded their heads in assent. Despite their personal disasters, they were still there for each other.

Emma looked at Anne and gave her a sympathetic smile. She alone was aware of the effort it had taken Anne to congratulate Fiona and wish her well. Emma also congratulated herself – she hadn't told Fiona that Anne couldn't have children, so Anne would see that she *could* keep a secret!

Anne sat tight-lipped, understanding Emma's sympathetic glance. She had to look away, since any gesture of sympathy was likely to make her burst into tears. Yet in another way, she found Emma's gesture surprisingly comforting. She gave her a nod to let her know she was aware she'd kept her secret. Maybe she didn't always have to be in control. Maybe someday she'd share her pain with Fiona, who'd surely understand, having been childless herself for so long. But right now, she couldn't spoil Fiona's happiness by raking up her own problems.

Suddenly, Anne smiled ironically to herself. For the first time in her life, she was doing something for somebody else. And it felt surprisingly good.

CHAPTER 85

Zoe's Diary

June 28

I've managed to protect Claire so far, but how long more can I do it? I feel sick, and in need of help myself. I've never felt so alone.

At home, Zoe avoided her mother as much as possible, since to face her meant accepting how badly she'd failed her. And Claire – how she wished she could confide in her! But she was far too young to understand the nature of their father's behaviour, or the threat he held over her sister.

Sometimes, Zoe wondered how long she could cope with her father's weekly demands, but every time she felt overwhelmed, she reminded herself that Claire's safety was why she'd no choice but to let him use her.

Zoe wished her mother might hear her vomiting in the bathroom each morning before school. But her mother seemed oblivious to her problem, and in another sense Zoe was relieved. Her poor mother had enough to cope with.

In school, the bullies had increased their name-calling, and she felt surrounded by enemies. Several times she'd had to rush out of class, and just made it to the toilets before getting sick. Later, the bullies jeered her on the way home, making puking noises and claiming she had a contagious disease.

Zoe was also worried because her periods had stopped. Perversely she felt she'd almost welcome the bullies' taunting if it meant she was bleeding again. In the library, she had taken down a book on human reproduction, devouring its pages anxiously at one of the reading tables. When she read the chapter that confirmed she was pregnant, she began to cry, and the librarian began making shushing noises.

Abandoning the book, Zoe ran out of the library and down to the beach – it was the only place where she could cry in peace.

What on earth was she going to do? She needed help, but she didn't feel she could burden her poor ill mother any further. She didn't like Dr Barker, but surely he'd know what she should do? She was scared about telling him who'd made her pregnant but, once he knew, he might be able to prevent what was happening to her in the woods every week.

Zoe timed her visit to coincide with the doctor's last appointment of the day. Hopefully, after the last patient left, he'd give her five minutes of his time before closing the surgery.

As the doctor was seeing out the last patient of the day, Zoe presented herself at his door.

"Dr Barker, I really need to see you," she said, as soon as the previous patient was out of earshot. "I'm sorry for calling so late, but it's really important."

Dr Barker sighed, but held the door open for her to enter. "Come in, come in, this had better be important. I've had a long day, you know."

Walking ahead of him into his surgery, Zoe sat down in the chair in front of his desk, and waited until he sat down facing her.

Zoe was trembling, and terrified about what she needed to say, but there was nothing for it. She had to tell him.

"Dr Barker, I think I'm pregnant, and I don't know what to do."

Dr Barker looked momentarily startled, then he covered his surprise with a nod.

"And who is the father?"

Zoe gulped. This was the really difficult part. Had she courage to tell him the truth? She knew that Dr Barker and her father had been friends for years. Would he believe her? Would he be angry with her? If he ordered her out, she didn't know what she'd do.

"I-it was m-my father."

For an instant, Dr Barker looked shocked. "Good heavens, does anyone else know?"

Zoe shook her head.

"Well, that's a relief. Now, you must keep this to yourself, if I'm to help you."

Zoe nodded anxiously. "Of course."

Dr Barker tapped the desk rhythmically with his pencil, and appeared to be deep in thought. Then he stopped tapping, put the pencil down and stared at her.

"Leave it with me, dear girl, I'll see what I can do," he said. Then he smiled unctuously. "Don't worry, Zoe, I'll sort everything out. Come back and see me at the same time tomorrow, and I'll have everything organised."

Zoe thanked him profusely. How could she ever have doubted him? She'd no idea how he intended to help her, but at least she wasn't alone anymore. Now she understood the meaning of the saying: 'A trouble shared is a trouble halved.' With a spring in her step, she made her way out of the surgery and to the front door.

Dr Barker laid a hand on her arm as he opened the door. "You won't forget that this is now our little secret, will you, Zoe?"

Zoe nodded gratefully. Since Dr Barker was going to help her, everything was going to be all right.

"Of course, Dr Barker. Thanks for your help. I'll see you tomorrow."

Dr Barker smiled as she waved goodbye, but when he closed the door his expression darkened. Finding a solution to this problem wasn't going to be easy.

Back in his surgery, he sat at his desk again, and began rhythmically tapping his pencil once more. Then he lifted the phone and dialled a number.

When the phone was answered, Dr Barker's comments were precise and to the point.

"Get your sorry ass over here tonight. You're in big trouble."

Then he hung up.

"You've been screwing that pretty little daughter of yours, haven't you?"

Billy Gray shrugged his shoulders, a cigarette dangling from his mouth.

"You stupid bastard – you've got her pregnant. Surely that possibility crossed your mind?"

Billy Gray looked alarmed. "I thought she was far too young for that kind of thing!" he whined.

"You've got to stop before they reach puberty." Dr Barker looked at him sternly, You're in a lot of trouble, Bill. You could go to prison for this, if you're found out."

"Jesus! What the hell am I going to do now?"

Dr Barker pursed his lips. "There's only one thing that can be done," he said ominously. "And for that, you're going to need my help."

CHAPTER 86

As she sat in her kitchen, Claire smoothed out the crumpled diary pages and gazed at the words in front of her. Now that they were finally in her possession, she was terrified to read them.

As Claire stared at Zoe's writing, she was transported back to her sister's world of terror and the bullies' daily onslaught. But on the second page, a new terror was revealed, and Claire's hands shook as she read the words.

So Anne's suggestion had been right – not only was her father a paedophile, he'd preyed on his own daughter! He must have come back to the area after being banished from the cottage by their mother. He'd obviously lied when he said he'd gone straight to Australia.

Claire wiped away a tear. She'd never realised the sacrifice their mother had made for her and Zoe. She'd ended her marriage so that her daughters could be safe, but turned to drink to relieve the pain of her own loss.

Another entry told of Zoe's weekly terror at having to turn up in the woods each week to be raped by her father – if she didn't, he'd sworn to have both daughters sent away to an orphanage. And if Zoe didn't comply, he'd seek out Claire instead.

Claire was filled with rage. What a mean and cruel threat to use against an innocent child! But why was she even surprised? Her father was evil through and through. Men like him stopped at nothing to get what they wanted.

The last few entries continued to reveal the enormity of what Zoe had endured, and it was even worse than Claire could ever have imagined . . . Her jaw was trembling, and she had to stop reading to wipe away her tears. Had Zoe finally killed herself because she couldn't face all that was happening to her?

Guilty tears filled Claire's eyes. How could she not have known the horrors that her sister was going through? But her mother hadn't known either, for Zoe had been careful to keep her torment to herself.

Then Claire came to Zoe's final diary entry, dated June 29th – the day before Zoe's body had been found in the sea. Claire blanched. Why had Zoe gone to Dr Barker? They'd always avoided him like the plague!

The writing veered off into a scribble, and Claire realised that these were the words Zoe had been writing when Jennifer wrenched the pages from the diary.

Claire would never forget that last fateful evening. Zoe had casually mentioned having an errand to run, and said she wouldn't be long. But she'd never returned, and Claire had lain awake all night, worried sick about her sister, yet reluctant to tell their mother in case Zoe got into trouble. But by early morning, she'd had to confess that Zoe had been gone all night, and despite all the drink their mother had consumed, she sobered up immediately. Within the hour, Zoe's body had been found at sea, and Dr Barker called out to identify her and certify her death from drowning.

Nevertheless, Claire was still puzzled. Earlier, she'd accepted that Zoe might have drowned herself because of all that had happened to her. But the last diary entry told a different story. Despite everything, Zoe hadn't been suicidal – she'd expected to come home that night, to cook Claire's supper! But if she hadn't intended to kill herself, how had she ended up in the sea? Had there been an accident? Had she ever reached Dr Barker's house?

Placing the crumpled pages aside, Claire picked up Zoe's diary and skimmed through it again. She'd misinterpreted that earlier entry – when her sister had written *It's been going on for ages now, and I don't know how much more I can take,* she'd assumed her sister was referring to the bullies. But now she realised Zoe had probably been referring to her father's abuse!

Claire wept quietly. Oh Zoe, she thought, I wish you were here so that I could hug you tightly, and never, ever let you go!

In a sudden flashback, Claire remembered the 'special' hugs and kisses her father had given her. She'd only been six, and she shuddered to think what he might have done to her, too, when she got older . . . Claire felt sick inside as she recalled all the misplaced love she'd stored in her heart for that man. A man who deserved nothing but contempt.

With a sick feeling in the pit of her stomach, Claire was forced to acknowledge that she'd been directing her anger at the wrong people. While the four bullies had made Zoe's life miserable, ultimately they hadn't been responsible for her death. Claire now felt guilty for what she'd done to them. Although she hadn't really done that much harm, she reasoned, apart from causing food poisoning at the garden party. Everything else they'd brought on themselves. She hadn't forced Clive Ellwood and Jennifer Corcroft to have an affair – she'd only photographed what she saw.

Nevertheless Claire accepted that, without her intervention, Clive's affair might never have been discovered, and Anne might have been saved all the humiliation. On the other hand, Anne was a strong woman, and Claire felt certain she'd rather know the truth.

But now, Claire had a new focus for all her hatred. A man who'd helped to create life, then allowed his sick impulses to destroy what he'd created. Her beautiful sister had been destroyed because of their father's evil desires. You sick bastard, she thought. You're living in my house – the house left to me by my tragic, broken-hearted mother whom I've maligned so often. Forgive me, Mum, I won't let him stay there a moment longer.

CHAPTER 87

Zoe's Diary

June 29

Dr Barker said to come back to his surgery this evening, when all his patients have gone. I don't like him and I'm scared, but I don't know what else to do. I'll have to ask Claire to cover for me while I'm gone, since I don't want to worry Mum. When I get back, I'll make Claire an especially nice supper. She deserves a ——

The following evening, when Zoe returned to Dr Barker's surgery, she was surprised – and shocked – to find her father there. Had the doctor betrayed her? She began backing out the door again, but her father grabbed her by the arm.

"Oh no, you little bitch – you're going nowhere!" he murmured, glancing at Dr Barker. "Are you ready, Dennis?"

Dr Barker nodded, and before Zoe realised what was happening, the two men had hoisted her up on the surgery table.

"Hold her down, Bill – this'll only take a few minutes –" Dr Barker said, producing several strange implements. Terrified, Zoe began struggling and kicking as Dr Barker approached, and the two men began pulling down her knickers.

"*Leave me alone! What are you doing?*" Zoe screamed.

"*It's all for the best, Zoe,*" Dr Barker said determinedly. "*This will be over in no time, and then you won't be pregnant anymore.*"

"*Leave me alone!*" Zoe screamed, and she began crying even more loudly.

"*Jesus, Bill – put your hand over her mouth!*" Dr Barker ordered. "*If someone hears this racket, we'll be in serious trouble!*"

As Dr Barker approached the table, Zoe was doing her best to break free.

"*Ow! You're a vicious little thing!*" exclaimed the doctor, as a well-aimed kick from Zoe caught him on the side of the head, "*Bill, for Christ's sake, hold her legs apart –*"

"*I can't hold her legs and cover her mouth at the same time!*" shouted her father angrily. "*For Christ's sake, Dennis, can't you give her a shot of anaesthetic or something?*"

Dr Barker grimaced, then nodded reluctantly. "*I was trying to avoid any after-effects – they might arouse suspicion when she goes home. Although that lush you married doesn't notice much. But I suppose you're right – it looks like the only way we're going to get this done –*"

Dr Barker returned to his medicine cabinet and began searching among the phials and bottles that were stored there.

Still crying and terrified, Zoe tried her best to escape from her father's grip. What were they trying to do to her? Why had she ever trusted Dr Barker?

As Dr Barker returned to the table, armed with a full syringe, Zoe made her final bid for freedom. Lashing out with all the strength she could muster, she kicked her father, and he momentarily let go, clutching his groin in pain. Zoe lunged sideways off the table, but the drop to the floor was greater than she'd anticipated. As she tried to compensate, she fell sideways and hit her head against the protruding fireplace. There was a sickening thud, then Zoe collapsed in a heap on the floor.

The two men gazed in shock at the inert body. For several seconds, neither was able to move, then they both reacted at once.

"Oh Christ, is she alright?"

"What the hell happened?"

A horrified Dr Barker knelt down and felt for a pulse in Zoe's neck. Then he stood up, shaking his head.

"She's dead," he said.

"Oh my God! What are we going to do now?" Zoe's father whimpered. "You said it was simple and straightforward – a quick clean-out and she'd be back to normal!"

"Shut up!" muttered Dr Barker. "This isn't the time for hysterics. We've got to work out what to do next . . ."

"I'm not even supposed to be in Trentham-on-Sea!" said Billy Gray, panic in his voice. "If my ex-wife hears I've been sniffing around Zoe, she'll definitely report me this time –"

"Bill, for Christ's sake, calm down! We've got to get rid of Zoe's body – that way, no one will know what happened. It was an accident – we both know that – but we can't let anyone know what we were doing. We'd both be up shit creek if anyone found out."

Billy Gray nodded, terror in his eyes. "What do you think we should do?"

"I don't know."

Dennis Barker sat down in his doctor's chair and buried his head in his hands. "Jesus, I should have taken the risk and sedated her straight away –"

In the silence that followed, neither man dared to look at Zoe's body on the floor, although they knew something would have to be done before long.

Suddenly, Dennis Barker looked at his watch. "There's one thing that might work," he said. "The tide is in around midnight, so we could take the body down to the sea and drop it off the cliff. When it surfaces in a day or so, I'll be the doctor called out and I'll be the one to fill out the death certificate. Let's just hope no one calls for a post mortem, because that would show there was no water in her lungs."

Billy Gray nodded, relieved at the doctor's suggestion. "And you'll make sure no one knows she was pregnant?" he added.

Dennis Barker nodded, looking distastefully down at Zoe's body. He wasn't helping because of any generosity on his part. But he was well aware that if Billy Gray went down, he himself would be quick to follow. Briefly, he wished he'd left Bill to stew in his own juices. But now that he was seriously implicated, he had a very vested interest in ensuring that Zoe's death was declared an accident.

"Come on, Bill, help me put her knickers back on before rigor mortis sets in," he said. "Then we'll wrap her in a sheet and wait here until the tide comes in."

Between them, they silently tended to Zoe's body. Now, all they had to do was wait until midnight.

"I wouldn't mind a whiskey," said Billy Gray, eyeing the bottle of triple-distilled malt on the doctor's top shelf. "My nerves are shattered."

"Don't even think of it!" said Dr Barker angrily. "We'll need all our wits about us until we get this little, er, matter taken care of." His shoulders slumped. "Later, Bill – when it's been taken care of, we'll finish the bottle together." Then the doctor looked pointedly at Billy Gray again. "We also need to get you as far away from here as possible. How does a ticket to Australia sound?"

CHAPTER 88

During the long drive to Trentham-on-Sea, Claire lost her nerve several times. On one occasion, she pulled her car into a lay-by and waited, heart pumping, until she'd got control of her nerves again. A second time, she stopped outside a small café, where she bought herself a take-away sandwich and a tea. As she unwrapped the sandwich, she almost scalded herself with the tea because her hands were shaking so much.

She wondered, for the millionth time, why she'd turned down David's offer to accompany her on this journey to confront her father. But deep inside, she knew this confrontation belonged to her and her father alone. She had a lifetime of memories and history to challenge, and for this David would definitely be in the way. When it was over, she'd return to him with an open and loving heart.

Eventually Claire arrived at the cottage. Using her key, she let herself inside, calling out her father's name. He appeared from the kitchen with a smile on his face, but his expression changed to one of puzzlement when he saw Claire's expression.

"I want you out of here – now!" Claire shouted. "I've found out the kind of man you are – you pervert!"

"Don't be silly," her father said, obviously deciding to brazen it out. "Trentham-on-Sea is where I belong."

"You must be joking! I don't want you within a mile of this house," she shouted, appalled by the sheer gall of the man. "Get out of here – *now!* I don't want anything more to do with you!"

For the first time, her father looked annoyed and disconcerted. He shrugged his shoulders. "I don't know what's got into you, Claire. I'm still the same man I was when you last saw me. You were happy enough then."

"That was before I discovered that you're a paedophile!" Claire screamed, her face red, and tears pricking her eyelids. "You raped your own daughter and a girl called Anne Morgan, and God knows who else!" Claire shouted, disgust making her voice rise higher. "Do you know that Anne can't have children because of you?"

Her father shrugged his shoulders. "That's the way I am," he said, looking as though the problem was not of his making, and that he had no responsibility for his actions.

"By that admission, I presume you mean that Trentham-on-Sea isn't the only place where you've molested children?" said Claire, her voice dripping with venom.

Some part of her had fantasised about being wrong, and that her father would be able to refute all the claims about his abuse. But now, all hope was finally and irrevocably gone. She was facing a sordid manipulator and abuser who felt no remorse for what he'd done.

"You prepared your script well for our first meeting, didn't you, Dad?" Claire screamed. "All that crap about Mum attacking you – you knew I was longing to find you, and you played on my need. You tried to make her the villain – you even hesitated before saying anything, so that I'd beg you to tell me!" Her voice was almost at breaking point. "You're a consummate actor, Dad – did you take acting lessons, or was I just so gullible that I'd have accepted any lies you told me? You deserve an Oscar for your brilliant performance – pity you didn't stick to acting, instead of abusing kids!"

Her father gave her a sneering look. "You're an ungrateful bitch – after all I've done for you! It's a pity my friend Dennis Barker isn't still alive – he'd take me in and show me some respect."

Claire ignored him, her voice rising higher. "Answer me, you sick bastard – what other children have you abused? I'm sure you didn't limit your proclivities to Trentham-on-Sea?"

He was getting angry now. "Don't you dare speak to me like that – I'm your father!"

Claire laughed harshly. "I'll call you whatever I like – you don't deserve the title *father*, you're a disgrace to decent fathers everywhere! As far as I'm concerned, you're not my father anymore – I don't want anything to do with you ever again!"

Her father was beginning to feel trapped now. They were still standing in the hall of the cottage, and he began eyeing the hallstand where his overcoat was hanging. Claire realised what he intended to do, and blocked his way out. He had questions to answer before she'd allow him to leave.

Her stomach was heaving at the thought of what this man had done, and she felt tainted by her blood relationship to him. Presumably the police should be informed about him, because if he wasn't on any sex register, he needed to be. Maybe she should have gone to the police before she'd come to the cottage . . .

Claire's few seconds of distraction gave her father the opportunity he was waiting for. Grabbing his coat, he pushed past her and rushed out of the house without a backward glance.

"I'm not finished with you yet!" Claire screamed, running after him. "I want answers! Zoe was your eldest daughter – didn't you care about her at all? You got her pregnant!"

"Ah yes, that was unfortunate," he said, hunching his shoulders against the strong wind as he headed up towards the cliff. "But you have to understand, Claire, your sister threw herself at me. She was so thrilled to see me – because, you see, your silly mother sent me away – and Zoe was willing to do anything to please me."

Claire shuddered with disgust. He was still justifying what he'd done by blaming it on Zoe and the other innocent children he'd harmed. Whoever said that evil was banal was speaking the truth. How could anyone see anything wrong with this sad, decrepit old man?

Claire ran after him, trying to keep up as he strode ahead. "Poor Mum tried to save Zoe and me by sending you away –"

The old man slowed down, smiling sardonically as she caught up with him. "Oh, your mother was such a fusspot. Just because I gave Zoe a kiss and a cuddle –"

"I seem to recall that you kissed *me* inappropriately, Dad."

Her father gave a sly smile. "You didn't think it was inappropriate back then, did you? You were only six, but you liked it! It's only now, since other people have started filling your head with nonsense, that you've decided it was wrong –"

"That's how people like you manage to do what you do," said Claire, a look of sheer disgust on her face. "You'd already started grooming Zoe and me!"

Her father laughed, as though she'd told him a funny joke, and Claire wanted to strangle him. People like him never changed.

"There never were any birthday cards, were there, Dad?"

Her father shrugged his shoulders again, as though her accusation wasn't worthy of an answer.

The wind continued to blow fiercely as he headed further out along the cliff. Running behind him, Claire was shivering with both the cold and the anger coursing through her. He had betrayed her and Zoe, and all the other children he'd harmed throughout his life. Although their mother had tried to save them, poor Zoe had been trapped by her neediness and longing for a father's love. A love he'd betrayed so shockingly.

"Why can't you at least be sorry for all the harm you've done?" Claire screamed, as the wind lashed against her, whipping her wet hair across her face.

Her father ignored her, but Claire could see that she was finally getting through to him, and angering him with her accusations.

"You took your two children's love, and you – you – tried to turn it into something nasty and dirty! All Zoe wanted was for us to be a family again, and you destroyed her! You'd have abused me too, if you'd had the chance!"

By now they'd reached the cliff top and, with a queasy feeling, Claire looked down at the waves breaking across the rocks at the bottom.

"What happened to Zoe, Dad?" Claire beseeched him. "If

you know, please tell me – you owe me the truth! I don't believe she committed suicide – the last place she went was Dr Barker's surgery, and the next day her body was found in the sea!" She stepped towards her father. "I *know* that Zoe intended coming home again – what did Dr Barker do to her?"

Her father looked startled. "How do you – what do you mean?"

Claire suspected he was playing for time. "Just answer the question – he was your friend – did he kill Zoe?"

"No, no – it was an accident!"

"So you *do* know what happened!"

Initially, her father looked as though he was going to deny it, then he sighed. "Why are you bothered about something that happened thirty years ago? After all this time, you can't prove anything –"

"Just tell me the truth – please!" Claire begged.

Her father shrugged, accepting he could no longer divert her questions. "Dennis was going to perform an abortion – I'd have been in trouble if the authorities found out I'd made her pregnant –"

"Go on – what happened?"

"Zoe was frightened when we tried to hold her down. She struggled, then fell and hit her head on the stone fireplace. She died instantly – there was nothing we could do."

Claire felt sick. "So after terrifying her, you threw her poor little body into the sea! And Dennis Barker protected you by certifying 'Death by drowning'!" She was seething now, the tears streaming down her face. "It's always been about you, hasn't it?" she screamed, "You're nothing but an evil, self-centred old man. David was right – the only person you care about is yourself!"

Her father suddenly looked upset. "David doesn't like me?"

"No, he hates you! He thinks you're pathetic!"

Claire was suddenly enjoying the effect her words were having. She'd found a way to break through her father's composure at last. Clearly she could hurt him through his monstrous ego. Despite his evilness, he still wanted people to like him.

Feeling triumphant at upsetting his feelings, Claire took a step towards him. He stepped back. But the long grass concealed a pothole, his foot caught in it, and he cried out as he stumbled backwards. Flailing his arms, he briefly managed to regain his balance, but then lost it again.

Claire watched in horror as the old man slipped, crying out as he stumbled, losing his footing again and sliding further down the embankment. Suddenly, he went over the edge of the cliff and his body seemed to pick up speed, crashing against boulders and eventually landing with a splash in the sea below. By now the tide was fully in, and the deep water swirled and eddied among the seaweed-covered rocks, foaming as it pounded off them, the salty smell rising through the air.

She heard a scream, but it was quickly carried away on the wind.

As Claire stared down from above, a tumult of feelings raced through her mind. This was the man who'd given life to her and Zoe, yet he'd taken away her sister's childhood, and ultimately her sister's life. But still, everything in her cried out to save him.

There was only one problem – Claire couldn't swim. Despite living by the sea as a child, neither she nor Zoe had ever bothered to learn. Frantically, she looked around for a branch, a piece of wood or anything he could cling to. But there was nothing on the barren cliff, and helplessly she watched him struggle, his eyes wide with fear. Right now, he was still her father, and she had to rescue him.

Running back down the cliff, Claire searched frantically for a passer-by to help her. But there was no one to be found anywhere on the deserted headland. Reaching the beach, she tore off her jacket as she ran along the sand, hoping she could make it to the rocks, throw in her jacket as a lifeline and pull her father to safety. But when she reached the rocks, the full tide was lashing against the rocks, but there was no longer any sign of him. Then she caught a brief glimpse of an arm before it disappeared completely beneath the waves.

For a long time Claire sat alone on the beach, almost in a state of fugue. To outsiders, she might have looked like a woman observing the scenery. But inwardly, she felt a deep sense of sorrow combined with a strange sense of release. She knew that later she'd cry a river of tears when the pain and shock caught up with her. But right now, nature was numbing her pain. It was almost as though she was in a bubble, and experiencing a strange sense of distance from the world around her.

Suddenly, the silence of the afternoon was fractured by the ringing of Claire's mobile phone. For a moment, she thought it might be David.

"Hello?"

"Claire, it's Hazel – look, I don't know how to tell you this, but remember you said your father worked in Australia? Well, I asked a friend in the police to check him out, and –" Hazel's voice broke. "Claire, your father's been in prison in Australia for years – for child abuse!"

Claire began to cry.

"Claire, are you alright? God, I'm sorry to have to tell you something so awful –"

As Hazel waited anxiously, Claire's sobs gradually abated.

"Thanks, Hazel, but it's okay," she managed to say at last. "I know all about him."

"You do? Oh, thank goodness – I mean, I'm glad I'm not the one telling you the bad news. You know, it bugged me, all those years ago, when your mother broke the television set –"

"What?" Claire suddenly perked up, remembering that day clearly.

"Zoe and I tried to find out what made her do it, but it's only now that I've discovered why," Hazel said. "The date always stuck in my mind, so I've been going through the newspaper archives and I discovered that your father was one of several men arrested on child abuse charges that day. Although they weren't named on the TV news, they were shown being led away by the police, and your father covered his head with his jacket to avoid being recognised."

Claire remembered her mother's words: "I bought him that jacket – I'd recognise it anywhere!" Her voice had dripped with venom. Despite being drunk, she'd still recognised the man hiding beneath the jacket.

"Did he go to prison?" Claire asked.

"No, the DPP wasn't able to prosecute because the police had beaten them up."

So her father had got away with it yet again, Claire thought. But at least they'd locked him up in Australia.

"Well, it's all over now, Hazel," Claire told her friend. "So there's no need for you to worry. I'll explain everything to you later."

"But –"

"Sorry, Hazel – reception isn't very good here," she lied. "Talk to you later."

Claire cut the call. She felt weary and didn't want to talk to anyone right now. For a long time, she sat gazing out to sea. The tide went out again, and Claire wondered if it had taken her father's body with it. Overhead, the gulls wheeled, and eventually their sad screeching seemed to wake her from her reverie. Feeling like an automaton, she stood up, walked slowly along the beach and back to her car, which was still parked outside the cottage. Only an hour had passed since she'd parked it there, but it felt like aeons since she'd arrived in Trentham-on-Sea.

Claire climbed into the car and turned on the ignition. She didn't even bother to check whether the cottage door was closed or not. She simply didn't care. The cottage and all its contents had been contaminated by her father's presence there, and she never wanted to set foot in it again. The only mementoes she needed were already stored in her heart. She'd never forget her mother, and her wonderful sister whose only mistake had been misplaced trust.

Claire felt humbled by the sacrifice her mother had made for her daughters, even though it hadn't been enough to save Zoe. By refusing to talk to them about their father, their mother thought she was protecting them. But it had been impossible to outwit a wily predator like their father, and her heavy drinking had prevented her from seeing what was happening to Zoe.

As Claire drove off, a strange sense of peace enveloped her. Now that her father was gone, the children who might have become his victims would be saved. Hopefully, her own children would never be victims of a paedophile. She'd fight tooth and nail to protect them from men like her father.

Claire drove her car in the direction of Trentham-on-Sea police station to report her father's death. It's over, Zoe, she whispered, as she drove along, the tears streaming down her face, I think you can rest in peace now. Suddenly, Zoe felt more real to her than she'd ever been since her death. She felt as though her sister was sitting beside her, and she glanced at the passenger seat, almost expecting to see Zoe there. In a way, she *was* there. She'd been Claire's unseen passenger and companion for most of her life.

"I'll never forget you, Zoe," Claire whispered, as her tears ran freely. "You'll always be with me – I'll know you're there in the wind that blows across the beach in summer, and in the heat of the fire that warms me in the winter. But most of all, you'll always be alive in the deepest recesses of my mind."

By the time she reached the police station, Claire was having difficulty putting the events of the last hour into words, and she falteringly informed the police sergeant of her father's death.

Suddenly she felt an extraordinary empathy with Anne Ellwood, who must have experienced similar mixed emotions after Jennifer fell off the church tower. In spite of her distress, Claire found herself briefly smiling at the irony of it. She'd never expected to find any similarities between her and Anne!

"Sit down, love, and I'll get you a cup of tea," the duty police officer told her, a concerned look on his face. "You've had a terrible shock. I'll notify the rescue services immediately, so they can search for your father's body."

When he brought her a cup of tea, Claire drank it with relish. Right now, it was just what she needed. Or maybe it just symbolised someone's caring response to her sadness.

"Let me ring someone to take you home," the kind sergeant said. "You need support at a time like this."

"Thanks – please contact David, my fiancé."

Having given him David's phone numbers, Claire sat back and drank some more of her tea while the sergeant phoned him. For the first time in her life, she hadn't protested at allowing someone else to help her. Maybe this was a turning point. Nor had she any doubt that David would drive to Trentham-on-Sea as soon as possible, and he'd make the long journey without complaint. That was the security of knowing someone loved you, regardless of everything else.

She finished drinking the tea, feeling strangely detached from everything. She didn't want to think about anything anymore. If this was what being in shock felt like, then she was finding it a very pleasurable state. Eventually, she drifted off into sleep, and it seemed only minutes before she awoke to find that David was just arriving.

Rushing in the door of the police station, he had a deeply worried look on his face. Without speaking, he ran to Claire and held her tight, and all the pain of the previous months seemed to ebb away in the safety of his arms. The evil at the heart of her family was gone at last, and she was free to begin a new life with the man she loved.

She was vaguely aware of the police sergeant filling David in on the details of what had happened. David looked horrified, and kept darting concerned glances at her. Undoubtedly he'd be annoyed that she'd lied to him and tackled her father alone. If only she'd listened to him when he admitted his dislike of her father! On the other hand, if she hadn't believed in her father, she'd never have learnt the truth about Zoe . . .

"We've parked Ms Ross's car in the station yard, so you can collect it at your leisure," the sergeant told David. "Right now, I think this lady needs plenty of rest."

Thanking him, David slipped his arm around Claire and led her out into the sunlight and towards his car. "Come on love, let's get you home," he whispered tenderly.

Claire smiled at him through her tears. Never had any words sounded more beautiful.

Epilogue

Claire woke up just as David entered her hospital room. He was smiling broadly, and carrying an enormous bouquet of flowers. "For the most wonderful wife in the world," he said, leaning over to kiss her.

Claire smiled happily. Was it only a year since they'd married? They'd both sold their apartments and bought a large old house needing lots of work. And as they'd plastered, painted and tiled, they'd hoped that some day they might fill it with the sounds of children's laughter. And now it wasn't just the two of them any longer . . .

"And how's my beautiful daughter today?" David asked, leaning over the cradle beside Claire's bed.

"She's doing great," she replied. "In fact, we're both going home tomorrow!"

David's face lit up with joy. "Then I'd better finish wallpapering the nursery!"

Claire smiled contentedly as she watched him lift up their baby daughter and hold her close to his heart. "Hello, Zoe," he whispered. "You don't know it yet, but you've made our lives complete!"

Claire smiled. The past had finally been laid to rest, and a wonderful new future was just beginning.

If you enjoyed
Never Say Goodbye by Linda Kavanagh,
why not try an exclusive 2 chapters of her forthcoming
title *Still Waters* being published in 2012.

Still Waters

LINDA
KAVANAGH

Still Waters

CHAPTER 1

A minute ago, everything had been fine in Ivy Heartley's life. Now her worst nightmare was finally coming true.

She'd been smiling happily as she'd opened the email from her sister-in-law Peggy, who was also a lifelong friend. She loved Peggy's newsy emails, filled with gossip about the village where they'd both grown up, and where Peggy still lived. Peggy had the ability to bring everything to life, and Ivy could almost see the events she described unfolding before her very eyes.

Ivy had been chuckling as she read the events of the previous week in Willow Haven. Peggy told her about the fund-raising drive for a new roof for the church, the disastrous garden party at the vicarage, and the thief who'd raided the church's allotment. She also learned that Mrs Evans had been taken to hospital with a suspected heart attack, and Clara Bellingham had just got engaged to Bill Huggins from Allcott, a nearby village.

Ivy regularly visited the village where she'd grown up. She and her husband – Peggy's brother – had left Willow Haven as soon as they'd finished school, and moved to London where Ivy studied at RADA. Now, almost twenty years later, they were both highly successful in their respective careers, and Joseph, their son, was at university. She was a highly paid soap star, and

Danny was founder and managing director of the Betterbuys supermarket chain. The tiny rented flat they'd once shared in London was now a distant memory, and today they lived in a luxurious mansion in Sussex.

Ivy stretched, and decided to make herself a cup of tea before she continued reading Peggy's long email. While she boiled the kettle and placed a tea bag in a cup, she'd revel in the anticipation. She smiled as she thought of the garden party at the Willow Haven vicarage – those events were usually so cringe-worthy, and she'd attended more of them than she cared to remember. As a celebrity, she was often called upon to open fetes or lend a touch of glamour to community social events, and she went back to Willow Haven every summer to launch the Community Sports Day.

Returning to the computer, Ivy sat down again and scrolled down Peggy's email as she sipped her tea. She read about Peggy's husband Ned and family, and about her father-in-law Fred Heartley's high blood pressure. Peggy kept a close eye on him, for which Ivy was grateful, since she and Danny were hundreds of miles away in London.

Suddenly, Ivy's heart gave a lurch as she read Peggy's final words: *Since the village has been expanding so much lately, there's talk of draining Harper's Lake. The space will be used for landfill, which means that eventually the land could be built on. Ned thinks it's a crazy idea, but the local council has voted in favour of it.*

Ivy's hands were now shaking, and she could no longer hold the cup. Putting it down, she realised she was in a cold sweat. "Oh my God," she whispered, "what am I going to do?" The past was finally catching up with her. The secret she'd kept hidden for most of her adult life was now about to destroy her. And not just her alone, but her entire family. Her career would be over, Danny's business could go to the wall, and he'd hate her for what she'd done. And Joseph, her son – how would he react when he discovered his mother's heinous secret? Peggy, too, would want nothing to do with her. And all because she didn't tell the truth all those years ago.

Suddenly, Ivy found herself shaking from head to toe. If the Council's plan went ahead, the ripples from the lake would spread out and devastate many lives in the process. Just as they had on that fateful day when her own life had changed forever.

CHAPTER 2

Rosa Dalton was sitting at her desk in the classroom, busy writing on the front page of one of her schoolbooks, her fluffy blonde hair almost touching the desk as she leaned over it. Class hadn't yet begun, and she was deeply absorbed in what she was doing, which was writing her name as 'Rosa Heartley' over and over again.

Everyone in the school knew that sixteen-year-old Rosa was crazy about Danny Heartley, and dreamed of marrying him and living happily ever after. He attended the local boys' school and was in the class ahead of Rosa and her friends. Every day she'd wait outside the girls' school in the hope of engaging him in conversation when he passed by on his way home. But despite Danny's disinterest, Rosa refused to accept defeat. If Danny would only ask her out, she'd show him what a wonderful girlfriend – and later, wife – she could be. She just needed the opportunity!

As the teacher arrived, Clara Bellingham, who was sitting behind Rosa, gave her a warning dig in the back, and Rosa quickly hid the book she'd been writing in. Flashing Clara a grateful smile, she turned to the page the teacher called out. It was Geometry today, and Rosa was bored before the class even began. All she could think of was Danny Heartley and his flashing blue eyes, and the shock of unruly blond hair that fell across his left eye.

"This morning, we're going to look at isosceles triangles – please turn to page 47 of your texts," Mrs Jones, the teacher, announced, but Rosa heard nothing. She didn't see the value of all this theory – after all, when she and Danny were married, they weren't going to be discussing geometry over the breakfast table, were they?

As the teacher droned on about the importance of understanding the concepts of angles and unequal sides, Rosa had a dreamy look on her face. Geometry had no place in her worldview – she regarded it as just another torment thought up by adults to keep young people from enjoying themselves.

She was having a lovely daydream about being married to Danny when the teacher noticed Rosa gazing out the window with a faraway look in her eyes.

"Rosa Dalton, explain what I've just been talking about." Mrs Jones had a triumphant gleam in her eye. She'd caught Rosa out, and she intended making the most of it.

At first Rosa didn't answer because she was too absorbed in her daydream, but the sudden silence and tittering at the back of the classroom gradually began to filter through to her consciousness and she glanced around, only to see Mrs Jones bearing down on her.

"Oh . . ."

"Stand up and repeat what I've just been explaining to the class for the last fifteen minutes."

"Oh er, I'm sorry, Mrs Jones," Rosa faltered, "I – I – didn't . . ."

"She didn't recognise her name, Mrs Jones!" shouted one of the girls at the back of the room. "If you'd called her Rosa Heartley, she'd have answered straight away!"

The classroom dissolved into laughter since everyone knew about Rosa's feelings for Danny Heartley. Angrily, Mrs Jones called for order as she returned to the podium.

"Sit down, you silly girl," she said haughtily to an embarrassed Rosa. "You'd better buck up and pay attention if you want to get decent exam results. There's more to life than boys, you know."

The other pupils began to snigger at the mention of boys, and Rosa turned puce.

Ivy Morton, who was sitting at the back of the class, felt sorry for Rosa. The girl was a daydreamer, but she had a bubbly personality, and was fun to be with. Although they'd never been close friends, she and Rosa hung out with the same group of boys, and Rosa was usually the centre of attention because of her outrageous jokes and coquettish behaviour. It was impossible to dislike her, even though she always tried to outshine the other girls and focus the boys' attention solely on her. She had a presence and a sense of her own importance, and Ivy, who desperately wanted to be an actress when she left school, often wondered if Rosa wasn't more suited to the profession than she was.

Rosa heaved a sigh of relief as the teacher began the lesson again. She tried to look nonchalant and unaffected by the teacher's comments – she didn't want anyone thinking she cared about what Mrs Jones had to say. On the other hand, she was well aware that she needed to knuckle down and start studying. But it was difficult when Danny Heartley occupied so much of her thoughts . . .

Since childhood, Rosa had wanted to be a flight attendant, and she'd never tired of telling anyone who'd listen that she hoped to work for one of the big airlines. Everyone assured her that, with her personality and looks, she'd be a shoo-in, and in her dreams Danny was always waiting at the airport to welcome her home from the exotic locations she'd been visiting. He'd be so proud of his high-flying wife . . .

Rosa sighed. But first, she had to catch Danny, and convince him that she was the girl for him. She couldn't understand what he saw in shy, mousy Ivy Morton, who'd never amount to anything. Much to Rosa's annoyance, Danny Heartley was always trying to talk to Ivy, who always ended up laughing at his antics as he tried to get her attention.

Rosa was relieved that Ivy didn't seem to return his feelings – or was the minx playing hard-to-get? Her heart plummeted at the thought that Ivy might simply be pretending indifference in order to snare Danny. If Ivy started going out with him, Rosa felt she'd never live down the shame. Since everyone knew how much she fancied Danny, the other students would either feel sorry for her, or be delighted she'd got her comeuppance. Either way, she wouldn't be able to face them day after day in school. If only she'd kept her feelings for Danny to herself! But she'd confided in a trusted friend, who'd told her own circle of friends, and suddenly the whole school knew about it. Before long, everyone in the boys' school knew too. But ultimately, all the embarrassment would be worth it if she and Danny finally got together . . .

Suddenly the school bell rang, and Rosa was catapulted back to reality. She sighed with relief – another day of torment was over.

Clara nudged her. "Are we going to the lake?"

Rosa nodded. This was the most important part of the day.

"See you in five," she whispered, hurrying out of the classroom and down the corridor to the school toilets. She needed to check her hair, apply some discreet make-up and lip gloss, and dab on some of the perfume she'd sneaked from her mother's dressing-table. Hopefully, Danny Heartley would be at the lake too . . .

Time after Time

LINDA KAVANAGH

As Caroline Leyden's wedding to Ken Barnes approaches she wants everything to be perfect and all her family to be there. But a 30-year-old photograph album reveals Gina, an aunt she has never met and Caroline gets the feeling her mother Stella and aunt Dolly want their sister and a scandal to remain hidden in the past.

Aware she has touched a raw family nerve, Caroline is compelled to track down Gina. It's a journey that will change the rest of her life.

Investigative reporter Alice Fitzsimons is in for a shock when her property developer husband Bill reveals the true state of their finances. Can their marriage survive? Alice is not sure – she needs time to think, so she goes backpacking alone around Argentina.

But who is the strange old woman who tells Alice she is in danger, and what is Alice going to do about Enrique the gorgeous widower policeman from Buenos Aires? While Alice is clearing her head and coming to a decision, strange things start to happen. Is someone trying to kill her?

Caroline and Alice have never met, but something connects them – it's hiding in the murky depths of the past just waiting for someone to unearth the truth and set it free. Maybe it's time to put an end to all the secrets and lies.

ISBN 978-1-84223-309-2